THE BIG SLEEP

THE
BIG SLEEP

RAYMOND CHANDLER

ALFRED · A · KNOPF
NEW YORK

1

It was about eleven o'clock in the morning, mid October, with the sun not shining and a look of hard wet rain in the clearness of the foothills. I was wearing my powder-blue suit, with dark blue shirt, tie and display handkerchief, black brogues, black wool socks with dark blue clocks on them. I was neat, clean, shaved and sober, and I didn't care who knew it. I was everything the well-dressed private detective ought to be. I was calling on four million dollars.

The main hallway of the Sternwood place was two stories high. Over the entrance doors, which would have let in a troop of Indian elephants, there was a broad stained-glass panel showing a knight in dark armor rescuing a lady who was tied to a tree and didn't have any clothes on but some very long and convenient hair. The knight had pushed the vizor of his helmet back to be sociable, and he was fiddling with the knots on the ropes that tied the lady to the tree and not getting anywhere. I stood there and thought that if I lived in the house, I would sooner or later have to climb up there and help him. He didn't seem to be really trying.

There were French doors at the back of the hall, beyond them a wide sweep of emerald grass to a white garage, in front of which a slim dark young chauffeur in shiny black leggings was dusting a maroon Packard convertible. Beyond the garage were some decorative trees trimmed as carefully as poodle dogs. Beyond them a large greenhouse with a domed roof. Then more trees and beyond everything the solid, uneven, comfortable line of the foothills.

On the east side of the hall a free staircase, tile-paved, rose to a gallery with a wrought-iron railing and another piece of stained-glass romance. Large hard chairs with rounded red plush seats were backed into the vacant spaces of the wall round about. They didn't look as if anybody had ever sat in them. In the middle of the west wall there was a big empty fireplace with a brass screen in four hinged panels, and over the fireplace a marble mantel with cupids at the corners. Above the mantel there was a large oil portrait, and above the portrait two bullet-torn or moth-eaten cavalry pennants crossed in a glass frame. The portrait was a stiffly posed job of an officer in full regimentals of about the time of the Mexican war. The officer had a neat black imperial, black mustachios, hot hard coal-black eyes, and the general look of a man it would pay to get along with. I thought this might be General Sternwood's grandfather. It could hardly be the General himself, even though I had heard he was pretty far gone in years to have a couple of daughters still in the dangerous twenties.

I was still staring at the hot black eyes when a door opened far back under the stairs. It wasn't the butler coming back. It was a girl.

She was twenty or so, small and delicately put together, but she looked durable. She wore pale blue slacks and they looked well on her. She walked as if she were floating. Her hair was a fine tawny wave cut much shorter than the current fashion of pageboy tresses curled in at the bottom. Her eyes were slate-gray, and had almost no expression when they looked at me. She came over near me and smiled with her mouth and she had little sharp predatory teeth, as white as fresh orange pith and as shiny as porcelain. They glistened between her thin too taut lips. Her face lacked color and didn't look too healthy.

"Tall, aren't you?" she said.

"I didn't mean to be."

Her eyes rounded. She was puzzled. She was thinking. I

could see, even on that short acquaintance, that thinking was always going to be a bother to her.

"Handsome too," she said. "And I bet you know it."

I grunted.

"What's your name?"

"Reilly," I said. "Doghouse Reilly."

"That's a funny name." She bit her lip and turned her head a little and looked at me along her eyes. Then she lowered her lashes until they almost cuddled her cheeks and slowly raised them again, like a theater curtain. I was to get to know that trick. That was supposed to make me roll over on my back with all four paws in the air.

"Are you a prizefighter?" she asked, when I didn't.

"Not exactly. I'm a sleuth."

"A—a—" She tossed her head angrily, and the rich color of it glistened in the rather dim light of the big hall. "You're making fun of me."

"Uh-uh."

"What?"

"Get on with you," I said. "You heard me."

"You didn't say anything. You're just a big tease." She put a thumb up and bit it. It was a curiously shaped thumb, thin and narrow like an extra finger, with no curve in the first joint. She bit it and sucked it slowly, turning it around in her mouth like a baby with a comforter.

"You're awfully tall," she said. Then she giggled with secret merriment. Then she turned her body slowly and lithely, without lifting her feet. Her hands dropped limp at her sides. She tilted herself towards me on her toes. She fell straight back into my arms. I had to catch her or let her crack her head on the tessellated floor. I caught her under her arms and she went rubber-legged on me instantly. I had to hold her close to hold her up. When her head was against my chest she screwed it around and giggled at me.

"You're cute," she giggled. "I'm cute too."

I didn't say anything. So the butler chose that convenient

moment to come back through the French doors and see me holding her.

It didn't seem to bother him. He was a tall, thin, silver man, sixty or close to it or a little past it. He had blue eyes as remote as eyes could be. His skin was smooth and bright and he moved like a man with very sound muscles. He walked slowly across the floor towards us and the girl jerked away from me. She flashed across the room to the foot of the stairs and went up them like a deer. She was gone before I could draw a long breath and let it out.

The butler said tonelessly: "The General will see you now, Mr. Marlowe."

I pushed my lower jaw up off my chest and nodded at him. "Who was that?"

"Miss Carmen Sternwood, sir."

"You ought to wean her. She looks old enough."

He looked at me with grave politeness and repeated what he had said.

2

We went out at the French doors and along a smooth red-flagged path that skirted the far side of the lawn from the garage. The boyish-looking chauffeur had a big black and chromium sedan out now and was dusting that. The path took us along to the side of the greenhouse and the butler opened a door for me and stood aside. It opened into a sort of vestibule that was about as warm as a slow oven. He came in after me, shut the outer door, opened an inner door and we went through that. Then it was really hot. The air was thick, wet, steamy and larded with the cloying smell of tropical orchids in bloom. The glass walls and roof were heavily misted and big drops of moisture splashed down on the plants. The light had an unreal greenish color, like light filtered through an aquarium tank. The plants filled the place, a forest of them, with nasty meaty leaves and stalks like the newly washed fingers of dead men. They smelled as overpowering as boiling alcohol under a blanket.

The butler did his best to get me through without being smacked in the face by the sodden leaves, and after a while we came to a clearing in the middle of the jungle, under the domed roof. Here, in a space of hexagonal flags, an old red Turkish rug was laid down and on the rug was a wheel chair, and in the wheel chair an old and obviously dying man watched us come with black eyes from which all fire had died long ago, but which still had the coal-black directness of the eyes in the portrait that hung above the mantel in the hall. The rest of his face was a leaden mask, with the bloodless lips and the sharp nose and the sunken temples and the outward-turning earlobes of approaching dissolution. His long narrow body was wrapped—in that heat—in a traveling rug and a faded red bathrobe. His thin clawlike hands were folded loosely on the rug, purple-nailed. A few locks of dry white hair clung to his scalp, like wild flowers fighting for life on a bare rock.

The butler stood in front of him and said: "This is Mr. Marlowe, General."

The old man didn't move or speak, or even nod. He just looked at me lifelessly. The butler pushed a damp wicker chair against the backs of my legs and I sat down. He took my hat with a deft scoop.

Then the old man dragged his voice up from the bottom of a well and said: "Brandy, Norris. How do you like your brandy, sir?"

"Any way at all," I said.

The butler went away among the abominable plants. The General spoke again, slowly, using his strength as carefully as an out-of-work showgirl uses her last good pair of stockings.

"I used to like mine with champagne. The champagne as cold as Valley Forge and about a third of a glass of brandy beneath it. You may take your coat off, sir. It's too hot in here for a man with blood in his veins."

I stood up and peeled off my coat and got a handkerchief out and mopped my face and neck and the backs of my wrists. St. Louis in August had nothing on that place. I sat down again and felt automatically for a cigarette and then stopped. The old man caught the gesture and smiled faintly.

"You may smoke, sir. I like the smell of tobacco."

I lit the cigarette and blew a lungful at him and he sniffed at it like a terrier at a rathole. The faint smile pulled at the shadowed corners of his mouth.

"A nice state of affairs when a man has to indulge his vices by proxy," he said dryly. "You are looking at a very dull survival of a rather gaudy life, a cripple paralyzed in both legs and with only half of his lower belly. There's very little that I can eat and my sleep is so close to waking that it is hardly worth the name. I seem to exist largely on heat, like a newborn spider, and the orchids are an excuse for the heat. Do you like orchids?"

"Not particularly," I said.

The General half-closed his eyes. "They are nasty things. Their flesh is too much like the flesh of men. And their perfume has the rotten sweetness of a prostitute."

I stared at him with my mouth open. The soft wet heat was like a pall around us. The old man nodded, as if his neck was afraid of the weight of his head. Then the butler came pushing back through the jungle with a teawagon, mixed me a brandy and soda, swathed the copper ice bucket with a damp napkin, and went away softly among the orchids. A door opened and shut behind the jungle.

I sipped the drink. The old man licked his lips watching me, over and over again, drawing one lip slowly across the other with a funereal absorption, like an undertaker dry-washing his hands.

"Tell me about yourself, Mr. Marlowe. I suppose I have a right to ask?"

"Sure, but there's very little to tell. I'm thirty-three years old, went to college once and can still speak English if there's any demand for it. There isn't much in my trade. I worked for Mr. Wilde, the District Attorney, as an investigator once. His chief investigator, a man named Bernie Ohls, called me and told me you wanted to see me. I'm unmarried because I don't like policemen's wives."

"And a little bit of a cynic," the old man smiled. "You didn't like working for Wilde?"

"I was fired. For insubordination. I test very high on insubordination, General."

"I always did myself, sir. I'm glad to hear it. What do you know about my family?"

"I'm told you are a widower and have two young daughters, both pretty and both wild. One of them has been married three times, the last time to an ex-bootlegger who went in the trade by the name of Rusty Regan. That's all I heard, General."

"Did any of it strike you as peculiar?"

"The Rusty Regan part, maybe. But I always got along with bootleggers myself."

He smiled his faint economical smile. "It seems I do too. I'm very fond of Rusty. A big curly-headed Irishman from Clonmel, with sad eyes and a smile as wide as Wilshire Boulevard. The first time I saw him I thought he might be what you are probably thinking he was, an adventurer who happened to get himself wrapped up in some velvet."

"You must have liked him," I said. "You learned to talk the language."

He put his thin bloodless hands under the edge of the rug. I put my cigarette stub out and finished my drink.

"He was the breath of life to me—while he lasted. He spent hours with me, sweating like a pig, drinking brandy by the quart and telling me stories of the Irish revolution. He had been an officer in the I.R.A. He wasn't even legally in the United States. It was a ridiculous marriage of course, and it probably didn't last a month, as a marriage. I'm telling you the family secrets, Mr. Marlowe."

"They're still secrets," I said. "What happened to him?"

The old man looked at me woodenly. "He went away, a month ago. Abruptly, without a word to anyone. Without saying good-by to me. That hurt a little, but he had been raised in a rough school. I'll hear from him one of these days. Meantime I am being blackmailed again."

I said: "Again?"

He brought his hands from under the rug with a brown envelope in them. "I should have been very sorry for anybody who tried to blackmail me while Rusty was around. A few months before he came—that is to say about nine or ten months ago—I paid a man named Joe Brody five thousand dollars to let my younger daughter Carmen alone."

"Ah," I said.

He moved his thin white eyebrows. "That means what?"

"Nothing," I said.

He went on staring at me, half frowning. Then he said: "Take this envelope and examine it. And help yourself to the brandy."

I took the envelope off his knees and sat down with it again. I wiped off the palms of my hands and turned it around. It was addressed to General Guy Sternwood, 3765 Alta Brea Crescent, West Hollywood, California. The address was in ink, in the slanted printing engineers use. The envelope was slit. I opened it up and took out a brown card and three slips of stiff paper. The card was of thin brown linen, printed in gold: "Mr. Arthur Gwynn Geiger." No address. Very small in the lower left-hand corner: "Rare Books and De Luxe Editions." I turned the card over. More of the slanted printing on the back. "Dear Sir: In spite of the legal uncollectibility of the enclosed, which frankly represent gambling debts, I assume you might wish them honored. Respectfully, A. G. Geiger."

I looked at the slips of stiffish white paper. They were promissory notes filled out in ink, dated on several dates early in the month before, September. "On Demand I promise to pay to Arthur Gwynn Geiger or Order the sum of One Thousand Dollars ($1000.00) without interest. Value Received. Carmen Sternwood."

The written part was in a sprawling moronic handwriting with a lot of fat curlicues and circles for dots. I mixed myself another drink and sipped it and put the exhibit aside.

"Your conclusions?" the General asked.

"I haven't any yet. Who is this Arthur Gwynn Geiger?"

"I haven't the faintest idea."

"What does Carmen say?"

"I haven't asked her. I don't intend to. If I did, she would suck her thumb and look coy."

I said: "I met her in the hall. She did that to me. Then she tried to sit in my lap."

Nothing changed in his expression. His clasped hands rested peacefully on the edge of the rug, and the heat, which made me feel like a New England boiled dinner, didn't seem to make him even warm.

"Do I have to be polite?" I asked. "Or can I just be natural?"

"I haven't noticed that you suffer from many inhibitions, Mr. Marlowe."

"Do the two girls run around together?"

"I think not. I think they go their separate and slightly divergent roads to perdition. Vivian is spoiled, exacting, smart and quite ruthless. Carmen is a child who likes to pull wings off flies. Neither of them has any more moral sense than a cat. Neither have I. No Sternwood ever had. Proceed."

"They're well educated, I suppose. They know what they're doing."

"Vivian went to good schools of the snob type and to college. Carmen went to half a dozen schools of greater and greater liberality, and ended up where she started. I presume they both had, and still have, all the usual vices. If I sound a little sinister as a parent, Mr. Marlowe, it is because my hold on life is too slight to include any Victorian hypocrisy." He leaned his head back and closed his eyes, then opened them again suddenly. "I need not add that a man who indulges in parenthood for the first time at the age of fifty-four deserves all he gets."

I sipped my drink and nodded. The pulse in his lean gray throat throbbed visibly and yet so slowly that it was hardly a pulse at all. An old man two thirds dead and still determined to believe he could take it.

"Your conclusions?" he snapped suddenly.

"I'd pay him."

"Why?"

"It's a question of a little money against a lot of annoyance. There has to be something behind it. But nobody's going to break your heart, if it hasn't been done already. And it would take an awful lot of chiselers an awful lot of time to rob you of enough so that you'd even notice it."

"I have pride, sir," he said coldly.

"Somebody's counting on that. It's the easiest way to fool them. That or the police. Geiger can collect on these notes, unless you can show fraud. Instead of that he makes you a present of them and admits they are gambling debts, which gives you a defense, even if he had kept the notes. If he's a crook, he knows his onions, and if he's an honest man doing a little loan business on the side, he ought to have his money. Who was this Joe Brody you paid the five thousand dollars to?"

"Some kind of gambler. I hardly recall. Norris would know. My butler."

"Your daughters have money in their own right, General?"

"Vivian has, but not a great deal. Carmen is still a minor under her mother's will. I give them both generous allowances."

I said: "I can take this Geiger off your back, General, if that's what you want. Whoever he is and whatever he has. It may cost you a little money, besides what you pay me. And of course it won't get you anything. Sugaring them never does. You're already listed on their book of nice names."

"I see." He shrugged his wide sharp shoulders in the faded red bathrobe. "A moment ago you said pay him. Now you say it won't get me anything."

"I mean it might be cheaper and easier to stand for a certain amount of squeeze. That's all."

"I'm afraid I'm rather an impatient man, Mr. Marlowe. What are your charges?"

"I get twenty-five a day and expenses—when I'm lucky."

"I see. It seems reasonable enough for removing morbid growths from people's backs. Quite a delicate operation. You realize that, I hope. You'll make your operation as little of a shock to the patient as possible? There might be several of them, Mr. Marlowe."

I finished my second drink and wiped my lips and my face. The heat didn't get any less hot with the brandy in me. The General blinked at me and plucked at the edge of his rug.

"Can I make a deal with this guy, if I think he's within hooting distance of being on the level?"

"Yes. The matter is now in your hands. I never do things by halves."

"I'll take him out," I said. "He'll think a bridge fell on him."

"I'm sure you will. And now I must excuse myself. I am tired." He reached out and touched the bell on the arm of his chair. The cord was plugged into a black cable that wound along the side of the deep dark green boxes in which the orchids grew and festered. He closed his eyes, opened them again in a brief bright stare, and settled back among his cushions. The lids dropped again and he didn't pay any more attention to me.

I stood up and lifted my coat off the back of the damp wicker chair and went off with it among the orchids, opened the two doors and stood outside in the brisk October air getting myself some oxygen. The chauffeur over by the garage had gone away. The butler came along the red path with smooth light steps and his back as straight as an ironing board. I shrugged into my coat and watched him come.

He stopped about two feet from me and said gravely: "Mrs. Regan would like to see you before you leave, sir. And in the matter of money the General has instructed me to give you a check for whatever seems desirable."

"Instructed you how?"

He looked puzzled, then he smiled. "Ah, I see, sir. You are, of course, a detective. By the way he rang his bell."

"You write his checks?"

"I have that privilege."

"That ought to save you from a pauper's grave. No money now, thanks. What does Mrs. Regan want to see me about?"

His blue eyes gave me a smooth level look. "She has a misconception of the purpose of your visit, sir."

"Who told her anything about my visit?"

"Her windows command the greenhouse. She saw us go in. I was obliged to tell her who you were."

"I don't like that," I said.

His blue eyes frosted. "Are you attempting to tell me my duties, sir?"

"No. But I'm having a lot of fun trying to guess what they are."

We stared at each other for a moment. He gave me a blue glare and turned away.

3

THIS ROOM was too big, the ceiling was too high, the doors were too tall, and the white carpet that went from wall to wall looked like a fresh fall of snow at Lake Arrowhead. There were full-length mirrors and crystal doodads all over the place. The ivory furniture had chromium on it, and the enormous ivory drapes lay tumbled on the white carpet a yard from the windows. The white made the ivory look dirty and the ivory made the white look bled out. The windows stared towards the darkening foothills. It was going to rain soon. There was pressure in the air already.

I sat down on the edge of a deep soft chair and looked at Mrs. Regan. She was worth a stare. She was trouble. She was stretched out on a modernistic chaise-longue with her slippers off, so I stared at her legs in the sheerest silk stockings. They seemed to be arranged to stare at. They were visible to the knee and one of them well beyond. The knees were dimpled, not bony and sharp. The calves were beautiful, the ankles long and slim and with enough melodic line for a tone poem. She was tall and rangy and strong-looking. Her head was against an ivory satin cushion. Her hair was black and wiry and parted in the middle and she had the hot black eyes of the portrait in the hall. She had a good mouth and a good chin. There was a sulky droop to her lips and the lower lip was full.

She had a drink. She took a swallow from it and gave me a cool level stare over the rim of the glass.

"So you're a private detective," she said. "I didn't know they really existed, except in books. Or else they were greasy little men snooping around hotels."

There was nothing in that for me, so I let it drift with the current. She put her glass down on the flat arm of the chaise-longue and flashed an emerald and touched her hair. She said slowly: "How did you like Dad?"

"I liked him," I said.

"He liked Rusty. I suppose you know who Rusty is?"

"Uh-huh."

"Rusty was earthy and vulgar at times, but he was very real. And he was a lot of fun for Dad. Rusty shouldn't have gone off like that. Dad feels very badly about it, although he won't say so. Or did he?"

"He said something about it."

"You're not much of a gusher, are you, Mr. Marlowe? But he wants to find him, doesn't he?"

I stared at her politely through a pause. "Yes and no," I said.

"That's hardly an answer. Do you think you can find him?"

"I didn't say I was going to try. Why not try the Missing Persons Bureau? They have the organization. It's not a one-man job."

"Oh, Dad wouldn't hear of the police being brought into it." She looked at me smoothly across her glass again, emptied it, and rang a bell. A maid came into the room by a side door. She was a middle-aged woman with a long yellow gentle face, a long nose, no chin, large wet eyes. She looked like a nice old horse that had been turned out to pasture after long service. Mrs. Regan waved the empty glass at her and she mixed another drink and handed it to her and left the room, without a word, without a glance in my direction.

When the door shut Mrs. Regan said: "Well, how will you go about it then?"

"How and when did he skip out?"

"Didn't Dad tell you?"

I grinned at her with my head on one side. She flushed. Her hot black eyes looked mad. "I don't see what there is to be cagey about," she snapped. "And I don't like your manners."

"I'm not crazy about yours," I said. "I didn't ask to see you. You sent for me. I don't mind your ritzing me or drinking your lunch out of a Scotch bottle. I don't mind your showing me your legs. They're very swell legs and it's a pleasure to make their acquaintance. I don't mind if you don't like my manners. They're pretty bad. I grieve over them during the long winter evenings. But don't waste your time trying to cross-examine me."

She slammed her glass down so hard that it slopped over on an ivory cushion. She swung her legs to the floor and stood up with her eyes sparking fire and her nostrils wide. Her mouth was open and her bright teeth glared at me. Her knuckles were white.

"People don't talk like that to me," she said thickly.

I sat there and grinned at her. Very slowly she closed her mouth and looked down at the spilled liquor. She sat down on the edge of the chaise-longue and cupped her chin in one hand.

"My God, you big dark handsome brute! I ought to throw a Buick at you."

I snicked a match on my thumbnail and for once it lit. I puffed smoke into the air and waited.

"I loathe masterful men," she said. "I simply loathe them."

"Just what is it you're afraid of, Mrs. Regan?"

Her eyes whitened. Then they darkened until they seemed to be all pupil. Her nostrils looked pinched.

"That wasn't what he wanted with you at all," she said in a strained voice that still had shreds of anger clinging to it. "About Rusty. Was it?"

"Better ask him."

She flared up again. "Get out! Damn you, get out!"

I stood up. "Sit down!" she snapped. I sat down. I flicked a finger at my palm and waited.

"Please," she said. "Please. You could find Rusty—if Dad wanted you to."

That didn't work either. I nodded and asked: "When did he go?"

"One afternoon a month back. He just drove away in his car without saying a word. They found the car in a private garage somewhere."

"They?"

She got cunning. Her whole body seemed to go lax. Then she smiled at me winningly. "He didn't tell you then." Her voice was almost gleeful, as if she had outsmarted me. Maybe she had.

"He told me about Mr. Regan, yes. That's not what he wanted to see me about. Is that what you've been trying to get me to say?"

"I'm sure I don't care what you say."

I stood up again. "Then I'll be running along." She didn't speak. I went over to the tall white door I had come in at. When I looked back she had her lip between her teeth and was worrying it like a puppy at the fringe of a rug.

I went out, down the tile staircase to the hall, and the butler drifted out of somewhere with my hat in his hand. I put it on while he opened the door for me.

"You made a mistake," I said. "Mrs. Regan didn't want to see me."

He inclined his silver head and said politely: "I'm sorry, sir. I make many mistakes." He closed the door against my back.

I stood on the step breathing my cigarette smoke and looking down a succession of terraces with flowerbeds and trimmed trees to the high iron fence with gilt spears that hemmed in the estate. A winding driveway dropped down between retaining walls to the open iron gates. Beyond the fence the hill sloped for several miles. On this lower level faint and far off I could just barely see some of the old wooden derricks of the oilfield from which the Sternwoods had made their money. Most of the field was public park now, cleaned up and donated to the city by General Sternwood. But a little of it was still producing in groups of wells pumping five or six barrels a day. The Sternwoods, having moved up the hill, could no longer smell the stale sump water or the oil, but they could still look out of their front windows and see what had made them rich. If they wanted to. I didn't suppose they would want to.

I walked down a brick path from terrace to terrace, followed along inside the fence and so out of the gates to where I had left my car under a pepper tree on the street. Thunder was crackling in the foothills now and the sky above them was purple-black. It was going to rain hard. The air had the damp foretaste of rain. I put the top up on my convertible before I started downtown.

She had lovely legs. I would say that for her. They were a couple of pretty smooth citizens, she and her father. He was probably just trying me out; the job he had given me was a lawyer's job. Even if Mr. Arthur Gwynn Geiger, *Rare Books and De Luxe Editions,* turned out to be a blackmailer, it was still a lawyer's job. Unless there was a lot more to it than met the eye. At a casual glance I thought I might have a lot of fun finding out.

I drove down to the Hollywood public library and did a little superficial research in a stuffy volume called Famous First Editions. Half an hour of it made me need my lunch.

4

A. G. GEIGER's place was a store frontage on the north side of
the boulevard near Las Palmas. The entrance door was set far
back in the middle and there was a copper trim on the windows, which were backed with Chinese screens, so I couldn't
see into the store. There was a lot of oriental junk in the windows. I didn't know whether it was any good, not being a collector of antiques, except unpaid bills. The entrance door was
plate glass, but I couldn't see much through that either, because
the store was very dim. A building entrance adjoined it on one
side and on the other was a glittering credit jewelry establishment. The jeweler stood in his entrance, teetering on his heels
and looking bored, a tall handsome white-haired Jew in lean
dark clothes, with about nine carats of diamond on his right
hand. A faint knowing smile curved his lips when I turned into
Geiger's store. I let the door close softly behind me and walked
on a thick blue rug that paved the floor from wall to wall. There
were blue leather easy chairs with smoke stands beside them.
A few sets of tooled leather bindings were set out on narrow
polished tables, between book ends. There were more tooled
bindings in glass cases on the walls. Nice-looking merchandise,
the kind a rich promoter would buy by the yard and have somebody paste his bookplate in. At the back there was a grained
wood partition with a door in the middle of it, shut. In the
corner made by the partition and one wall, a woman sat behind
a small desk with a carved wooden lantern on it.

She got up slowly and swayed towards me in a tight black dress that didn't reflect any light. She had long thighs and she walked with a certain something I hadn't often seen in book-stores. She was an ash blonde with greenish eyes, beaded lashes, hair waved smoothly back from ears in which large jet buttons glittered. Her fingernails were silvered. In spite of her get-up she looked as if she would have a hall bedroom accent.

She approached me with enough sex appeal to stampede a business men's lunch and tilted her head to finger a stray, but not very stray, tendril of softly glowing hair. Her smile was tentative, but could be persuaded to be nice.

"Was it something?" she enquired.

I had my horn-rimmed sunglasses on. I put my voice high and let a bird twitter in it. "Would you happen to have a Ben Hur 1860?"

She didn't say: "Huh?" but she wanted to. She smiled bleakly. "A first edition?"

"Third," I said. "The one with the erratum on page 116."

"I'm afraid not—at the moment."

"How about a Chevalier Audubon 1840—the full set, of course?"

"Er—not at the moment," she purred harshly. Her smile was now hanging by its teeth and eyebrows and wondering what it would hit when it dropped.

"You *do* sell books?" I said in my polite falsetto.

She looked me over. No smile now. Eyes medium to hard. Pose very straight and stiff. She waved silver fingernails at the glassed-in shelves. "What do they look like—grapefruit?" she enquired tartly.

"Oh, that sort of thing hardly interests me, you know. Prob-ably has duplicate sets of steel engravings, tuppence colored and a penny plain. The usual vulgarity. No. I'm sorry. No."

"I see." She tried to jack the smile back up on her face. She was as sore as an alderman with the mumps. "Perhaps Mr. Geiger—but he's not in at the moment." Her eyes studied me carefully. She knew as much about rare books as I knew about handling a flea circus.

"He might be in later?"

"I'm afraid not until late."

"Too bad," I said. "Ah, too bad. I'll sit down and smoke a cigarette in one of these charming chairs. I have rather a blank afternoon. Nothing to think about but my trigonometry lesson."

"Yes," she said. "Ye-es, of course."

I stretched out in one and lit a cigarette with the round nickel lighter on the smoking stand. She still stood, holding her lower lip with her teeth, her eyes vaguely troubled. She nodded at last, turned slowly and walked back to her little desk in the corner. From behind the lamp she stared at me. I crossed my ankles and yawned. Her silver nails went out to the cradle phone on the desk, didn't touch it, dropped and began to tap on the desk.

Silence for about five minutes. The door opened and a tall hungry-looking bird with a cane and a big nose came in neatly, shut the door behind him against the pressure of the door closer, marched over to the corner and placed a wrapped parcel on the desk. He took a pinseal wallet with gold corners from his pocket and showed the blonde something. She pressed a button on the desk. The tall bird went to the door in the paneled partition and opened it barely enough to slip through.

I finished my cigarette and lit another. The minutes dragged by. Horns tooted and grunted on the boulevard. A big red interurban car grumbled past. A traffic light gonged. The blonde leaned on her elbow and cupped a hand over her eyes and stared at me behind it. The partition door opened and the tall bird with the cane slid out. He had another wrapped parcel, the shape of a large book. He went over to the desk and paid money. He left as he had come, walking on the balls of his feet, breathing with his mouth open, giving me a sharp side glance as he passed.

I got to my feet, tipped my hat to the blonde and went out after him. He walked west, swinging his cane in a small tight arc just above his right shoe. He was easy to follow. His coat was cut from a rather loud piece of horse robe with shoulders so wide that his neck stuck up out of it like a celery stalk and his head wobbled on it as he walked. We went a block and a half. At the Highland Avenue traffic signal I pulled up beside him and let him see me. He gave me a casual, then a suddenly sharpened side glance, and quickly turned away. We crossed Highland with the green light and made another block. He stretched his long legs and had twenty yards on me at the corner. He turned right. A hundred feet up the hill he stopped and hooked his cane over his arm and fumbled a leather cigarette case out of an inner pocket. He put a cigarette in his mouth, dropped his match, looked back when he picked it up, saw me watching him from the corner, and straightened up as if somebody had booted him from behind. He almost raised dust going up the block, walking with long gawky strides and jabbing his cane into the sidewalk. He turned left again. He had at least half a block on me when I reached the place where he had turned. He had me wheezing. This was a narrow tree-lined street with a retaining wall on one side and three bungalow courts on the other.

He was gone. I loafed along the block peering this way and that. At the second bungalow court I saw something. It was called "The La Baba," a quiet dim place with a double row of tree-shaded bungalows. The central walk was lined with Italian cypresses trimmed short and chunky, something the shape of the oil jars in Ali Baba and the Forty Thieves. Behind the third jar a loud-patterned sleeve edge moved.

I leaned against a pepper tree in the parkway and waited. The thunder in the foothills was rumbling again. The glare of lightning was reflected on piled-up black clouds off to the south. A few tentative raindrops splashed down on the sidewalk and made spots as large as nickels. The air was as still as the air in General Sternwood's orchid house.

The sleeve behind the tree showed again, then a big nose and one eye and some sandy hair without a hat on it. The eye stared at me. It disappeared. Its mate reappeared like a woodpecker on the other side of the tree. Five minutes went by. It got him. His type are half nerves. I heard a match strike and then whistling started. Then a dim shadow slipped along the grass to the next tree. Then he was out on the walk coming straight towards me, swinging the cane and whistling. A sour whistle with jitters in it. I stared vaguely up at the dark sky. He passed within ten feet of me and didn't give me a glance. He was safe now. He had ditched it.

I watched him out of sight and went up the central walk of the La Baba and parted the branches of the third cypress. I drew out a wrapped book and put it under my arm and went away from there. Nobody yelled at me.

5

BACK ON the boulevard I went into a drugstore phone booth
and looked up Mr. Arthur Gwynn Geiger's residence. He lived
on Laverne Terrace, a hillside street off Laurel Canyon Boulevard. I dropped my nickel and dialed his number just for fun.
Nobody answered. I turned to the classified section and noted a
couple of bookstores within blocks of where I was.

The first I came to was on the north side, a large lower floor
devoted to stationery and office supplies, a mass of books on
the mezzanine. It didn't look the right place. I crossed the
street and walked two blocks east to the other one. This was
more like it, a narrowed cluttered little shop stacked with books
from floor to ceiling and four or five browsers taking their time
putting thumb marks on the new jackets. Nobody paid any
attention to them. I shoved on back into the store, passed
through a partition and found a small dark woman reading a
law book at a desk.

I flipped my wallet open on her desk and let her look at the
buzzer pinned to the flap. She looked at it, took her glasses
off and leaned back in her chair. I put the wallet away. She
had the fine-drawn face of an intelligent Jewess. She stared at
me and said nothing.

I said: "Would you do me a favor, a very small favor?"

"I don't know. What is it?" She had a smoothly husky voice.

"You know Geiger's store across the street, two blocks west?"

"I think I may have passed it."

"It's a bookstore," I said. "Not your kind of bookstore. You know darn well."

She curled her lip slightly and said nothing. "You know Geiger by sight?" I asked.

"I'm sorry. I don't know Mr. Geiger."

"Then you couldn't tell me what he looks like?"

Her lip curled some more. "Why should I?"

"No reason at all. If you don't want to, I can't make you."

She looked out through the partition door and leaned back again. "That was a sheriff's star, wasn't it?"

"Honorary deputy. Doesn't mean a thing. It's worth a dime cigar."

"I see." She reached for a pack of cigarettes and shook one loose and reached for it with her lips. I held a match for her. She thanked me, leaned back again and regarded me through smoke. She said carefully:

"You wish to know what he looks like and you don't want to interview him?"

"He's not there," I said.

"I presume he will be. After all, it's his store."

"I don't want to interview him just yet," I said.

She looked out through the open doorway again. I said: "Know anything about rare books?"

"You could try me."

"Would you have a Ben Hur, 1860, Third Edition, the one with the duplicated line on page 116?"

She pushed her yellow law book to one side and reached a fat volume up on the desk, leafed it through, found her page, and studied it. "Nobody would," she said without looking up. "There isn't one."

"Right."

"What in the world are you driving at?"

"The girl in Geiger's store didn't know that."

She looked up. "I see. You interest me. Rather vaguely."

"I'm a private dick on a case. Perhaps I ask too much. It didn't seem much to me somehow."

She blew a soft gray smoke ring and poked her finger

through. It came to pieces in frail wisps. She spoke smoothly, indifferently. "In his early forties, I should judge. Medium height, fattish. Would weigh about a hundred and sixty pounds. Fat face, Charlie Chan moustache, thick soft neck. Soft all over. Well dressed, goes without a hat, affects a knowledge of antiques and hasn't any. Oh yes. His left eye is glass."

"You'd make a good cop," I said.

She put the reference book back on an open shelf at the end of her desk, and opened the law book in front of her again. "I hope not," she said. She put her glasses on.

I thanked her and left. The rain had started. I ran for it, with the wrapped book under my arm. My car was on a side street pointing at the boulevard almost opposite Geiger's store. I was well sprinkled before I got there. I tumbled into the car and ran both windows up and wiped my parcel off with my handkerchief. Then I opened it up.

I knew about what it would be, of course. A heavy book, well bound, handsomely printed in handset type on fine paper. Larded with full-page arty photographs. Photos and letterpress were alike of an indescribable filth. The book was not new. Dates were stamped on the front endpaper, in and out dates. A rent book. A lending library of elaborate smut.

I rewrapped the book and locked it up behind the seat. A racket like that, out in the open on the boulevard, seemed to mean plenty of protection. I sat there and poisoned myself with cigarette smoke and listened to the rain and thought about it.

6

Rain filled the gutters and splashed knee-high off the sidewalk. Big cops in slickers that shone like gun barrels had a lot of fun carrying giggling girls across the bad places. The rain drummed hard on the roof of the car and the burbank top began to leak. A pool of water formed on the floorboards for me to keep my feet in. It was too early in the fall for that kind of rain. I struggled into a trench coat and made a dash for the nearest drugstore and bought myself a pint of whiskey. Back in the car I used enough of it to keep warm and interested. I was long overparked, but the cops were too busy carrying girls and blowing whistles to bother about that.

In spite of the rain, or perhaps even because of it, there was business done at Geiger's. Very nice cars stopped in front and very nice-looking people went in and out with wrapped parcels. They were not all men.

He showed about four o'clock. A cream-colored coupe stopped in front of the store and I caught a glimpse of the fat face and the Charlie Chan moustache as he dodged out of it and into the store. He was hatless and wore a belted green leather raincoat. I couldn't see his glass eye at that distance. A tall and very good-looking kid in a jerkin came out of the store and rode the coupe off around the corner and came back walking, his glistening black hair plastered with rain.

Another hour went by. It got dark and the rain-clouded lights of the stores were soaked up by the black street. Street-car bells jangled crossly. At around five-fifteen the tall boy in the jerkin came out of Geiger's with an umbrella and went after the cream-colored coupe. When he had it in front Geiger came out and the tall boy held the umbrella over Geiger's bare head. He folded it, shook it off and handed it into the car. He dashed back into the store. I started my motor.

The coupe went west on the boulevard, which forced me to make a left turn and a lot of enemies, including a motorman who stuck his head out into the rain to bawl me out. I was two blocks behind the coupe before I got in the groove. I hoped Geiger was on his way home. I caught sight of him two or three times and then made him turning north into Laurel Canyon Drive. Halfway up the grade he turned left and took a curving ribbon of wet concrete which was called Laverne Terrace. It was a narrow street with a high bank on one side and a scattering of cabin-like houses built down the slope on the other side, so that their roofs were not very much above road level. Their front windows were masked by hedges and shrubs. Sodden trees dripped all over the landscape.

Geiger had his lights on and I hadn't. I speeded up and passed him on a curve, picked a number off a house as I went by and turned at the end of the block. He had already stopped. His car lights were tilted in at the garage of a small house with a square box hedge so arranged that it masked the front door completely. I watched him come out of the garage with his umbrella up and go in through the hedge. He didn't act as if he expected anybody to be tailing him. Light went on in the house. I drifted down to the next house above it, which seemed empty but had no signs out. I parked, aired out the convertible, had a drink from my bottle, and sat. I didn't know what I was waiting for, but something told me to wait. Another army of sluggish minutes dragged by.

Two cars came up the hill and went over the crest. It seemed to be a very quiet street. At a little after six more bright lights bobbed through the driving rain. It was pitch black by then. A car dragged to a stop in front of Geiger's house. The filaments of its lights glowed dimly and died. The door opened and a woman got out. A small slim woman in a vagabond hat and a transparent raincoat. She went in through the box maze. A bell rang faintly, light through the rain, a closing door, silence.

I reached a flash out of my car pocket and went downgrade and looked at the car. It was a Packard convertible, maroon or dark brown. The left window was down. I felt for the license holder and poked light at it. The registration read: Carmen Sternwood, 3765 Alta Brea Crescent, West Hollywood. I went back to my car again and sat and sat. The top dripped on my knees and my stomach burned from the whiskey. No more cars came up the hill. No lights went on in the house before which I was parked. It seemed like a nice neighborhood to have bad habits in.

At seven-twenty a single flash of hard white light shot out of Geiger's house like a wave of summer lightning. As the darkness folded back on it and ate it up a thin tinkling scream echoed out and lost itself among the rain-drenched trees. I was out of the car and on my way before the echoes died.

There was no fear in the scream. It had a sound of half-pleasurable shock, an accent of drunkenness, an overtone of pure idiocy. It was a nasty sound. It made me think of men in white and barred windows and hard narrow cots with leather wrist and ankle straps fastened to them. The Geiger hideaway was perfectly silent again when I hit the gap in the hedge and dodged around the angle that masked the front door. There was an iron ring in a lion's mouth for a knocker. I reached for it, I had hold of it. At that exact instant, as if somebody had been waiting for a cue, three shots boomed in the house. There was a sound that might have been a long harsh sigh. Then a soft messy thump. And then rapid footsteps in the house— going away.

The door fronted on a narrow run, like a footbridge over a gully, that filled the gap between the house wall and the edge of the bank. There was no porch, no solid ground, no way to get around to the back. The back entrance was at the top of a flight of wooden steps that rose from the alley-like street below. I knew this because I heard a clatter of feet on the steps, going down. Then I heard the sudden roar of a starting car. It faded swiftly into the distance. I thought the sound was echoed by another car, but I wasn't sure. The house in front of me was as silent as a vault. There wasn't any hurry. What was in there was in there.

I straddled the fence at the side of the runway and leaned far out to the draped but unscreened French window and tried to look in at the crack where the drapes came together. I saw lamplight on a wall and one end of a bookcase. I got back on the runway and took all of it and some of the hedge and gave the front door the heavy shoulder. This was foolish. About the only part of a California house you can't put your foot through is the front door. All it did was hurt my shoulder and make me mad. I climbed over the railing again and kicked the French window in, used my hat for a glove and pulled out most of the lower small pane of glass. I could now reach in and draw a bolt that fastened the window to the sill. The rest was easy. There was no top bolt. The catch gave. I climbed in and pulled the drapes off my face.

Neither of the two people in the room paid any attention to the way I came in, although only one of them was dead.

7

IT WAS a wide room, the whole width of the house. It had a low beamed ceiling and brown plaster walls decked out with strips of Chinese embroidery and Chinese and Japanese prints in grained wood frames. There were low bookshelves, there was a thick pinkish Chinese rug in which a gopher could have spent a week without showing his nose above the nap. There were floor cushions, bits of odd silk tossed around, as if whoever lived there had to have a piece he could reach out and thumb. There was a broad low divan of old rose tapestry. It had a wad of clothes on it, including lilac-colored silk underwear. There was a big carved lamp on a pedestal, two other standing lamps with jade-green shades and long tassels. There was a black desk with carved gargoyles at the corners and behind it a yellow satin cushion on a polished black chair with carved arms and back. The room contained an odd assortment of odors, of which the most emphatic at the moment seemed to be the pungent aftermath of cordite and the sickish aroma of ether.

On a sort of low dais at one end of the room there was a high-backed teakwood chair in which Miss Carmen Stern-wood was sitting on a fringed orange shawl. She was sitting very straight, with her hands on the arms of the chair, her knees close together, her body stiffly erect in the pose of an Egyptian goddess, her chin level, her small bright teeth shining between her parted lips. Her eyes were wide open. The dark slate color of the iris had devoured the pupil. They were mad eyes. She seemed to be unconscious, but she didn't have the pose of unconsciousness. She looked as if, in her mind, she was doing something very important and making a fine job of it. Out of her mouth came a tinny chuckling noise which didn't change her expression or even move her lips.

She was wearing a pair of long jade earrings. They were nice earrings and had probably cost a couple of hundred dollars. She wasn't wearing anything else.

She had a beautiful body, small, lithe, compact, firm, rounded. Her skin in the lamplight had the shimmering luster of a pearl. Her legs didn't quite have the raffish grace of Mrs. Regan's legs, but they were very nice. I looked her over without either embarrassment or ruttishness. As a naked girl she was not there in that room at all. She was just a dope. To me she was always just a dope.

I stopped looking at her and looked at Geiger. He was on his back on the floor, beyond the fringe of the Chinese rug, in front of a thing that looked like a totem pole. It had a profile like an eagle and its wide round eye was a camera lens. The lens was aimed at the naked girl in the chair. There was a blackened flash bulb clipped to the side of the totem pole. Geiger was wearing Chinese slippers with thick felt soles, and his legs were in black satin pajamas and the upper part of him wore a Chinese embroidered coat, the front of which was mostly blood. His glass eye shone brightly up at me and was by far the most lifelike thing about him. At a glance none of the three shots I heard had missed. He was very dead.

The flash bulb was the sheet lightning I had seen. The crazy scream was the doped and naked girl's reaction to it. The three shots had been somebody else's idea of how the proceedings might be given a new twist. The idea of the lad who had gone down the back steps and slammed into a car and raced away. I could see merit in his point of view.

A couple of fragile gold-veined glasses rested on a red lacquer tray on the end of the black desk, beside a potbellied flagon of brown liquid. I took the stopper out and sniffed at it. It smelled of ether and something else, possibly laudanum. I

had never tried the mixture but it seemed to go pretty well
with the Geiger menage.

I listened to the rain hitting the roof and the north windows.
Beyond was no other sound, no cars, no siren, just the rain
beating. I went over to the divan and peeled off my trench
coat and pawed through the girl's clothes. There was a pale
green rough wool dress of the pull-on type, with half sleeves.
I thought I might be able to handle it. I decided to pass up
her underclothes, not from feelings of delicacy, but because I
couldn't see myself putting her pants on and snapping her
brassiere. I took the dress over to the teak chair on the dais.
Miss Sternwood smelled of ether also, at a distance of several
feet. The tinny chuckling noise was still coming from her and
a little froth oozed down her chin. I slapped her face. She
blinked and stopped chuckling. I slapped her again.

"Come on," I said brightly. "Let's be nice. Let's get dressed."

She peered at me, her slaty eyes as empty as holes in a
mask. "Gugugoterell," she said.

I slapped her around a little more. She didn't mind the slaps.
They didn't bring her out of it. I set to work with the dress.
She didn't mind that either. She let me hold her arms up and
she spread her fingers out wide, as if that was cute. I got her
hands through the sleeves, pulled the dress down over her
back, and stood her up. She fell into my arms giggling. I set
her back in the chair and got her stockings and shoes on her.

"Let's take a little walk," I said. "Let's take a nice little walk."

We took a little walk. Part of the time her earrings banged
against my chest and part of the time we did the splits in uni-
son, like adagio dancers. We walked over to Geiger's body and
back. I had her look at him. She thought he was cute. She giggled and tried to tell me so, but she just bubbled. I walked her
over to the divan and spread her out on it. She hiccuped twice,
giggled a little and went to sleep. I stuffed her belongings into
my pockets and went over behind the totem pole thing. The
camera was there all right, set inside it, but there was no plateholder in the camera. I looked around on the floor, thinking he
might have got it out before he was shot. No plateholder. I

took hold of his limp chilling hand and rolled him a little. No plateholder. I didn't like this development.

I went into a hall at the back of the room and investigated the house. There was a bathroom on the right and a locked door, a kitchen at the back. The kitchen window had been jimmied. The screen was gone and the place where the hook had pulled out showed on the sill. The back door was unlocked. I left it unlocked and looked into a bedroom on the left side of the hall. It was neat, fussy, womanish. The bed had a flounced cover. There was perfume on the triple-mirrored dressing table, beside a handkerchief, some loose money, a man's brushes, a keyholder. A man's clothes were in the closet and a man's slippers under the flounced edge of the bed cover. Mr. Geiger's room. I took the keyholder back to the living room and went through the desk. There was a locked steel box in the deep drawer. I used one of the keys on it. There was nothing in it but a blue leather book with an index and a lot of writing in code, in the same slanting printing that had written to General Sternwood. I put the notebook in my pocket, wiped the steel box where I had touched it, locked the desk up, pocketed the keys, turned the gas logs off in the fireplace, wrapped myself in my coat and tried to rouse Miss Sternwood. It couldn't be done. I crammed her vagabond hat on her head and swathed her in her coat and carried her out to her car. I went back and put all the lights out and shut the front door, dug her keys out of her bag and started the Packard. We went off down the hill without lights. It was less than ten minutes' drive to Alta Brea Crescent. Carmen spent them snoring and breathing ether in my face. I couldn't keep her head off my shoulder. It was all I could do to keep it out of my lap.

8

THERE WAS dim light behind narrow leaded panes in the side door of the Sternwood mansion. I stopped the Packard under the porte-cochere and emptied my pockets out on the seat. The girl snored in the corner, her hat tilted rakishly over her nose, her hands hanging limp in the folds of the raincoat. I got out and rang the bell. Steps came slowly, as if from a long dreary distance. The door opened and the straight, silvery butler looked out at me. The light from the hall made a halo of his hair.

He said: "Good evening, sir," politely and looked past me at the Packard. His eyes came back to look at my eyes.

"Is Mrs. Regan in?"

"No, sir."

"The General is asleep, I hope?"

"Yes. The evening is his best time for sleeping."

"How about Mrs. Regan's maid?"

"Mathilda? She's here, sir."

"Better get her down here. The job needs the woman's touch. Take a look in the car and you'll see why."

He took a look in the car. He came back. "I see," he said. "I'll get Mathilda."

"Mathilda will do right by her," I said.

"We all try to do right by her," he said.

"I guess you have had practice," I said.

He let that one go. "Well, good-night," I said. "I'm leaving it in your hands."

"Very good, sir. May I call you a cab?"

"Positively," I said, "not. As a matter of fact I'm not here. You're just seeing things."

He smiled then. He gave me a duck of his head and I turned and walked down the driveway and out of the gates.

Ten blocks of that, winding down curved rain-swept streets, under the steady drip of trees, past lighted windows in big houses in ghostly enormous grounds, vague clusters of eaves and gables and lighted windows high on the hillside, remote and inaccessible, like witch houses in a forest. I came out at a service station glaring with wasted light, where a bored attendant in a white cap and a dark blue windbreaker sat hunched on a stool, inside the steamed glass, reading a paper. I started in, then kept going. I was as wet as I could get already. And on a night like that you can grow a beard waiting for a taxi. And taxi drivers remember.

I made it back to Geiger's house in something over half an hour of nimble walking. There was nobody there, no car on the street except my own car in front of the next house. It looked as dismal as a lost dog. I dug my bottle of rye out of it and poured half of what was left down my throat and got inside to light a cigarette. I smoked half of it, threw it away, got out again and went down to Geiger's. I unlocked the door and stepped into the still warm darkness and stood there, dripping quietly on the floor and listening to the rain. I groped to a lamp and lit it.

The first thing I noticed was that a couple of strips of embroidered silk were gone from the wall. I hadn't counted them, but the spaces of brown plaster stood out naked and obvious. I went a little farther and put another lamp on. I looked at the totem pole. At its foot, beyond the margin of the Chinese rug, on the bare floor another rug had been spread. It hadn't been there before. Geiger's body had. Geiger's body was gone.

That froze me. I pulled my lips back against my teeth and leered at the glass eye in the totem pole. I went through the

house again. Everything was exactly as it had been. Geiger
wasn't in his flounced bed or under it or in his closet. He wasn't
in the kitchen or the bathroom. That left the locked door on
the right of the hall. One of Geiger's keys fitted the lock. The
room inside was interesting, but Geiger wasn't in it. It was interesting because it was so different from Geiger's room. It was
a hard bare masculine bedroom with a polished wood floor, a
couple of small throw rugs in an Indian design, two straight
chairs, a bureau in dark grained wood with a man's toilet set
and two black candles in foot-high brass candlesticks. The
bed was narrow and looked hard and had a maroon batik cover.
The room felt cold. I locked it up again, wiped the knob off
with my handkerchief, and went back to the totem pole. I knelt
down and squinted along the nap of the rug to the front door.
I thought I could see two parallel grooves pointing that way,
as though heels had dragged. Whoever had done it had meant
business. Dead men are heavier than broken hearts.

It wasn't the law. They would have been there still, just
about getting warmed up with their pieces of string and chalk
and their cameras and dusting powders and their nickel cigars.
They would have been very much there. It wasn't the killer. He
had left too fast. He must have seen the girl. He couldn't be
sure she was too batty to see him. He would be on his way to
distant places. I couldn't guess the answer, but it was all right
with me if somebody wanted Geiger missing instead of just
murdered. It gave me a chance to find out if I could tell it
leaving Carmen Sternwood out. I locked up again, choked my
car to life and rode off home to a shower, dry clothes and a late
dinner. After that I sat around in the apartment and drank
too much hot toddy trying to crack the code in Geiger's blue
indexed notebook. All I could be sure of was that it was a list
of names and addresses, probably of the customers. There were
over four hundred of them. That made it a nice racket, not to
mention any blackmail angles, and there were probably plenty
of those. Any name on the list might be a prospect as the killer.
I didn't envy the police their job when it was handed to them.

I went to bed full of whiskey and frustration and dreamed about a man in a bloody Chinese coat who chased a naked girl with long jade earrings while I ran after them and tried to take a photograph with an empty camera.

9

THE NEXT morning was bright, clear and sunny. I woke up with a motorman's glove in my mouth, drank two cups of coffee and went through the morning papers. I didn't find any reference to Mr. Arthur Gwynn Geiger in either of them. I was shaking the wrinkles out of my damp suit when the phone rang. It was Bernie Ohls, the D.A.'s chief investigator, who had given me the lead to General Sternwood.

"Well, how's the boy?" he began. He sounded like a man who had slept well and didn't owe too much money.

"I've got a hangover," I said.

"Tsk, tsk." He laughed absently and then his voice became a shade too casual, a cagey cop voice. "Seen General Sternwood yet?"

"Uh-huh."

"Done anything for him?"

"Too much rain," I answered, if that was an answer.

"They seem to be a family things happen to. A big Buick belonging to one of them is washing about in the surf off Lido fish pier."

I held the telephone tight enough to crack it. I also held my breath.

"Yeah," Ohls said cheerfully. "A nice new Buick sedan all messed up with sand and sea water. . . . Oh, I almost forgot. There's a guy inside it."

I let my breath out so slowly that it hung on my lip. "Regan?" I asked.

"Huh? Who? Oh, you mean the ex-legger the eldest girl picked up and went and married. I never saw him. What would he be doing down there?"

"Quit stalling. What would anybody be doing down there?"

"I don't know, pal. I'm dropping down to look see. Want to go along?"

"Yes."

"Snap it up," he said. "I'll be in my hutch."

Shaved, dressed and lightly breakfasted I was at the Hall of Justice in less than an hour. I rode up to the seventh floor and went along to the group of small offices used by the D.A.'s men. Ohls' was no larger than the others, but he had it to himself. There was nothing on his desk but a blotter, a cheap pen set, his hat and one of his feet. He was a medium-sized blondish man with stiff white eyebrows, calm eyes and well-kept teeth. He looked like anybody you would pass on the street. I happened to know he had killed nine men—three of them when he was covered, or somebody thought he was.

He stood up and pocketed a flat tin of toy cigars called Entractes, jiggled the one in his mouth up and down and looked at me carefully along his nose, with his head thrown back.

"It's not Regan," he said. "I checked. Regan's a big guy, as tall as you and a shade heavier. This is a young kid."

I didn't say anything.

"What made Regan skip out?" Ohls asked. "You interested in that?"

"I don't think so," I said.

"When a guy out of the liquor traffic marries into a rich family and then waves good-by to a pretty dame and a couple million legitimate bucks—that's enough to make even me think. I guess you thought that was a secret."

"Uh-huh."

"Okey, keep buttoned, kid. No hard feelings." He came around the desk tapping his pockets and reaching for his hat.

"I'm not looking for Regan," I said.

He fixed the lock on his door and we went down to the official parking lot and got into a small blue sedan. We drove out Sunset, using the siren once in a while to beat a signal. It was a crisp morning, with just enough snap in the air to make life seem simple and sweet, if you didn't have too much on your mind. I had.

It was thirty miles to Lido on the coast highway, the first ten of them through traffic. Ohls made the run in three quarters of an hour. At the end of that time we skidded to a stop in front of a faded stucco arch and I took my feet out of the floorboards and we got out. A long pier railed with white two-by-fours stretched seaward from the arch. A knot of people leaned out at the far end and a motorcycle officer stood under the arch keeping another group of people from going out on the pier. Cars were parked on both sides of the highway, the usual ghouls, of both sexes. Ohls showed the motorcycle officer his badge and we went out on the pier, into a loud fish smell which one night's hard rain hadn't even dented.

"There she is—on the power barge," Ohls said, pointing with one of his toy cigars.

A low black barge with a wheelhouse like a tug's was crouched against the pilings at the end of the pier. Something that glistened in the morning sunlight was on its deck, with hoist chains still around it, a large black and chromium car. The arm of the hoist had been swung back into position and lowered to deck level. Men stood around the car. We went down slippery steps to the deck.

Ohls said hello to a deputy in green khaki and a man in plain clothes. The barge crew of three men leaned against the front of the wheelhouse and chewed tobacco. One of them was rubbing at his wet hair with a dirty bath-towel. That would be the man who had gone down into the water to put the chains on.

We looked the car over. The front bumper was bent, one headlight smashed, the other bent up but the glass still unbroken. The radiator shell had a big dent in it, and the paint and nickel were scratched up all over the car. The upholstery was sodden and black. None of the tires seemed to be damaged.

The driver was still draped around the steering post with his head at an unnatural angle to his shoulders. He was a slim dark-haired kid who had been good-looking not so long ago. Now his face was bluish white and his eyes were a faint dull gleam under the lowered lids and his open mouth had sand in it. On the left side of his forehead there was a dull bruise that stood out against the whiteness of the skin.

Ohls backed away, made a noise in his throat and put a match to his little cigar. "What's the story?"

The uniformed man pointed up at the rubbernecks on the end of the pier. One of them was fingering a place where the white two-by-fours had been broken through in a wide space. The splintered wood showed yellow and clean, like fresh-cut pine.

"Went through there. Must have hit pretty hard. The rain stopped early down here, around nine p.m. The broken wood's dry inside. That puts it after the rain stopped. She fell in plenty of water not to be banged up worse, not more than half tide or she'd have drifted farther, and not more than half tide going out or she'd have crowded the piles. That makes it around ten last night. Maybe nine-thirty, not earlier. She shows under the water when the boys come down to fish this morning, so we get the barge to hoist her out and we find the dead guy."

The plainclothesman scuffed at the deck with the toe of his shoe. Ohls looked sideways along his eyes at me, and twitched his little cigar like a cigarette.

"Drunk?" he asked, of nobody in particular.

The man who had been toweling his head went over to the rail and cleared his throat in a loud hawk that made everybody look at him. "Got some sand," he said, and spat. "Not as much as the boy friend got—but some."

The uniformed man said: "Could have been drunk. Showing off all alone in the rain. Drunks will do anything."

"Drunk, hell," the plainclothesman said. "The hand throttle's set halfway down and the guy's been sapped on the side of the head. Ask me and I'll call it murder."

Ohls looked at the man with the towel. "What do you think, buddy?"

The man with the towel looked flattered. He grinned. "I say suicide, Mac. None of my business, but you ask me, I say suicide. First off the guy plowed an awful straight furrow down that pier. You can read his tread marks all the way nearly. That puts it after the rain like the Sheriff said. Then he hit the pier hard and clean or he don't go through and land right side up. More likely turned over a couple of times. So he had plenty of speed and hit the rail square. That's more than half-throttle. He could have done that with his hand falling and he could have hurt his head falling too."

Ohls said: "You got eyes, buddy. Frisked him?" he asked the deputy. The deputy looked at me, then at the crew against the wheelhouse. "Okey, save that," Ohls said.

A small man with glasses and a tired face and a black bag came down the steps from the pier. He picked out a fairly clean spot on the deck and put the bag down. Then he took his hat off and rubbed the back of his neck and stared out to sea, as if he didn't know where he was or what he had come for.

Ohls said: "There's your customer, Doc. Dove off the pier last night. Around nine to ten. That's all we know."

The small man looked in at the dead man morosely. He fingered the head, peered at the bruise on the temple, moved the head around with both hands, felt the man's ribs. He lifted a lax dead hand and stared at the fingernails. He let it fall and watched it fall. He stepped back and opened his bag and took out a printed pad of D.O.A. forms and began to write over a carbon.

"Broken neck's the apparent cause of death," he said, writing. "Which means there won't be much water in him. Which means he's due to start getting stiff pretty quick now he's out in the air. Better get him out of the car before he does. You won't like doing it after."

Ohls nodded. "How long dead, Doc?"

"I wouldn't know."

Ohls looked at him sharply and took the little cigar out of his mouth and looked at that sharply. "Pleased to know you, Doc. A coroner's man that can't guess within five minutes has me beat."

The little man grinned sourly and put his pad in his bag and clipped his pencil back on his vest. "If he ate dinner last night, I'll tell you—if I know what time he ate it. But not within five minutes."

"How would he get that bruise—falling?"

The little man looked at the bruise again. "I don't think so. That blow came from something covered. And it had already bled subcutaneously while he was alive."

"Blackjack, huh?"

"Very likely."

The little M.E.'s man nodded, picked his bag off the deck and went back up the steps to the pier. An ambulance was backing into position outside the stucco arch. Ohls looked at me and said: "Let's go. Hardly worth the ride, was it?"

We went back along the pier and got into Ohls' sedan again. He wrestled it around on the highway and drove back towards town along a three-lane highway washed clean by the rain, past low rolling hills of yellow-white sand terraced with pink moss. Seaward a few gulls wheeled and swooped over something in the surf and far out a white yacht looked as if it was hanging in the sky.

Ohls cocked his chin at me and said: "Know him?"

"Sure. The Sternwood chauffeur. I saw him dusting that very car out there yesterday."

"I don't want to crowd you, Marlowe. Just tell me, did the job have anything to do with him?"

"No. I don't even know his name."

"Owen Taylor. How do I know? Funny about that. About a year or so back we had him in the cooler on a Mann Act rap. It seems he run Sternwood's hotcha daughter, the young one, off to Yuma. The sister ran after them and brought them back and had Owen heaved into the icebox. Then next day she comes down to the D.A. and gets him to beg the kid off with the U. S. 'cutor. She says the kid meant to marry her sister and wanted to, only the sister can't see it. All *she* wanted was to kick a few high ones off the bar and have herself a party. So we let the kid go and then darned if they don't have him come back to work. And a little later we get the routine report on his prints from Washington, and he's got a prior back in Indiana, attempted hold-up six years ago. He got off with a six months in the county jail, the very one Dillinger bust out of. We hand that to the Sternwoods and they keep him on just the same. What do you think of that?"

"They seem to be a screwy family," I said. "Do they know about last night?"

"No. I gotta go up against them now."

"Leave the old man out of it, if you can."

"Why?"

"He has enough troubles and he's sick."

"You mean Regan?"

I scowled. "I don't know anything about Regan, I told you. I'm not looking for Regan. Regan hasn't bothered anybody that I know of."

Ohls said: "Oh," and stared thoughtfully out to sea and the sedan nearly went off the road. For the rest of the drive back to town he hardly spoke. He dropped me off in Hollywood near the Chinese Theater and turned back west to Alta Brea Crescent. I ate lunch at a counter and looked at an afternoon paper and couldn't find anything about Geiger in it.

After lunch I walked east on the boulevard to have another look at Geiger's store.

10

THE LEAN black-eyed credit jeweler was standing in his entrance
in the same position as the afternoon before. He gave me the
same knowing look as I turned in. The store looked just the
same. The same lamp glowed on the small desk in the corner
and the same ash blonde in the same black suede-like dress got
up from behind it and came towards me with the same tentative smile on her face.

"Was it—?" she said and stopped. Her silver nails twitched
at her side. There was an overtone of strain in her smile. It
wasn't a smile at all. It was a grimace. She just thought it was
a smile.

"Back again," I chirped airily, and waved a cigarette. "Mr.
Geiger in today?"

"I'm—I'm afraid not. No—I'm afraid not. Let me see—you
wanted . . . ?"

I took my dark glasses off and tapped them delicately on the
inside of my left wrist. If you can weigh a hundred and ninety
pounds and look like a fairy, I was doing my best.

"That was just a stall about those first editions," I whispered.
"I have to be careful. I've got something he'll want. Something he's wanted for a long time."

The silver fingernails touched the blonde hair over one small
jet-buttoned ear. "Oh, a salesman," she said. "Well—you might
come in tomorrow. I think he'll be here tomorrow."

"Drop the veil," I said. "I'm in the business too."

Her eyes narrowed until they were a faint greenish glitter, like a forest pool far back in the shadow of trees. Her fingers clawed at her palm. She stared at me and chopped off a breath.

"Is he sick? I could go up to the house," I said impatiently. "I haven't got forever."

"You—a—you—a—" her throat jammed. I thought she was going to fall on her nose. Her whole body shivered and her face fell apart like a bride's pie crust. She put it together again slowly, as if lifting a great weight, by sheer will power. The smile came back, with a couple of corners badly bent.

"No," she breathed. "No. He's out of town. That—wouldn't be any use. Can't you—come in—tomorrow?"

I had my mouth open to say something when the partition door opened a foot. The tall dark handsome boy in the jerkin looked out, pale-faced and tight-lipped, saw me, shut the door quickly again, but not before I had seen on the floor behind him a lot of wooden boxes lined with newspapers and packed loosely with books. A man in very new overalls was fussing with them. Some of Geiger's stock was being moved out.

When the door shut I put my dark glasses on again and touched my hat. "Tomorrow, then. I'd like to give you a card, but you know how it is."

"Ye-es. I know how it is." She shivered a little more and made a faint sucking noise between her bright lips. I went out of the store and west on the boulevard to the corner and north on the street to the alley which ran behind the stores. A small black truck with wire sides and no lettering on it was backed up to Geiger's place. The man in the very new overalls was just heaving a box up on the tailboard. I went back to the boulevard and along the block next to Geiger's and found a taxi standing at a fireplug. A fresh-faced kid was reading a horror magazine behind the wheel. I leaned in and showed him a dollar: "Tail job?"

He looked me over. "Cop?"

"Private."

He grinned. "My meat, Jack." He tucked the magazine over his rear view mirror and I got into the cab. We went around the block and pulled up across from Geiger's alley, beside another fireplug.

There were about a dozen boxes on the truck when the man in overalls closed the screened doors and hooked the tailboard up and got in behind the wheel.

"Take him," I told my driver.

The man in overalls gunned his motor, shot a glance up and down the alley and ran away fast in the other direction. He turned left out of the alley. We did the same. I caught a glimpse of the truck turning east on Franklin and told my driver to close in a little. He didn't or couldn't do it. I saw the truck two blocks away when we got to Franklin. We had it in sight to Vine and across Vine and all the way to Western. We saw it twice after Western. There was a lot of traffic and the fresh-faced kid tailed from too far back. I was telling him about that without mincing words when the truck, now far ahead, turned north again. The street at which it turned was called Brittany Place. When we got to Brittany Place the truck had vanished.

The fresh-faced kid made comforting sounds at me through the panel and we went up the hill at four miles an hour looking for the truck behind bushes. Two blocks up, Brittany Place swung to the east and met Randall Place in a tongue of land on which there was a white apartment house with its front on Randall Place and its basement garage opening on Brittany. We were going past that and the fresh-faced kid was telling me the truck couldn't be far away when I looked through the arched entrance of the garage and saw it back in the dimness with its rear doors open again.

We went around to the front of the apartment house and I got out. There was nobody in the lobby, no switchboard. A wooden desk was pushed back against the wall beside a panel of gilt mailboxes. I looked the names over. A man named Joseph Brody had Apartment 405. A man named Joe Brody had received five thousand dollars from General Sternwood to stop playing with Carmen and find some other little girl to play with. It could be the same Joe Brody. I felt like giving odds on it.

I went around an elbow of wall to the foot of tiled stairs and the shaft of the automatic elevator. The top of the elevator was level with the floor. There was a door beside the shaft lettered "Garage." I opened it and went down narrow steps to the basement. The automatic elevator was propped open and the man in new overalls was grunting hard as he stacked heavy boxes in it. I stood beside him and lit a cigarette and watched him. He didn't like my watching him.

After a while I said: "Watch the weight, bud. She's only tested for half a ton. Where's the stuff going?"

"Brody, four-o-five," he grunted. "Manager?"

"Yeah. Looks like a nice lot of loot."

He glared at me with pale white rimmed eyes. "Books," he snarled. "A hundred pounds a box, easy, and me with a seventy-five pound back."

"Well, watch the weight," I said.

He got into the elevator with six boxes and shut the doors. I went back up the steps to the lobby and out to the street and the cab took me downtown again to my office building. I gave the fresh-faced kid too much money and he gave me a dog-eared business card which for once I didn't drop into the majolica jar of sand beside the elevator bank.

I had a room and a half on the seventh floor at the back. The half-room was an office split in two to make reception rooms. Mine had my name on it and nothing else, and that only on the reception room. I always left this unlocked, in case I had a client, and the client cared to sit down and wait.

I had a client.

11

She wore brownish speckled tweeds, a mannish shirt and tie, hand-carved walking shoes. Her stockings were just as sheer as the day before, but she wasn't showing as much of her legs. Her black hair was glossy under a brown Robin Hood hat that might have cost fifty dollars and looked as if you could have made it with one hand out of a desk blotter.

"Well, you *do* get up," she said, wrinkling her nose at the faded red settee, the two odd semi-easy chairs, the net curtains that needed laundering and the boy's size library table with the venerable magazines on it to give the place a professional touch. "I was beginning to think perhaps you worked in bed, like Marcel Proust."

"Who's he?" I put a cigarette in my mouth and stared at her. She looked a little pale and strained, but she looked like a girl who could function under a strain.

"A French writer, a connoisseur in degenerates. You wouldn't know him."

"Tut, tut," I said. "Come into my boudoir."

She stood up and said: "We didn't get along very well yesterday. Perhaps I was rude."

"We were both rude," I said. I unlocked the communicating door and held it for her. We went into the rest of my suite, which contained a rust-red carpet, not very young, five green filing cases, three of them full of California climate, an advertising calendar showing the Quints rolling around on a sky-blue floor, in pink dresses, with seal-brown hair and sharp black eyes as large as mammoth prunes. There were three near-walnut chairs, the usual desk with the usual blotter, pen set, ashtray and telephone, and the usual squeaky swivel chair behind it.

"You don't put on much of a front," she said, sitting down at the customer's side of the desk.

I went over to the mail slot and picked up six envelopes, two letters and four pieces of advertising matter. I hung my hat on the telephone and sat down.

"Neither do the Pinkertons," I said. "You can't make much money at this trade, if you're honest. If you have a front, you're making money—or expect to."

"Oh—are you honest?" she asked and opened her bag. She picked a cigarette out of a French enamel case, lit it with a pocket lighter, dropped case and lighter back into the bag and left the bag open.

"Painfully."

"How did you get into this slimy kind of business then?"

"How did you come to marry a bootlegger?"

"My God, let's not start quarreling again. I've been trying to get you on the phone all morning. Here and at your apartment."

"About Owen?"

Her face tightened sharply. Her voice was soft. "Poor Owen," she said. "So you know about that."

"A D.A.'s man took me down to Lido. He thought I might know something about it. But he knew much more than I did. He knew Owen wanted to marry your sister—once."

She puffed silently at her cigarette and considered me with steady black eyes. "Perhaps it wouldn't have been a bad idea," she said quietly. "He was in love with her. We don't find much of that in our circle."

"He had a police record."

She shrugged. She said negligently: "He didn't know the right people. That's all a police record means in this rotten crime-ridden country."

"I wouldn't go that far."

She peeled her right glove off and bit her index finger at the first joint, looking at me with steady eyes. "I didn't come to see you about Owen. Do you feel yet that you can tell me what my father wanted to see you about?"

"Not without his permission."

"Was it about Carmen?"

"I can't even say that." I finished filling a pipe and put a match to it. She watched the smoke for a moment. Then her hand went into her open bag and came out with a thick white envelope. She tossed it across the desk.

"You'd better look at it anyway," she said.

I picked it up. The address was typewritten to Mrs. Vivian Regan, 3765 Alta Brea Crescent, West Hollywood. Delivery had been by messenger service and the office stamp showed 8.35 a.m. as the time out. I opened the envelope and drew out the shiny 4¼ by 3¼ photo that was all there was inside.

It was Carmen sitting in Geiger's high-backed teakwood chair on the dais, in her earrings and her birthday suit. Her eyes looked even a little crazier than as I remembered them. The back of the photo was blank. I put it back in the envelope.

"How much do they want?" I asked.

"Five thousand—for the negative and the rest of the prints. The deal has to be closed tonight, or they give the stuff to some scandal sheet."

"The demand came how?"

"A woman telephoned me, about half an hour after this thing was delivered."

"There's nothing in the scandal sheet angle. Juries convict without leaving the box on that stuff nowadays. What else is there?"

"Does there have to be something else?"

"Yes."

She stared at me, a little puzzled. "There is. The woman said there was a police jam connected with it and I'd better lay it on the line fast, or I'd be talking to my little sister through a wire screen."

"Better," I said. "What kind of jam?"

"I don't know."

"Where is Carmen now?"

"She's at home. She was sick last night. She's still in bed, I think."

"Did she go out last night?"

"No. I was out, but the servants say she wasn't. I was down at Las Olindas, playing roulette at Eddie Mars' Cypress Club. I lost my shirt."

"So you like roulette. You would."

She crossed her legs and lit another cigarette. "Yes. I like roulette. All the Sternwoods like losing games, like roulette and marrying men that walk out on them and riding steeplechases at fifty-eight years old and being rolled on by a jumper and crippled for life. The Sternwoods have money. All it has bought them is a rain check."

"What was Owen doing last night with your car?"

"Nobody knows. He took it without permission. We always let him take a car on his night off, but last night wasn't his night off." She made a wry mouth. "Do you think—?"

"He knew about this nude photo? How would I be able to say? I don't rule him out. Can you get five thousand in cash right away?"

"Not unless I tell Dad—or borrow it. I could probably borrow it from Eddie Mars. He ought to be generous with me, heaven knows."

"Better try that. You may need it in a hurry."

She leaned back and hung an arm over the back of the chair. "How about telling the police?"

"It's a good idea. But you won't do it."

"Won't I?"

"No. You have to protect your father and your sister. You don't know what the police might turn up. It might be something they couldn't sit on. Though they usually try in blackmail cases."

"Can you do anything?"

"I think I can. But I can't tell you why or how."

"I like you," she said suddenly. "You believe in miracles. Would you have a drink in the office?"

I unlocked my deep drawer and got out my office bottle and two pony glasses. I filled them and we drank. She snapped her bag shut and pushed her chair back.

"I'll get the five grand," she said. "I've been a good customer of Eddie Mars. There's another reason why he should be nice to me, which you may not know." She gave me one of those smiles the lips have forgotten before they reach the eyes. "Eddie's blonde wife is the lady Rusty ran away with."

I didn't say anything. She stared tightly at me and added: "That doesn't interest you?"

"It ought to make it easier to find him—if I was looking for him. You don't think he's in this mess, do you?"

She pushed her empty glass at me. "Give me another drink. You're the hardest guy to get anything out of. You don't even move your ears."

I filled the little glass. "You've got all you wanted out of me —a pretty good idea I'm not looking for your husband."

She put the drink down very quickly. It made her gasp—or gave her an opportunity to gasp. She let a breath out slowly.

"Rusty was no crook. If he had been, it wouldn't have been for nickels. He carried fifteen thousand dollars, in bills. He called it his mad money. He had it when I married him and he had it when he left me. No—Rusty's not in on any cheap blackmail racket."

She reached for the envelope and stood up. "I'll keep in touch with you," I said. "If you want to leave me a message, the phone girl at my apartment house will take care of it."

We walked over to the door. Tapping the white envelope against her knuckles, she said: "You still feel you can't tell me what Dad—"

"I'd have to see him first."

She took the photo out and stood looking at it, just inside the door. "She has a beautiful little body, hasn't she?"

"Uh-huh."

She leaned a little towards me. "You ought to see mine," she said gravely.

"Can it be arranged?"

She laughed suddenly and sharply and went halfway through the door, then turned her head to say coolly: "You're as cold-blooded a beast as I ever met, Marlowe. Or can I call you Phil?"

"Sure."

"You can call me Vivian."

"Thanks, Mrs. Regan."

"Oh, go to hell, Marlowe." She went on out and didn't look back.

I let the door shut and stood with my hand on it, staring at the hand. My face felt a little hot. I went back to the desk and put the whiskey away and rinsed out the two pony glasses and put them away.

I took my hat off the phone and called the D.A.'s office and asked for Bernie Ohls.

He was back in his cubbyhole. "Well, I let the old man alone," he said. "The butler said he or one of the girls would tell him. This Owen Taylor lived over the garage and I went through his stuff. Parents at Dubuque, Iowa. I wired the Chief of Police there to find out what they want done. The Sternwood family will pay for it."

"Suicide?" I asked.

"No can tell. He didn't leave any notes. He had no leave to take the car. Everybody was home last night but Mrs. Regan. She was down at Las Olindas with a playboy named Larry Cobb. I checked on that. I know a lad on one of the tables."

"You ought to stop some of that flash gambling," I said.

"With the syndicate we got in this county? Be your age, Marlowe. That sap mark on the boy's head bothers me. Sure you can't help me on this?"

I liked his putting it that way. It let me say no without actually lying. We said good-by and I left the office, bought all three afternoon papers and rode a taxi down to the Hall of Justice to get my car out of the lot. There was nothing in any of the papers about Geiger. I took another look at his blue notebook, but the code was just as stubborn as it had been the night before.

12

THE TREES on the upper side of Laverne Terrace had fresh green leaves after the rain. In the cool afternoon sunlight I could see the steep drop of the hill and the flight of steps down which the killer had run after his three shots in the darkness. Two small houses fronted on the street below. They might or might not have heard the shots.

There was no activity in front of Geiger's house or anywhere along the block. The box hedge looked green and peaceful and the shingles on the roof were still damp. I drove past slowly, gnawing at an idea. I hadn't looked in the garage the night before. Once Geiger's body slipped away I hadn't really wanted to find it. It would force my hand. But dragging him to the garage, to his own car and driving that off into one of the hundred odd lonely canyons around Los Angeles would be a good way to dispose of him for days or even for weeks. That supposed two things: a key to his car and two in the party. It would narrow the sector of search quite a lot, especially as I had had his personal keys in my pocket when it happened.

I didn't get a chance to look at the garage. The doors were shut and padlocked and something moved behind the hedge as I drew level. A woman in a green and white check coat and a small button of a hat on soft blonde hair stepped out of the maze and stood looking wild-eyed at my car, as if she hadn't heard it come up the hill. Then she turned swiftly and dodged back out of sight. It was Carmen Sternwood, of course.

I went on up the street and parked and walked back. In the daylight it seemed an exposed and dangerous thing to do. I went in through the hedge. She stood there straight and silent against the locked front door. One hand went slowly up to her teeth and her teeth bit at her funny thumb. There were purple smears under her eyes and her face was gnawed white by nerves.

She half smiled at me. She said: "Hello," in a thin, brittle voice. "Wha—what—?" That tailed off and she went back to the thumb.

"Remember me?" I said. "Doghouse Reilly, the man that grew too tall. Remember?"

She nodded and a quick jerky smile played across her face.

"Let's go in," I said. "I've got a key. Swell, huh?"

"Wha—wha—?"

I pushed her to one side and put the key in the door and opened it and pushed her in through it. I shut the door again and stood there sniffing. The place was horrible by daylight. The Chinese junk on the walls, the rug, the fussy lamps, the teakwood stuff, the sticky riot of colors, the totem pole, the flagon of ether and laudanum—all this in the daytime had a stealthy nastiness, like a fag party.

The girl and I stood looking at each other. She tried to keep a cute little smile on her face but her face was too tired to be bothered. It kept going blank on her. The smile would wash off like water off sand and her pale skin had a harsh granular texture under the stunned and stupid blankness of her eyes. A whitish tongue licked at the corners of her mouth. A pretty, spoiled and not very bright little girl who had gone very, very wrong, and nobody was doing anything about it. To hell with the rich. They made me sick. I rolled a cigarette in my fingers and pushed some books out of the way and sat on the end of the black desk. I lit my cigarette, puffed a plume of smoke and watched the thumb and tooth act for a while in silence. Carmen stood in front of me, like a bad girl in the principal's office.

"What are you doing here?" I asked her finally.

She picked at the cloth of her coat and didn't answer.

"How much do you remember of last night?"

She answered that—with a foxy glitter rising at the back of her eyes. "Remember what? I was sick last night. I was home." Her voice was a cautious throaty sound that just reached my ears.

"Like hell you were."

Her eyes flicked up and down very swiftly.

"Before you went home," I said. "Before I took you home. Here. In that chair—" I pointed to it—"on that orange shawl. You remember all right."

A slow flush crept up her throat. That was something. She could blush. A glint of white showed under the clogged gray irises. She chewed hard on her thumb.

"You—were the one?" she breathed.

"Me. How much of it stays with you?"

She said vaguely: "Are you the police?"

"No. I'm a friend of your father's."

"You're not the police?"

"No."

She let out a thin sigh. "Wha—what do you want?"

"Who killed him?"

Her shoulders jerked, but nothing more moved in her face. "Who else—knows?"

"About Geiger? I don't know. Not the police, or they'd be camping here. Maybe Joe Brody."

It was a stab in the dark but it got a yelp out of her. "Joe Brody! Him!"

Then we were both silent. I dragged at my cigarette and she ate her thumb.

"Don't get clever, for God's sake," I urged her. "This is a spot for a little old-fashioned simplicity. Did Brody kill him?"

"Kill who?"

"Oh, Christ," I said.

She looked hurt. Her chin came down an inch. "Yes," she said solemnly. "Joe did it."

"Why?"

"I don't know." She shook her head, persuading herself that she didn't know.

"Seen much of him lately?"

Her hands went down and made small white knots. "Just once or twice. I hate him."

"Then you know where he lives."

"Yes."

"And you don't like him any more?"

"I hate him!"

"Then you'd like him for the spot."

A little blank again. I was going too fast for her. It was hard not to. "Are you willing to tell the police it was Joe Brody?" I probed.

Sudden panic flamed all over her face. "If I can kill the nude photo angle, of course," I added soothingly.

She giggled. That gave me a nasty feeling. If she had screeched or wept or even nosedived to the floor in a dead faint, that would have been all right. She just giggled. It was suddenly a lot of fun. She had had her photo taken as Isis and somebody had swiped it and somebody had bumped Geiger off in front of her and she was drunker than a Legion convention, and it was suddenly a lot of nice clean fun. So she giggled. Very cute. The giggles got louder and ran around the corners of the room like rats behind the wainscoting. She started to go hysterical. I slid off the desk and stepped up close to her and gave her a smack on the side of the face.

"Just like last night," I said. "We're a scream together. Reilly and Sternwood, two stooges in search of a comedian."

The giggles stopped dead, but she didn't mind the slap any more than last night. Probably all her boy friends got around to slapping her sooner or later. I could understand how they might. I sat down on the end of the black desk again.

"Your name isn't Reilly," she said seriously. "It's Philip Marlowe. You're a private detective. Viv told me. She showed me your card." She smoothed the cheek I had slapped. She smiled at me, as if I was nice to be with.

"Well, you do remember," I said. "And you came back to look for that photo and you couldn't get into the house. Didn't you?"

Her chin ducked down and up. She worked the smile. I was having the eye put on me. I was being brought into camp. I was going to yell "Yippee!" in a minute and ask her to go to Yuma.

"The photo's gone," I said. "I looked last night, before I took you home. Probably Brody took it with him. You're not kidding me about Brody?"

She shook her head earnestly.

"It's a pushover," I said. "You don't have to give it another thought. Don't tell a soul you were here, last night or today. Not even Vivian. Just forget you were here. Leave it to Reilly."

"Your name isn't—" she began, and then stopped and shook her head vigorously in agreement with what I had said or with what she had just thought of. Her eyes became narrow and almost black and as shallow as enamel on a cafeteria tray. She had had an idea. "I have to go home now," she said, as if we had been having a cup of tea.

"Sure."

I didn't move. She gave me another cute glance and went on towards the front door. She had her hand on the knob when we both heard a car coming. She looked at me with questions in her eyes. I shrugged. The car stopped, right in front of the house. Terror twisted her face. There were steps and the bell rang. Carmen stared back at me over her shoulder, her hand clutching the door knob, almost drooling with fear. The bell kept on ringing. Then the ringing stopped. A key tickled at the door and Carmen jumped away from it and stood frozen. The door swung open. A man stepped through it briskly and stopped dead, staring at us quietly, with complete composure.

13

HE WAS a gray man, all gray, except for his polished black shoes and two scarlet diamonds in his gray satin tie that looked like the diamonds on roulette layouts. His shirt was gray and his double-breasted suit of soft, beautifully cut flannel. Seeing Carmen he took a gray hat off and his hair underneath it was gray and as fine as if it had been sifted through gauze. His thick gray eyebrows had that indefinably sporty look. He had a long chin, a nose with a hook to it, thoughtful gray eyes that had a slanted look because the fold of skin over his upper lid came down over the corner of the lid itself.

He stood there politely, one hand touching the door at his back, the other holding the gray hat and flapping it gently against his thigh. He looked hard, not the hardness of the tough guy. More like the hardness of a well-weathered horseman. But he was no horseman. He was Eddie Mars.

He pushed the door shut behind him and put that hand in the lap-seamed pocket of his coat and left the thumb outside to glisten in the rather dim light of the room. He smiled at Carmen. He had a nice easy smile. She licked her lips and stared at him. The fear went out of her face. She smiled back.

"Excuse the casual entrance," he said. "The bell didn't seem to rouse anybody. Is Mr. Geiger around?"

I said: "No. We don't know just where he is. We found the door a little open. We stepped inside."

He nodded and touched his long chin with the brim of his hat. "You're friends of his, of course?"

"Just business acquaintances. We dropped by for a book."

"A book, eh?" He said that quickly and brightly and, I thought, a little slyly, as if he knew all about Geiger's books. Then he looked at Carmen again and shrugged.

I moved towards the door. "We'll trot along now," I said. I took hold of her arm. She was staring at Eddie Mars. She liked him.

"Any message—if Geiger comes back?" Eddie Mars asked gently.

"We won't bother you."

"That's too bad," he said, with too much meaning. His gray eyes twinkled and then hardened as I went past him to open the door. He added in a casual tone: "The girl can dust. I'd like to talk to you a little, soldier."

I let go of her arm. I gave him a blank stare. "Kidder, eh?" he said nicely. "Don't waste it. I've got two boys outside in a car that always do just what I want them to."

Carmen made a sound at my side and bolted through the door. Her steps faded rapidly downhill. I hadn't seen her car, so she must have left it down below. I started to say: "What the hell—!"

"Oh, skip it," Eddie Mars sighed. "There's something wrong around here. I'm going to find out what it is. If you want to pick lead out of your belly, get in my way."

"Well, well," I said, "a tough guy."

"Only when necessary, soldier." He wasn't looking at me any more. He was walking around the room, frowning, not paying any attention to me. I looked out above the broken pane of the front window. The top of a car showed over the hedge. Its motor idled.

Eddie Mars found the purple flagon and the two gold-veined glasses on the desk. He sniffed at one of the glasses, then at the flagon. A disgusted smile wrinkled his lips. "The lousy pimp," he said tonelessly.

He looked at a couple of books, grunted, went on around

the desk and stood in front of the little totem pole with the camera eye. He studied it, dropped his glance to the floor in front of it. He moved the small rug with his foot, then bent swiftly, his body tense. He went down on the floor with one gray knee. The desk hid him from me partly. There was a sharp exclamation and he came up again. His arm flashed under his coat and a black Luger appeared in his hand. He held it in long brown fingers, not pointing it at me, not pointing it at anything.

"Blood," he said. "Blood on the floor there, under the rug. Quite a lot of blood."

"Is that so?" I said, looking interested.

He slid into the chair behind the desk and hooked the mulberry-colored phone towards him and shifted the Luger to his left hand. He frowned sharply at the telephone, bringing his thick gray eyebrows close together and making a hard crease in the weathered skin at the top of his hooked nose. "I think we'll have some law," he said.

I went over and kicked at the rug that lay where Geiger had lain. "It's old blood," I said. "Dried blood."

"Just the same we'll have some law."

"Why not?" I said.

His eyes went narrow. The veneer had flaked off him, leaving a well-dressed hard boy with a Luger. He didn't like my agreeing with him.

"Just who the hell are you, soldier?"

"Marlowe is the name. I'm a sleuth."

"Never heard of you. Who's the girl?"

"Client. Geiger was trying to throw a loop on her with some blackmail. We came to talk it over. He wasn't here. The door being open we walked in to wait. Or did I tell you that?"

"Convenient," he said. "The door being open. When you didn't have a key."

"Yes. How come *you* had a key?"

"Is that any of your business, soldier?"

"I could make it my business."

He smiled tightly and pushed his hat back on his gray hair.
"And I could make your business my business."

"You wouldn't like it. The pay's too small."

"All right, bright eyes. I own this house. Geiger is my tenant.
Now what do you think of that?"

"You know such lovely people."

"I take them as they come. They come all kinds." He glanced
down at the Luger, shrugged and tucked it back under his arm.
"Got any good ideas, soldier?"

"Lots of them. Somebody gunned Geiger. Somebody got
gunned by Geiger, who ran away. Or it was two other fellows.
Or Geiger was running a cult and made blood sacrifices in front
of that totem pole. Or he had chicken for dinner and liked to
kill his chickens in the front parlor."

The gray man scowled at me.

"I give up," I said. "Better call your friends downtown."

"I don't get it," he snapped. "I don't get your game here."

"Go ahead, call the buttons. You'll get a big reaction from
it."

He thought that over without moving. His leps went back
against his teeth. "I don't get that, either," he said tightly.

"Maybe it just isn't your day. I know you, Mr. Mars. The
Cypress Club at Las Olindas. Flash gambling for flash people.
The local law in your pocket and a well-greased line into L.A.
In other words, protection. Geiger was in a racket that needed
that too. Perhaps you spared him a little now and then, seeing
he's your tenant."

His mouth became a hard white grimace. "Geiger was in
what racket?"

"The smut book racket."

He stared at me for a long level minute. "Somebody got to
him," he said softly. "You know something about it. He didn't
show at the store today. They don't know where he is. He
didn't answer the phone here. I came up to see about it. I find
blood on the floor, under a rug. And you and a girl here."

"A little weak," I said. "But maybe you can sell the story to
a willing buyer. You missed a little something, though. Some-

body moved his books out of the store today—the nice books he rented out."

He snapped his fingers sharply and said: "I should have thought of that, soldier. You seem to get around. How do you figure it?"

"I think Geiger was rubbed. I think that is his blood. And the books being moved out gives a motive for hiding the body for a while. Somebody is taking over the racket and wants a little time to organize."

"They can't get away with it," Eddie Mars said grimly.

"Who says so? You and a couple of gunmen in your car outside? This is a big town now, Eddie. Some very tough people have checked in here lately. The penalty of growth."

"You talk too damned much," Eddie Mars said. He bared his teeth and whistled twice, sharply. A car door slammed outside and running steps came through the hedge. Mars flicked the Luger out again and pointed it at my chest. "Open the door."

The knob rattled and a voice called out. I didn't move. The muzzle of the Luger looked like the mouth of the Second Street tunnel, but I didn't move. Not being bullet proof is an idea I had had to get used to.

"Open it yourself, Eddie. Who the hell are you to give me orders? Be nice and I might help you out."

He came to his feet rigidly and moved around the end of the desk and over to the door. He opened it without taking his eyes off me. Two men tumbled into the room, reaching busily under their arms. One was an obvious pug, a good-looking pale-faced boy with a bad nose and one ear like a club steak. The other man was slim, blond, deadpan, with close-set eyes and no color in them.

Eddie Mars said: "See if this bird is wearing any iron."

The blond flicked a short-barreled gun out and stood pointing it at me. The pug sidled over flatfooted and felt my pockets with care. I turned around for him like a bored beauty modeling an evening gown.

"No gun," he said in a burry voice.

"Find out who he is."

The pug slipped a hand into my breast pocket and drew out my wallet. He flipped it open and studied the contents. "Name's Philip Marlowe, Eddie. Lives at the Hobart Arms on Franklin. Private license, deputy's badge and all. A shamus." He slipped the wallet back in my pocket, slapped my face lightly and turned away.

"Beat it," Eddie Mars said.

The two gunmen went out again and closed the door. There was the sound of them getting back into the car. They started its motor and kept it idling once more.

"All right. Talk," Eddie Mars snapped. The peaks of his eyebrows made sharp angles against his forehead.

"I'm not ready to give out. Killing Geiger to grab his racket would be a dumb trick and I'm not sure it happened that way, assuming he has been killed. But I'm sure that whoever got the books knows what's what, and I'm sure that the blonde lady down at his store is scared batty about something or other. And I have a guess who got the books."

"Who?"

"That's the part I'm not ready to give out. I've got a client, you know."

He wrinkled his nose. "That—" he chopped it off quickly.

"I expected you would know the girl," I said.

"Who got the books, soldier?"

"Not ready to talk, Eddie. Why should I?"

He put the Luger down on the desk and slapped it with his open palm. "This," he said. "And I might make it worth your while."

"That's the spirit. Leave the gun out of it. I can always hear the sound of money. How much are you clinking at me?"

"For doing what?"

"What did you want done?"

He slammed the desk hard. "Listen, soldier. I ask you a question and you ask me another. We're not getting anywhere. I want to know where Geiger is, for my own personal reasons. I didn't like his racket and I didn't protect him. I happen to own this house. I'm not so crazy about that right now. I can believe that whatever you know about all this is under glass, or there would be a flock of johns squeaking sole leather around this dump. You haven't got anything to sell. My guess is you need a little protection yourself. So cough up."

It was a good guess, but I wasn't going to let him know it. I lit a cigarette and blew the match out and flicked it at the glass eye of the totem pole. "You're right," I said. "If anything has happened to Geiger, I'll have to give what I have to the law. Which puts it in the public domain and doesn't leave me anything to sell. So with your permission I'll just drift."

His face whitened under the tan. He looked mean, fast and tough for a moment. He made a movement to lift the gun. I added casually: "By the way, how is Mrs. Mars these days?"

I thought for a moment I had kidded him a little too far. His hand jerked at the gun, shaking. His face was stretched out by hard muscles. "Beat it," he said quite softly. "I don't give a damn where you go or what you do when you get there. Only take a word of advice, soldier. Leave me out of your plans or you'll wish your name was Murphy and you lived in Limerick."

"Well, that's not so far from Clonmel," I said. "I hear you had a pal came from there."

He leaned down on the desk, frozen-eyed, unmoving. I went over to the door and opened it and looked back at him. His eyes had followed me, but his lean gray body had not moved. There was hate in his eyes. I went out and through the hedge and up the hill to my car and got into it. I turned it around and drove up over the crest. Nobody shot at me. After a few blocks I turned off, cut the motor and sat for a few moments. Nobody followed me either. I drove back into Hollywood.

14

IT WAS ten minutes to five when I parked near the lobby entrance of the apartment house on Randall Place. A few windows were lit and radios were bleating at the dusk. I rode the automatic elevator up to the fourth floor and went along a wide hall carpeted in green and paneled in ivory. A cool breeze blew down the hall from the open screened door to the fire escape.

There was a small ivory pushbutton beside the door marked "405." I pushed it and waited what seemed a long time. Then the door opened noiselessly about a foot. There was a steady, furtive air in the way it opened. The man was long-legged, long-waisted, high-shouldered and he had dark brown eyes in a brown expressionless face that had learned to control its expressions long ago. Hair like steel wool grew far back on his head and gave him a great deal of domed brown forehead that might at a careless glance have seemed a dwelling place for brains. His somber eyes probed at me impersonally. His long thin brown fingers held the edge of the door. He said nothing.

I said: "Geiger?"

Nothing in the man's face changed that I could see. He brought a cigarette from behind the door and tucked it between his lips and drew a little smoke from it. The smoke came towards me in a lazy, contemptuous puff and behind it words in a cool, unhurried voice that had no more inflection that the voice of a faro dealer.

"You said what?"

"Geiger. Arthur Gwynn Geiger. The guy that has the books."

The man considered that without any haste. He glanced down at the tip of his cigarette. His other hand, the one that had been holding the door, dropped out of sight. His shoulder had a look as though his hidden hand might be making motions.

"Don't know anybody by that name," he said. "Does he live around here?"

I smiled. He didn't like the smile. His eyes got nasty. I said: "You're Joe Brody?"

The brown face hardened. "So what? Got a grift, brother— or just amusing yourself?"

"So you're Joe Brody," I said. "And you don't know anybody named Geiger. That's very funny."

"Yeah? You got a funny sense of humor maybe. Take it away and play on it somewhere else."

I leaned against the door and gave him a dreamy smile. "You got the books, Joe. I got the sucker list. We ought to talk things over."

He didn't shift his eyes from my face. There was a faint sound in the room behind him, as though a metal curtain ring clicked lightly on a metal rod. He glanced sideways into the room. He opened the door wider.

"Why not—if you think you've got something?" he said coolly. He stood aside from the door. I went past him into the room.

It was a cheerful room with good furniture and not too much of it. French windows in the end wall opened on a stone porch and looked across the dusk at the foothills. Near the windows a closed door in the west wall and near the entrance door another door in the same wall. This last had a plush curtain drawn across it on a thin brass rod below the lintel.

That left the east wall, in which there were no doors. There was a davenport backed against the middle of it, so I sat down on the davenport. Brody shut the door and walked crab-fashion to a tall oak desk studded with square nails. A cedar-wood box with gilt hinges lay on the lowered leaf of the desk. He carried the box to an easy chair midway between the other two doors and sat down. I dropped my hat on the davenport and waited.

"Well, I'm listening," Brody said. He opened the cigar box and dropped his cigarette stub into a dish at his side. He put a long thin cigar in his mouth. "Cigar?" He tossed one at me through the air.

I reached for it. Brody took a gun out of the cigar box and pointed it at my nose. I looked at the gun. It was a black Police .38. I had no argument against it at the moment.

"Neat, huh?" Brody said. "Just kind of stand up a minute. Come forward just about two yards. You might grab a little air while you're doing that." His voice was the elaborately casual voice of the tough guy in pictures. Pictures have made them all like that.

"Tsk, tsk," I said, not moving at all. "Such a lot of guns around town and so few brains. You're the second guy I've met within hours who seems to think a gat in the hand means a world by the tail. Put it down and don't be silly, Joe."

His eyebrows came together and he pushed his chin at me. His eyes were mean.

"The other guy's name is Eddie Mars," I said. "Ever hear of him?"

"No." Brody kept the gun pointed at me.

"If he ever gets wise to where you were last night in the rain, he'll wipe you off the way a check raiser wipes a check."

"What would I be to Eddie Mars?" Brody asked coldly. But he lowered the gun to his knee.

"Not even a memory," I said.

We stared at each other. I didn't look at the pointed black slipper that showed under the plush curtain on the doorway to my left.

Brody said quietly: "Don't get me wrong. I'm not a tough guy—just careful. I don't know hell's first whisper about you. You might be a lifetaker for all I know."

"You're not careful enough," I said. "That play with Geiger's books was terrible."

He drew a long slow breath and let it out silently. Then he leaned back and crossed his long legs and held the Colt on his knee.

"Don't kid yourself I won't use this heat, if I have to," he said. "What's your story?"

"Have your friend with the pointed slippers come on in. She gets tired holding her breath."

Brody called out without moving his eyes off my stomach. "Come on in, Agnes."

The curtain swung aside and the green-eyed, thigh-swinging ash blonde from Geiger's store joined us in the room. She looked at me with a kind of mangled hatred. Her nostrils were pinched and her eyes had darkened a couple of shades. She looked very unhappy.

"I knew damn well you were trouble," she snapped at me. "I told Joe to watch his step."

"It's not his step, it's the back of his lap he ought to watch," I said.

"I suppose that's funny," the blonde squealed.

"It has been," I said. "But it probably isn't any more."

"Save the gags," Brody advised me. "Joe's watchin' his step plenty. Put some light on so I can see to pop this guy, if it works out that way."

The blonde snicked on a light in a big square standing lamp. She sank down into a chair beside the lamp and sat stiffly, as if her girdle was too tight. I put my cigar in my mouth and bit the end off. Brody's Colt took a close interest in me while I got matches out and lit the cigar. I tasted the smoke and said:

"The sucker list I spoke of is in code. I haven't cracked it yet, but there are about five hundred names. You got twelve boxes of books that I know of. You should have at least five hundred books. There'll be a bunch more out on loan, but say five hundred is the full crop, just to be cautious. If it's a good active list and you could run it even fifty per cent down the line, that would be one hundred and twenty-five thousand rentals. Your girl friend knows all about that. I'm only guessing. Put the average rental as low as you like, but it won't be less than a dollar. That merchandise costs money. At a dollar a rental you take one hundred and twenty-five grand and you still have your capital. I mean, you still have Geiger's capital. That's enough to spot a guy for."

The blonde yelped: "You're crazy, you goddam egg-headed—!"

Brody put his teeth sideways at her and snarled: "Pipe down, for Chrissake. Pipe down!"

She subsided into an outraged mixture of slow anguish and bottled fury. Her silvery nails scraped on her knees.

"It's no racket for bums," I told Brody almost affectionately. "It takes a smooth worker like you, Joe. You've got to get confidence and keep it. People who spend their money for second-hand sex jags are as nervous as dowagers who can't find the rest room. Personally I think the blackmail angles are a big mistake. I'm for shedding all that and sticking to legitimate sales and rentals."

Brody's dark brown stare moved up and down my face. His Colt went on hungering for my vital organs. "You're a funny guy," he said tonelessly. "Who has this lovely racket?"

"You have," I said. "Almost."

The blonde choked and clawed her ear. Brody didn't say anything. He just looked at me.

"What?" the blonde yelped. "You sit there and try to tell us Mr. Geiger ran that kind of business right down on the main drag? You're nuts!"

I leered at her politely. "Sure I do. Everybody knows the racket exists. Hollywood's made to order for it. If a thing like that has to exist, then right out on the street is where all practical coppers want it to exist. For the same reason they favor red light districts. They know where to flush the game when they want to."

"My God," the blonde wailed. "You let this cheesehead sit there and insult me, Joe? You with a gun in your hand and him holding nothing but a cigar and his thumb?"

"I like it," Brody said. "The guy's got good ideas. Shut your trap and keep it shut, or I'll slap it shut for you with this." He flicked the gun around in an increasingly negligent manner.

The blonde gasped and turned her face to the wall. Brody looked at me and said cunningly: "*How* have I got that lovely racket?"

"You shot Geiger to get it. Last night in the rain. It was dandy shooting weather. The trouble is he wasn't alone when you whiffed him. Either you didn't notice that, which seems unlikely, or you got the wind up and lammed. But you had nerve enough to take the plate out of his camera and you had nerve enough to come back later on and hide his corpse, so you could tidy up on the books before the law knew it had a murder to investigate."

"Yah," Brody said contemptuously. The Colt wobbled on his knee. His brown face was as hard as a piece of carved wood. "You take chances, mister. It's kind of goddamned lucky for you I *didn't* bop Geiger."

"You can step off for it just the same," I told him cheerfully. "You're made to order for the rap."

Brody's voice rustled. "Think you got me framed for it?"

"Positive."

"How come?"

"There's somebody who'll tell it that way. I told you there was a witness. Don't go simple on me, Joe."

He exploded then. "That goddamned little hot pants!" he yelled. "She would, god damn her! She would—just that!"

I leaned back and grinned at him. "Swell. I thought you had those nude photos of her."

He didn't say anything. The blonde didn't say anything. I let them chew on it. Brody's face cleared slowly, with a sort of grayish relief. He put his Colt down on the end table beside his chair but kept his right hand close to it. He knocked ash from his cigar on the carpet and stared at me with eyes that were a tight shine between narrowed lids.

"I guess you think I'm dumb," Brody said.

"Just average, for a grifter. Get the pictures."

"What pictures?"

I shook my head. "Wrong play, Joe. Innocence gets you nowhere. You were either there last night, or you got the nude photo from somebody that was there. You knew *she* was there, because you had your girl friend threaten Mrs. Regan with a police rap. The only ways you could know enough to do that would be by seeing what happened or by holding the photo and knowing where and when it was taken. Cough up and be sensible."

"I'd have to have a little dough," Brody said. He turned his head a little to look at the green-eyed blonde. Not now green-eyed and only superficially a blonde. She was as limp as a fresh-killed rabbit.

"No dough," I said.

He scowled bitterly. "How'd you get to me?"

I flicked my wallet out and let him look at my buzzer. "I was working on Geiger—for a client. I was outside last night, in the rain. I heard the shots. I crashed in. I didn't see the killer. I saw everything else."

"And kept your lip buttoned," Brody sneered.

I put my wallet away. "Yes," I admitted. "Up till now. Do I get the photos or not?"

"About these books," Brody said. "I don't get that."

"I tailed them here from Geiger's store. I have a witness."

"That punk kid?"

"What punk kid?"

He scowled again. "The kid that works at the store. He skipped out after the truck left. Agnes don't even know where he flops."

"That helps," I said, grinning at him. "That angle worried me a little. Either of you ever been in Geiger's house—before last night?"

"Not even last night," Brody said sharply. "So she says I gunned him, eh?"

"With the photos in hand I might be able to convince her she was wrong. There was a little drinking being done."

Brody sighed. "She hates my guts. I bounced her out. I got paid, sure, but I'd of had to do it anyway. She's too screwy for a simple guy like me." He cleared his throat. "How about a little dough? I'm down to nickels. Agnes and me gotta move on."

"Not from my client."

"Listen—"

"Get the pictures, Brody."

"Oh, hell," he said. "You win." He stood up and slipped the Colt into his side pocket. His left hand went up inside his coat. He was holding it there, his face twisted with disgust, when the door buzzer rang and kept on ringing.

15

HE DIDN'T like that. His lower lip went in under his teeth, and his eyebrows drew down sharply at the corners. His whole face became sharp and foxy and mean.

The buzzer kept up its song. I didn't like it either. If the visitors should happen to be Eddie Mars and his boys, I might get chilled off just for being there. If it was the police, I was caught with nothing to give them but a smile and a promise. And if it was some of Brody's friends—supposing he had any—they might turn out to be tougher than he was.

The blonde didn't like it. She stood up in a surge and chipped at the air with one hand. Nerve tension made her face old and ugly.

Watching me, Brody jerked a small drawer in the desk and picked a bone-handled automatic out of it. He held it at the blonde. She slid over to him and took it, shaking.

"Sit down next to him," Brody snapped. "Hold it on him low down, away from the door. If he gets funny use your own judgment. We ain't licked yet, baby."

"Oh, Joe," the blonde wailed. She came over and sat next to me on the davenport and pointed the gun at my leg artery. I didn't like the jerky look in her eyes.

The door buzzer stopped humming and a quick impatient rapping on the wood followed it. Brody put his hand in his pocket, on his gun, and walked over to the door and opened it with his left hand. Carmen Sternwood pushed him back into the room by putting a little revolver against his lean brown lips.

Brody backed away from her with his mouth working and an expression of panic on his face. Carmen shut the door behind her and looked neither at me nor at Agnes. She stalked Brody carefully, her tongue sticking out a little between her teeth. Brody took both hands out of his pockets and gestured placatingly at her. His eyebrows designed themselves into an odd assortment of curves and angles. Agnes turned the gun away from me and swung it at Carmen. I shot my hand out and closed my fingers down hard over her hand and jammed my thumb on the safety catch. It was already on. I kept it on. There was a short silent tussle, to which neither Brody nor Carmen paid any attention whatever. I had the gun. Agnes breathed deeply and shivered the whole length of her body. Carmen's face had a bony scraped look and her breath hissed. Her voice said without tone:

"I want my pictures, Joe."

Brody swallowed and tried to grin. "Sure, kid, sure." He said it in a small flat voice that was as much like the voice he had used to me as a scooter is like a ten-ton truck.

Carmen said: "You shot Arthur Geiger. I saw you. I want my pictures." Brody turned green.

"Hey, wait a minute, Carmen," I yelped.

Blonde Agnes came to life with a rush. She ducked her head and sank her teeth in my right hand. I made more noises and shook her off.

"Listen, kid," Brody whined. "Listen a minute—"

The blonde spat at me and threw herself on my leg and tried to bite that. I cracked her on the head with the gun, not very hard, and tried to stand up. She rolled down my legs and wrapped her arms around them. I fell back on the davenport. The blonde was strong with the madness of love or fear, or a mixture of both, or maybe she was just strong.

Brody grabbed for the little revolver that was so close to his face. He missed. The gun made a sharp rapping noise that was not very loud. The bullet broke glass in a folded-back

French window. Brody groaned horribly and fell down on the floor and jerked Carmen's feet from under her. She landed in a heap and the little revolver went skidding off into a corner. Brody jumped up on his knees and reached for his pocket.

I hit Agnes on the head with less delicacy than before, kicked her off my feet, and stood up. Brody flicked his eyes at me. I showed him the automatic. He stopped trying to get his hand into his pocket.

"Christ!" he whined. "Don't let her kill me!"

I began to laugh. I laughed like an idiot, without control. Blonde Agnes was sitting up on the floor with her hands flat on the carpet and her mouth wide open and a wick of metallic blond hair down over her right eye. Carmen was crawling on her hands and knees, still hissing. The metal of her little revolver glistened against the baseboard over in the corner. She crawled towards it relentlessly.

I waved my share of the guns at Brody and said: "Stay put. You're all right."

I stepped past the crawling girl and picked the gun up. She looked up at me and began to giggle. I put her gun in my pocket and patted her on the back. "Get up, angel. You look like a Pekinese."

I went over to Brody and put the automatic against his midriff and reached his Colt out of his side pocket. I now had all the guns that had been exposed to view. I stuffed them into my pockets and held my hand out to him.

"Give."

He nodded, licking his lips, his eyes still scared. He took a fat envelope out of his breast pocket and gave it to me. There was a developed plate in the envelope and five glossy prints.

"Sure these are all?"

He nodded again. I put the envelope in my own breast pocket and turned away. Agnes was back on the davenport, straightening her hair. Her eyes ate Carmen with a green distillation of hate. Carmen was up on her feet too, coming towards me with her hand out, still giggling and hissing. There was a little froth at the corners of her mouth. Her small white teeth glinted close to her lips.

"Can I have them now?" she asked me with a coy smile.

"I'll take care of them for you. Go on home."

"Home?"

I went to the door and looked out. The cool night breeze was blowing peacefully down the hall. No excited neighbors hung out of doorways. A small gun had gone off and broken a pane of glass, but noises like that don't mean much any more. I held the door open and jerked my head at Carmen. She came towards me, smiling uncertainly.

"Go on home and wait for me," I said soothingly.

She put her thumb up. Then she nodded and slipped past me into the hall. She touched my cheek with her fingers as she went by. "You'll take care of Carmen, won't you?" she cooed.

"Check."

"You're cute."

"What you see is nothing," I said. "I've got a Bali dancing girl tattooed on my right thigh."

Her eyes rounded. She said: "Naughty," and wagged a finger at me. Then she whispered: "Can I have my gun?"

"Not now. Later. I'll bring it to you."

She grabbed me suddenly around the neck and kissed me on the mouth. "I like you," she said. "Carmen likes you a lot." She ran off down the hall as gay as a thrush, waved at me from the stairs and ran down the stairs out of my sight.

I went back into Brody's apartment.

16

I WENT over to the folded-back French window and looked at the small broken pane in the upper part of it. The bullet from Carmen's gun had smashed the glass like a blow. It had not made a hole. There was a small hole in the plaster which a keen eye would find quickly enough. I pulled the drapes over the broken pane and took Carmen's gun out of my pocket. It was a Banker's Special, .22 caliber, hollow point cartridges. It had a pearl grip, and a small round silver plate set into the butt was engraved: "Carmen from Owen." She made saps of all of them.

I put the gun back in my pocket and sat down close to Brody and stared into his bleak brown eyes. A minute passed. The blonde adjusted her face by the aid of a pocket mirror. Brody fumbled around with a cigarette and jerked: "Satisfied?"

"So far. Why did you put the bite on Mrs. Regan instead of the old man?"

"Tapped the old man once. About six, seven months ago. I figure maybe he gets sore enough to call in some law."

"What made you think Mrs. Regan wouldn't tell him about it?"

He considered that with some care, smoking his cigarette and keeping his eyes on my face. Finally he said: "How well you know her?"

"I've met her twice. You must know her a lot better to take a chance on that squeeze with the photo."

"She skates around plenty. I figure maybe she has a couple of soft spots she don't want the old man to know about. I figure she can raise five grand easy."

"A little weak," I said. "But pass it. You're broke, eh?"

"I been shaking two nickels together for a month, trying to get them to mate."

"What you do for a living?"

"Insurance. I got desk room in Puss Walgreen's office, Fulwider Building, Western and Santa Monica."

"When you open up, you open up. The books here in your apartment?"

He snapped his teeth and waved a brown hand. Confidence was oozing back into his manner. "Hell, no. In storage."

"You had a man bring them here and then you had a storage outfit come and take them away again right afterwards?"

"Sure. I don't want them moved direct from Geiger's place, do I?"

"You're smart," I said admiringly. "Anything incriminating in the joint right now?"

He looked worried again. He shook his head sharply.

"That's fine," I told him. I looked across at Agnes. She had finished fixing her face and was staring at the wall, blank-eyed, hardly listening. Her face had the drowsiness which strain and shock induce, after their first incidence.

Brody flicked his eyes warily. "Well?"

"How'd you come by the photo?"

He scowled. "Listen, you got what you came after, got it plenty cheap. You done a nice neat job. Now go peddle it to your top man. I'm clean. I don't know nothing about any photo, do I, Agnes?"

The blonde opened her eyes and looked at him with vague but uncomplimentary speculation. "A half smart guy," she said with a tired sniff. "That's all I ever draw. Never once a guy that's smart all the way around the course. Never once."

I grinned at her. "Did I hurt your head much?"

"You and every other man I ever met."

I looked back at Brody. He was pinching his cigarette between his fingers, with a sort of twitch. His hand seemed to be shaking a little. His brown poker face was still smooth.

"We've got to agree on a story," I said. "For instance, Carmen wasn't here. That's very important. She wasn't here. That was a vision you saw."

"Huh!" Brody sneered. "If you say so, pal, and if—" he put his hand out palm up and cupped the fingers and rolled the thumb gently against the index and middle fingers.

I nodded. "We'll see. There might be a small contribution. You won't count it in grands, though. Now where did you get the picture?"

"A guy slipped it to me."

"Uh-huh. A guy you just passed in the street. You wouldn't know him again. You never saw him before."

Brody yawned. "It dropped out of his pocket," he leered.

"Uh-huh. Got an alibi for last night, poker pan?"

"Sure. I was right here. Agnes was with me. Okey, Agnes?"

"I'm beginning to feel sorry for you again," I said.

His eyes flicked wide and his mouth hung loose, the cigarette balanced on his lower lip.

"You think you're smart and you're so goddamned dumb," I told him. "Even if you don't dance off up in Quentin, you have such a bleak long lonely time ahead of you."

His cigarette jerked and dropped ash on his vest.

"Thinking about how smart you are," I said.

"Take the air," he growled suddenly. "Dust. I got enough chinning with you. Beat it."

"Okey." I stood up and went over to the tall oak desk and took his two guns out of my pockets, laid them side by side on the blotter so that the barrels were exactly parallel. I reached my hat off the floor beside the davenport and started for the door.

Brody yelped: "Hey!"

I turned and waited. His cigarette was jiggling like a doll on a coiled spring. "Everything's smooth, ain't it?" he asked.

"Why, sure. This is a free country. You don't have to stay out of jail, if you don't want to. That is, if you're a citizen. Are you a citizen?"

He just stared at me, jiggling the cigarette. The blonde Agnes turned her head slowly and stared at me along the same level. Their glances contained almost the exact same blend of foxiness, doubt and frustrated anger. Agnes reached her silvery nails up abruptly and yanked a hair out of her head and broke it between her fingers, with a bitter jerk.

Brody said tightly: "You're not going to any cops, brother. Not if it's the Sternwoods you're working for. I've got too much stuff on that family. You got your pictures and you got your hush. Go and peddle your papers."

"Make your mind up," I said. "You told me to dust, I was on my way out, you hollered at me and I stopped, and now I'm on my way out again. Is that what you want?"

"You ain't got anything on me," Brody said.

"Just a couple of murders. Small change in your circle."

He didn't jump more than an inch, but it looked like a foot. The white cornea showed all around the tobacco-colored iris of his eyes. The brown skin of his face took on a greenish tinge in the lamplight.

Blonde Agnes let out a low animal wail and buried her head in a cushion on the end of the davenport. I stood there and admired the long line of her thighs.

Brody moistened his lips slowly and said: "Sit down, pal. Maybe I have a little more for you. What's that crack about two murders mean?"

I leaned against the door. "Where were you last night about seven-thirty, Joe?"

His mouth drooped sulkily and he stared down at the floor. "I was watching a guy, a guy who had a nice racket I figured he needed a partner in. Geiger. I was watching him now and then to see had he any tough connections. I figure he has friends or he don't work the racket as open as he does. But they don't go to his house. Only dames."

"You didn't watch hard enough," I said. "Go on."

"I'm there last night on the street below Geiger's house.

It's raining hard and I'm buttoned up in my coupe and I don't see anything. There's a car in front of Geiger's and another car a little way up the hill. That's why I stay down below. There's a big Buick parked down where I am and after a while I go over and take a gander into it. It's registered to Vivian Regan. Nothing happens, so I scram. That's all." He waved his cigarette. His eyes crawled up and down my face.

"Could be," I said. "Know where that Buick is now?"

"Why would I?"

"In the Sheriff's garage. It was lifted out of twelve feet of water off Lido fish pier this a.m. There was a dead man in it. He had been sapped and the car pointed out the pier and the hand throttle pulled down."

Brody was breathing hard. One of his feet tapped restlessly. "Jesus, guy, you can't pin that one on me," he said thickly.

"Why not? This Buick was down back of Geiger's according to you. Well, Mrs. Regan didn't have it out. Her chauffeur, a lad named Owen Taylor, had it out. He went over to Geiger's place to have words with him, because Owen Taylor was sweet on Carmen, and he didn't like the kind of games Geiger was playing with her. He let himself in the back way with a jimmy and a gun and he caught Geiger taking a photo of Carmen without any clothes on. So his gun went off, as guns will, and Geiger fell down dead and Owen ran away, but not without the photo negative Geiger had just taken. So you ran after him and took the photo from him. How else would you have got hold of it?"

Brody licked his lips. "Yeah," he said. "But that don't make me knock him off. Sure, I heard the shots and saw this killer come slamming down the back steps into the Buick and off. I took out after him. He hit the bottom of the canyon and went west on Sunset. Beyond Beverly Hills he skidded off the road and had to stop and I came up and played copper. He had a gun but his nerve was bad and I sapped him down. So I went through his clothes and found out who he was and I lifted the plateholder, just out of curiosity. I was wondering what it was all about and getting my neck wet when he came out of it all of a sudden and knocked me off the car. He was out of sight when I picked myself up. That's the last I saw of him."

"How did you know it was Geiger he shot?" I asked gruffly.

Brody shrugged. "I figure it was, but I can be wrong. When I had the plate developed and saw what was on it, I was pretty damn sure. And when Geiger didn't come down to the store this morning and didn't answer his phone I was plenty sure. So I figure it's a good time to move his books out and make a quick touch on the Sternwoods for travel money and blow for a while."

I nodded. "That seems reasonable. Maybe you didn't murder anybody at that. Where did you hide Geiger's body?"

He jumped his eyebrows. Then he grinned. "Nix, nix. Skip it. You think I'd go back there and handle him, not knowing when a couple carloads of law would come tearing around the corner? Nix."

"Somebody hid the body," I said.

Brody shrugged. The grin stayed on his face. He didn't believe me. While he was still not believing me the door buzzer started to ring again. Brody stood up sharply, hard-eyed. He glanced over at his guns on the desk.

"So she's back again," he growled.

"If she is, she doesn't have her gun," I comforted him. "Don't you have any other friends?"

"Just about one," he growled. "I got enough of this puss in the corner game." He marched to the desk and took the Colt. He held it down at his side and went to the door. He put his left hand to the knob and twisted it and opened the door a foot and leaned into the opening, holding the gun tight against his thigh.

A voice said: "Brody?"

Brody said something I didn't hear. The two quick reports were muffled. The gun must have been pressed tight against Brody's body. He tilted forward against the door and the weight of his body pushed it shut with a bang. He slid down the wood. His feet pushed the carpet away behind him. His left hand dropped off the knob and the arm slapped the floor with a thud. His head was wedged against the door. He didn't move. The Colt clung to his right hand.

I jumped across the room and rolled him enough to get the door open and crowd through. A woman peered out of a door almost opposite. Her face was full of fright and she pointed along the hall with a clawlike hand.

I raced down the hall and heard thumping feet going down the tile steps and went down after the sound. At the lobby level the front door was closing itself quietly and running feet slapped the sidewalk outside. I made the door before it was shut, clawed it open again and charged out.

A tall hatless figure in a leather jerkin was running diagonally across the street between the parked cars. The figure turned and flame spurted from it. Two heavy hammers hit the stucco wall beside me. The figure ran on, dodged between two cars, vanished.

A man came up beside me and barked: "What happened?"

"Shooting going on," I said.

"Jesus!" He scuttled into the apartment house.

I walked quickly down the sidewalk to my car and got in and started it. I pulled out from the curb and drove down the hill, not fast. No other car started up on the other side of the street. I thought I heard steps, but I wasn't sure about that. I rode down the hill a block and a half, turned at the intersection and started back up. The sound of a muted whistling came to me faintly along the sidewalk. Then steps. I double parked and slid out between two cars and went down low. I took Carmen's little revolver out of my pocket.

The sound of the steps grew louder, and the whistling went on cheerfully. In a moment the jerkin showed. I stepped out between the two cars and said: "Got a match, buddy?"

The boy spun towards me and his right hand darted up to go inside the jerkin. His eyes were a wet shine in the glow of the round electroliers. Moist dark eyes shaped like almonds, and a pallid handsome face with wavy black hair growing low on the forehead in two points. A very handsome boy indeed, the boy from Geiger's store.

He stood there looking at me silently, his right hand on the edge of the jerkin, but not inside it yet. I held the little revolver down at my side.

"You must have thought a lot of that queen," I said.

"Go —— yourself," the boy said softly, motionless between the parked cars and the five-foot retaining wall on the inside of the sidewalk.

A siren wailed distantly coming up the long hill. The boy's head jerked towards the sound. I stepped in close and put my gun into his jerkin.

"Me or the cops?" I asked him.

His head rolled a little sideways as if I had slapped his face. "Who are you?" he snarled.

"Friend of Geiger's."

"Get away from me, you son of a bitch."

"This is a small gun, kid. I'll give it you through the navel and it will take three months to get you well enough to walk. But you'll get well. So you can walk to the nice new gas chamber up in Quentin."

He said: "Go —— yourself." His hand moved inside the jerkin. I pressed harder on his stomach. He let out a long soft sigh, took his hand away from the jerkin and let it fall limp at his side. His wide shoulders sagged. "What you want?" he whispered.

I reached inside the jerkin and plucked out the automatic. "Get into my car, kid."

He stepped past me and I crowded him from behind. He got into the car.

"Under the wheel, kid. You drive."

He slid under the wheel and I got into the car beside him. I said: "Let the prowl car pass up the hill. They'll think we moved over when we heard the siren. Then turn her down hill and we'll go home."

I put Carmen's gun away and leaned the automatic against the boy's ribs. I looked back through the window. The whine of the siren was very loud now. Two red lights swelled in the middle of the street. They grew larger and blended into one and the car rushed by in a wild flurry of sound.

"Let's go," I said.

The boy swung the car and started off down the hill.

"Let's go home," I said. "To Laverne Terrace."

His smooth lips twitched. He swung the car west on Franklin. "You're a simple-minded lad. What's your name?"

"Carol Lundgren," he said lifelessly.

"You shot the wrong guy, Carol. Joe Brody didn't kill your queen."

He spoke three words to me and kept on driving.

17

A moon half gone from the full glowed through a ring of mist among the high branches of the eucalyptus trees on Laverne Terrace. A radio sounded loudly from a house low down the hill. The boy swung the car over to the box hedge in front of Geiger's house, killed the motor and sat looking straight before him with both hands on the wheel. No light showed through Geiger's hedge.

I said: "Anybody home, son?"

"You ought to know."

"How would I know?"

"Go —— yourself."

"That's how people get false teeth."

He showed me his in a tight grin. Then he kicked the door open and got out. I scuttled out after him. He stood with his fists on his hips, looking silently at the house above the top of the hedge.

"All right," I said. "You have a key. Let's go on in."

"Who said I had a key?"

"Don't kid me, son. The fag gave you one. You've got a nice clean manly little room in there. He shooed you out and locked it up when he had lady visitors. He was like Caesar, a husband to women and a wife to men. Think I can't figure people like him and you out?"

I still held his automatic more or less pointed at him, but he swung on me just the same. It caught me flush on the chin.

I backstepped fast enough to keep from falling, but I took
plenty of the punch. It was meant to be a hard one, but a pansy
has no iron in his bones, whatever he looks like.

I threw the gun down at the kid's feet and said: "Maybe you
need this."

He stooped for it like a flash. There was nothing slow about
his movements. I sank a fist in the side of his neck. He toppled
over sideways, clawing for the gun and not reaching it. I picked
it up again and threw it in the car. The boy came up on all
fours, leering with his eyes too wide open. He coughed and
shook his head.

"You don't want to fight," I told him. "You're giving away
too much weight."

He wanted to fight. He shot at me like a plane from a cata-
pult, reaching for my knees in a diving tackle. I sidestepped
and reached for his neck and took it into chancery. He scraped
the dirt hard and got his feet under him enough to use his
hands on me where it hurt. I twisted him around and heaved
him a little higher. I took hold of my right wrist with my left
hand and turned my right hipbone into him and for a moment
it was a balance of weights. We seemed to hang there in the
misty moonlight, two grotesque creatures whose feet scraped
on the road and whose breath panted with effort.

I had my right forearm against his windpipe now and all
the strength of both arms in it. His feet began a frenetic shuffle
and he wasn't panting any more. He was ironbound. His left
foot sprawled off to one side and the knee went slack. I held
on half a minute longer. He sagged on my arm, an enormous
weight I could hardly hold up. Then I let go. He sprawled at
my feet, out cold. I went to the car and got a pair of handcuffs
out of the glove compartment and twisted his wrists behind
him and snapped them on. I lifted him by the armpits and
managed to drag him in behind the hedge, out of sight from
the street. I went back to the car and moved it a hundred feet
up the hill and locked it.

He was still out when I got back. I unlocked the door,
dragged him into the house, shut the door. He was beginning

to gasp now. I switched a lamp on. His eyes fluttered open and focused on me slowly.

I bent down, keeping out of the way of his knees and said: "Keep quiet or you'll get the same and more of it. Just lie quiet and hold your breath. Hold it until you can't hold it any longer and then tell yourself that you have to breathe, that you're black in the face, that your eyeballs are popping out, and that you're going to breathe right now, but that you're sitting strapped in the chair in the clean little gas chamber up in San Quentin and when you take that breath you're fighting with all your soul not to take it, it won't be air you'll get, it will be cyanide fumes. And that's what they call humane execution in our state now."

"Go —— yourself," he said with a soft stricken sigh.

"You're going to cop a plea, brother, don't ever think you're not. And you're going to say just what we want you to say and nothing we don't want you to say."

"Go —— yourself."

"Say that again and I'll put a pillow under your head."

His mouth twitched. I left him lying on the floor with his wrists shackled behind him and his cheek pressed into the rug and an animal brightness in his visible eye. I put on another lamp and stepped into the hallway at the back of the living room. Geiger's bedroom didn't seem to have been touched. I opened the door, not locked now, of the bedroom across the hall from it. There was a dim flickering light in the room and a smell of sandalwood. Two cones of incense ash stood side by side on a small brass tray on the bureau. The light came from the two tall black candles in the foot-high candlesticks. They were standing on straight-backed chairs, one on either side of the bed.

Geiger lay on the bed. The two missing strips of Chinese tapestry made a St. Andrew's Cross over the middle of his body, hiding the blood-smeared front of his Chinese coat. Below the cross his black-pajama'd legs lay stiff and straight. His feet were in the slippers with thick white felt soles. Above the cross his arms were crossed at the wrists and his hands lay flat against his shoulders, palms down, fingers close together and stretched out evenly. His mouth was closed and his Charlie Chan moustache was as unreal as a toupee. His broad nose was pinched and white. His eyes were almost closed, but not entirely. The faint glitter of his glass eye caught the light and winked at me.

I didn't touch him. I didn't go very near him. He would be as cold as ice and as stiff as a board.

The black candles guttered in the draft from the open door. Drops of black wax crawled down their sides. The air of the room was poisonous and unreal. I went out and shut the door again and went back to the living room. The boy hadn't moved. I stood still, listening for sirens. It was all a question of how soon Agnes talked and what she said. If she talked about Geiger, the police would be there any minute. But she might not talk for hours. She might even have got away.

I looked down at the boy. "Want to sit up, son?"

He closed his eye and pretended to go to sleep. I went over to the desk and scooped up the mulberry-colored phone and dialed Bernie Ohls' office. He had left to go home at six o'clock. I dialed the number of his home. He was there.

"This is Marlowe," I said. "Did your boys find a revolver on Owen Taylor this morning?"

I could hear him clearing his throat and then I could hear him trying to keep the surprise out of his voice. "That would come under the heading of police business," he said.

"If they did, it had three empty shells in it."

"How the hell did you know that?" Ohls asked quietly.

"Come over to 7244 Laverne Terrace, off Laurel Canyon Boulevard. I'll show you where the slugs went."

"Just like that, huh?"

"Just like that."

Ohls said: "Look out the window and you'll see me coming round the corner. I thought you acted a little cagey on that one."

"Cagey is no word for it," I said.

18

OHLS STOOD looking down at the boy. The boy sat on the couch leaning sideways against the wall. Ohls looked at him silently, his pale eyebrows bristling and stiff and round like the little vegetable brushes the Fuller Brush man gives away.

He asked the boy: "Do you admit shooting Brody?"

The boy said his favorite three words in a muffled voice.

Ohls sighed and looked at me. I said: "He doesn't have to admit that. I have his gun."

Ohls said: "I wish to Christ I had a dollar for every time I've had that said to me. What's funny about it?"

"It's not meant to be funny," I said.

"Well, that's something," Ohls said. He turned away. "I've called Wilde. We'll go over and see him and take this punk. He can ride with me and you can follow on behind in case he tries to kick me in the face."

"How do you like what's in the bedroom?"

"I like it fine," Ohls said. "I'm kind of glad that Taylor kid went off the pier. I'd hate to have to help send him to the deathhouse for rubbing that skunk."

I went back into the small bedroom and blew out the black candles and let them smoke. When I got back to the living room Ohls had the boy up on his feet. The boy stood glaring at him with sharp black eyes in a face as hard and white as cold mutton fat.

"Let's go," Ohls said and took him by the arm as if he didn't like touching him. I put the lamps out and followed them out of the house. We got into our cars and I followed Ohls' twin tail-lights down the long curving hill. I hoped this would be my last trip to Laverne Terrace.

Taggart Wilde, the District Attorney, lived at the corner of Fourth and Lafayette Park, in a white frame house the size of a carbarn, with a red sandstone porte-cochere built on to one side and a couple of acres of soft rolling lawn in front. It was one of those solid old-fashioned houses which it used to be the thing to move bodily to new locations as the city grew westward. Wilde came of an old Los Angeles family and had probably been born in the house when it was on West Adams or Figueroa or St. James Park.

There were two cars in the driveway already, a big private sedan and a police car with a uniformed chauffeur who leaned smoking against his rear fender and admired the moon. Ohls went over and spoke to him and the chauffeur looked in at the boy in Ohls' car.

We went up to the house and rang the bell. A slick-haired blond man opened the door and led us down the hall and through a huge sunken living room crowded with heavy dark furniture and along another hall on the far side of it. He knocked at a door and stepped inside, then held the door wide and we went into a paneled study with an open French door at the end and a view of dark garden and mysterious trees. A smell of wet earth and flowers came in at the window. There were large dim oils on the walls, easy chairs, books, a smell of good cigar smoke which blended with the smell of wet earth and flowers.

Taggart Wilde sat behind a desk, a middle-aged plump man with clear blue eyes that managed to have a friendly expression without really having any expression at all. He had a cup of black coffee in front of him and he held a dappled thin cigar between the neat careful fingers of his left hand. Another man sat at the corner of the desk in a blue leather chair, a cold-eyed hatchet-faced man, as lean as a rake and as hard as the manager of a loan office. His neat well-kept face looked as if it had been shaved within the hour. He wore a well-pressed brown suit and there was a black pearl in his tie. He had the long nervous fingers of a man with a quick brain. He looked ready for a fight.

Ohls pulled a chair up and sat down and said: "Evening, Cronjager. Meet Phil Marlowe, a private eye who's in a jam." Ohls grinned.

Cronjager looked at me without nodding. He looked me over as if he was looking at a photograph. Then he nodded his chin about an inch. Wilde said: "Sit down, Marlowe. I'll try to handle Captain Cronjager, but you know how it is. This is a big city now."

I sat down and lit a cigarette. Ohls looked at Cronjager and asked: "What did you get on the Randall Place killing?"

The hatchet-faced man pulled one of his fingers until the knuckle cracked. He spoke without looking up. "A stiff, two slugs in him. Two guns that hadn't been fired. Down on the street we got a blonde trying to start a car that didn't belong to her. Hers was right next to it, the same model. She acted rattled so the boys brought her in and she spilled. She was in there when this guy Brody got it. Claims she didn't see the killer."

"That all?" Ohls asked.

Cronjager raised his eyebrows a little. "Only happened about an hour ago. What did you expect—moving pictures of the killing?"

"Maybe a description of the killer," Ohls said.

"A tall guy in a leather jerkin—if you call that a description."

"He's outside in my heap," Ohls said. "Handcuffed. Marlowe put the arm on him for you. Here's his gun." Ohls took the boy's automatic out of his pocket and laid it on a corner of Wilde's desk. Cronjager looked at the gun but didn't reach for it.

Wilde chuckled. He was leaning back and puffing his dappled cigar without letting go of it. He bent forward to sip from his coffee cup. He took a silk handkerchief from the breast pocket of the dinner jacket he was wearing and touched his lips with it and tucked it away again.

"There's a couple more deaths involved," Ohls said, pinching the soft flesh at the end of his chin.

Cronjager stiffened visibly. His surly eyes became points of steely lights.

Ohls said: "You heard about a car being lifted out of the Pacific Ocean off Lido pier this a.m. with a dead guy in it?"

Cronjager said: "No," and kept on looking nasty.

"The dead guy in the car was chauffeur to a rich family," Ohls said. "The family was being blackmailed on account of one of the daughters. Mr. Wilde recommended Marlowe to the family, through me. Marlowe played it kind of close to the vest."

"I love private dicks that play murders close to the vest," Cronjager snarled. "You don't have to be so goddamned coy about it."

"Yeah," Ohls said. "I don't have to be so goddamned coy about it. It's not so goddamned often I get a chance to be coy with a city copper. I spend most of my time telling them where to put their feet so they won't break an ankle."

Cronjager whitened around the corners of his sharp nose. His breath made a soft hissing sound in the quiet room. He said very quietly: "You haven't had to tell any of *my* men where to put their feet, smart guy."

"We'll see about that," Ohls said. "This chauffeur I spoke of that's drowned off Lido shot a guy last night in your territory. A guy named Geiger who ran a dirty book racket in a store on Hollywood Boulevard. Geiger was living with the punk I got outside in my car. I mean living with him, if you get the idea."

Cronjager was staring at him levelly now. "That sounds like it might grow up to be a dirty story," he said.

"It's my experience most police stories are," Ohls growled and turned to me, his eyebrows bristling. "You're on the air, Marlowe. Give it to him."

I gave it to him.

I left out two things, not knowing just why, at the moment,

I left out one of them. I left out Carmen's visit to Brody's apartment and Eddie Mars' visit to Geiger's in the afternoon. I told the rest of it just as it happened.

Cronjager never took his eyes off my face and no expression of any kind crossed his as I talked. At the end of it he was perfectly silent for a long minute. Wilde was silent, sipping his coffee, puffing gently at his dappled cigar. Ohls stared at one of his thumbs.

Cronjager leaned slowly back in his chair and crossed one ankle over his knee and rubbed the ankle bone with his thin nervous hand. His lean face wore a harsh frown. He said with deadly politeness:

"So all you did was not report a murder that happened last night and then spend today foxing around so that this kid of Geiger's could commit a second murder this evening."

"That's all," I said. "I was in a pretty tough spot. I guess I did wrong, but I wanted to protect my client and I hadn't any reason to think the boy would go gunning for Brody."

"That kind of thinking is police business, Marlowe. If Geiger's death had been reported last night, the books could never have been moved from the store to Brody's apartment. The kid wouldn't have been led to Brody and wouldn't have killed him. Say Brody was living on borrowed time. His kind usually are. But a life is a life."

"Right," I said. "Tell that to your coppers next time they shoot down some scared petty larceny crook running away up an alley with a stolen spare."

Wilde put both his hands down on his desk with a solid smack. "That's enough of that," he snapped. "What makes you so sure, Marlowe, that this Taylor boy shot Geiger? Even if the gun that killed Geiger was found on Taylor's body or in the car, it doesn't absolutely follow that he was the killer. The gun might have been planted—say by Brody, the actual killer."

"It's physically possible," I said, "but morally impossible. It assumes too much coincidence and too much that's out of character for Brody and his girl, and out of character for what he was trying to do. I talked to Brody for a long time. He was a crook, but not a killer type. He had two guns, but he wasn't wearing either of them. He was trying to find a way to cut in on Geiger's racket, which naturally he knew all about from the girl. He says he was watching Geiger off and on to see if he had any tough backers. I believe him. To suppose he killed Geiger in order to get his books, then scrammed with the nude photo Geiger had just taken of Carmen Sternwood, then planted the gun on Owen Taylor and pushed Taylor into the ocean off Lido, is to suppose a hell of a lot too much. Taylor had the motive, jealous rage, and the opportunity to kill Geiger. He was out in one of the family cars without permission. He killed Geiger right in front of the girl, which Brody would never have done, even if he had been a killer. I can't see anybody with a purely commercial interest in Geiger doing that. But Taylor would have done it. The nude photo business was just what would have made him do it."

Wilde chuckled and looked along his eyes at Cronjager. Cronjager cleared his throat with a snort. Wilde asked: "What's this business about hiding the body? I don't see the point of that."

I said: "The kid hasn't told us, but he must have done it. Brody wouldn't have gone into the house after Geiger was shot. The boy must have got home when I was away taking Carmen to her house. He was afraid of the police, of course, being what he is, and he probably thought it a good idea to have the body hidden until he had removed his effects from the house. He dragged it out of the front door, judging by the marks on the rug, and very likely put it in the garage. Then he packed up whatever belongings he had there and took them away. And later on, sometime in the night and before the body stiffened, he had a revulsion of feeling and thought he hadn't treated his dead friend very nicely. So he went back and laid him out on the bed. That's all guessing, of course."

Wilde nodded. "Then this morning he goes down to the store as if nothing had happened and keeps his eyes open. And when Brody moved the books out he found out where they were going and assumed that whoever got them had killed

Geiger just for that purpose. He may even have known more about Brody and the girl than they suspected. What do you think, Ohls?"

Ohls said: "We'll find out—but that doesn't help Cronjager's troubles. What's eating him is all this happened last night and he's only just been rung in on it."

Cronjager said sourly: "I think I can find some way to deal with that angle too." He looked at me sharply and immediately looked away again.

Wilde waved his cigar and said: "Let's see the exhibits, Marlowe."

I emptied my pockets and put the catch on his desk: the three notes and Geiger's card to General Sternwood, Carmen's photos, and the blue notebook with the code list of names and addresses. I had already given Geiger's keys to Ohls.

Wilde looked at what I gave him, puffing gently at his cigar. Ohls lit one of his own toy cigars and blew smoke peacefully at the ceiling. Cronjager leaned on the desk and looked at what I had given Wilde.

Wilde tapped the three notes signed by Carmen and said: "I guess these were just a come-on. If General Sternwood paid them, it would be through fear of something worse. Then Geiger would have tightened the screws. Do you know what he was afraid of?" He was looking at me.

I shook my head.

"Have you told your story complete in all relevant details?"

"I left out a couple of personal matters. I intend to keep on leaving them out, Mr. Wilde."

Cronjager said: "Hah!" and snorted with deep feeling.

"Why?" Wilde asked quietly.

"Because my client is entitled to that protection, short of anything but a Grand Jury. I have a license to operate as a private detective. I suppose that word 'private' has some meaning. The Hollywood Division has two murders on its hands, both solved. They have both killers. They have the motive, the instrument in each case. The blackmail angle has got to be suppressed, as far as the names of the parties are concerned."

"Why?" Wilde asked again.

"That's okey," Cronjager said dryly. "We're glad to stooge for a shamus of his standing."

I said: "I'll show you." I got up and went back out of the house to my car and got the book from Geiger's store out of it. The uniformed police driver was standing beside Ohls' car. The boy was inside it, leaning back sideways in the corner.

"Has he said anything?" I asked.

"He made a suggestion," the copper said and spat. "I'm letting it ride."

I went back into the house, put the book on Wilde's desk and opened up the wrappings. Cronjager was using a telephone on the end of the desk. He hung up and sat down as I came in.

Wilde looked through the book, wooden-faced, closed it and pushed it towards Cronjager. Cronjager opened it, looked at a page or two, shut it quickly. A couple of red spots the size of half dollars showed on his cheekbones.

I said: "Look at the stamped dates on the front endpaper."

Cronjager opened the book again and looked at them. "Well?"

"If necessary," I said, "I'll testify under oath that that book came from Geiger's store. The blonde, Agnes, will admit what kind of business the store did. It's obvious to anybody with eyes that that store is just a front for something. But the Hollywood police allowed it to operate, for their own reasons. I dare say the Grand Jury would like to know what those reasons are."

Wilde grinned. He said: "Grand Juries do ask those embarrassing questions sometimes—in a rather vain effort to find out just why cities are run as they are run."

Cronjager stood up suddenly and put his hat on. "I'm one against three here," he snapped. "I'm a homicide man. If this Geiger was running indecent literature, that's no skin off my nose. But I'm ready to admit it won't help my division any to have it washed over in the papers. What do you birds want?"

Wilde looked at Ohls. Ohls said calmly: "I want to turn a prisoner over to you. Let's go."

He stood up. Cronjager looked at him fiercely and stalked out of the room. Ohls went after him. The door closed again. Wilde tapped on his desk and stared at me with his clear blue eyes.

"You ought to understand how any copper would feel about a cover-up like this," he said. "You'll have to make statements of all of it—at least for the files. I think it may be possible to keep the two killings separate and to keep General Sternwood's name out of both of them. Do you know why I'm not tearing your ear off?"

"No. I expected to get both ears torn off."

"What are you getting for it all?"

"Twenty-five dollars a day and expenses."

"That would make fifty dollars and a little gasoline so far."

"About that."

He put his head on one side and rubbed the back of his left little finger along the lower edge of his chin.

"And for that amount of money you're willing to get yourself in Dutch with half the law enforcement of this country?"

"I don't like it," I said. "But what the hell am I to do? I'm on a case. I'm selling what I have to sell to make a living. What little guts and intelligence the Lord gave me and a willingness to get pushed around in order to protect a client. It's against my principles to tell as much as I've told tonight, without consulting the General. As for the cover-up, I've been in police business myself, as you know. They come a dime a dozen in any big city. Cops get very large and emphatic when an outsider tries to hide anything, but they do the same things themselves every other day, to oblige their friends or anybody with a little pull. And I'm not through. I'm still on the case. I'd do the same thing again, if I had to."

"Providing Cronjager doesn't get your license," Wilde grinned. "You said you held back a couple of personal matters. Of what import?"

"I'm still on the case," I said, and stared straight into his eyes.

Wilde smiled at me. He had the frank daring smile of an

Irishman. "Let me tell you something, son. My father was a close friend of old Sternwood. I've done all my office permits—and maybe a good deal more—to save the old man from grief. But in the long run it can't be done. Those girls of his are bound certain to hook up with something that can't be hushed, especially that little blonde brat. They ought not to be running around loose. I blame the old man for that. I guess he doesn't realize what the world is today. And there's another thing I might mention while we're talking man to man and I don't have to growl at you. I'll bet a dollar to a Canadian dime that the General's afraid his son-in-law, the ex-bootlegger, is mixed up in this somewhere, and what he really hoped you would find out is that he isn't. What do you think of that?"

"Regan didn't sound like a blackmailer, what I heard of him. He had a soft spot where he was and he walked out on it."

Wilde snorted. "The softness of that spot neither you nor I could judge. If he was a certain sort of man, it would not have been so very soft. Did the General tell you he was looking for Regan?"

"He told me he wished he knew where he was and that he was all right. He liked Regan and was hurt the way he bounced off without telling the old man good-by."

Wilde leaned back and frowned. "I see," he said in a changed voice. His hand moved the stuff on his desk around, laid Geiger's blue notebook to one side and pushed the other exhibits toward me. "You may as well take these," he said. "I've no further use for them."

19

It was close to eleven when I put my car away and walked around to the front of the Hobart Arms. The plate-glass door was put on the lock at ten, so I had to get my keys out. Inside, in the square barren lobby, a man put a green evening paper down beside a potted palm and flicked a cigarette butt into the tub the palm grew in. He stood up and waved his hat at me and said: "The boss wants to talk to you. You sure keep your friends waiting, pal."

I stood still and looked at his flattened nose and club steak ear.

"What about?"

"What do you care? Just keep your nose clean and everything will be jake." His hand hovered near the upper buttonhole of his open coat.

"I smell of policemen," I said. "I'm too tired to talk, too tired to eat, too tired to think. But if you think I'm not too tired to take orders from Eddie Mars—try getting your gat out before I shoot your good ear off."

"Nuts. You ain't got no gun." He stared at me levelly. His dark wiry brows closed in together and his mouth made a downward curve.

"That was then," I told him. "I'm not always naked."

He waved his left hand. "Okey. You win. I wasn't told to blast anybody. You'll hear from him."

"Too late will be too soon," I said, and turned slowly as he passed me on his way to the door. He opened it and went out without looking back. I grinned at my own foolishness, went along to the elevator and upstairs to the apartment. I took Carmen's little gun out of my pocket and laughed at it. Then I cleaned it thoroughly, oiled it, wrapped it in a piece of canton flannel and locked it up. I made myself a drink and was drinking it when the phone rang. I sat down beside the table on which it stood.

"So you're tough tonight," Eddie Mars' voice said.

"Big, fast, tough and full of prickles. What can I do for you?"

"Cops over there—you know where. You keep me out of it?"

"Why should I?"

"I'm nice to be nice to, soldier. I'm not nice not to be nice to."

"Listen hard and you'll hear my teeth chattering."

He laughed dryly. "Did you—or did you?"

"I did. I'm damned if I know why. I guess it was just complicated enough without you."

"Thanks, soldier. Who gunned him?"

"Read it in the paper tomorrow—maybe."

"I want to know now."

"Do you get everything you want?"

"No. Is that an answer, soldier?"

"Somebody you never heard of gunned him. Let it go at that."

"If that's on the level, someday I may be able to do you a favor."

"Hang up and let me go to bed."

He laughed again. "You're looking for Rusty Regan, aren't you?"

"A lot of people seem to think I am, but I'm not."

"If you were, I could give you an idea. Drop in and see me down at the beach. Any time. Glad to see you."

"Maybe."

"Be seeing you then." The phone clicked and I sat holding it with a savage patience. Then I dialed the Sternwoods' number and heard it ring four or five times and then the butler's suave voice saying: "General Sternwood's residence."

"This is Marlowe. Remember me? I met you about a hundred years ago—or was it yesterday?"

"Yes, Mr. Marlowe. I remember, of course."

"Is Mrs. Regan home?"

"Yes, I believe so. Would you—"

I cut in on him with a sudden change of mind. "No. You give her the message. Tell her I have the pictures, all of them, and that everything is all right."

"Yes . . . yes. . . ." The voice seemed to shake a little. "You have the pictures—all of them—and everything is all right. . . . Yes, sir. I may say—thank you very much, sir."

The phone rang back in five minutes. I had finished my drink and it made me feel as if I could eat the dinner I had forgotten all about; I went out leaving the telephone ringing. It was ringing when I came back. It rang at intervals until half-past twelve. At that time I put my lights out and opened the windows up and muffled the phone bell with a piece of paper and went to bed. I had a bellyful of the Sternwood family.

I read all three of the morning papers over my eggs and bacon the next morning. Their accounts of the affair came as close to the truth as newspaper stories usually come—as close as Mars is to Saturn. None of the three connected Owen Taylor, driver of the Lido Pier Suicide Car, with the Laurel Canyon Exotic Bungalow Slaying. None of them mentioned the Sternwoods, Bernie Ohls or me. Owen Taylor was "chauffeur to a wealthy family." Captain Cronjager of the Hollywood Division got all the credit for solving the two slayings in his district, which were supposed to arise out of a dispute over the proceeds from a wire service maintained by one Geiger in the back of the bookstore on Hollywood Boulevard. Brody had shot Geiger and Carol Lundgren had shot Brody in revenge. Police were holding Carol Lundgren in custody. He had confessed. He had a bad record—probably in high school. Police were also holding one Agnes Lozelle, Geiger's secretary, as a material witness.

It was a nice write-up. It gave the impression that Geiger had been killed the night before, that Brody had been killed about an hour later, and that Captain Cronjager had solved both murders while lighting a cigarette. The suicide of Taylor made Page One of Section II. There was a photo of the sedan on the deck of the power lighter, with the license plate blacked out, and something covered with a cloth lying on the deck beside the running board. Owen Taylor had been despondent and in poor health. His family lived in Dubuque, and his body would be shipped there. There would be no inquest.

20

Captain Gregory of the Missing Persons Bureau laid my card down on his wide flat desk and arranged it so that its edges exactly paralleled the edges of the desk. He studied it with his head on one side, grunted, swung around in his swivel chair and looked out of his window at the barred top floor of the Hall of Justice half a block away. He was a burly man with tired eyes and the slow deliberate movements of a night watchman. His voice was toneless, flat and uninterested.

"Private dick, eh?" he said, not looking at me at all, but looking out of his window. Smoke wisped from the blackened bowl of a briar that hung on his eye tooth. "What can I do for you?"

"I'm working for General Guy Sternwood, 3765 Alta Brea Crescent, West Hollywood."

Captain Gregory blew a little smoke from the corner of his mouth without removing the pipe. "On what?"

"Not exactly on what you're working on, but I'm interested. I thought you could help me."

"Help you on what?"

"General Sternwood's a rich man," I said. "He's an old friend of the D.A.'s father. If he wants to hire a full-time boy to run errands for him, that's no reflection on the police. It's just a luxury he is able to afford himself."

"What makes you think I'm doing anything for him?"

I didn't answer that. He swung around slowly and heavily in his swivel chair and put his large feet flat on the bare linoleum that covered his floor. His office had the musty smell of years of routine. He stared at me bleakly.

"I don't want to waste your time, Captain," I said and pushed my chair back—about four inches.

He didn't move. He kept on staring at me out of his washed-out tired eyes. "You know the D.A.?"

"I've met him. I worked for him once. I know Bernie Ohls, his chief investigator, pretty well."

Captain Gregory reached for a phone and mumbled into it: "Get me Ohls at the D.A.'s office."

He sat holding the phone down on its cradle. Moments passed. Smoke drifted from his pipe. His eyes were heavy and motionless like his hand. The bell tinkled and he reached for my card with his left hand. "Ohls? . . . Al Gregory at headquarters. A guy named Philip Marlowe is in my office. His card says he's a private investigator. He wants information from me. . . . Yeah? What does he look like? . . . Okey, thanks."

He dropped the phone and took his pipe out of his mouth and tamped the tobacco with the brass cap of a heavy pencil. He did it carefully and solemnly, as if that was as important as anything he would have to do that day. He leaned back and stared at me some more.

"What you want?"

"An idea of what progress you're making, if any."

He thought that over. "Regan?" he asked finally.

"Sure."

"Know him?"

"I never saw him. I hear he's a good-looking Irishman in his late thirties, that he was once in the liquor racket, that he married General Sternwood's older daughter and that they didn't click. I'm told he disappeared about a month back."

"Sternwood oughta think himself lucky instead of hiring private talent to beat around in the tall grass."

"The General took a big fancy to him. Such things happen. The old man is crippled and lonely. Regan used to sit around with him and keep him company."

"What you think you can do that we can't do?"

"Nothing at all, in so far as finding Regan goes. But there's a rather mysterious blackmail angle. I want to make sure Regan isn't involved. Knowing where he is or isn't might help."

"Brother, I'd like to help you, but I don't know where he is. He pulled down the curtain and that's that."

"Pretty hard to do against your organization, isn't it, Captain?"

"Yeah—but it can be done—for a while." He touched a bell button on the side of his desk. A middle-aged woman put her head in at a side door. "Get me the file on Terence Regan, Abba."

The door closed. Captain Gregory and I looked at each other in some more heavy silence. The door opened again and the woman put a tabbed green file on his desk. Captain Gregory nodded her out, put a pair of heavy horn-rimmed glasses on his veined nose and turned the papers in the file over slowly. I rolled a cigarette around in my fingers.

"He blew on the 16th of September," he said. "The only thing important about that is it was the chauffeur's day off and nobody saw Regan take his car out. It was late afternoon, though. We found the car four days later in a garage belonging to a ritzy bungalow court place near the Sunset Towers. A garage man reported it to the stolen car detail, said it didn't belong there. The place is called the Casa de Oro. There's an angle to that I'll tell you about in a minute. We couldn't find out anything about who put the car in there. We print the car but don't find any prints that are on file anywhere. The car in that garage don't jibe with foul play, although there's a reason to suspect foul play. It jibes with something else I'll tell you about in a minute."

I said: "That jibes with Eddie Mars' wife being on the missing list."

He looked annoyed. "Yeah. We investigate the tenants and find she's living there. Left about the time Regan did, within two days anyway. A guy who sounds a bit like Regan had been seen with her, but we don't get a positive identification. It's goddamned funny in this police racket how an old woman can look out of a window and see a guy running and pick him out of a line-up six months later, but we can show hotel help a clear photo and they just can't be sure."

"That's one of the qualifications for good hotel help," I said.

"Yeah. Eddie Mars and his wife didn't live together, but they were friendly, Eddie says. Here's some of the possibilities. First off Regan carried fifteen grand, packed it in his clothes all the time. Real money, they tell me. Not just a top card and a bunch of hay. That's a lot of jack but this Regan might be the boy to have it around so he could take it out and look at it when somebody was looking at him. Then again maybe he wouldn't give a damn. His wife says he never made a nickel off of old man Sternwood except room and board and a Packard 120 his wife gave him. Tie that for an ex-legger in the rich gravy."

"It beats me," I said.

"Well, here we are with a guy who ducks out and has fifteen grand in his pants and folks know it. Well, that's money. I might duck out myself, if I had fifteen grand, and me with two kids in high school. So the first thought is somebody rolls him for it and rolls him too hard, so they have to take him out in the desert and plant him among the cactuses. But I don't like that too well. Regan carried a gat and had plenty of experience using it, and not just in a greasy-faced liquor mob. I understand he commanded a whole brigade in the Irish troubles back in 1922 or whenever it was. A guy like that wouldn't be white meat to a heister. Then, his car being in that garage makes whoever rolled him know he was sweet on Eddie Mars' wife, which he was, I guess, but it ain't something every poolroom bum would know."

"Got a photo?" I asked.

"Him, not her. That's funny too. There's a lot of funny angles to this case. Here." He pushed a shiny print across the desk and I looked at an Irish face that was more sad than merry and more reserved than brash. Not the face of a tough guy and not the face of a man who could be pushed around much by anybody. Straight dark brows with strong bone under them. A forehead wide rather than high, a mat of dark clustering hair, a thin short nose, a wide mouth. A chin that had strong lines but was small for the mouth. A face that looked a little taut, the face of a man who would move fast and play for keeps. I passed the print back. I would know that face, if I saw it.

Captain Gregory knocked his pipe out and refilled it and tamped the tobacco down with his thumb. He lit it, blew smoke and began to talk again.

"Well, there could be people who would know he was sweet on Eddie Mars' frau. Besides Eddie himself. For a wonder *he* knew it. But he don't seem to give a damn. We check him pretty thoroughly around that time. Of course Eddie wouldn't have knocked him off out of jealousy. The set-up would point to him too obvious."

"It depends how smart he is," I said. "He might try the double bluff."

Captain Gregory shook his head. "If he's smart enough to get by in his racket, he's too smart for that. I get your idea. He pulls the dumb play because he thinks we wouldn't expect him to pull the dumb play. From a police angle that's wrong. Because he'd have us in his hair so much it would interfere with his business. *You* might think a dumb play would be smart. I might think so. The rank and file wouldn't. They'd make his life miserable. I've ruled it out. If I'm wrong, you can prove it on me and I'll eat my chair cushion. Till then I'm leaving Eddie in the clear. Jealousy is a bad motive for his type. Top-flight racketeers have business brains. They learn to do things that are good policy and let their personal feelings take care of themselves. I'm leaving that out."

"What are you leaving in?"

"The dame and Regan himself. Nobody else. She was a blonde then, but she won't be now. We don't find her car, so they probably left in it. They had a long start on us—fourteen days. Except for that car of Regan's I don't figure we'd have got the case at all. Of course I'm used to them that way, especially in good-class families. And of course everything I've done has had to be under the hat."

He leaned back and thumped the arms of his chair with the heels of his large heavy hands.

"I don't see nothing to do but wait," he said. "We've got readers out, but it's too soon to look for results. Regan had fifteen grand we know of. The girl had some, maybe a lot in rocks. But they'll run out of dough some day. Regan will cash a check, drop a marker, write a letter. They're in a strange town and they've got new names, but they've got the same old appetites. They got to get back in the fiscal system."

"What did the girl do before she married Eddie Mars?"

"Torcher."

"Can't you get any old professional photos?"

"No. Eddie must of had some, but he won't loosen up. He wants her let alone. I can't make him. He's got friends in town, or he wouldn't be what he is." He grunted. "Any of this do you any good?"

I said: "You'll never find either of them. The Pacific Ocean is too close."

"What I said about my chair cushion still goes. We'll find him. It may take time. It could take a year or two."

"General Sternwood may not live that long," I said.

"We've done all we could, brother. If he wants to put out a reward and spend some money, we might get results. The city don't give me the kind of money it takes." His large eyes peered at me and his scratchy eyebrows moved. "You serious about thinking Eddie put them both down?"

I laughed. "No. I was just kidding. I think what you think, Captain. That Regan ran away with a woman who meant more to him than a rich wife he didn't get along with. Besides, she isn't rich yet."

"You met her, I suppose?"

"Yes. She'd make a jazzy week-end, but she'd be wearing for a steady diet."

He grunted and I thanked him for his time and information

and left. A gray Plymouth sedan tailed me away from the City Hall. I gave it a chance to catch up with me on a quiet street. It refused the offer, so I shook it off and went about my business.

21

I DIDN'T go near the Sternwood family. I went back to the office and sat in my swivel chair and tried to catch up on my foot-dangling. There was a gusty wind blowing in at the windows and the soot from the oil burners of the hotel next door was down-drafted into the room and rolling across the top of the desk like tumbleweed drifting across a vacant lot. I was thinking about going out to lunch and that life was pretty flat and that it would probably be just as flat if I took a drink and that taking a drink all alone at that time of day wouldn't be any fun anyway. I was thinking this when Norris called up. In his carefully polite manner he said that General Sternwood was not feeling very well and that certain items in the newspaper had been read to him and he assumed that my investigation was now completed.

"Yes, as regards Geiger," I said. "I didn't shoot him, you know."

"The General didn't suppose you did, Mr. Marlowe."

"Does the General know anything about those photographs Mrs. Regan was worrying about?"

"No, sir. Decidedly not."

"Did you know what the General gave me?"

"Yes, sir. Three notes and a card, I believe."

"Right. I'll return them. As to the photos I think I'd better just destroy them."

"Very good, sir. Mrs. Regan tried to reach you a number of times last night—"

"I was out getting drunk," I said.

"Yes. Very necessary, sir, I'm sure. The General has instructed me to send you a check for five hundred dollars. Will that be satisfactory?"

"More than generous," I said.

"And I presume we may now consider the incident closed?"

"Oh sure. Tight as a vault with a busted time lock."

"Thank you, sir. I am sure we all appreciate it. When the General is feeling a little better—possibly tomorrow—he would like to thank you in person."

"Fine," I said. "I'll come out and drink some more of his brandy, maybe with champagne."

"I shall see that some is properly iced," the old boy said, almost with a smirk in his voice.

That was that. We said good-by and hung up. The coffee shop smell from next door came in at the windows with the soot but failed to make me hungry. So I got out my office bottle and took the drink and let my self-respect ride its own race.

I counted it up on my fingers. Rusty Regan had run away from a lot of money and a handsome wife to go wandering with a vague blonde who was more or less married to a racketeer named Eddie Mars. He had gone suddenly without good-bys and there might be any number of reasons for that. The General had been too proud, or, at the first interview he gave me, too careful, to tell me the Missing Persons Bureau had the matter in hand. The Missing Persons people were dead on their feet on it and evidently didn't think it was worth bothering over. Regan had done what he had done and that was his business. I agreed with Captain Gregory that Eddie Mars would have been very unlikely to involve himself in a double murder just because another man had gone to town with the blonde he was not even living with. It might have annoyed him, but business is business, and you have to hold your teeth clamped around Hollywood to keep from chewing on stray blondes. If there had been a lot of money involved, that would be different. But fifteen grand wouldn't be a lot of money to Eddie Mars. He was no two-bit chiseler like Brody.

Geiger was dead and Carmen would have to find some other shady character to drink exotic blends of hooch with. I didn't suppose she would have any trouble. All she would have to do would be to stand on the corner for five minutes and look coy. I hoped that the next grifter who dropped the hook on her would play her a little more smoothly, a little more for the long haul rather than the quick touch.

Mrs. Regan knew Eddie Mars well enough to borrow money from him. That was natural, if she played roulette and was a good loser. Any gambling house owner would lend a good client money in a pinch. Apart from this they had an added bond of interest in Regan. He was her husband and he had gone off with Eddie Mars' wife.

Carol Lundgren, the boy killer with the limited vocabulary, was out of circulation for a long, long time, even if they didn't strap him in a chair over a bucket of acid. They wouldn't, because he would take a plea and save the county money. They all do when they don't have the price of a big lawyer. Agnes Lozelle was in custody as a material witness. They wouldn't need her for that, if Carol took a plea, and if he pleaded guilty on arraignment, they would turn her loose. They wouldn't want to open up any angles on Geiger's business, apart from which they had nothing on her.

That left me. I had concealed a murder and suppressed evidence for twenty-four hours, but I was still at large and had a five-hundred-dollar check coming. The smart thing for me to do was to take another drink and forget the whole mess.

That being the obviously smart thing to do, I called Eddie Mars and told him I was coming down to Las Olindas that evening to talk to him. That was how smart I was.

I got down there about nine, under a hard high October moon that lost itself in the top layers of a beach fog. The Cypress Club was at the far end of the town, a rambling frame mansion that had once been the summer residence of a rich man named De Cazens, and later had been a hotel. It was now a big dark outwardly shabby place in a thick grove of wind-twisted Monterey cypresses, which gave it its name. It had enormous scrolled porches, turrets all over the place, stained-glass trims around the big windows, big empty stables at the back, a general air of nostalgic decay. Eddie Mars had left the outside much as he had found it, instead of making it over to look like an MGM set. I left my car on a street with sputtering arc lights and walked into the grounds along a damp gravel path to the main entrance. A doorman in a double-breasted guard's coat let me into a huge dim silent lobby from which a white oak staircase curved majestically up to the darkness of an upper floor. I checked my hat and coat and waited, listening to music and confused voices behind heavy double doors. They seemed a long way off, and not quite of the same world as the building itself. Then the slim pasty-faced blond man who had been with Eddie Mars and the pug at Geiger's place came through a door under the staircase, smiled at me bleakly and took me back with him along a carpeted hall to the boss's office.

This was a square room with a deep old bay window and a stone fireplace in which a fire of juniper logs burned lazily. It was wainscoted in walnut and had a frieze of faded damask above the paneling. The ceiling was high and remote. There was a smell of cold sea.

Eddie Mars' dark sheenless desk didn't belong in the room, but neither did anything made after 1900. His carpet had a Florida suntan. There was a bartop radio in the corner and a Sèvres china tea set on a copper tray beside a samovar. I wondered who that was for. There was a door in the corner that had a time lock on it.

Eddie Mars grinned at me sociably and shook hands and moved his chin at the vault. "I'm a pushover for a heist mob here except for that thing," he said cheerfully. "The local johns drop in every morning and watch me open it. I have an arrangement with them."

"You hinted you had something for me," I said. "What is it?"

"What's your hurry? Have a drink and sit down."

"No hurry at all. You and I haven't anything to talk about but business."

"You'll have the drink and like it," he said. He mixed a couple and put mine down beside a red leather chair and stood crosslegged against the desk himself, one hand in the side pocket of his midnight-blue dinner jacket, the thumb outside and the nail glistening. In dinner clothes he looked a little harder than in gray flannel, but he still looked like a horseman. We drank and nodded at each other.

"Ever been here before?" he asked.

"During prohibition. I don't get any kick out of gambling."

"Not with money," he smiled. "You ought to look in tonight. One of your friends is outside betting the wheels. I hear she's doing pretty well. Vivian Regan."

I sipped my drink and took one of his monogrammed cigarettes.

"I kind of liked the way you handled that yesterday," he said. "You made me sore at the time but I could see afterwards how right you were. You and I ought to get along. How much do I owe you?"

"For doing what?"

"Still careful, eh? I have my pipe line into headquarters, or I wouldn't be here. I get them the way they happen, not the way you read them in the papers." He showed me his large white teeth.

"How much have you got?" I asked.

"You're not talking money?"

"Information was the way I understood it."

"Information about what?"

"You have a short memory. Regan."

"Oh, that." He waved his glistening nails in the quiet light from one of those bronze lamps that shoot a beam at the ceiling. "I hear you got the information already. I felt I owed you a fee. I'm used to paying for nice treatment."

"I didn't drive down here to make a touch. I get paid for what I do. Not much by your standards, but I make out. One customer at a time is a good rule. You didn't bump Regan off, did you?"

"No. Did you think I did?"

"I wouldn't put it past you."

He laughed. "You're kidding."

I laughed. "Sure, I'm kidding. I never saw Regan, but I saw his photo. You haven't got the men for the work. And while we're on that subject don't send me any more gun punks with orders. I might get hysterical and blow one down."

He looked through his glass at the fire, set it down on the end of the desk and wiped his lips with a sheer lawn handkerchief.

"You talk a good game," he said. "But I dare say you can break a hundred and ten. You're not really interested in Regan, are you?"

"No, not professionally. I haven't been asked to be. But I know somebody who would like to know where he is."

"She doesn't give a damn," he said.

"I mean her father."

He wiped his lips again and looked at the handkerchief almost as if he expected to find blood on it. He drew his thick gray eyebrows close together and fingered the side of his weatherbeaten nose.

"Geiger was trying to blackmail the General," I said. "The General wouldn't say so, but I figure he was at least half scared Regan might be behind it."

Eddie Mars laughed. "Uh-uh. Geiger worked that one on everybody. It was strictly his own idea. He'd get notes from people that looked legal—were legal, I dare say, except that he wouldn't have dared sue on them. He'd present the notes, with a nice flourish, leaving himself empty-handed. If he drew an ace, he had a prospect that scared and he went to work. If he didn't draw an ace, he just dropped the whole thing."

"Clever guy," I said. "He dropped it all right. Dropped it and fell on it. How come *you* know all this?"

He shrugged impatiently. "I wish to Christ I didn't know

half the stuff that's brought to me. Knowing other people's business is the worst investment a man can make in my circle. Then if it was just Geiger you were after, you're washed up on that angle."

"Washed up and paid off."

"I'm sorry about that. I wish old Sternwood would hire himself a soldier like you on a straight salary, to keep those girls of his home at least a few nights a week."

"Why?"

His mouth looked sulky. "They're plain trouble. Take the dark one. She's a pain in the neck around here. If she loses, she plunges and I end up with a fistful of paper which nobody will discount at any price. She has no money of her own except an allowance and what's in the old man's will is a secret. If she wins, she takes my money home with her."

"You get it back the next night," I said.

"I get some of it back. But over a period of time I'm loser."

He looked earnestly at me, as if that was important to me. I wondered why he thought it necessary to tell me at all. I yawned and finished my drink.

"I'm going out and look the joint over," I said.

"Yes, do." He pointed to a door near the vault door. "That leads to a door behind the tables."

"I'd rather go in the way the suckers enter."

"Okey. As you please. We're friends, aren't we, soldier?"

"Sure." I stood up and we shook hands.

"Maybe I can do you a real favor some day," he said. "You got it all from Gregory this time."

"So you own a piece of him too."

"Oh not that bad. We're just friends."

I stared at him for a moment, then went over to the door I had come in at. I looked back at him when I had it open.

"You don't have anybody tailing me around in a gray Plymouth sedan, do you?"

His eyes widened sharply. He looked jarred. "Hell, no. Why should I?"

"I couldn't imagine," I said, and went on out. I thought his surprise looked genuine enough to be believed. I thought he even looked a little worried. I couldn't think of any reason for that.

22

It was about ten-thirty when the little yellow-sashed Mexican orchestra got tired of playing a low-voiced, prettied-up rhumba that nobody was dancing to. The gourd player rubbed his finger tips together as if they were sore and got a cigarette into his mouth almost with the same movement. The other four, with a timed simultaneous stoop, reached under their chairs for glasses from which they sipped, smacking their lips and flashing their eyes. Tequila, their manner said. It was probably mineral water. The pretense was as wasted as the music. Nobody was looking at them.

The room had been a ballroom once and Eddie Mars had changed it only as much as his business compelled him. No chromium glitter, no indirect lighting from behind angular cornices, no fused glass pictures, or chairs in violent leather and polished metal tubing, none of the pseudo-modernistic circus of the typical Hollywood night trap. The light was from heavy crystal chandeliers and the rose-damask panels of the wall were still the same rose damask, a little faded by time and darkened by dust, that had been matched long ago against the parquetry floor, of which only a small glass-smooth space in front of the little Mexican orchestra showed bare. The rest was covered by a heavy old-rose carpeting that must have cost plenty. The parquetry was made of a dozen kinds of hardwood, from Burma teak through half a dozen shades of oak and ruddy wood that looked like mahogany, and fading out to the hard pale wild lilac of the California hills, all laid in elaborate patterns, with the accuracy of a transit.

It was still a beautiful room and now there was roulette in it instead of measured, old-fashioned dancing. There were three tables close to the far wall. A low bronze railing joined them and made a fence around the croupiers. All three tables were working, but the crowd was at the middle one. I could see Vivian Regan's black head close to it, from across the room where I was leaning against the bar and turning a small glass of bacardi around on the mahogany.

The bartender leaned beside me watching the cluster of well-dressed people at the middle table. "She's pickin' 'em tonight, right on the nose," he said. "That tall blackheaded frail."

"Who is she?"

"I wouldn't know her name. She comes here a lot though."

"The hell you wouldn't know her name."

"I just work here, mister," he said without any animosity. "She's all alone too. The guy was with her passed out. They took him out to his car."

"I'll take her home," I said.

"The hell you will. Well, I wish you luck anyways. Should I gentle up that bacardi or do you like it the way it is?"

"I like it the way it is as well as I like it at all," I said.

"Me, I'd just as leave drink croup medicine," he said.

The crowd parted and two men in evening clothes pushed their way out and I saw the back of her neck and her bare shoulders in the opening. She wore a low-cut dress of dull green velvet. It looked too dressy for the occasion. The crowd closed and hid all but her black head. The two men came across the room and leaned against the bar and asked for Scotch and soda. One of them was flushed and excited. He was mopping his face with a black-bordered handkerchief. The double satin stripes down the side of his trousers were wide enough for tire tracks.

"Boy, I never saw such a run," he said in a jittery voice.

"Eight wins and two stand-offs in a row on that red. That's roulette, boy, that's roulette."

"It gives me the itch," the other one said. "She's betting a grand at a crack. She can't lose." They put their beaks in their drinks, gurgled swiftly and went back.

"So wise the little men are," the barkeep drawled. "A grand a crack, huh. I saw an old horseface in Havana once—"

The noise swelled over at the middle table and a chiseled foreign voice rose above it saying: "If you will just be patient a moment, madam. The table cannot cover your bet. Mr. Mars will be here in a moment."

I left my bacardi and padded across the carpet. The little orchestra started to play a tango, rather loud. No one was dancing or intending to dance. I moved through a scattering of people in dinner clothes and full evening dress and sports clothes and business suits to the end table at the left. It had gone dead. Two croupiers stood behind it with their heads together and their eyes sideways. One moved a rake back and forth aimlessly over the empty layout. They were both staring at Vivian Regan.

Her long lashes twitched and her face looked unnaturally white. She was at the middle table, exactly opposite the wheel. There was a disordered pile of money and chips in front of her. It looked like a lot of money. She spoke to the croupier with a cool, insolent, ill-tempered drawl.

"What kind of a cheap outfit is this, I'd like to know. Get busy and spin that wheel, highpockets. I want one more play and I'm playing table stakes. You take it away fast enough I've noticed, but when it comes to dishing it out you start to whine."

The croupier smiled a cold polite smile that had looked at thousands of boors and millions of fools. His tall dark disinterested manner was flawless. He said gravely: "The table cannot cover your bet, madam. You have over sixteen thousand dollars there."

"It's your money," the girl jeered. "Don't you want it back?"

A man beside her tried to tell her something. She turned

swiftly and spat something at him and he faded back into the crowd red-faced. A door opened in the paneling at the far end of the enclosed place made by the bronze railing. Eddie Mars came through the door with a set indifferent smile on his face, his hands thrust into the pockets of his dinner jacket, both thumbnails glistening outside. He seemed to like that pose. He strolled behind the croupiers and stopped at the corner of the middle table. He spoke with lazy calm, less politely than the croupier.

"Something the matter, Mrs. Regan?"

She turned her face to him with a sort of lunge. I saw the curve of her cheek stiffen, as if with an almost unbearable inner tautness. She didn't answer him.

Eddie Mars said gravely: "If you're not playing any more, you must let me send someone home with you."

The girl flushed. Her cheekbones stood out white in her face. Then she laughed off-key. She said bitterly:

"One more play, Eddie. Everything I have on the red. I like red. It's the color of blood."

Eddie Mars smiled faintly, then nodded and reached into his inner breast pocket. He drew out a large pinseal wallet with gold corners and tossed it carelessly along the table to the croupier. "Cover her bet in even thousands," he said, "if no one objects to this turn of the wheel being just for the lady."

No one objected. Vivian Regan leaned down and pushed all her winnings savagely with both hands on to the large red diamond on the layout.

The croupier leaned over the table without haste. He counted and stacked her money and chips, placed all but a few chips and bills in a neat pile and pushed the rest back off the layout with his rake. He opened Eddie Mars' wallet and drew out two flat packets of thousand-dollar bills. He broke one, counted six bills out, added them to the unbroken packet, put the four loose bills in the wallet and laid it aside as carelessly as if it had been a packet of matches. Eddie Mars didn't touch the wallet. Nobody moved except the croupier. He spun the wheel lefthanded and sent the ivory ball skittering along the upper edge with a casual flirt of his wrist. Then he drew his hands back and folded his arms.

Vivian's lips parted slowly until her teeth caught the light and glittered like knives. The ball drifted lazily down the slope of the wheel and bounced on the chromium ridges above the numbers. After a long time and then very suddenly motion left it with a dry click. The wheel slowed, carrying the ball around with it. The croupier didn't unfold his arms until the wheel had entirely ceased to revolve.

"The red wins," he said formally, without interest. The little ivory ball lay in Red 25, the third number from the Double Zero. Vivian Regan put her head back and laughed triumphantly.

The croupier lifted his rake and slowly pushed the stack of thousand-dollar bills across the layout, added them to the stake, pushed everything slowly out of the field of play.

Eddie Mars smiled, put his wallet back in his pocket, turned on his heel and left the room through the door in the paneling.

A dozen people let their breath out at the same time and broke for the bar. I broke with them and got to the far end of the room before Vivian had gathered up her winnings and turned away from the table. I went out into the large quiet lobby, got my hat and coat from the check girl, dropped a quarter in her tray and went out on the porch. The doorman loomed up beside me and said: "Can I get your car for you, sir?"

I said: "I'm just going for a walk."

The scrollwork along the edge of the porch was wet with the fog. The fog dripped from the Monterey cypresses that shadowed off into nothing towards the cliff above the ocean. You could see a scant dozen feet in any direction. I went down the porch steps and drifted off through the trees, following an indistinct path until I could hear the wash of the surf licking at the fog, low down at the bottom of the cliff. There wasn't a gleam of light anywhere. I could see a dozen trees clearly at one time, another dozen dimly, then nothing at all but the fog. I circled to the left and drifted back towards the gravel path that went around to the stables where they parked the cars. When I could make out the outlines of the house I stopped. A little in front of me I had heard a man cough.

My steps hadn't made any sound on the soft moist turf. The man coughed again, then stifled the cough with a handkerchief or a sleeve. While he was still doing that I moved forward closer to him. I made him out, a vague shadow close to the path. Something made me step behind a tree and crouch down. The man turned his head. His face should have been a white blur when he did that. It wasn't. It remained dark. There was a mask over it.

I waited, behind the tree.

23

LIGHT STEPS, the steps of a woman, came along the invisible pathway and the man in front of me moved forward and seemed to lean against the fog. I couldn't see the woman, then I could see her indistinctly. The arrogant carriage of her head seemed familiar. The man stepped out very quickly. The two figures blended in the fog, seemed to be part of the fog. There was dead silence for a moment. Then the man said:

"This is a gun, lady. Gentle now. Sound carries in the fog. Just hand me the bag."

The girl didn't make a sound. I moved forward a step. Quite suddenly I could see the foggy fuzz on the man's hat brim. The girl stood motionless. Then her breathing began to make a rasping sound, like a small file on soft wood.

"Yell," the man said, "and I'll cut you in half."

She didn't yell. She didn't move. There was a movement from him, and a dry chuckle. "It better be in here," he said. A catch clicked and a fumbling sound came to me. The man turned and came towards my tree. When he had taken three or four steps he chuckled again. The chuckle was something out of my own memories. I reached a pipe out of my pocket and held it like a gun.

I called out softly: "Hi, Lanny."

The man stopped dead and started to bring his hand up. I said: "No. I told you never to do that, Lanny. You're covered."

Nothing moved. The girl back on the path didn't move. I didn't move. Lanny didn't move.

"Put the bag down between your feet, kid," I told him. "Slow and easy."

He bent down. I jumped out and reached him still bent over. He straightened up against me breathing hard. His hands were empty.

"Tell me I can't get away with it," I said. I leaned against him and took the gun out of his overcoat pocket. "Somebody's always giving me guns," I told him. "I'm weighted down with them till I walk all crooked. Beat it."

Our breaths met and mingled, our eyes were like the eyes of two tomcats on a wall. I stepped back.

"On your way, Lanny. No hard feelings. You keep it quiet and I keep it quiet. Okey?"

"Okey," he said thickly.

The fog swallowed him. The faint sound of his steps and then nothing. I picked the bag up and felt in it and went towards the path. She still stood there motionless, a gray fur coat held tight around her throat with an ungloved hand on which a ring made a faint glitter. She wore no hat. Her dark parted hair was part of the darkness of the night. Her eyes too.

"Nice work, Marlowe. Are you my bodyguard now?" Her voice had a harsh note.

"Looks that way. Here's the bag."

She took it. I said: "Have you a car with you?"

She laughed. "I came with a man. What are you doing here?"

"Eddie Mars wanted to see me."

"I didn't know you knew him. Why?"

"I don't mind telling you. He thought I was looking for somebody he thought had run away with his wife."

"Were you?"

"No."

"Then what did you come for?"

"To find out why he thought I was looking for somebody he thought had run away with his wife."

"Did you find out?"

"No."

"You leak information like a radio announcer," she said. "I suppose it's none of my business—even if the man was my husband. I thought you weren't interested in that."

"People keep throwing it at me."

She clicked her teeth in annoyance. The incident of the masked man with the gun seemed to have made no impression on her at all. "Well, take me to the garage," she said. "I have to look in at my escort."

We walked along the path and around a corner of the building and there was light ahead, then around another corner and came to a bright enclosed stable yard lit with two floodlights. It was still paved with brick and still sloped down to a grating in the middle. Cars glistened and a man in a brown smock got up off a stool and came forward.

"Is my boy friend still blotto?" Vivian asked him carelessly.

"I'm afraid he is, miss. I put a rug over him and run the windows up. He's okey, I guess. Just kind of resting."

We went over to a big Cadillac and the man in the smock pulled the rear door open. On the wide back seat, loosely arranged, covered to the chin with a plaid robe, a man lay snoring with his mouth open. He seemed to be a big blond man who would hold a lot of liquor.

"Meet Mr. Larry Cobb," Vivian said. "Mister Cobb—Mister Marlowe."

I grunted.

"Mr. Cobb was my escort," she said. "Such a nice escort, Mr. Cobb. So attentive. You should see him sober. *I* should see him sober. Somebody should see him sober. I mean, just for the record. So it could become a part of history, that brief flashing moment, soon buried in time, but never forgotten— when Larry Cobb was sober."

"Yeah," I said.

"I've even thought of marrying him," she went on in a high strained voice, as if the shock of the stick-up was just beginning to get to her. "At odd times when nothing pleasant would come into my mind. We all have those spells. Lots of money, you know. A yacht, a place on Long Island, a place at Newport, a place at Bermuda, places dotted here and there all over the world probably—just a good Scotch bottle apart. And to Mr. Cobb a bottle of Scotch is not very far."

"Yeah," I said. "Does he have a driver to take him home?"

"Don't say 'yeah.' It's common." She looked at me with arched eyebrows. The man in the smock was chewing his lower lip hard. "Oh, undoubtedly a whole platoon of drivers. They probably do squads right in front of the garage every morning, buttons shining, harness gleaming, white gloves immaculate—a sort of West Point elegance about them."

"Well, where the hell is this driver?" I asked.

"He drove hisself tonight," the man in the smock said, almost apologetically. "I could call his home and have somebody come down for him."

Vivian turned around and smiled at him as if he had just presented her with a diamond tiara. "That would be lovely," she said. "Would you do that? I really wouldn't want Mr. Cobb to die like that—with his mouth open. Someone might think he died of thirst."

The man in the smock said: "Not if they sniffed him, miss."

She opened her bag and grabbed a handful of paper money and pushed it at him. "You'll take care of him, I'm sure."

"Jeeze," the man said, pop-eyed. "I sure will, miss."

"Regan is the name," she said sweetly. "Mrs. Regan. You'll probably see me again. Haven't been here long, have you?"

"No'm." His hands were doing frantic things with the fistful of money he was holding.

"You'll get to love it here," she said. She took hold of my arm. "Let's ride in your car, Marlowe."

"It's outside on the street."

"Quite all right with me, Marlowe. I love a nice walk in the fog. You meet such interesting people."

"Oh, nuts," I said.

She held on to my arm and began to shake. She held me hard all the way to the car. She had stopped shaking by the time we reached it. I drove down a curving lane of trees on the blind side of the house. The lane opened on De Cazens Boulevard, the main drag of Las Olindas. We passed under the ancient sputtering arc lights and after a while there was a town, buildings, dead-looking stores, a service station with a light over a night bell, and at last a drugstore that was still open.

"You better have a drink," I said.

She moved her chin, a point of paleness in the corner of the seat. I turned diagonally into the curb and parked. "A little black coffee and a smattering of rye would go well," I said.

"I could get as drunk as two sailors and love it."

I held the door for her and she got out close to me, brushing my cheek with her hair. We went into the drugstore. I bought a pint of rye at the liquor counter and carried it over to the stools and set it down on the cracked marble counter.

"Two coffees," I said. "Black, strong and made this year."

"You can't drink liquor in here," the clerk said. He had a washed-out blue smock, was thin on top as to hair, had fairly honest eyes and his chin would never hit a wall before he saw it.

Vivian Regan reached into her bag for a pack of cigarettes and shook a couple loose just like a man. She held them towards me.

"It's against the law to drink liquor in here," the clerk said.

I lit the cigarettes and didn't pay any attention to him. He drew two cups of coffee from a tarnished nickel urn and set them in front of us. He looked at the bottle of rye, muttered under his breath and said wearily: "Okey, I'll watch the street while you pour it."

He went and stood at the display window with his back to us and his ears hanging out.

"My heart's in my mouth doing this," I said, and unscrewed the top of the whiskey bottle and loaded the coffee. "The law enforcement in this town is terrific. All through prohibition Eddie Mars' place was a night club and they had two uniformed men in the lobby every night—to see that the guests didn't bring their own liquor instead of buying it from the house."

The clerk turned suddenly and walked back behind the counter and went in behind the little glass window of the prescription room.

We sipped our loaded coffee. I looked at Vivian's face in the mirror back of the coffee urn. It was taut, pale, beautiful and wild. Her lips were red and harsh.

"You have wicked eyes," I said. "What's Eddie Mars got on you?"

She looked at me in the mirror. "I took plenty away from him tonight at roulette—starting with five grand I borrowed from him yesterday and didn't have to use."

"That might make him sore. You think he sent that loogan after you?"

"What's a loogan?"

"A guy with a gun."

"Are you a loogan?"

"Sure," I laughed. "But strictly speaking a loogan is on the wrong side of the fence."

"I often wonder if there is a wrong side."

"We're losing the subject. What has Eddie Mars got on you?"

"You mean a hold on me of some sort?"

"Yes."

Her lip curled. "Wittier, please, Marlowe. Much wittier."

"How's the General? I don't pretend to be witty."

"Not too well. He didn't get up today. You could at least stop questioning me."

"I remember a time when I thought the same about you. How much does the General know?"

"He probably knows everything."

"Norris would tell him?"

"No. Wilde, the District Attorney, was out to see him. Did you burn those pictures?"

"Sure. You worry about your little sister, don't you—from time to time."

"I think she's all I do worry about. I worry about Dad in a way, to keep things from him."

"He hasn't many illusions," I said, "but I suppose he still has pride."

"We're his blood. That's the hell of it." She stared at me in the mirror with deep, distant eyes. "I don't want him to die despising his own blood. It was always wild blood, but it wasn't always rotten blood."

"Is it now?"

"I guess you think so."

"Not yours. You're just playing the part."

She looked down. I sipped some more coffee and lit another cigarette for us. "So you shoot people," she said quietly. "You're a killer."

"Me? How?"

"The papers and the police fixed it up nicely. But I don't believe everything I read."

"Oh, you think I accounted for Geiger—or Brody—or both of them."

She didn't say anything. "I didn't have to," I said. "I might have, I suppose, and got away with it. Neither of them would have hesitated to throw lead at me."

"That makes you just a killer at heart, like all cops."

"Oh, nuts."

"One of those dark deadly quiet men who have no more feelings that a butcher has for slaughtered meat. I knew it the first time I saw you."

"You've got enough shady friends to know different."

"They're all soft compared to you."

"Thanks, lady. You're no English muffin yourself."

"Let's get out of this rotten little town."

I paid the check, put the bottle of rye in my pocket, and we left. The clerk still didn't like me.

We drove away from Las Olindas through a series of little dank beach towns with shack-like houses built down on the sand close to the rumble of the surf and larger houses built back on the slopes behind. A yellow window shone here and there, but most of the houses were dark. A smell of kelp came in off the water and lay on the fog. The tires sang on the moist concrete of the boulevard. The world was a wet emptiness.

We were closed to Del Rey before she spoke to me for the first time since we left the drugstore. Her voice had a muffled sound, as if something was throbbing deep under it.

"Drive down by the Del Rey beach club. I want to look at the water. It's the next street on the left."

There was a winking yellow light at the intersection. I turned the car and slid down a slope with a high bluff on one side, interurban tracks to the right, a low straggle of lights far off beyond the tracks, and then very far off a glitter of pier lights and a haze in the sky over a city. That way the fog was almost gone. The road crossed the tracks where they turned to run under the bluff, then reached a paved strip of waterfront highway that bordered an open and uncluttered beach. Cars were parked along the sidewalk, facing out to sea, dark. The lights of the beach club were a few hundred yards away.

I braked the car against the curb and switched the headlights off and sat with my hands on the wheel. Under the thinning fog the surf curled and creamed, almost without sound, like a thought trying to form itself on the edge of consciousness.

"Move closer," she said almost thickly.

I moved out from under the wheel into the middle of the seat. She turned her body a little away from me as if to peer out of the window. Then she let herself fall backwards, without a sound, into my arms. Her head almost struck the wheel. Her eyes were closed, her face was dim. Then I saw that her eyes opened and flickered, the shine of them visible even in the darkness.

"Hold me close, you beast," she said.

I put my arms around her loosely at first. Her hair had a harsh feeling against my face. I tightened my arms and lifted her up. I brought her face slowly up to my face. Her eyelids were flickering rapidly, like moth wings.

I kissed her tightly and quickly. Then a long slow clinging

kiss. Her lips opened under mine. Her body began to shake in my arms.

"Killer," she said softly, her breath going into my mouth.

I strained her against me until the shivering of her body was almost shaking mine. I kept on kissing her. After a long time she pulled her head away enough to say: "Where do you live?"

"Hobart Arms. Franklin near Kenmore."

"I've never seen it."

"Want to?"

"Yes," she breathed.

"What has Eddie Mars got on you?"

Her body stiffened in my arms and her breath made a harsh sound. Her head pulled back until her eyes, wide open, ringed with white, were staring at me.

"So that's the way it is," she said in a soft dull voice.

"That's the way it is. Kissing is nice, but your father didn't hire me to sleep with you."

"You son of a bitch," she said calmly, without moving.

I laughed in her face. "Don't think I'm an icicle," I said. "I'm not blind or without senses. I have warm blood like the next guy. You're easy to take—too damned easy. What has Eddie Mars got on you?"

"If you say that again, I'll scream."

"Go ahead and scream."

She jerked away and pulled herself upright, far back in the corner of the car.

"Men have been shot for little things like that, Marlowe."

"Men have been shot for practically nothing. The first time we met I told you I was a detective. Get it through your lovely head. I work at it, lady. I don't play at it."

She fumbled in her bag and got a handkerchief out and bit on it, her head turned away from me. The tearing sound of the handkerchief came to me. She tore it with her teeth, slowly, time after time.

"What makes you think he has anything on me?" she whispered, her voice muffled by the handkerchief.

"He lets you win a lot of money and sends a gunpoke around

to take it back for him. You're not more than mildly surprised. You didn't even thank me for saving it for you. I think the whole thing was just some kind of an act. If I wanted to flatter myself, I'd say it was at least partly for my benefit."

"You think he can win or lose as he pleases."

"Sure. On even money bets, four times out of five."

"Do I have to tell you I loathe your guts, Mister Detective?"

"You don't owe me anything. I'm paid off."

She tossed the shredded handkerchief out of the car window. "You have a lovely way with women."

"I liked kissing you."

"You kept your head beautifully. That's so flattering. Should I congratulate you, or my father?"

"I liked kissing you."

Her voice became an icy drawl. "Take me away from here, if you will be so kind. I'm quite sure I'd like to go home."

"You won't be a sister to me?"

"If I had a razor, I'd cut your throat—just to see what ran out of it."

"Caterpillar blood," I said.

I started the car and turned it and drove back across the interurban tracks to the highway and so on into town and up to West Hollywood. She didn't speak to me. She hardly moved all the way back. I drove through the gates and up the sunken driveway to the porte-cochere of the big house. She jerked the car door open and was out of it before it had quite stopped. She didn't speak even then. I watched her back as she stood against the door after ringing the bell. The door opened and Norris looked out. She pushed past him quickly and was gone. The door banged shut and I was sitting there looking at it.

I turned back down the driveway and home.

24

THE APARTMENT house lobby was empty this time. No gunman waiting under the potted palm to give me orders. I took the automatic elevator up to my floor and walked along the hallway to the tune of a muted radio behind a door. I needed a drink and was in a hurry to get one. I didn't switch the light on inside the door. I made straight for the kitchenette and brought up short in three or four feet. Something was wrong. Something on the air, a scent. The shades were down at the windows and the street light leaking in at the sides made a dim light in the room. I stood still and listened. The scent on the air was a perfume, a heavy cloying perfume.

There was no sound, no sound at all. Then my eyes adjusted themselves more to the darkness and I saw there was something across the floor in front of me that shouldn't have been there. I backed, reached the wall switch with my thumb and flicked the light on.

The bed was down. Something in it giggled. A blonde head was pressed into my pillow. Two bare arms curved up and the hands belonging to them were clasped on top of the blonde head. Carmen Sternwood lay on her back, in my bed, giggling at me. The tawny wave of her hair was spread out on the pillow as if by a careful and artificial hand. Her slaty eyes peered at me and had the effect, as usual, of peering from behind a barrel. She smiled. Her small sharp teeth glinted.

"Cute, aren't I?" she said.

I said harshly: "Cute as a Filipino on Saturday night."

I went over a floor lamp and pulled the switch, went back to put off the ceiling light, and went across the room again to the chessboard on a card table under the lamp. There was a problem laid out on the board, a six-mover. I couldn't solve it, like a lot of my problems. I reached down and moved a knight, then pulled my hat and coat off and threw them somewhere. All this time the soft giggling went on from the bed, that sound that made me think of rats behind a wainscoting in an old house.

"I bet you can't even guess how I got in."

I dug a cigarette out and looked at her with bleak eyes. "I bet I can. You came through the keyhole, just like Peter Pan."

"Who's he?"

"Oh, a fellow I used to know around the poolroom."

She giggled. "You're cute, aren't you?" she said.

I began to say: "About that thumb—" but she was ahead of me. I didn't have to remind her. She took her right hand from behind her head and started sucking the thumb and eyeing me with very round and naughty eyes.

"I'm all undressed," she said, after I had smoked and stared at her for a minute.

"By God," I said, "it was right at the back of my mind. I was groping for it. I almost had it, when you spoke. In another minute I'd have said 'I bet you're all undressed.' I always wear my rubbers in bed myself, in case I wake up with a bad conscience and have to sneak away from it."

"You're cute." She rolled her head a little, kittenishly. Then she took her left hand from under her head and took hold of the covers, paused dramatically, and swept them aside. She was undressed all right. She lay there on the bed in the lamplight, as naked and glistening as a pearl. The Sternwood girls were giving me both barrels that night.

I pulled a shred of tobacco off the edge of my lower lip.

"That's nice," I said. "But I've already seen it all. Remember? I'm the guy that keeps finding you without any clothes on."

She giggled some more and covered herself up again. "Well, how *did* you get in?" I asked her.

"The manager let me in. I showed him your card. I'd stolen it from Vivian. I told him you told me to come here and wait for you. I was—I was mysterious." She glowed with delight.

"Neat," I said. "Managers are like that. Now I know how you got in tell me how you're going to go out."

She giggled. "Not going—not for a long time. . . . I like it here. You're cute."

"Listen," I pointed my cigarette at her. "Don't make me dress you again. I'm tired. I appreciate all you're offering me. It's just more than I could possibly take. Doghouse Reilly never let a pal down that way. I'm your friend. I won't let you down —in spite of yourself. You and I have to keep on being friends, and this isn't the way to do it. Now will you dress like a nice little girl?"

She shook her head from side to side.

"Listen," I plowed on, "you don't really care anything about me. You're just showing how naughty you can be. But you don't have to show me. I knew it already. I'm the guy that found—"

"Put the light out," she giggled.

I threw my cigarette on the floor and stamped on it. I took a handkerchief out and wiped the palms of my hands. I tried it once more.

"It isn't on account of the neighbors," I told her. "They don't really care a lot. There's a lot of stray broads in any apartment house and one more won't make the building rock. It's a question of professional pride. You know—professional pride. I'm working for your father. He's a sick man, very frail, very helpless. He sort of trusts me not to pull any stunts. Won't you please get dressed, Carmen?"

"Your name isn't Doghouse Reilly," she said. "It's Philip Marlowe. You can't fool me."

I looked down at the chessboard. The move with the knight was wrong. I put it back where I had moved it from. Knights had no meaning in this game. It wasn't a game for knights.

I looked at her again. She lay still now, her face pale against the pillow, her eyes large and dark and empty as rain barrels in a drought. One of her small five-fingered thumbless hands picked at the cover restlessly. There was a vague glimmer of doubt starting to get born in her somewhere. She didn't know about it yet. It's so hard for women—even nice women—to realize that their bodies are not irresistible.

I said: "I'm going out in the kitchen and mix a drink. Want one?"

"Uh-huh." Dark silent mystified eyes stared at me solemnly, the doubt growing larger in them, creeping into them noiselessly, like a cat in long grass stalking a young blackbird.

"If you're dressed when I get back, you'll get the drink. Okey?"

Her teeth parted and a faint hissing noise came out of her mouth. She didn't answer me. I went out to the kitchenette and got out some Scotch and fizzwater and mixed a couple of highballs. I didn't have anything really exciting to drink, like nitroglycerin or distilled tiger's breath. She hadn't moved when I got back with the glasses. The hissing had stopped. Her eyes were dead again. Her lips started to smile at me. Then she sat up suddenly and threw all the covers off her body and reached.

"Gimme."

"When you're dressed. Not *until* you're dressed."

I put the two glasses down on the card table and sat down myself and lit another cigarette. "Go ahead. I won't watch you."

I looked away. Then I was aware of the hissing noise very sudden and sharp. It startled me into looking at her again. She sat there naked, propped on her hands, her mouth open a little, her face like scraped bone. The hissing noise came tearing out of her mouth as if she had nothing to do with it. There was something behind her eyes, blank as they were, that I had never seen in a woman's eyes.

Then her lips moved very slowly and carefully, as if they

were artificial lips and had to be manipulated with springs.

She called me a filthy name.

I didn't mind that. I didn't mind what she called me, what anybody called me. But this was the room I had to live in. It was all I had in the way of a home. In it was everything that was mine, that had any association for me, any past, anything that took the place of a family. Not much; a few books, pictures, radio, chessmen, old letters, stuff like that. Nothing. Such as they were they had all my memories.

I couldn't stand her in that room any longer. What she called me only reminded me of that.

I said carefully: "I'll give you three minutes to get dressed and out of here. If you're not out by then, I'll throw you out—by force. Just the way you are, naked. And I'll throw your clothes after you into the hall. Now—get started."

Her teeth chattered and the hissing noise was sharp and animal. She swung her feet to the floor and reached for her clothes on a chair beside the bed. She dressed. I watched her. She dressed with stiff awkward fingers—for a woman—but quickly at that. She was dressed in a little over two minutes. I timed it.

She stood there beside the bed, holding a green bag tight against a fur-trimmed coat. She wore a rakish green hat crooked on her head. She stood there for a moment and hissed at me, her face still like scraped bone, her eyes still empty and yet full of some jungle emotion. Then she walked quickly to the door and opened it and went out, without speaking, without looking back. I heard the elevator lurch into motion and move in the shaft.

I walked to the windows and pulled the shades up and opened the windows wide. The night air came drifting in with a kind of stale sweetness that still remembered automobile exhausts and the streets of the city. I reached for my drink and drank it slowly. The apartment house door closed itself down below me. Steps tinkled on the quiet sidewalk. A car started up not far away. It rushed off into the night with a rough clashing of gears. I went back to the bed and looked down at it. The imprint of her head was still in the pillow, of her small corrupt body still on the sheets.

I put my empty glass down and tore the bed to pieces savagely.

25

It was raining again the next morning, a slanting gray rain like a swung curtain of crystal beads. I got up feeling sluggish and tired and stood looking out of the windows, with a dark harsh taste of Sternwoods still in my mouth. I was as empty of life as a scarecrow's pockets. I went out to the kitchenette and drank two cups of black coffee. You can have a hangover from other things than alcohol. I had one from women. Women made me sick.

I shaved and showered and dressed and got my raincoat out and went downstairs and looked out of the front door. Across the street, a hundred feet up, a gray Plymouth sedan was parked. It was the same one that had tried to trail me around the day before, the same one that I had asked Eddie Mars about. There might be a cop in it, if a cop had that much time on his hands and wanted to waste it following me around. Or it might be a smoothie in the detective business trying to get a noseful of somebody else's case in order to chisel a way into it. Or it might be the Bishop of Bermuda disapproving of my night life.

I went out back and got my convertible from the garage and drove it around front past the gray Plymouth. There was a small man in it, alone. He started up after me. He worked better in the rain. He stayed close enough so that I couldn't make a short block and leave that before he entered it, and he stayed back far enough so that other cars were between us most of the time. I drove down to the boulevard and parked in the lot next to my building and came out of there with my raincoat collar up and my hat brim low and the raindrops tapping icily at my face in between. The Plymouth was across the way at a fireplug. I walked down to the intersection and crossed with the green light and walked back, close to the edge of the sidewalk and the parked cars. The Plymouth hadn't moved. Nobody got out of it. I reached it and jerked open the door on the curb side.

A small bright-eyed man was pressed back into the corner behind the wheel. I stood and looked in at him, the rain thumping my back. His eyes blinked behind the swirling smoke of a cigarette. His hands tapped restlessly on the thin wheel.

I said: "Can't you make your mind up?"

He swallowed and the cigarette bobbed between his lips. "I don't think I know you," he said, in a tight little voice.

"Marlowe's the name. The guy you've been trying to follow around for a couple of days."

"I ain't following anybody, doc."

"This jalopy is. Maybe you can't control it. Have it your own way. I'm now going to eat breakfast in the coffee shop across the street, orange juice, bacon and eggs, toast, honey, three or four cups of coffee and a toothpick. I am then going up to my office, which is on the seventh floor of the building right opposite you. If you have anything that's worrying you beyond endurance, drop up and chew it over. I'll only be oiling my machine gun."

I left him blinking and walked away. Twenty minutes later I was airing the scrubwoman's Soirée d'Amour out of my office and opening up a thick rough envelope addressed in a fine old-fashioned pointed handwriting. The envelope contained a brief formal note and a large mauve check for five hundred dollars, payable to Philip Marlowe and signed, Guy de Brisay Sternwood, by Vincent Norris. That made it a nice morning. I was making out a bank slip when the buzzer told me somebody had entered my two by four reception room. It was the little man from the Plymouth.

"Fine," I said. "Come in and shed your coat."

He slid past me carefully as I held the door, as carefully as though he feared I might plant a kick in his minute buttocks. We sat down and faced each other across the desk. He was a very small man, not more than five feet three and would hardly weigh as much as a butcher's thumb. He had tight brilliant eyes that wanted to look hard, and looked as hard as oysters on the half shell. He wore a double-breasted dark gray suit that was too wide in the shoulders and had too much lapel. Over this, open, an Irish tweed coat with some badly worn spots. A lot of foulard tie bulged out and was rain-spotted above his crossed lapels.

"Maybe you know me," he said. "I'm Harry Jones."

I said I didn't know him. I pushed a flat tin of cigarettes at him. His small neat fingers speared one like a trout taking the fly. He lit it with the desk lighter and waved his hand.

"I been around," he said. "Know the boys and such. Used to do a little liquor-running down from Hueneme Point. A tough racket, brother. Riding the scout car with a gun in your lap and a wad on your hip that would choke a coal chute. Plenty of times we paid off four sets of law before we hit Beverly Hills. A tough racket."

"Terrible," I said.

He leaned back and blew smoke at the ceiling from the small tight corner of his small tight mouth.

"Maybe you don't believe me," he said.

"Maybe I don't," I said. "And maybe I do. And then again maybe I haven't bothered to make my mind up. Just what is the build-up supposed to do to me?"

"Nothing," he said tartly.

"You've been following me around for a couple of days," I said. "Like a fellow trying to pick up a girl and lacking the last inch of nerve. Maybe you're selling insurance. Maybe you knew a fellow called Joe Brody. That's a lot of maybes, but I have a lot on hand in my business."

His eyes bulged and his lower lip almost fell in his lap. "Christ, how'd you know that?" he snapped.

"I'm psychic. Shake your business up and pour it. I haven't got all day."

The brightness of his eyes almost disappeared between the suddenly narrowed lids. There was silence. The rain pounded down on the flat tarred roof over the Mansion House lobby below my windows. His eyes opened a little, shined again, and his voice was full of thought.

"I was trying to get a line on you, sure," he said. "I've got something to sell—cheap, for a couple of C notes. How'd you tie me to Joe?"

I opened a letter and read it. It offered me a six months' correspondence course in fingerprinting at a special professional discount. I dropped it into the waste basket and looked at the little man again. "Don't mind me. I was just guessing. You're not a cop. You don't belong to Eddie Mars' outfit. I asked him last night. I couldn't think of anybody else but Joe Brody's friends who would be that much interested in me."

"Jesus," he said and licked his lower lip. His face had turned white as paper when I mentioned Eddie Mars. His mouth drooped open and his cigarette hung to the corner of it by some magic, as if it had grown there. "Aw, you're kidding me," he said at last, with the sort of smile the operating room sees.

"All right. I'm kidding you." I opened another letter. This one wanted to send me a daily newsletter from Washington, all inside stuff, straight from the cookhouse. "I suppose Agnes is loose," I added.

"Yeah. She sent me. You interested?"

"Well—she's a blonde."

"Nuts. You made a crack when you were up there that night —the night Joe got squibbed off. Something about Brody must have known something good about the Sternwoods or he wouldn't have taken the chance on that picture he sent them."

"Uh-huh. So he had? What was it?"

"That's what the two hundred bucks pays for."

I dropped some more fan mail into the basket and lit myself a fresh cigarette.

"We gotta get out of town," he said. "Agnes is a nice girl. You can't hold that stuff on her. It's not so easy for a dame to get by these days."

"She's too big for you," I said. "She'll roll on you and smother you."

"That's kind of a dirty crack, brother," he said with something that was near enough to dignity to make me stare at him.

I said: "You're right. I've been meeting the wrong kind of people lately. Let's cut out the gabble and get down to cases. What have you got for the money?"

"Would you pay for it?"

"If it does what?"

"If it helps you find Rusty Regan."

"I'm not looking for Rusty Regan."

"Says you. Want to hear it or not?"

"Go ahead and chirp. I'll pay for anything I use. Two C notes buys a lot of information in my circle."

"Eddie Mars had Regan bumped off," he said calmly, and leaned back as if he had just been made a vice-president.

I waved a hand in the direction of the door. "I wouldn't even argue with you," I said. "I wouldn't waste the oxygen. On your way, small size."

He leaned across the desk, white lines at the corners of his mouth. He snubbed his cigarette out carefully, over and over again, without looking at it. From behind a communicating door came the sound of a typewriter clacking monotonously to the bell, to the shift, line after line.

"I'm not kidding," he said.

"Beat it. Don't bother me. I have work to do."

"No you don't," he said sharply. "I ain't that easy. I came here to speak my piece and I'm speaking it. I knew Rusty myself. Not well, well enough to say 'How's a boy?' and he'd answer me or he wouldn't, according to how he felt. A nice guy though. I always liked him. He was sweet on a singer named Mona Grant. Then she changed her name to Mars. Rusty got sore and married a rich dame that hung around the joints like she couldn't sleep well at home. You know all about her, tall, dark, enough looks for a Derby winner, but the type would put a lot of pressure on a guy. High-strung. Rusty wouldn't get along with her. But Jesus, he'd get along with her old man's dough, wouldn't he? That's what you think. This Regan was a cockeyed sort of buzzard. He had long-range eyes. He was looking over into the next valley all the time. He wasn't scarcely around where he was. I don't think he gave a damn about dough. And coming from me, brother, that's a compliment."

The little man wasn't so dumb after all. A three for a quarter grifter wouldn't even think such thoughts, much less know how to express them.

I said: "So he ran away."

"He started to run away, maybe. With this girl Mona. She wasn't living with Eddie Mars, didn't like his rackets. Especially the side lines, like blackmail, bent cars, hideouts for hot boys from the east, and so on. The talk was Regan told Eddie one night, right out in the open, that if he ever messed Mona up in any criminal rap, he'd be around to see him."

"Most of this is on the record, Harry," I said. "You can't expect money for that."

"I'm coming to what isn't. So Regan blew. I used to see him every afternoon in Vardi's drinking Irish whiskey and staring at the wall. He don't talk much any more. He'd give me a bet now and then, which was what I was there for, to pick up bets for Puss Walgreen."

"I thought he was in the insurance business."

"That's what it says on the door. I guess he'd sell you insurance at that, if you tramped on him. Well, about the middle of September I don't see Regan anymore. I don't notice it right away. You know how it is. A guy's there and you see him and then he ain't there and you don't see him until something makes you think of it. What makes me think about it is I hear a guy say laughing that Eddie Mars' woman lammed out with Rusty Regan and Mars is acting like he was best man, instead of being sore. So I tell Joe Brody and Joe was smart."

"Like hell he was," I said.

"Not copper smart, but still smart. He's out for the dough. He gets to figuring could he get a line somehow on the two lovebirds he could maybe collect twice—once from Eddie Mars and once from Regan's wife. Joe knew the family a little."

"Five grand worth," I said. "He nicked them for that a while back."

"Yeah?" Harry Jones looked mildly surprised. "Agnes ought to of told me that. There's a frail for you. Always holding out. Well, Joe and me watch the papers and we don't see anything, so we know old Sternwood has a blanket on it. Then one day I see Lash Canino in Vardi's. Know him?"

I shook my head.

"There's a boy that is tough like some guys think they are tough. He does a job for Eddie Mars when Mars needs him— trouble-shooting. He'd bump a guy off between drinks. When Mars don't need him he don't go near him. And he don't stay in L.A. Well it might be something and it might not. Maybe they got a line on Regan and Mars has just been sitting back with a smile on his puss, waiting for the chance. Then again it might be something else entirely. Anyway I tell Joe and Joe gets on Canino's tail. He can tail. Me, I'm no good at it. I'm giving that one away. No charge. And Joe tails Canino out to the Sternwood place and Canino parks outside the estate and a car come up beside him with a girl in it. They talk for a while and Joe thinks the girl passes something over, like maybe dough. The girl beats it. It's Regan's wife. Okey, she knows Canino and Canino knows Mars. So Joe figures Canino knows something about Regan and is trying to squeeze a little on the side for himself. Canino blows and Joe loses him. End of Act One."

"What does this Canino look like?"

"Short, heavy set, brown hair, brown eyes, and always wears brown clothes and a brown hat. Even wears a brown suede raincoat. Drives a brown coupe. Everything brown for Mr. Canino."

"Let's have Act Two," I said.

"Without some dough that's all."

"I don't see two hundred bucks in it. Mrs. Regan married an ex-bootlegger out of the joints. She'd know other people of his sort. She knows Eddie Mars well. If she thought anything had happened to Regan, Eddie would be the very man she'd go to, and Canino might be the man Eddie would pick to handle the assignment. Is that all you have?"

"Would you give the two hundred to know where Eddie's wife is?" the little man asked calmly.

He had all my attention now. I almost cracked the arms of my chair leaning on them.

"Even if she was alone?" Harry Jones added in a soft, rather sinister tone. "Even if she never run away with Regan at all, and was being kept now about forty miles from L.A. in a hide-out—so the law would keep on thinking she had dusted with him? Would you pay two hundred bucks for that, shamus?"

I licked my lips. They tasted dry and salty. "I think I would," I said. "Where?"

"Agnes found her," he said grimly. "Just by a lucky break. Saw her out riding and managed to tail her home. Agnes will tell you where that is—when she's holding the money in her hand."

I made a hard face at him. "You could tell the coppers for nothing, Harry. They have some good wreckers down at Central these days. If they killed you trying, they still have Agnes."

"Let 'em try," he said. "I ain't so brittle."

"Agnes must have something I didn't notice."

"She's a grifter, shamus. I'm a grifter. We're all grifters. So we sell each other out for a nickel. Okey. See can you make me." He reached for another of my cigarettes, placed it neatly between his lips and lit it with a match the way I do myself, missing twice on his thumbnail and then using his foot. He puffed evenly and stared at me level-eyed, a funny little hard guy I could have thrown from home plate to second base. A small man in a big man's world. There was something I liked about him.

"I haven't pulled anything in here," he said steadily. "I come in talking two C's. That's still the price. I come because I thought I'd get a take it or leave it, one right gee to another. Now you're waving cops at me. You oughta be ashamed of yourself."

I said: "You'll get the two hundred—for that information. I have to get the money myself first."

He stood up and nodded and pulled his worn little Irish tweed coat tight around his chest. "That's okey. After dark is better anyway. It's a leery job—buckin' guys like Eddie Mars. But a guy has to eat. The book's been pretty dull lately. I think the big boys have told Puss Walgreen to move on. Suppose you come over there to the office, Fulwider Building, Western and Santa Monica, four-twenty-eight at the back. You bring the money, I'll take you to Agnes."

"Can't you tell me yourself? I've seen Agnes."

"I promised her," he said simply. He buttoned his overcoat, cocked his hat jauntily, nodded again and strolled to the door. He went out. His steps died along the hall.

I went down to the bank and deposited my five-hundred-dollar check and drew out two hundred in currency. I went upstairs again and sat in my chair thinking about Harry Jones and his story. It seemed a little too pat. It had the austere simplicity of fiction rather than the tangled woof of fact. Captain Gregory ought to have been able to find Mona Mars, if she was that close to his beat. Supposing, that is, he had tried.

I thought about it most of the day. Nobody came into the office. Nobody called me on the phone. It kept on raining.

26

AT SEVEN the rain had stopped for a breathing spell, but the gutters were still flooded. On Santa Monica the water was level with the sidewalk and a thin film of it washed over the top of the curbing. A traffic cop in shining black rubber from boots to cap sloshed through the flood on his way from the shelter of a sodden awning. My rubber heels slithered on the sidewalk as I turned into the narrow lobby of the Fulwider Building. A single drop light burned far back, beyond an open, once gilt elevator. There was a tarnished and well-missed spittoon on a gnawed rubber mat. A case of false teeth hung on the mustard-colored wall like a fuse box in a screen porch. I shook the rain off my hat and looked at the building directory beside the case of teeth. Numbers with names and numbers without names. Plenty of vacancies or plenty of tenants who wished to remain anonymous. Painless dentists, shyster detective agencies, small sick businesses that had crawled there to die, mail order schools that would teach you how to become a railroad clerk or a radio technician or a screen writer—if the postal inspectors didn't catch up with them first. A nasty building. A building in which the smell of stale cigar butts would be the cleanest odor.

An old man dozed in the elevator, on a ramshackle stool, with a burst-out cushion under him. His mouth was open, his veined temples glistened in the weak light. He wore a blue uniform coat that fitted him the way a stall fits a horse. Under that gray trousers with frayed cuffs, white cotton socks and black kid shoes, one of which was slit across a bunion. On the stool he slept miserably, waiting for a customer. I went past him softly, the clandestine air of the building prompting me, found the fire door and pulled it open. The fire stairs hadn't been swept in a month. Bums had slept on them, eaten on them, left crusts and fragments of greasy newspaper, matches, a gutted imitation-leather pocketbook. In a shadowy angle against the scribbled wall a pouched ring of pale rubber had fallen and had not been disturbed. A very nice building.

I came out at the fourth floor sniffing for air. The hallway had the same dirty spittoon and frayed mat, the same mustard walls, the same memories of low tide. I went down the line and turned a corner. The name: "L. D. Walgreen—Insurance," showed on a dark pebbled glass door, on a second dark door, on a third behind which there was a light. One of the dark doors said: "Entrance."

A glass transom was open above the lighted door. Through it the sharp birdlike voice of Harry Jones spoke, saying:

"Canino? . . . Yeah, I've seen you around somewhere. Sure."

I froze. The other voice spoke. It had a heavy purr, like a small dynamo behind a brick wall. It said: "I thought you would." There was a vaguely sinister note in that voice.

A chair scraped on linoleum, steps sounded, the transom above me squeaked shut. A shadow melted from behind the pebbled glass.

I went back to the first of the three doors marked with the name Walgreen. I tried it cautiously. It was locked. It moved in a loose frame, an old door fitted many years past, made of half-seasoned wood and shrunken now. I reached my wallet out and slipped the thick hard window of celluloid from over my driver's license. A burglar's tool the law had forgotten to proscribe. I put my gloves on, leaned softly and lovingly against the door and pushed the knob hard away from the frame. I pushed the celluloid plate into the wide crack and felt for the slope of the spring lock. There was a dry click, like a small icicle breaking. I hung there motionless, like a lazy fish in the water. Nothing happened inside. I turned the knob and pushed the door back into darkness. I shut it behind me as carefully as I had opened it.

The lighted oblong of an uncurtained window faced me, cut by the angle of a desk. On the desk a hooded typewriter took form, then the metal knob of a communicating door. This was unlocked. I passed into the second of the three offices. Rain rattled suddenly against the closed window. Under its noise I crossed the room. A tight fan of light spread from an inch opening of the door into the lighted office. Everything very convenient. I walked like a cat on a mantel and reached the hinged side of the door, put an eye to the crack and saw nothing but light against the angle of the wood.

The purring voice was now saying quite pleasantly: "Sure, a guy could sit on his fanny and crab what another guy done if he knows what it's all about. So you go to see this peeper. Well, that was your mistake. Eddie don't like it. The peeper told Eddie some guy in a gray Plymouth was tailing him. Eddie naturally wants to know who and why, see."

Harry Jones laughed lightly. "What makes it his business?"

"That don't get you no place."

"You know why I went to the peeper. I already told you. Account of Joe Brody's girl. She has to blow and she's shatting on her uppers. She figures the peeper can get her some dough. I don't have any."

The purring voice said gently: "Dough for what? Peepers don't give that stuff out to punks."

"He could raise it. He knows rich people." Harry Jones laughed, a brave little laugh.

"Don't fuss with me, little man." The purring voice had an edge, like sand in the bearings.

"Okey, okey. You know the dope on Brody's bump-off. That screwy kid done it all right, but the night it happened this Marlowe was right there in the room."

"That's known, little man. He told it to the law."

"Yeah—here's what isn't. Brody was trying to peddle a nudist photo of the young Sternwood girl. Marlowe got wise to him. While they were arguing about it the young Sternwood girl dropped around herself—with a gat. She took a shot at Brody. She lets one fly and breaks a window. Only the peeper didn't tell the coppers about that. And Agnes didn't neither. She figures it's railroad fare for her not to."

"This ain't got anything to do with Eddie?"

"Show me how."

"Where's this Agnes at?"

"Nothing doing."

"You tell me, little man. Here, or in the back room where the boys pitch dimes against the wall."

"She's my girl now, Canino. I don't put my girl in the middle for anybody."

A silence followed. I listened to the rain lashing the windows. The smell of cigarette smoke came through the crack of the door. I wanted to cough. I bit hard on a handkerchief.

The purring voice said, still gentle: "From what I hear this blonde broad was just a shill for Geiger. I'll talk it over with Eddie. How much you tap the peeper for?"

"Two centuries."

"Get it?"

Harry Jones laughed again. "I'm seeing him tomorrow. I have hopes."

"Where's Agnes?"

"Listen—"

"Where's Agnes?"

Silence.

"Look at it, little man."

I didn't move. I wasn't wearing a gun. I didn't have to see through the crack of the door to know that a gun was what the purring voice was inviting Harry Jones to look at. But I did think Mr. Canino would do anything with his gun beyond showing it. I waited.

"I'm looking at it," Harry Jones said, his voice squeezed tight as if it could hardly get past his teeth. "And I don't see anything I didn't see before. Go ahead and blast and see what it gets you."

"A Chicago overcoat is what it would get *you*, little man."

Silence.

"Where's Agnes?"

Harry Jones sighed. "Okey," he said wearily. "She's in an apartment house at 28 Court Street, up on Bunker Hill. Apartment 301. I guess I'm yellow all right. Why should I front for that twist?"

"No reason. You got good sense. You and me'll go out and talk to her. All I want is to find out is she dummying up on you, kid. If it's the way you say it is, everything is jakeloo. You can put the bite on the peeper and be on your way. No hard feelings?"

"No," Harry Jones said. "No hard feelings, Canino."

"Fine. Let's dip the bill. Got a glass?" The purring voice was now as false as an usherette's eyelashes and as slippery as a watermelon seed. A drawer was pulled open. Something jarred on wood. A chair squeaked. A scuffing sound on the floor. "This is bond stuff," the purring voice said.

There was a gurgling sound. "Moths in your ermine, as the ladies say."

Harry Jones said softly: "Success."

I heard a short sharp cough. Then a violent retching. There was a small thud on the floor, as if a thick glass had fallen. My fingers curled against my raincoat.

The purring voice said gently: "You ain't sick from just one drink, are you, pal?"

Harry Jones didn't answer. There was labored breathing for a short moment. Then thick silence folded down. Then a chair scraped.

"So long, little man," said Mr. Canino.

Steps, a click, the wedge of light died at my feet, a door opened and closed quietly. The steps faded, leisurely and assured.

I stirred around the edge of the door and pulled it wide and looked into blackness relieved by the dim shine of a window.

The corner of a desk glittered faintly. A hunched shape took form in a chair behind it. In the close air there was a heavy clogged smell, almost a perfume. I went across to the corridor door and listened. I heard the distant clang of the elevator.

I found the light switch and light glowed in a dusty glass bowl hanging from the ceiling by three brass chains. Harry Jones looked at me across the desk, his eyes wide open, his face frozen in a tight spasm, the skin bluish. His small dark head was tilted to one side. He sat upright against the back of the chair.

A street-car bell clanged at an almost infinite distance and the sound came buffeted by innumerable walls. A brown half pint of whiskey stood on the desk with the cap off. Harry Jones' glass glinted against a castor of the desk. The second glass was gone.

I breathed shallowly, from the top of my lungs, and bent above the bottle. Behind the charred smell of the bourbon another odor lurked, faintly, the odor of bitter almonds. Harry Jones dying had vomited on his coat. That made it cyanide.

I walked around him carefully and lifted a phone book from a hook on the wooden frame of the window. I let it fall again, reached the telephone as far as it would go from the little dead man. I dialed information. The voice answered.

"Can you give me the phone number of Apartment 301, 28 Court Street?"

"One moment, please." The voice came to me borne on the smell of bitter almonds. A silence. "The number is Wentworth 2528. It is listed under Glendower Apartments."

I thanked the voice and dialed the number. The bell rang three times, then the line opened. A radio blared along the wire and was muted. A burly male voice said: "Hello."

"Is Agnes there?"

"No Agnes here, buddy. What number you want?"

"Wentworth two-five-two-eight."

"Right number, wrong gal. Ain't that a shame?" The voice cackled.

I hung up and reached for the phone book again and looked

up the Glendower Apartments. I dialed the manager's number.
I had a blurred vision of Mr. Canino driving fast through rain
to another appointment with death.

"Glendower Apartments. Mr. Schiff speaking."

"This is Wallis, Police Identification Bureau. Is there a girl
named Agnes Lozelle registered in your place?"

"Who did you say you were?"

I told him again.

"If you give me your number, I'll—"

"Cut the comedy," I said sharply, "I'm in a hurry. Is there
or isn't there?"

"No. There isn't." The voice was as stiff as a breadstick.

"Is there a tall blonde with green eyes registered in the flop?"

"Say, this isn't any flop—"

"Oh, can it, *can it!*" I rapped at him in a police voice. "You
want me to send the vice squad over there and shake the joint
down? I know all about Bunker Hill apartment houses,
mister. Especially the ones that have phone numbers listed for
each apartment."

"Hey, take it easy, officer. I'll co-operate. There's a couple
of blondes here, sure. Where isn't there? I hadn't noticed their
eyes much. Would yours be alone?"

"Alone, or with a little chap about five feet three, a hundred
and ten, sharp black eyes, wears double-breasted dark gray
suit and Irish tweed overcoat, gray hat. My information is
Apartment 301, but all I get there is the big razzoo."

"Oh, she ain't there. There's a couple of car salesmen living
in three-o-one."

"Thanks, I'll drop around."

"Make it quiet, won't you? Come to my place, direct?"

"Much obliged, Mr. Schiff." I hung up.

I wiped sweat off my face. I walked to the far corner of
the office and stood with my face to the wall, patted it with
a hand. I turned around slowly and looked across at little
Harry Jones grimacing in his chair.

"Well, you fooled him, Harry," I said out loud, in a voice that
sounded queer to me. "You lied to him and you drank your

cyanide like a little gentleman. You died like a poisoned rat, Harry, but you're no rat to me."

I had to search him. It was a nasty job. His pockets yielded nothing about Agnes, nothing that I wanted at all. I didn't think they would, but I had to be sure. Mr. Canino might be back. Mr. Canino would be the kind of self-confident gentleman who would not mind returning to the scene of his crime.

I put the light out and started to open the door. The phone bell rang jarringly down on the baseboard. I listened to it, my jaw muscles drawn into a knot, aching. Then I shut the door and put the light on again and went across to it.

"Yeah?"

A woman's voice. Her voice. "Is Harry around?"

"Not for a minute, Agnes."

She waited a while on that. Then she said slowly: "Who's talking?"

"Marlowe, the guy that's trouble to you."

"Where is he?" sharply.

"I came over to give him two hundred bucks in return for certain information. The offer holds. I have the money. Where are you?"

"Didn't he tell you?"

"No."

"Perhaps you'd better ask him. Where is he?"

"I can't ask him. Do you know a man named Canino?"

Her gasp came as clearly as though she had been beside me.

"Do you want the two C's or not?" I asked.

"I—I want it pretty bad, mister."

"All right then. Tell me where to bring it."

"I—I—" Her voice trailed off and came back with a panic rush. "Where's Harry?"

"Got scared and blew. Meet me somewhere—anywhere at all—I have the money."

"I don't believe you—about Harry. It's a trap."

"Oh stuff. I could have had Harry hauled in long ago. There isn't anything to make a trap for. Canino got a line on Harry somehow and he blew. I want quiet, you want quiet, Harry wants quiet." Harry already had it. Nobody could take it away from him. "You don't think I'd stooge for Eddie Mars, do you, angel?"

"No-o, I guess not. Not that. I'll meet you in half an hour. Beside Bullocks Wilshire, the east entrance to the parking lot."

"Right," I said.

I dropped the phone in its cradle. The wave of almond odor flooded me again, and the sour smell of vomit. The little dead man sat silent in his chair, beyond fear, beyond change.

I left the office. Nothing moved in the dingy corridor. No pebbled glass door had light behind it. I went down the fire stairs to the second floor and from there looked down at the lighted roof of the elevator cage. I pressed the button. Slowly the car lurched into motion. I ran down the stairs again. The car was above me when I walked out of the building.

It was raining hard again. I walked into it with the heavy drops slapping my face. When one of them touched my tongue I knew that my mouth was open and the ache at the side of my jaws told me it was open wide and strained back, mimicking the rictus of death carved upon the face of Harry Jones.

27

"Give me the money."

The motor of the gray Plymouth throbbed under her voice and the rain pounded above it. The violet light at the top of Bullocks green-tinged tower was far above us, serene and withdrawn from the dark, dripping city. Her black-gloved hand reached out and I put the bills in it. She bent over to count them under the dim light of the dash. A bag clicked open, clicked shut. She let a spent breath die on her lips. She leaned towards me.

"I'm leaving, copper. I'm on my way. This is a get-away stake and God how I need it. What happened to Harry?"

"I told you he ran away. Canino got wise to him somehow. Forget Harry. I've paid and I want my information."

"You'll get it. Joe and I were out riding Foothill Boulevard Sunday before last. It was late and the lights coming up and the usual mess of cars. We passed a brown coupe and I saw the girl who was driving it. There was a man beside her, a dark short man. The girl was a blonde. I'd seen her before. She was Eddie Mars' wife. The guy was Canino. You wouldn't forget either of them, if you ever saw them. Joe tailed the coupe from in front. He was good at that. Canino, the watchdog, was taking her out for air. A mile or so east of Realito a road turns towards the foothills. That's orange country to the south but to the north it's as bare as hell's back yard and smack up against the hills there's a cyanide plant where they make the stuff for fumigation.

Just off the highway there's a small garage and paintshop run by a gee named Art Huck. Hot car drop, likely. There's a frame house beyond this, and beyond the house nothing but the foothills and the bare stone outcrop and the cyanide plant a couple of miles on. That's the place where she's holed up. They turned off on this road and Joe swung around and went back and we saw the car turn off the road where the frame house was. We sat there half an hour looking through the cars going by. Nobody came back out. When it was quite dark Joe sneaked up there and took a look. He said there were lights in the house and a radio was going and just the one car out in front, the coupe. So we beat it."

She stopped talking and I listened to the swish of tires on Wilshire. I said: "They might have shifted quarters since then but that's what you have to sell—that's what you have to sell. Sure you knew her?"

"If you ever see her, you won't make a mistake the second time. Good-by, copper, and wish me luck. I got a raw deal."

"Like hell you did," I said, and walked away across the street to my own car.

The gray Plymouth moved forward, gathered speed, and darted around the corner on to Sunset Place. The sound of its motor died, and with it blonde Agnes wiped herself off the slate for good, so far as I was concerned. Three men dead, Geiger, Brody and Harry Jones, and the woman went riding off in the rain with my two hundred in her bag and not a mark on her. I kicked my starter and drove on downtown to eat. I ate a good dinner. Forty miles in the rain is a hike, and I hoped to make it a round trip.

I drove north across the river, on into Pasadena, through Pasadena and almost at once I was in orange groves. The tumbling rain was solid white spray in the headlights. The windshield wiper could hardly keep the glass clear enough to see through. But not even the drenched darkness could hide the flawless lines of the orange trees wheeling away like endless spokes into the night.

Cars passed with a tearing hiss and a wave of dirty spray. The highway jerked through a little town that was all packing houses and sheds, and railway sidings nuzzling them. The groves thinned out and dropped away to the south and the road climbed and it was cold and to the north the black foothills crouched closer and sent a bitter wind whipping down their flanks. Then faintly out of the dark two yellow vapor lights glowed high up in the air and a neon sign between them said: "Welcome to Realito."

Frame houses were spaced far back from a wide main street, then a sudden knot of stores, the lights of a drugstore behind fogged glass, the fly-cluster of cars in front of the movie theater, a dark bank on a corner with a clock sticking out over the sidewalk and a group of people standing in the rain looking at its windows, as if they were some kind of a show. I went on. Empty fields closed in again.

Fate stage-managed the whole thing. Beyond Realito, just about a mile beyond, the highway took a curve and the rain fooled me and I went too close to the shoulder. My right front tire let go with an angry hiss. Before I could stop the right rear went with it. I jammed the car to a stop, half on the pavement, half on the shoulder, got out and flashed a spotlight around. I had two flats and one spare. The flat butt of a heavy galvanized tack stared at me from the front tire.

The edge of the pavement was littered with them. They had been swept off, but not far enough off.

I snapped the flash off and stood there breathing rain and looking up a side road at a yellow light. It seemed to come from a skylight. The skylight could belong to a garage, the garage could be run by a man named Art Huck, and there could be a frame house next door to it. I tucked my chin down in my collar and started towards it, then went back to unstrap the license holder from the steering post and put it in my pocket. I leaned lower under the wheel. Behind a weighted flap, directly under my right leg as I sat in the car, there was a hidden compartment. There were two guns in it. One belonged to Eddie Mars' boy Lanny and one belonged to me. I took Lanny's. It would have had more practice than mine. I stuck it nose down in an inside pocket and started up the side road.

The garage was a hundred yards from the highway. It showed the highway a blank side wall. I played the flash on it quickly. "Art Huck—Auto Repairs and Painting." I chuckled, then Harry Jones' face rose up in front of me, and I stopped chuckling. The garage doors were shut, but there was an edge of light under them and a thread of light where the halves met. I went on past. The frame house was there, light in two front windows, shades down. It was set well back from the road, behind a thin clump of trees. A car stood on the gravel drive in front. It was dark, indistinct, but it would be a brown coupe and it would belong to Mr. Canino. It squatted there peacefully in front of the narrow wooden porch.

He would let her take it out for a spin once in a while, and sit beside her, probably with a gun handy. The girl Rusty Regan ought to have married, that Eddie Mars couldn't keep, the girl that hadn't run away with Regan. Nice Mr. Canino.

I trudged back to the garage and banged on the wooden door with the butt of my flash. There was a hung instant of silence, as heavy as thunder. The light inside went out. I stood there grinning and licking the rain off my lip. I clicked the spot on the middle of the doors. I grinned at the circle of white. I was where I wanted to be.

A voice spoke through the door, a surly voice: "What you want?"

"Open up. I've got two flats back on the highway and only one spare. I need help."

"Sorry, mister. We're closed up. Realito's a mile west. Better try there."

I didn't like that. I kicked the door hard. I kept on kicking it. Another voice made itself heard, a purring voice, like a small dynamo behind a wall. I liked this voice. It said: "A wise guy, huh? Open up, Art."

A bolt squealed and half of the door bent inward. My flash burned briefly on a gaunt face. Then something that glittered swept down and knocked the flash out of my hand. A gun had peaked at me. I dropped low where the flash burned on the wet ground and picked it up.

The surly voice said: "Kill that spot, bo. Folks get hurt that way."

I snapped the flash off and straightened. Light went on inside the garage, outlined a tall man in coveralls. He backed away from the open door and kept a gun leveled at me.

"Step inside and shut the door, stranger. We'll see what we can do."

I stepped inside, and shut the door behind my back. I looked at the gaunt man, but not at the other man who was shadowy over by a workbench, silent. The breath of the garage was sweet and sinister with the smell of hot pyroxylin paint.

"Ain't you got no sense?" the gaunt man chided me. "A bank job was pulled at Realito this noon."

"Pardon," I said, remembering the people staring at the bank in the rain. "I didn't pull it. I'm a stranger here."

"Well, there was," he said morosely. "Some say it was a couple of punk kids and they got 'em cornered back here in the hills."

"It's a nice night for hiding," I said. "I suppose they threw tacks out. I got some of them. I thought you just needed the business."

"You didn't ever get socked in the kisser, did you?" the gaunt man asked me briefly.

"Not by anybody your weight."

The purring voice from over in the shadows said: "Cut out the heavy menace, Art. This guy's in a jam. You run a garage, don't you?"

"Thanks," I said, and didn't look at him even then.

"Okey, okey," the man in the coveralls grumbled. He tucked his gun through a flap in his clothes and bit a knuckle, staring at me moodily over it. The smell of the pyroxylin paint was as sickening as ether. Over in the corner, under a drop light, there was a big new-looking sedan with a paint gun lying on its fender.

I looked at the man by the workbench now. He was short and thick-bodied with strong shoulders. He had a cool face and cool dark eyes. He wore a belted brown suede raincoat that was heavily spotted with rain. His brown hat was tilted rakishly.

He leaned his back against the workbench and looked me over without haste, without interest, as if he was looking at a slab of cold meat. Perhaps he thought of people that way.

He moved his dark eyes up and down slowly and then glanced at his fingernails one by one, holding them up against the light and studying them with care, as Hollywood has taught it should be done. He spoke around a cigarette.

"Got two flats, huh? That's tough. They swept them tacks, I thought."

"I skidded a little on the curve."

"Stranger in town you said?"

"Traveling through. On the way to L.A. How far is it?"

"Forty miles. Seems longer this weather. Where from, stranger?"

"Santa Rosa."

"Come the long way, eh? Tahoe and Lone Pine?"

"Not Tahoe. Reno and Carson City."

"Still the long way." A fleeting smile curved his lips.

"Any law against it?" I asked him.

"Huh? No, sure not. Guess you think we're nosey. Just on account of that heist back there. Take a jack and get his flats, Art."

"I'm busy," the gaunt man growled. "I've got work to do. I got this spray job. And it's raining, you might have noticed."

The man in brown said pleasantly: "Too damp for a good spray job, Art. Get moving."

I said: "They're front and rear, on the right side. You could use the spare for one spot, if you're busy."

"Take two jacks, Art," the brown man said.

"Now, listen—" Art began to bluster.

The brown man moved his eyes, looked at Art with a soft quiet-eyed stare, lowered them again almost shyly. He didn't speak. Art rocked as if a gust of wind had hit him. He stamped over to the corner and put a rubber coat over his coveralls, a sou'wester on his head. He grabbed a socket wrench and a hand jack and wheeled a dolly jack over to the doors.

He went out silently, leaving the door yawning. The rain

blustered in. The man in brown strolled over and shut it and strolled back to the workbench and put his hips exactly where they had been before. I could have taken him then. We were alone. He didn't know who I was. He looked at me lightly and threw his cigarette on the cement floor and stamped on it without looking down.

"I bet you could use a drink," he said. "Wet the inside and even up." He reached a bottle from the workbench behind him and set it on the edge and set two glasses beside it. He poured a stiff jolt into each and held one out.

Walking like a dummy I went over and took it. The memory of the rain was still cold on my face. The smell of hot paint drugged the close air of the garage.

"That Art," the brown man said. "He's like all mechanics. Always got his face in a job he ought to have done last week. Business trip?"

I sniffed my drink delicately. It had the right smell. I watched him drink some of his before I swallowed mine. I rolled it around on my tongue. There was no cyanide in it. I emptied the little glass and put it down beside him and moved away.

"Partly," I said. I walked over to the half-painted sedan with the big metal paint gun lying along its fender. The rain hit the flat roof hard. Art was out in it, cursing.

The brown man looked at the big car. "Just a panel job, to start with," he said casually, his purring voice still softer from the drink. "But the guy had dough and his driver needed a few bucks. You know the racket."

I said: "There's only one that's older." My lips felt dry. I didn't want to talk. I lit a cigarette. I wanted my tires fixed. The minutes passed on tiptoe. The brown man and I were two strangers chance-met, looking at each other across a little dead man named Harry Jones. Only the brown man didn't know that yet.

Feet crunched outside and the door was pushed open. The light hit pencils of rain and made silver wires of them. Art trundled two muddy flats in sullenly, kicked the door shut, let one of the flats fall over on its side. He looked at me savagely.

"You sure pick spots for a jack to stand on," he snarled.

The brown man laughed and took a rolled cylinder of nickels out of his pocket and tossed it up and down on the palm of his hand.

"Don't crab so much," he said dryly. "Fix those flats."

"I'm fixin' them, ain't I?"

"Well, don't make a song about it."

"Yah!" Art peeled his rubber coat and sou'wester off and threw them away from him. He heaved one tire up on a spreader and tore the rim loose viciously. He had the tube out and cold-patched in nothing flat. Still scowling, he strode over to the wall beside me and grabbed an air hose, put enough air into the tube to give it body and let the nozzle of the air hose smack against the whitewashed wall.

I stood watching the roll of wrapped coins dance in Canino's hand. The moment of crouched intensity had left me. I turned my head and watched the gaunt mechanic beside me toss the air-stiffened tube up and catch it with his hands wide, one one each side of the tube. He looked it over sourly, glanced at a big galvanized tub of dirty water in the corner and grunted.

The teamwork must have been very nice. I saw no signal, no glance of meaning, no gesture that might have a special import. The gaunt man had the stiffened tube high in the air, staring at it. He half turned his body, took one long quick step, and slammed it down over my head and shoulders, a perfect ringer.

He jumped behind me and leaned hard on the rubber. His weight dragged on my chest, pinned my upper arms tight to my sides. I could move my hands, but I couldn't reach the gun in my pocket.

The brown man came almost dancing towards me across the floor. His hand tightened over the roll of nickels. He came up to me without sound, without expression. I bent forward and tried to heave Art off his feet.

The fist with the weighted tube inside it went through my spread hands like a stone through a cloud of dust. I had the stunned moment of shock when the lights danced and the visible world went out of focus but was still there. He hit me again.

There was no sensation in my head. The bright glare got brighter. There was nothing but hard aching white light. Then there was darkness in which something red wriggled like a germ under a microscope. Then there was nothing bright or wriggling, just darkness and emptiness and a rushing wind and a falling as of great trees.

28

IT SEEMED there was a woman and she was sitting near a lamp, which was where she belonged, in a good light. Another light shone hard on my face, so I closed my eyes again and tried to look at her through the lashes. She was so platinumed that her hair shone like a silver fruit bowl. She wore a green knitted dress with a broad white collar turned over it. There was a sharp-angled glossy bag at her feet. She was smoking and a glass of amber fluid was tall and pale at her elbow.

I moved my head a little, carefully. It hurt, but not more than I expected. I was trussed like a turkey ready for the oven. Handcuffs held my wrists behind me and a rope went from them to my ankles and then over the end of the brown davenport on which I was sprawled. The rope dropped out of sight over the davenport. I moved enough to make sure it was tied down.

I stopped these furtive movements and opened my eyes again and said: "Hello."

The woman withdrew her gaze from some distant mountain peak. Her small firm chin turned slowly. Her eyes were the blue of mountain lakes. Overhead the rain still pounded, with a remote sound, as if it was somebody else's rain.

"How do you feel?" It was a smooth silvery voice that matched her hair. It had a tiny tinkle in it, like bells in a doll's house. I thought that was silly as soon as I thought of it.

"Great," I said. "Somebody built a filling station on my jaw."

"What did you expect, Mr. Marlowe—orchids?"

"Just a plain pine box," I said. "Don't bother with bronze or silver handles. And don't scatter my ashes over the blue Pacific. I like the worms better. Did you know that worms are of both sexes and that any worm can love any other worm?"

"You're a little light-headed," she said, with a grave stare.

"Would you mind moving this light?"

She got up and went behind the davenport. The light went off. The dimness was a benison.

"I don't think you're so dangerous," she said. She was tall rather than short, but no bean-pole. She was slim, but not a dried crust. She went back to her chair.

"So you know my name."

"You slept well. They had plenty of time to go through your pockets. They did everything but embalm you. So you're a detective."

"Is that all they have on me?"

She was silent. Smoke floated dimly from the cigarette. She moved it in the air. Her hand was small and had shape, not the usual bony garden tool you see on women nowadays.

"What time is it?" I asked.

She looked sideways at her wrist, beyond the spiral of smoke, at the edge of the grave luster of the lamplight. "Ten-seventeen. You have a date?"

"I wouldn't be surprised. Is this the house next to Art Huck's garage?"

"Yes."

"What are the boys doing—digging a grave?"

"They had to go somewhere."

"You mean they left you here alone?"

Her head turned slowly again. She smiled. "You don't look dangerous."

"I thought they were keeping you a prisoner."

It didn't seem to startle her. It even slightly amused her. "What made you think that?"

"I know who you are."

Her very blue eyes flashed so sharply that I could almost see the sweep of their glance, like the sweep of a sword. Her mouth tightened. But her voice didn't change.

"Then I'm afraid you're in a bad spot. And I hate killing."

"And you Eddie Mars' wife? Shame on you."

She didn't like that. She glared at me. I grinned. "Unless you can unlock these bracelets, which I'd advise you not to do, you might spare me a little of that drink you're neglecting."

She brought the glass over. Bubbles rose in it like false hopes. She bent over me. Her breath was as delicate as the eyes of a fawn. I gulped from the glass. She took it away from my mouth and watched some of the liquid run down my neck.

She bent over me again. Blood began to move around in me, like a prospective tenant looking over a house.

"Your face looks like a collision mat," she said.

"Make the most of it. It won't last long even this good."

She swung her head sharply and listened. For an instant her face was pale. The sounds were only the rain drifting against the walls. She went back across the room and stood with her side to me, bent forward a little, looking down at the floor.

"Why did you come here and stick your neck out?" she asked quietly. "Eddie wasn't doing you any harm. You know perfectly well that if I hadn't hid out here, the police would have been certain Eddie murdered Rusty Regan."

"He did," I said.

She didn't move, didn't change position an inch. Her breath made a harsh quick sound. I looked around the room. Two doors, both in the same wall, one half open. A carpet of red and tan squares, blue curtains at the windows, a wallpaper with bright green pine trees on it. The furniture looked as if it had come from one of those places that advertise on bus benches. Gay, but full of resistance.

She said softly: "Eddie didn't do anything to him. I haven't seen Rusty in months. Eddie's not that sort of man."

"You left his bed and board. You were living alone. People at the place where you lived identified Regan's photo."

"That's a lie," she said coldly.

I tried to remember whether Captain Gregory had said that or not. My head was too fuzzy. I couldn't be sure.

"And it's none of your business," she added.

"The whole thing is my business. I'm hired to find out."

"Eddie's not that sort of man."

"Oh, you like racketeers."

"As long as people will gamble there will be places for them to gamble."

"That's just protective thinking. Once outside the law you're all the way outside. You think he's just a gambler. I think he's a pornographer, a blackmailer, a hot car broker, a killer by remote control, and a suborner of crooked cops. He's whatever looks good to him, whatever has the cabbage pinned to it. Don't try to sell me on any high-souled racketeers. They don't come in that pattern."

"He's not a killer." Her nostrils flared.

"Not personally. He has Canino. Canino killed a man tonight, a harmless little guy who was trying to help somebody out. I almost saw him killed."

She laughed wearily.

"All right," I growled. "Don't believe it. If Eddie is such a nice guy, I'd like to get to talk to him without Canino around. You know what Canino will do—beat my teeth out and then kick me in the stomach for mumbling."

She put her head back and stood there thoughtful and withdrawn, thinking something out.

"I thought platinum hair was out of style," I bored on, just to keep sound alive in the room, just to keep from listening.

"It's a wig, silly. While mine grows out." She reached up and yanked it off. Her own hair was clipped short all over, like a boy's. She put the wig back on.

"Who did that to you?"

She looked surprised. "I had it done. Why?"

"Yes. Why?"

"Why, to show Eddie I was willing to do what he wanted me to do—hide out. That he didn't need to have me guarded. I wouldn't let him down. I love him."

"Good grief," I groaned. "And you have me right here in the room with you."

She turned a hand over and stared at it. Then abruptly she walked out of the room. She came back with a kitchen knife. She bent and sawed at my rope.

"Canino has the key to the handcuffs," she breathed. "I can't do anything about those."

She stepped back, breathing rapidly. She had cut the rope at every knot.

"You're a kick," she said. "Kidding with every breath—the spot you're in."

"I thought Eddie wasn't a killer."

She turned away quickly and went back to her chair by the lamp and sat down and put her face in her hands. I swung my feet to the floor and stood up. I tottered around, stiff-legged. The nerve on the left side of my face was jumping in all its branches. I took a step. I could still walk. I could run, if I had to.

"I guess you mean me to go," I said.

She nodded without lifting her head.

"You'd better go with me—if you want to keep on living."

"Don't waste time. He'll be back any minute."

"Light a cigarette for me."

I stood beside her, touching her knees. She came to her feet with a sudden lurch. Our eyes were only inches apart.

"Hello, Silver-Wig," I said softly.

She stepped back, around the chair, and swept a package of cigarettes up off the table. She jabbed one loose and pushed it roughly into my mouth. Her hand was shaking. She snapped a small green leather lighter and held it to the cigarette. I drew in the smoke, staring into her lake-blue eyes. While she was still close to me I said:

"A little bird named Harry Jones led me to you. A little bird that used to hop in and out of cocktail bars picking up horse bets for crumbs. Picking up information too. This little bird picked up an idea about Canino. One way and another he and his friends found out where you were. He came to me to sell

the information because he knew—how he knew is a long story
—that I was working for General Sternwood. I got his information, but Canino got the little bird. He's a dead little bird now,
with his feathers ruffled and his neck limp and a pearl of
blood on his beak. Canino killed him. But Eddie Mars wouldn't
do that, would he, Silver-Wig? He never killed anybody. He
just hires it done."

"Get out," she said harshly. "Get out of here quick."

Her hand clutched in midair on the green lighter. The fingers strained. The knuckles were as white as snow.

"But Canino doesn't know I know that," I said. "About the
little bird. All he knows is I'm nosing around."

Then she laughed. It was almost a racking laugh. It shook
her as the wind shakes a tree. I thought there was puzzle-
ment in it, not exactly surprise, but as if a new idea had been
added to something already known and it didn't fit. Then I
thought that was too much to get out of a laugh.

"It's very funny," she said breathlessly. "Very funny, because,
you see—I still love him. Women—" She began to laugh again.

I listened hard, my head throbbing. Just the rain still. "Let's
go," I said. "Fast."

She took two steps back and her face set hard. "Get out, you!
Get out! You can walk to Realito. You can make it—and you
can keep your mouth shut—for an hour or two at least. You
owe me that much."

"Let's go," I said. "Got a gun, Silver-Wig?"

"You know I'm not going. You know that. Please, please get
out of here quickly."

I stepped up close to her, almost pressing against her.
"You're going to stay here after turning me loose? Wait for that
killer to come back so you can say so sorry? A man who kills
like swatting a fly. Not much. You're going with me, Silver-
Wig."

"No."

"Suppose," I said thinly, "your handsome husband *did* kill
Regan? Or suppose Canino did, without Eddie's knowing it.

Just suppose. How long will *you* last, after turning me loose?"

"I'm not afraid of Canino. I'm still his boss's wife."

"Eddie's a handful of mush," I snarled. "Canino would take him with a teaspoon. He'll take him the way the cat took the canary. A handful of mush. The only time a girl like you goes for a wrong gee is when he's a handful of mush."

"Get out!" she almost spit at me.

"Okey." I turned away from her and moved out through the half-open door into a dark hallway. Then she rushed after me and pushed past to the front door and opened it. She peered out into the wet blackness and listened. She motioned me forward.

"Good-by," she said under her breath. "Good luck in everything but one thing. Eddie didn't kill Rusty Regan. You'll find him alive and well somewhere, when he wants to be found."

I leaned against her and pressed her against the wall with my body. I pushed my mouth against her face. I talked to her that way.

"There's no hurry. All this was arranged in advance, rehearsed to the last detail, timed to the split second. Just like a radio program. No hurry at all. Kiss me, Silver-Wig."

Her face under my mouth was like ice. She put her hands up and took hold of my head and kissed me hard on the lips. Her lips were like ice, too.

I went out through the door and it closed behind me, without sound, and the rain blew in under the porch, not as cold as her lips.

29

The garage next door was dark. I crossed the gravel drive and a patch of sodden lawn. The road ran with small rivulets of water. It gurgled down a ditch on the far side. I had no hat. That must have fallen in the garage. Canino hadn't bothered to give it back to me. He hadn't thought I would need it anymore. I imagined him driving back jauntily through the rain, alone, having left the gaunt and sulky Art and the probably stolen sedan in a safe place. She loved Eddie Mars and she was hiding to protect him. So he would find her there when he came back, calm beside the light and the untasted drink, and me tied up on the davenport. He would carry her stuff out to the car and go through the house carefully to make sure nothing incriminating was left. He would tell her to go out and wait. She wouldn't hear a shot. A blackjack is just as effective at short range. He would tell her he had left me tied up and I would get loose after a while. He would think she was that dumb. Nice Mr. Canino.

The raincoat was open in front and I couldn't button it, being handcuffed. The skirts flapped against my legs like the wings of a large and tired bird. I came to the highway. Cars went by in a wide swirl of water illuminated by headlights. The tearing noise of their tires died swiftly. I found my convertible where I had left it, both tires fixed and mounted, so it could be driven away, if necessary. They thought of everything. I got into it and leaned down sideways under the wheel and fumbled aside the flap of leather that covered the pocket. I got the other gun, stuffed it up under my coat and started back. The world was small, shut in, black. A private world for Canino and me.

Halfway there the headlights nearly caught me. They turned swiftly off the highway and I slid down the bank into the wet ditch and flopped there breathing water. The car hummed by without slowing. I lifted my head, heard the rasp of its tires as it left the road and took the gravel of the driveway. The motor died, the lights died, a door slammed. I didn't hear the house door shut, but a fringe of light trickled through the clump of trees, as though a shade had been moved aside from a window, or the light had been put on in the hall.

I came back to the soggy grass plot and sloshed across it. The car was between me and the house, the gun was down at my side, pulled as far around as I could get it, without pulling my left arm out by the roots. The car was dark, empty, warm. Water gurgled pleasantly in the radiator. I peered in at the door. The keys hung on the dash. Canino was very sure of himself. I went around the car and walked carefully across the gravel to the window and listened. I couldn't hear any voices, any sound but the swift bong-bong of the raindrops hitting the metal elbows at the bottom of the rain gutters.

I kept on listening. No loud voices, everything quiet and refined. He would be purring at her and she would be telling him she had let me go and I had promised to let them get away. He wouldn't believe me, as I wouldn't believe him. So he wouldn't be in there long. He would be on his way and take her with him. All I had to do was wait for him to come out.

I couldn't do it. I shifted the gun to my left hand and leaned down to scoop up a handful of gravel. I tossed it against the screen of the window. It was a feeble effort. Very little of it reached the glass above the screen, but the loose rattle of that little was like a dam bursting.

I ran back to the car and got on the running board behind it. The house had already gone dark. That was all. I dropped quietly on the running board and waited. No soap. Canino was too cagey.

I straightened up and got into the car backwards, fumbled around for the ignition key and turned it. I reached with my foot, but the starter button had to be on the dash. I found it at last, pulled it and the starter ground. The warm motor caught at once. It purred softly, contentedly. I got out of the car again and crouched down by the rear wheels.

I was shivering now but I knew Canino wouldn't like that last effect. He needed that car badly. A darkened window slid down inch by inch, only some shifting of light on the glass showing it moved. Flame spouted from it abruptly, the blended roar of three swift shots. Glass starred in the coupe. I yelled with agony. The yell went off into a wailing groan. The groan became a wet gurgle, choked with blood. I let the gurgle die sickeningly, on choked gasp. It was nice work. I liked it. Canino liked it very much. I heard him laugh. It was a large booming laugh, not at all like the purr of his speaking voice.

Then silence for a little while, except for the rain and the quietly throbbing motor of the car. Then the house door crawled open, a deeper blackness in the black night. A figure showed in it cautiously, something white around the neck. It was her collar. She came out on the porch stiffly, a wooden woman. I caught the pale shine of her silver wig. Canino came crouched methodically behind her. It was so deadly it was almost funny.

She came down the steps. Now I could see the white stiffness of her face. She started towards the car. A bulwark of defense for Canino, in case I could still spit in his eye. Her voice spoke through the lisp of the rain, saying slowly, without any tone: "I can't see a thing, Lash. The windows are misted."

He grunted something and the girl's body jerked hard, as though he had jammed a gun into her back. She came on again and drew near the lightless car. I could see him behind her now, his hat, a side of his face, the bulk of his shoulder. The girl stopped rigid and screamed. A beautiful thin tearing scream that rocked me like a left hook.

"I can see him!" she screamed. "Through the window. Behind the wheel, Lash!"

He fell for it like a bucket of lead. He knocked her roughly to one side and jumped forward, throwing his hand up. Three more spurts of flame cut the darkness. More glass scarred. One bullet went on through and smacked into a tree on my side. A ricochet whined off into the distance. But the motor went quietly on.

He was low down, crouched against the gloom, his face a grayness without form that seemed to come back slowly after the glare of the shots. If it was a revolver he had, it might be empty. It might not. He had fired six times, but he might have reloaded inside the house. I hoped he had. I didn't want him with an empty gun. But it might be an automatic.

I said: "Finished?"

He whirled at me. Perhaps it would have been nice to allow him another shot or two, just like a gentleman of the old school. But his gun was still up and I couldn't wait any longer. Not long enough to be a gentleman of the old school. I shot him four times, the Colt straining against my ribs. The gun jumped out of his hand as if it had been kicked. He reached both his hands for his stomach. I could hear them smack hard against his body. He fell like that, straight forward, holding himself together with his broad hands. He fell face down in the wet gravel. And after that there wasn't a sound from him.

Silver-Wig didn't make a sound either. She stood rigid, with the rain swirling at her. I walked around Canino and kicked his gun, without any purpose. Then I walked after it and bent over sideways and picked it up. That put me close beside her. She spoke moodily, as if she was talking to herself.

"I—I was afraid you'd come back."

I said: "We had a date. I told you it was all arrranged." I began to laugh like a loon.

Then she was bending down over him, touching him. And after a little while she stood up with a small key on a thin chain.

She said bitterly: "Did you have to kill him?"

I stopped laughing as suddenly as I had started. She went behind me and unlocked the handcuffs.

"Yes," she said softly. "I suppose you did."

30

THIS WAS another day and the sun was shining again.

Captain Gregory of the Missing Persons Bureau looked heavily out of his office window at the barred upper floor of the Hall of Justice, white and clean after the rain. Then he turned ponderously in his swivel chair and tamped his pipe with a heat-scarred thumb and stared at me bleakly.

"So you got yourself in another jam."

"Oh, you heard about it."

"Brother, I sit here all day on my fanny and I don't look as if I had a brain in my head. But you'd be surprised what I hear. Shooting this Canino was all right I guess, but I don't figure the homicide boys pinned any medals on you."

"There's been a lot of killing going on around me," I said. "I haven't been getting my share of it."

He smiled patiently. "Who told you this girl out there was Eddie Mars' wife?"

I told him. He listened carefully and yawned. He tapped his gold-studded mouth with a palm like a tray. "I guess you figure I ought to of found her."

"That's a fair deduction."

"Maybe I knew," he said. "Maybe I thought if Eddie and his woman wanted to play a little game like that, it would be smart —or as smart as I ever get—to let them think they were getting away with it. And then again maybe you think I was letting Eddie get away with it for more personal reasons." He held his big hand out and revolved the thumb against the index and second fingers.

"No," I said. "I didn't really think that. Not even when Eddie seemed to know all about our talk here the other day."

He raised his eyebrows as if raising them was an effort, a trick he was out of practice on. It furrowed his whole forehead and when it smoothed out it was full of white lines that turned reddish as I watched them.

"I'm a copper," he said. "Just a plain ordinary copper. Reasonably honest. As honest as you could expect a man to be in a world where it's out of style. That's mainly why I asked you to come in this morning. I'd like you to believe that. Being a copper I like to see the law win. I'd like to see the flashy well-dressed muggs like Eddie Mars spoiling their manicures in the rock quarry at Folsom, alongside of the poor little slumbred hard guys that got knocked over on their first caper and never had a break since. That's what I'd like. You and me both lived too long to think I'm likely to see it happen. Not in this town, not in any town half this size, in any part of this wide, green and beautiful U.S.A. We just don't run our country that way."

I didn't say anything. He blew smoke with a backward jerk of his head, looked at the mouthpiece of his pipe and went on:

"But that don't mean I think Eddie Mars bumped off Regan or had any reason to or would have done it if he had. I just figured maybe he knows something about it, and maybe sooner or later something will sneak out into the open. Hiding his wife out at Realito was childish, but it's the kind of childishness a smart monkey thinks is smart. I had him in here last night, after the D.A. got through with him. He admitted the whole thing. He said he knew Canino as a reliable protection guy and that's what he had him for. He didn't know anything about his hobbies or want to. He didn't know Harry Jones. He didn't know Joe Brody. He did know Geiger, of course, but claims he didn't know about his racket. I guess you heard all that."

"Yes."

"You played it smart down there at Realito, brother. Not trying to cover up. We keep a file on unidentified bullets nowadays. Someday you might use that gun again. Then you'd be over a barrel."

"I played it smart," I said, and leered at him.

He knocked his pipe out and stared down at it broodingly. "What happened to the girl?" he asked, not looking up.

"I don't know. They didn't hold her. We made statements, three sets of them, for Wilde, for the Sheriff's office, for the Homicide Bureau. They turned her loose. I haven't seen her since. I don't expect to."

"Kind of a nice girl, they say. Wouldn't be one to play dirty games."

"Kind of a nice girl," I said.

Captain Gregory sighed and rumpled his mousy hair. "There's just one more thing," he said almost gently. "You look like a nice guy, but you play too rough. If you really want to help the Sternwood family—leave 'em alone."

"I think you're right, Captain."

"How you feel?"

"Swell," I said. "I was standing on various pieces of carpet most of the night, being balled out. Before that I got soaked to the skin and beaten up. I'm in perfect condition."

"What the hell did you expect, brother?"

"Nothing else." I stood up and grinned at him and started for the door. When I had almost reached it he cleared his throat suddenly and said in a harsh voice: "I'm wasting my breath, huh? You still think you can find Regan."

I turned around and looked him straight in the eyes. "No, I don't think I can find Regan. I'm not even going to try. Does that suit you?"

He nodded slowly. Then he shrugged. "I don't know what the hell I even said that for. Good luck, Marlowe. Drop around any time."

"Thanks, Captain."

I went down out of the City Hall and got my car from the parking lot and drove home to the Hobart Arms. I lay down on

the bed with my coat off and stared at the ceiling and listened
to the traffic sounds on the street outside and watched the sun
move slowly across a corner of the ceiling. I tried to go to sleep,
but sleep didn't come. I got up and took a drink, although
it was the wrong time of day, and lay down again. I still couldn't
go to sleep. My brain ticked like a clock. I sat up on the side
of the bed and stuffed a pipe and said out loud:

"That old buzzard knows something."

The pipe tasted as bitter as lye. I put it aside and lay down
again. My mind drifted through waves of false memory, in
which I seemed to do the same thing over and over again, go
to the same places, meet the same people, say the same words
to them, over and over again, and yet each time it seemed real,
like something actually happening, and for the first time. I was
driving hard along the highway through the rain, with Silver-
Wig in the corner of the car, saying nothing, so that by the
time we reached Los Angeles we seemed to be utter strangers
again. I was getting out at an all night drugstore and phoning
Bernie Ohls that I had killed a man at Realito and was on my
way over to Wilde's house with Eddie Mars' wife, who had seen
me do it. I was pushing the car along the silent, rain-polished
streets to Lafayette Park and up under the porte-cochere of
Wilde's big frame house and the porch light was already on,
Ohls having telephoned ahead that I was coming. I was in
Wilde's study and he was behind his desk in a flowered
dressing-gown and a tight hard face and a dappled cigar moved
in his fingers and up to the bitter smile on his lips. Ohls was
there and a slim gray scholarly man from the Sheriff's office
who looked and talked more like a professor of economics than
a cop. I was telling the story and they were listening quietly
and Silver-Wig sat in a shadow with her hands folded in her
lap, looking at nobody. There was a lot of telephoning. There
were two men from the Homicide Bureau who looked at me
as if I was some kind of strange beast escaped from a traveling
circus. I was driving again, with one of them beside me, to the
Fulwider Building. We were there in the room where Harry
Jones was still in the chair behind the desk, the twisted stiff-

ness of his dead face and the sour-sweet smell in the room. There was a medical examiner, very young and husky, with red bristles on his neck. There was a fingerprint man fussing around and I was telling him not to forget the latch of the transom. (He found Canino's thumb print on it, the only print the brown man had left to back up my story.)

I was back again at Wilde's house, signing a typewritten statement his secretary had run off in another room. Then the door opened and Eddie Mars came in and an abrupt smile flashed to his face when he saw Silver-Wig, and he said: "Hello, sugar," and she didn't look at him or answer him. Eddie Mars fresh and cheerful, in a dark business suit, with a fringed white scarf hanging outside his tweed overcoat. Then they were gone, everybody was gone out of the room but myself and Wilde, and Wilde was saying in a cold, angry voice: "This is the last time, Marlowe. The next fast one you pull I'll throw you to the lions, no matter whose heart it breaks."

It was like that, over and over again, lying on the bed and watching the patch of sunlight slide down the corner of the wall. Then the phone rang, and it was Norris, the Sternwood butler, with his usual untouchable voice.

"Mr. Marlowe? I telephoned your office without success, so I took the liberty of trying to reach you at home."

"I was out most of the night," I said. "I haven't been down."

"Yes, sir. The General would like to see you this morning, Mr. Marlowe, if it's convenient."

"Half an hour or so," I said. "How is he?"

"He's in bed, sir, but not doing badly."

"Wait till he sees me," I said, and hung up.

I shaved, changed clothes and started for the door. Then I went back and got Carmen's little pearl-handled revolver and dropped it into my pocket. The sunlight was so bright that it danced. I got to the Sternwood place in twenty minutes and drove up under the arch at the side door. It was eleven-fifteen. The birds in the ornamental trees were crazy with song after the rain, the terraced lawns were as green as the Irish flag, and the whole estate looked as though it had been made about ten minutes before. I rang the bell. It was five days since I had rung it for the first time. It felt like a year.

A maid opened the door and led me along a side hall to the main hallway and left me there, saying Mr. Norris would be down in a moment. The main hallway looked just the same. The portrait over the mantel had the same hot black eyes and the knight in the stained-glass window still wasn't getting anywhere untying the naked damsel from the tree.

In a few minutes Norris appeared, and he hadn't changed either. His acid-blue eyes were as remote as ever, his grayish-pink skin looked healthy and rested, and he moved as if he was twenty years younger than he really was. I was the one who felt the weight of the years.

We went up the tiled staircase and turned the opposite way from Vivian's room. With each step the house seemed to grow larger and more silent. We reached a massive old door that looked as if it had come out of a church. Norris opened it softly and looked in. Then he stood aside and I went in past him across what seemed to be about a quarter of a mile of carpet to a huge canopied bed like the one Henry the Eighth died in.

General Sternwood was propped up on pillows. His bloodless hands were clasped on top of the sheet. They looked gray against it. His black eyes were still full of fight and the rest of his face still looked like the face of a corpse.

"Sit down, Mr. Marlowe." His voice sounded weary and a little stiff.

I pulled a chair close to him and sat down. All the windows were shut tight. The room was sunless at that hour. Awnings cut off what glare there might be from the sky. The air had the faint sweetish smell of old age.

He stared at me silently for a long minute. He moved a hand, as if to prove to himself that he could still move it, then folded it back over the other. He said lifelessly:

"I didn't ask you to look for my son-in-law, Mr. Marlowe."

"You wanted me to, though."

"I didn't ask you to. You assume a great deal. I usually ask for what I want."

I didn't say anything.

"You have been paid," he went on coldly. "The money is of no consequence one way or the other. I merely feel that you have, no doubt unintentionally, betrayed a trust."

He closed his eyes on that. I said: "Is that all you wanted to see me about?"

He opened his eyes again, very slowly, as though the lids were made of lead. "I suppose you are angry at that remark," he said.

I shook my head. "You have an advantage over me, General. It's an advantage I wouldn't want to take away from you, not a hair of it. It's not much, considering what you have to put up with. You can say anything you like to me and I wouldn't think of getting angry. I'd like to offer you your money back. It may mean nothing to you. It might mean something to me."

"What does it mean to you?"

"It means I have refused payment for an unsatisfactory job. That's all."

"Do you do many unsatisfactory jobs?"

"A few. Everyone does."

"Why did you go to see Captain Gregory?"

I leaned back and hung an arm over the back of the chair. I studied his face. It told me nothing. I didn't know the answer to his question—no satisfactory answer.

I said: "I was convinced you put those Geiger notes up to me chiefly as a test, and that you were a little afraid Regan might somehow be involved in an attempt to blackmail you. I didn't know anything about Regan then. It wasn't until I talked to Captain Gregory that I realized Regan wasn't that sort of guy in all probability."

"That is scarcely answering my question."

I nodded. "No. That is scarcely answering your question. I guess I just don't like to admit that I played a hunch. The morning I was here, after I left you out in the orchid house, Mrs. Regan sent for me. She seemed to assume I was hired to look for her husband and she didn't seem to like it. She let drop however that 'they' had found his car in a certain garage.

The 'they' could only be the police. Consequently the police must know something about it. If they did, the Missing Persons Bureau would be the department that would have the case. I didn't know whether you had reported it, of course, or somebody else, or whether they had found the car through somebody reporting it abandoned in a garage. But I know cops, and I knew that if they got that much, they would get a little more—especially as your driver happened to have a police record. I didn't know how much more they would get. That started me thinking about the Missing Persons Bureau. What convinced me was something in Mr. Wilde's manner the night we had the conference over at his house about Geiger and so on. We were alone for a minute and he asked me whether you had told me you were looking for Regan. I said you had told me you wished you knew where he was and that he was all right. Wilde pulled his lip in and looked funny. I knew just as plainly as though he had said it that by 'looking for Regan' he meant using the machinery of the law to look for him. Even then I tried to go up against Captain Gregory in such a way that I wouldn't tell him anything he didn't know already."

"And you allowed Captain Gregory to think I had employed you to find Rusty?"

"Yeah. I guess I did—when I was sure he had the case."

He closed his eyes. They twitched a little. He spoke with them closed. "And do you consider that ethical?"

"Yes," I said. "I do."

The eyes opened again. The piercing blackness of them was startling coming suddenly out of that dead face. "Perhaps I don't understand," he said.

"Maybe you don't. The head of a Missing Persons Bureau isn't a talker. He wouldn't be in that office if he was. This one is a very smart cagey guy who tries, with a lot of success at first, to give the impression he's a middle-aged hack fed up with his job. The game I play is not spillikins. There's always a large element of bluff connected with it. Whatever I might say to a cop, he would be apt to discount it. And to *that* cop it wouldn't make much difference what I said. When you hire a boy in my line of work it isn't like hiring a window-washer and showing him eight windows and saying: 'Wash those and you're through.' You don't know what I have to go through or over or under to do your job for you. I do it my way. I do my best to protect you and I may break a few rules, but I break them in your favor. The client comes first, unless he's crooked. Even then all I do is hand the job back to him and keep my mouth shut. After all you didn't tell me *not* to go to Captain Gregory."

"That would have been rather difficult," he said with a faint smile.

"Well, what have I done wrong? Your man Norris seemed to think when Geiger was eliminated the case was over. I don't see it that way. Geiger's method of approach puzzled me and still does. I'm not Sherlock Holmes or Philo Vance. I don't expect to go over ground the police have covered and pick up a broken pen point and build a case from it. If you think there is anybody in the detective business making a living doing that sort of thing, you don't know much about cops. It's not things like that they overlook, if they overlook anything. I'm not saying they often overlook anything when they're really allowed to work. But if they do, it's apt to be something looser and vaguer, like a man of Geiger's type sending you his evidence of debt and asking you to pay like a gentleman—Geiger, a man in a shady racket, in a vulnerable position, protected by a racketeer and having at least some negative protection from some of the police. Why did he do that? Because he wanted to find out if there was anything putting pressure on you. If there was, you would pay him. If not, you would ignore him and wait for his next move. But there was something putting a pressure on you. Regan. You were afraid he was not what he had appeared to be, that he had stayed around and been nice to you just long enough to find out how to play games with your bank account."

He started to say something but I interrupted him. "Even at that it wasn't your money you cared about. It wasn't even your daughters. You've more or less written them off. It's that you're still too proud to be played for a sucker—and you really liked Regan."

There was a silence. Then the General said quietly: "You talk too damn much, Marlowe. Am I to understand you are still trying to solve that puzzle?"

"No. I've quit. I've been warned off. The boys think I play too rough. That's why I thought I should give you back your money—because it isn't a completed job by my standards."

He smiled. "Quit, nothing," he said. "I'll pay you another thousand dollars to find Rusty. He doesn't have to come back. I don't even have to know where he is. A man has a right to live his own life. I don't blame him for walking out on my daughter, nor even for going so abruptly. It was probably a sudden impulse. I want to know that he is all right wherever he is. I want to know it from him directly, and if he should happen to need money, I should want him to have that also. Am I clear?"

I said: "Yes, General."

He rested a little while, lax on the bed, his eyes closed and dark-lidded, his mouth tight and bloodless. He was used up. He was pretty nearly licked. He opened his eyes again and tried to grin at me.

"I guess I'm a sentimental old goat," he said. "And no soldier at all. I took a fancy to that boy. He seemed pretty clean to me. I must be a little too vain about my judgment of character. Find him for me, Marlowe. Just find him."

"I'll try," I said. "You'd better rest now. I've talked your arm off."

I got up quickly and walked across the wide floor and out. He had his eyes shut again before I opened the door. His hands lay limp on the sheet. He looked a lot more like a dead man than most dead men look. I shut the door quietly and went back along the upper hall and down the stairs.

31

THE BUTLER appeared with my hat. I put it on and said: "What do you think of him?"

"He's not as weak as he looks, sir."

"If he was, he'd be ready for burial. What did this Regan fellow have that bored into him so?"

The butler looked at me levelly and yet with a queer lack of expression. "Youth, sir," he said. "And the soldier's eye."

"Like yours," I said.

"If I may say so, sir, not unlike yours."

"Thanks. How are the ladies this morning?"

He shrugged politely.

"Just what I thought," I said, and he opened the door for me.

I stood outside on the step and looked down the vistas of grassed terraces and trimmed trees and flowerbeds to the tall metal railing at the bottom of the gardens. I saw Carmen about halfway down, sitting on a stone bench, with her head between her hands, looking forlorn and alone.

I went down the red brick steps that led from terrace to terrace. I was quite close before she heard me. She jumped up and whirled like a cat. She wore the light blue slacks she had worn the first time I saw her. Her blonde hair was the same loose tawny wave. Her face was white. Red spots flared in her cheeks as she looked at me. Her eyes were slaty.

"Bored?" I said.

She smiled slowly, rather shyly, then nodded quickly. Then she whispered: "You're not mad at me?"

"I thought you were mad at me."

She put her thumb up and giggled. "I'm not." When she giggled I didn't like her any more. I looked around. A target hung on a tree about thirty feet away, with some darts sticking to it. There were three or four more on the stone bench where she had been sitting.

"For people with money you and your sister don't seem to have much fun," I said.

She looked at me under her long lashes. This was the look that was supposed to make me roll over on my back. I said: "You like throwing those darts?"

"Uh-huh."

"That reminds me of something." I looked back towards the house. By moving about three feet I made a tree hide me from it. I took her little pearl-handled gun out of my pocket. "I brought you back your artillery. I cleaned it and loaded it up. Take my tip—don't shoot it at people, unless you get to be a better shot. Remember?"

Her face went paler and her thin thumb dropped. She looked at me, then at the gun I was holding. There was a fascination in her eyes. "Yes," she said, and nodded. Then suddenly: "Teach me to shoot."

"Huh?"

"Teach me how to shoot. I'd like that."

"Here? It's against the law."

She came close to me and took the gun out of my hand, cuddled her hand around the butt. Then she tucked it quickly inside her slacks, almost with a furtive movement, and looked around.

"I know where," she said in a secret voice. "Down by some of the old wells." She pointed off down the hill. "Teach me?"

I looked into her slaty blue eyes. I might as well have looked at a couple of bottle-tops. "All right. Give me back the gun until I see if the place looks all right."

She smiled and made a mouth, then handed it back with a

secret naughty air, as if she was giving me a key to her room. We walked up the steps and around to my car. The gardens seemed deserted. The sunshine was as empty as a headwaiter's smile. We got into the car and I drove down the sunken drive-way and out through the gates.

"Where's Vivian?" I asked.

"Not up yet." She giggled.

I drove on down the hill through the quiet opulent streets with their faces washed by the rain, bore east to La Brea, then south. We reached the place she meant in about ten minutes.

"In there." She leaned out of the window and pointed.

It was a narrow dirt road, not much more than a track, like the entrance to some foothill ranch. A wide five-barred gate was folded back against a stump and looked as if it hadn't been shut in years. The road was fringed with tall eucalyptus trees and deeply rutted. Trucks had used it. It was empty and sunny now, but not yet dusty. The rain had been too hard and too recent. I followed the ruts along and the noise of city traffic grew curiously and quickly faint, as if this were not in the city at all, but far away in a daydream land. Then the oil-stained, motionless walking-beam of a squat wooden derrick stuck up over a branch. I could see the rusty old steel cable that con-nected this walking-beam with half a dozen others. The beams didn't move, probably hadn't moved for a year. The wells were no longer pumping. There was a pile of rusted pipe, a loading platform that sagged at one end, half a dozen empty oil drums lying in a ragged pile. There was the stagnant, oil-scummed water of an old sump iridescent in the sunlight.

"Are they going to make a park of all this?" I asked.

She dipped her chin down and gleamed at me.

"It's about time. The smell of that sump would poison a herd of goats. This the place you had in mind?"

"Uh-huh. Like it?"

"It's beautiful." I pulled up beside the loading platform. We got out. I listened. The hum of the traffic was a distant web of sound, like the buzzing of bees. The place was as lonely as a churchyard. Even after the rain the tall eucalyptus trees still looked dusty. They always look dusty. A branch broken off by the wind had fallen over the edge of the sump and the flat leathery leaves dangled in the water.

I walked around the sump and looked into the pumphouse. There was some junk in it, nothing that looked like recent activity. Outside a big wooden bull wheel was tilted against the wall. It looked like a good place all right.

I went back to the car. The girl stood beside it preening her hair and holding it out in the sun. "Gimme," she said, and held her hand out.

I took the gun out and put it in her palm. I bent down and picked up a rusty can.

"Take it easy now," I said. "It's loaded in all five. I'll go over and set this can in that square opening in the middle of that big wooden wheel. See?" I pointed. She ducked her head, delighted. "That's about thirty feet. Don't start shooting until I get back beside you. Okey?"

"Okey," she giggled.

I went back around the sump and set the can up in the middle of the bull wheel. It made a swell target. If she missed the can, which she was certain to do, she would probably hit the wheel. That would stop a small slug completely. However, she wasn't going to hit even that.

I went back towards her around the sump. When I was about ten feet from her, at the edge of the sump, she showed me all her sharp little teeth and brought the gun up and started to hiss.

I stopped dead, the sump water stagnant and stinking at my back.

"Stand there, you son of a bitch," she said.

The gun pointed at my chest. Her hand seemed to be quite steady. The hissing sound grew louder and her face had the scraped bone look. Aged, deteriorated, become animal, and not a nice animal.

I laughed at her. I started to walk towards her. I saw her small finger tighten on the trigger and grow white at the tip. I was about six feet away from her when she started to shoot.

The sound of the gun made a sharp slap, without body, a brittle crack in the sunlight. I didn't see any smoke. I stopped again and grinned at her.

She fired twice more, very quickly. I don't think any of the shots would have missed. There were five in the little gun. She had fired four. I rushed her.

I didn't want the last one in my face, so I swerved to one side. She gave it to me quite carefully, not worried at all. I think I felt the hot breath of the powder blast a little.

I straightened up. "My, but you're cute," I said.

Her hand holding the empty gun began to shake violently. The gun fell out of it. Her mouth began to shake. Her whole face went to pieces. Then her head screwed up towards her left ear and froth showed on her lips. Her breath made a whining sound. She swayed.

I caught her as she fell. She was already unconscious. I pried her teeth open with both hands and stuffed a wadded handkerchief in between them. It took all my strength to do it. I lifted her up and got her into the car, then went back for the gun and dropped it into my pocket. I climbed in under the wheel, backed the car and drove back the way we had come along the rutted road, out of the gateway, back up the hill and so home.

Carmen lay crumpled in the corner of the car, without motion. I was halfway up the drive to the house before she stirred. Then her eyes suddenly opened wide and wild. She sat up.

"What happened?" she gasped.

"Nothing. Why?"

"Oh, yes it did," she giggled. "I wet myself."

"They always do," I said.

She looked at me with a sudden sick speculation and began to moan.

32

THE GENTLE-EYED, horse-faced maid let me into the long gray and white upstairs sitting room with the ivory drapes tumbled extravagantly on the floor and the white carpet from wall to wall. A screen star's boudoir, a place of charm and seduction, artificial as a wooden leg. It was empty at the moment. The door closed behind me with the unnatural softness of a hospital door. A breakfast table on wheels stood by the chaise-longue. Its silver glittered. There were cigarette ashes in the coffee cup. I sat down and waited.

It seemed a long time before the door opened again and Vivian came in. She was in oyster-white lounging pajamas trimmed with white fur, cut as flowingly as a summer sea frothing on the beach of some small and exclusive island.

She went past me in long smooth strides and sat down on the edge of the chaise-longue. There was a cigarette in her lips, at the corner of her mouth. Her nails today were copper red from quick to tip, without half moons.

"So you're just a brute after all," she said quietly, staring at me. "An utter callous brute. You killed a man last night. Never mind how I heard it. I heard it. And now you have to come out here and frighten my kid sister into a fit."

I didn't say a word. She began to fidget. She moved over to a slipper chair and put her head back against a white cushion that lay along the back of the chair against the wall. She blew pale gray smoke upwards and watched it float towards the ceiling and come apart in wisps that were for a little while distinguishable from the air and then melted and were nothing. Then very slowly she lowered her eyes and gave me a cool hard glance.

"I don't understand you," she said. "I'm thankful as hell one of us kept his head the night before last. It's bad enough to have a bootlegger in my past. Why don't you for Christ's sake say something?"

"How is she?"

"Oh, she's all right, I suppose. Fast asleep. She always goes to sleep. What did you do to her?"

"Not a thing. I came out of the house after seeing your father and she was out in front. She had been throwing darts at a target on a tree. I went down to speak to her because I had something that belonged to her. A little revolver Owen Taylor gave her once. She took it over to Brody's place the other evening, the evening he was killed. I had to take it away from her there. I didn't mention it, so perhaps you didn't know it."

The black Sternwood eyes got large and empty. It was her turn not to say anything.

"She was pleased to get her little gun back and she wanted me to teach her how to shoot and she wanted to show me the old oil wells down the hill where your family made some of its money. So we went down there and the place was pretty creepy, all rusted metal and old wood and silent wells and greasy scummy sumps. Maybe that upset her. I guess you've been there yourself. It was kind of eerie."

"Yes—it is." It was a small breathless voice now.

"So we went in there and I stuck a can up in a bull wheel for her to pop at. She threw a wingding. Looked like a mild epileptic fit to me."

"Yes." The same minute voice. "She has them once in a while. Is that all you wanted to see me about?"

"I guess you still wouldn't tell me what Eddie Mars has on you."

"Nothing at all. And I'm getting a little tired of that question," she said coldly.

"Do you know a man named Canino?"

She drew her fine black brows together in thought. "Vaguely. I seem to remember the name."

"Eddie Mars' trigger man. A tough hombre, they said. I guess he was. Without a little help from a lady I'd be where he is—in the morgue."

"The ladies seem to—" She stopped dead and whitened. "I can't joke about it," she said simply.

"I'm not joking, and if I seem to talk in circles, it just seems that way. It all ties together—everything. Geiger and his cute little blackmail tricks, Brody and his pictures, Eddie Mars and his roulette tables, Canino and the girl Rusty Regan didn't run away with. It all ties together."

"I'm afraid I don't even know what you're talking about."

"Suppose you did—it would be something like this. Geiger got his hooks into your sister, which isn't very difficult, and got some notes from her and tried to blackmail your father with them, in a nice way. Eddie Mars was behind Geiger, protecting him and using him for a cat's-paw. Your father sent for me instead of paying up, which showed he wasn't scared about anything. Eddie Mars wanted to know that. He had something on you and he wanted to know if he had it on the General too. If he had, he could collect a lot of money in a hurry. If not, he would have to wait until you got your share of the family fortune, and in the meantime be satisfied with whatever spare cash he could take away from you across the roulette table. Geiger was killed by Owen Taylor, who was in love with your silly little sister and didn't like the kind of games Geiger played with her. That didn't mean anything to Eddie. He was playing a deeper game than Geiger knew anything about, or than Brody knew anything about, or anybody except you and Eddie and a tough guy named Canino. Your husband disappeared and Eddie, knowing everybody knew there had been bad blood between him and Regan, hid his wife out at Realito and put Canino to guard her, so that it would look as if she had run

away with Regan. He even got Regan's car into the garage of
the place where Mona Mars had been living. But that sounds
a little silly taken merely as an attempt to divert suspicion that
Eddie had killed your husband or had him killed. It isn't so
silly, really. He had another motive. He was playing for a million or so. He knew where Regan had gone and why and he
didn't want the police to have to find out. He wanted them to
have an explanation of the disappearance that would keep
them satisfied. Am I boring you?"

"You tire me," she said in a dead, exhausted voice. "God,
how you tire me!"

"I'm sorry. I'm not just fooling around trying to be clever.
Your father offered me a thousand dollars this morning to find
Regan. That's a lot of money to me, but I can't do it."

Her mouth jumped open. Her breath was suddenly strained
and harsh. "Give me a cigarette," she said thickly. "Why?" The
pulse in her throat had begun to throb.

I gave her a cigarette and lit a match and held it for her. She
drew in a lungful of smoke and let it out raggedly and then
the cigarette seemed to be forgotten between her fingers. She
never drew on it again.

"Well, the Missing Persons Bureau can't find him," I said.
"It's not so easy. What they can't do it's not likely that I can
do."

"Oh." There was a shade of relief in her voice.

"That's one reason. The Missing Persons people think he
just disappeared on purpose, pulled down the curtain, as they
call it. They don't think Eddie Mars did away with him."

"Who said anybody did away with him?"

"We're coming to it," I said.

For a brief instant her face seemed to come to pieces, to
become merely a set of features without form or control. Her
mouth looked like the prelude to a scream. But only for an
instant. The Sternwood blood had to be good for something
more than her black eyes and her recklessness.

I stood up and took the smoking cigarette from between her
fingers and killed it in an ashtray. Then I took Carmen's little

gun out of my pocket and laid it carefully, with exaggerated care, on her white satin knee. I balanced it there, and stepped back with my head on one side like a window-dresser getting the effect of a new twist of a scarf around a dummy's neck.

I sat down again. She didn't move. Her eyes came down millimeter by millimeter and looked at the gun.

"It's harmless," I said. "All five chambers empty. She fired them all. She fired them all at me."

The pulse jumped wildly in her throat. Her voice tried to say something and couldn't. She swallowed.

"From a distance of five or six feet," I said. "Cute little thing, isn't she? Too bad I had loaded the gun with blanks." I grinned nastily. "I had a hunch about what she would do—if she got the chance."

She brought her voice back from a long way off. "You're a horrible man," she said. "Horrible."

"Yeah. You're her big sister. What are you going to do about it?"

"You can't prove a word of it."

"Can't prove what?"

"That she fired at you. You said you were down there around the wells with her, alone. You can't prove a word of what you say."

"Oh that," I said. "I wasn't thinking of trying. I was thinking of another time—when the shells in the little gun had bullets in them."

Her eyes were pools of darkness, much emptier than darkness.

"I was thinking of the day Regan disappeared," I said. "Late in the afternoon. When he took her down to those old wells to teach her to shoot and put up a can somewhere and told her to pop at it and stood near her while she shot. And she didn't shoot at the can. She turned the gun and shot him, just the way she tried to shoot me today, and for the same reason."

She moved a little and the gun slid off her knee and fell to the floor. It was one of the loudest sounds I ever heard. Her eyes were riveted on my face. Her voice was a stretched whisper of agony. "Carmen! . . . Merciful God, Carmen! . . . Why?"

"Do I really have to tell you why she shot at me?"

"Yes." Her eyes were still terrible. "I'm—I'm afraid you do."

"Night before last when I got home she was in my apartment. She'd kidded the manager into letting her in to wait for me. She was in my bed—naked. I threw her out on her ear. I guess maybe Regan did the same thing to her sometime. But you can't do that to Carmen."

She drew her lips back and made a half-hearted attempt to lick them. It made her, for a brief instant, look like a frightened child. The lines of her cheeks sharpened and her hand went up slowly like an artificial hand worked by wires and its fingers closed slowly and stiffly around the white fur at her collar. They drew the fur tight against her throat. After that she just sat staring.

"Money," she croaked. "I suppose you want money."

"How much money?" I tried not to sneer.

"Fifteen thousand dollars?"

I nodded. "That would be about right. That would be the established fee. That was what he had in his pockets when she shot him. That would be what Mr. Canino got for disposing of the body when you went to Eddie Mars for help. But that would be small change to what Eddie expects to collect one of these days, wouldn't it?"

"You son of a bitch!" she said.

"Uh-uh. I'm a very smart guy. I haven't a feeling or a scruple in the world. All I have the itch for is money. I am so money greedy that for twenty-five bucks a day and expenses, mostly gasoline and whiskey, I do my thinking myself, what there is of it; I risk my whole future, the hatred of the cops and of Eddie Mars and his pals, I dodge bullets and eat saps, and say thank you very much, if you have any more trouble, I hope you'll think of me, I'll just leave one of my cards in case anything comes up. I do all this for twenty-five bucks a day—and maybe just a little to protect what little pride a broken and sick old man has left in his blood, in the thought that his blood is not poison, and that although his two little girls are a trifle wild, as many nice girls are these days, they are not perverts or killers. And that makes me a son of a bitch. All right. I don't care anything about that. I've been called that by people of all sizes and shapes, including your little sister. She called me worse than that for not getting into bed with her. I got five hundred dollars from your father, which I didn't ask for, but he can afford to give it to me. I can get another thousand for finding Mr. Rusty Regan, if I could find him. Now you offer me fifteen grand. That makes me a big shot. With fifteen grand I could own a home and a new car and four suits of clothes. I might even take a vacation without worrying about losing a case. That's fine. What are you offering it to me for? Can I go on being a son of a bitch, or do I have to become a gentleman, like that lush that passed out in his car the other night?"

She was as silent as a stone woman.

"All right," I went on heavily. "Will you take her away? Somewhere far off from here where they can handle her type, where they will keep guns and knives and fancy drinks away from her? Hell, she might even get herself cured, you know. It's been done."

She got up and walked slowly to the windows. The drapes lay in heavy ivory folds beside her feet. She stood among the folds and looked out, towards the quiet darkish foothills. She stood motionless, almost blending into the drapes. Her hands hung loose at her sides. Utterly motionless hands. She turned and came back along the room and walked past me blindly. When she was behind me she caught her breath sharply and spoke.

"He's in the sump," she said. "A horrible decayed thing. I did it. I did just what you said. I went to Eddie Mars. She came home and told me about it, just like a child. She's not normal. I knew the police would get it all out of her. In a little while she would even brag about it. And if dad knew, he would call them instantly and tell them the whole story. And sometime in that night he would die. It's not his dying—it's what he would be thinking just before he died. Rusty wasn't a bad fellow. I didn't love him. He was all right, I guess. He just didn't mean anything to me, one way or another, alive or dead, compared with keeping it from dad."

"So you let her run around loose," I said, "getting into other jams."

"I was playing for time. Just for time. I played the wrong way, of course. I thought she might even forget it herself. I've heard they do forget what happens in those fits. Maybe she has forgotten it. I knew Eddie Mars would bleed me white, but I didn't care. I had to have help and I could only get it from somebody like him. . . . There have been times when I hardly believed it all myself. And other times when I had to get drunk quickly—whatever time of day it was. Awfully damn quickly."

"You'll take her away," I said. "And do that awfully damn quickly."

She still had her back to me. She said softly now: "What about you?"

"Nothing about me. I'm leaving. I'll give you three days. If you're gone by then—okey. If you're not, out it comes. And don't think I don't mean that."

She turned suddenly. "I don't know what to say to you. I don't know how to begin."

"Yeah. Get her out of here and see that she's watched every minute. Promise?"

"I promise. Eddie—"

"Forget Eddie. I'll go see him after I get some rest. I'll handle Eddie."

"He'll try to kill you."

"Yeah," I said. "His best boy couldn't. I'll take a chance on the others. Does Norris know?"

"He'll never tell."

"I thought he knew."

I went quickly away from her down the room and out and down the tiled staircase to the front hall. I didn't see anybody when I left. I found my hat alone this time. Outside the bright gardens had a haunted look, as though small wild eyes were watching me from behind the bushes, as though the sunshine   H 10 itself had a mysterious something in its light. I got into my car and drove off down the hill.

What did it matter where you lay once you were dead? In a dirty sump or in a marble tower on top of a high hill? You were dead, you were sleeping the big sleep, you were not bothered by things like that. Oil and water were the same as wind and air to you. You just slept the big sleep, not caring about the nastiness of how you died or where you fell. Me, I was part of the nastiness now. Far more a part of it than Rusty Regan was. But the old man didn't have to be. He could lie quiet in his canopied bed, with his bloodless hands folded on the sheet, waiting. His heart was a brief, uncertain murmur. His thoughts were as gray as ashes. And in a little while he too, like Rusty Regan, would be sleeping the big sleep.

On the way downtown I stopped at a bar and had a couple of double Scotches. They didn't do me any good. All they did was make me think of Silver-Wig, and I never saw her again.

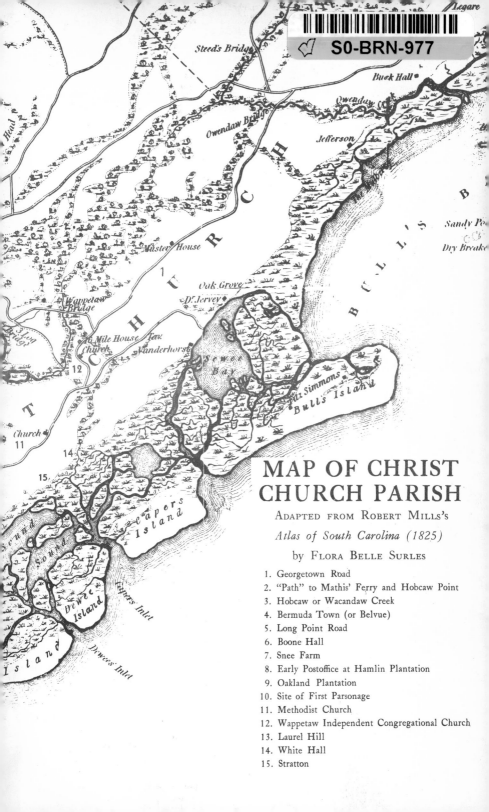

MAP OF CHRIST CHURCH PARISH

ADAPTED FROM ROBERT MILLS'S

Atlas of South Carolina (1825)

by FLORA BELLE SURLES

1. Georgetown Road
2. "Path" to Mathis' Ferry and Hobcaw Point
3. Hobcaw or Wacandaw Creek
4. Bermuda Town (or Belvue)
5. Long Point Road
6. Boone Hall
7. Snee Farm
8. Early Postoffice at Hamlin Plantation
9. Oakland Plantation
10. Site of First Parsonage
11. Methodist Church
12. Wappetaw Independent Congregational Church
13. Laurel Hill
14. White Hall
15. Stratton

CHRIST CHURCH

—*C. R. Banks*

CHRIST CHURCH, 1960

CHRIST CHURCH,
1706-1959

A Plantation Parish of
the South Carolina Establishment

By

ANNE KING GREGORIE

THE DALCHO HISTORICAL SOCIETY

CHARLESTON

1961

Publications

of

The Dalcho Historical Society
of the Protestant Episcopal Church
in South Carolina

Number 15

Diocesan House
138 Wentworth Street, Charleston

Manufactured by
The R. L. Bryan Company
Columbia

To the memory of my parents

FERDINAND AND ANNE PALMER PORCHER GREGORIE

who loved this church

The Dalcho Historical Society gratefully acknowledges the support of these contributors toward the publication of this book.

CONTRIBUTORS THROUGH
THE WOMEN OF CHRIST CHURCH

Mr. and Mrs. John J. Gray
Dr. and Mrs. Wilson Greene
Mr. and Mrs. B. L. Greenway
Mr. and Mrs. Ralph M. Hale
Mr. and Mrs. Osgood D. Hamlin
Mr. and Mrs. Cecil Johnson
Miss Martha P. Langley
Mr. Samuel D. Langley
Mr. and Mrs. A. B. McConnell
Mrs. W. W. McIver
Mr. and Mrs. William E. Pennewill
Mr. and Mrs. Francis P. Porcher
Mr. and Mrs. P. G. Porcher
Mrs. Granville T. Prior
Mr. E. M. Royall
Dr. and Mrs. J. Hertz Warren

CONTRIBUTORS THROUGH
THE DALCHO HISTORICAL SOCIETY

Miss Mary Heyward
Miss Flora Belle Surles

Some of these contributions are memorials.

FOREWORD

This sketch of Christ Church is based upon the extant records, chiefly the minutes of the vestry, which unfortunately are missing from August 6, 1759, to April, 1797; from May 16, 1897, to September 25, 1899; and from October 29, 1909, to August 15, 1915. Some supplementary material for the early years has been had from British reproductions in the Library of Congress.

A very interesting group of records is that which Thomas Barksdale placed in the custody of the Court of Chancery, Charleston, in 1846. This collection includes his own financial records, chiefly pertaining to the church endowment, during his long years as church treasurer; various letters concerning church affairs, and other records which he had received from William Hort, former chairman and secretary-treasurer of the vestry; and a few records antedating the year 1800, among which was the document signed by Thomas Lynch, Jr.

With his usual methodical efficiency, Mr. Barksdale placed these records in a box, carefully labeled. Twenty-one years later, in August 1877, this "box of old papers" came into the hands of the vestry in Mount Pleasant, whose chairman appointed Edward O. Hall and C. H. Rivers to examine the papers and report upon their nature at the next vestry meeting. In September the committee reported that it "could find nothing of any value, and recommended that they be preserved on account of their antiquity."

Apparently the old box thereafter was passed from secretary to secretary until it came into the custody of the

Rev. Mr. Hartzell when he was secretary, who placed it in a room on the ground floor of the rectory at Amen Corner in Mount Pleasant. When the rectory was destroyed by fire in 1907, the box was rescued and delivered to Willington E. Freeman, secretary of the vestry from 1904 until his death in 1916. He kept it in a room on the ground floor of his home, where it remained until some years after his death. When the box was discovered by Mrs. Freeman, she delivered it to Mr. J. Oswald Freeman, her brother-in-law, who was then secretary. Having an interest in the history of the church, Mr. Freeman went through the papers and placed some of them on exhibit at a congregational meeting of St. Andrew's Chapel. When the monetary value of the Lynch signature became known, it was placed in a safety deposit box in a bank until it was sold.

The registers of Christ Church also are not complete. The oldest are in the custody of the historiographer of the diocese, but copies of them, made at an early date, are in an old record book which contains both the registers and the minutes, from 1708 until after Mr. E. O. Hall copied an old register into it in 1880. The registers for the rectorate of the Rev. Gilbert Jones are missing and may have been destroyed in 1782 with the missing minutes when the British burned "the house of one of the Church Officers," probably John Sandford Dart.

The register of the Rev. John Richard Fell also is missing, although as late as 1925, Mr. J. Oswald Freeman in his minutes quoted from it: "Moultrie Rutledge Rivers . . . was Christened in this Chapel by the Rev. J. R. Fell and Rev. T. F. Gadsden on Sunday afternoon July 19th 1868." Existing registers, 1694-1836, were published in *The South Carolina Historical and Genealogical Magazine*, XVIII-XXII.

When Christ Church and St. Andrew's Chapel were separated in 1954, the chapel kept the original minutes and registers, from 1835 until 1954. Christ Church, however, now has copies of all that exist. The Woman's Auxiliary of Christ Church completed the task of copying in 1958 when it paid for an excellent typed copy of the vestry minutes dating from May 13, 1836, to September 20, 1954 .

In preparing this manuscript, the writer has had the assistance of her friend, Flora Belle Surles in taking notes from the journals of the Diocesan Conventions and from the admirable abstracts of colonial land records prepared by Clara A. Langley from original massive volumes in the office of the Register of Mesne Conveyance, Charleston. Miss Surles also typed the final draft of this manuscript for the printer, and shared the labor of copying inscriptions from tombstones in Christ Church cemetery.

Acknowledgements are due Dr. George W. Williams, president of the Dalcho Society, for his encouragement and assistance; to C. Richard Banks, secretary-treasurer of that society for his fine photographs used as illustrations in this book; and to Mrs. Ferdinand Gregorie and Mr. Philip G. Porcher for a critical reading of the manuscript.

ANNE KING GREGORIE

The manuscript of this history had been submitted to the Dalcho Society and was awaiting publication when on December 4, 1960, Dr. Gregorie died. Knowing well the financial straits in which many historical societies are confined, she made provision in her will for a generous bequest to the Society towards the publication of her parish history. Additional funds were made available through the generosity and the activities of the Woman's Auxiliary of the parish.

Dr. Gregorie's manuscript and wishes have been respected scrupulously; changes have been confined to those the author would almost certainly have made in proof herself.

The thanks of the Society go to Miss Surles and to Mrs. Ferdinand Gregorie, executrix of the estate, for their essential help.

G. W. W.

January, 1961.

CONTENTS

ILLUSTRATIONS

With the exception of the old prints and the photographs of Boone
Hall, Snee Farm, and Seaside Plantation, all the illustrations are by

CHARLES RICHARD BANKS

[xii]

CHRIST CHURCH OF THE CHURCH OF ENGLAND

ONE

A SMALL TIMBER CHURCH IN THE PINE WOODS

When Carolina was settled in 1670, religious freedom for the people of the province was amply safeguarded, and Quakers, French Huguenots, and other Dissenters who had suffered religious persecution, were among the adventurers who came as early settlers. But both the royal Charter and the Fundamental Constitutions of Carolina indicated that only the Church of England could legally become the established church of the province, to be supported from tax funds of the public treasury.

During the first thirty years of Carolina's existence, the members of the Anglican church and numerous Dissenters were too busy getting themselves established in the New World to quarrel about religious differences, and for eighteen of those thirty years Dissenters were governors of the colony.[1]

After the turn of the century, however, the disturbances in Europe over questions of religious beliefs began to be reflected in South Carolina. In 1699, Nicholas Trott, a bigoted Anglican, arrived in Charleston and soon was exerting great influence as chief justice. In the early spring of 1703, Sir Nathaniel Johnson, another ardent churchman, arrived as governor, appointed by the Lords Proprietors, but he was remotely under Queen Anne, a truly pious devotee of the Church of England, of which she had become the head the previous year.

[3]

Although St. Philip's Church in Charleston had been recognized as the official church since 1698, when the Assembly named its rector for life at an annual salary from the public treasury, the Anglicans now wanted churches for the settlements which extended beyond the limits of Charleston. In 1704, therefore, by act of the Assembly, the Church of England was made the established Church of South Carolina. Lay commissioners were named in the act to lay out six parishes and provide the churches, burial grounds, parsonages, and glebe lands from public funds. They were also empowered to displace unsuitable rectors.[2] This provision and another which required members of the Commons House to conform to the Church of England, the English House of Lords found to be contrary to the charter, and Queen Anne declared the law null and void.[3]

When the Assembly convened in Charleston in March 1706, Sir Nathaniel Johnson's message to the Commons House voiced the hope that the members would do their duty "both to God and the Publick" and finish in the first place "what may be still thought neccessary toward the Sure and Lasting Establishment in this Province of our Inffant Church of England."[4] The Governor's message was well received, and in reply the Commons House of Assembly said:

> With joy we take notice how particularly in the First place your Honor has Recommended Religion as it is the protestant Religion Established by law in the Church of England. And Wee the Representatives of the people Following your good Example will Endeavour to Consider it, as Parliaments in all ages have done, that is, as a part of Our Laws and a necessary part of Our Government.

CHRIST CHURCH, INTERIOR

The Silver of Christ Church

It is no Doubt a Duty we owe to God and our-
selves, to the present Age and to Posterity, to Improve the Opportunities God has given us of Fence-
ing our Vinyard; and makeing the Hedge about it
as Strong as we can.[5]

In November 1706, a new Church Act was duly ratified, and the Church of England became the official or
Established Church of South Carolina. The cost of building the churches and parsonages and other necessary expenses were to be paid by the province from a tax on
skins and furs, but contributions from individuals were
expected to aid.[6]

The Church Act was designed to meet political as well
as religious needs of the people. The parish church as a
public building was to be the center for the administration
of some local government in each parish, for at that time
there was not a courthouse in the province, not even in
Charleston. Proclamations and public notices of various
kinds were to be read in the churches, and governmental
advertisements were to be placed on the church door.
Vital statistics were to be kept by a church officer called
a register, who was to enter records of baptisms, births,
marriages, deaths, and burials upon official church registers. Poor relief was to be administered by church wardens from "sacrament money" donated by communicants
at the Lord's supper, and from funds collected from assessments upon the parishioners' property levied by the
vestrymen, who also were to use money from fines and
forfeitures. Destitute orphans were to be apprenticed to
various trades by the vestry.[7] Under the Church Act,
vestrymen and church wardens were public officials, to
be elected annually by the parishioners on Easter Monday; and as a safeguard against neglect of their duties,

they were required under penalty of fines to hold four meetings a year, at eleven o'clock in the forenoon, on the first Tuesday in January, April, July, and October.

Later, when members of the Assembly were to be elected, election writs were addressed to the wardens, notices of election were affixed to the church doors, polls were set up on the church grounds, and church wardens were election managers, required to keep a book in which names of qualified voters were recorded. After the election, they had to go to Charleston and report the results of the election to the Commons House within the first two days of the session. Parishes were election districts, and Christ Church Parish had two representatives.[8]

A benevolent organization in London which greatly aided the Established Church in South Carolina was the Society for the Propagation of the Gospel in Foreign Parts, whose long name is abbreviated as the S. P. G., and often referred to simply as the Society. Founded in 1701, the Society sent missionaries to the English colonies, where many young churches gratefully elected them as rectors. The supplementary salaries provided by the Society greatly assisted the colonies, and notably South Carolina, in supporting the Established Church.

The English colonies ecclesiastically were an extension of the Diocese of London, so the Established Church in South Carolina was under the jurisdiction of the Bishop of London. As he was too far away for personal supervision, he sent to Charleston his representative, called a commissary. The first commissary was the Rev. Gideon Johnston, who arrived as soon as practicable after the enactment of the Church Act. The commissary could not confirm church members or ordain priests, but he supervised the clergy, held visitations, and exercised general authority as the official head of the clergy in the province.

The democratic principles that were evident in the Church Act of 1706 displeased Commissary Johnston, who found them "so odd and unlike the English Constitution." He especially objected to the power given to the parishioners to elect their rectors, "which power," he wrote, "I confess has never gone down well with me, nor shall I ever be reconciled to it." He argued first, that the parishioners generally were "not proper Judges in this matter"; and second, that they might reject ministers sent at their request by the Bishop of London or by the benevolent Society. Thus, he continued, the Episcopal authority "is vilified and trampled underfoot," and the Society "is slighted and put to unnecessary expense," while the rejected minister "is exposed to many hazards and difficulties, if not to certain ruin."[9]

Christ Church Parish was one of the ten parishes created by the Church Act of 1706, which described it as simply "South-east of Wandoe river."

To organize the parishes and carry out the provisions of the law, twenty-four laymen were named in the Act as Church Commissioners, three of whom resided in Christ Church Parish: Thomas Barton, George Logan, and John A. Motte. Mr. Barton and Captain Motte were also members of the Assembly which had passed the Church Act, and George Logan was the public receiver, or treasurer of the province.

As the first step in organizing Christ Church Parish, the Church Commissioners were authorized to draw upon the public receiver for £333.6.8, to be used in purchasing a site for the church and a glebe for the parsonage, to begin construction of the church and parsonage, and to fence the churchyard.[10] As this sum was insufficient, the purchase of the glebe was postponed until more funds should become available from the Assembly and from private subscriptions.

The site chosen for Christ Church was only six miles from Charleston Harbor and was on the path which followed the watershed between the Wando River and the sea. The non-central location of the church was due to the fact that the boundaries of the parish were not yet defined. The foundations of the church, a small "Timber building" forty feet long and twenty-four feet wide, were laid in 1707.[11] Black cypress, an abundant wood in general use at the time and the most enduring, was probably the chosen material.

The first services in the parish were held the next year by the Rev. Edward Marston, former rector of St. Philip's, Charleston, who, after a violent quarrel with the Assembly, had been removed from his charge. He had then crossed the harbor to Christ Church Parish and was sojourning on the Wando River in sight of Charleston at a place called Bermuda Town, which had been laid out before 1699 for a town that never developed. The site, nevertheless, has retained the name Bermuda to this day. The Rev. Dr. Francis LeJau of St. James' Church, on Goose Creek, in a letter of September 1708, said that Mr. Marston was "in possession of a Parish called Bermudas Town," but elected for only twelve months. The parishioners of Christ Church were willing to elect him as their rector, but he declined, and later the vestry wrote, "time showed us that it was happy for us that he was not chosen, he not giving over his litigious Contentious Temper."[12]

For the first vestrymen of Christ Church, the parishioners, as required by law, elected seven "sober and discreet persons": Thomas Barton, William Capers, Leonard Hickman, John Simes, Richard Fairchild, John Boone, and John A. Motte, who met at the church on July 12, 1708, to qualify by taking the required oaths of office. Captain Motte and Mr. Barton, as Church Commissioners, had already taken official oaths and signed the test, an oath designed to make it impossible for a Roman Catholic to hold a public office. Mr. Barton produced a certificate that he had taken the required oaths. Captain Motte and Major Boone refused to take the oath as vestrymen. Captain Capers, Mr. Hickman, Mr. Simes, and Mr. Fairchild then took all the oaths before Mr. Barton.

First in the series was the oath of allegiance to good Queen Anne:

> I, William Capers, do sincerely promise and swear that I will be faithful and bear true allegiance to her Majesty Queen Anne &c.

Next, they took the oath of supremacy:

> I, William Capers, do swear that I do from my Heart abhor, detest, and abjure, as impious and heretical that damnable Doctrine and Position that Princes excommunicated or deprived by the Pope or any Authority of the See of Rome may be deposed or murdered by their Subjects or any other whatsoever. And I do Declare that no Foreign Prince, person, Prelate, State, or Potentate, hath or ought to have any Jurisdiction, power, superiority, Preeminence, or Authority, Ecclesiastical or Civil, within this province or any other of her Majesty's Realms or Dominions.

Then they each took the vestryman's oath:

> I, William Capers, do solemnly swear and declare that I will justly and truly execute the Office or Trust of a Vestryman of the Parish of Christ Church

according to the best of my skill, Knowledge, and Power, without prejudice, favour, or affection.

Lastly, they each signed the test:

We the underwritten do solemnly and sincerely in the presence of God profess, testify, and declare That We do believe that in the Sacrament of the Lords Supper there is not any Transubstantiation of the Elements of Bread and Wine into the Body and Blood of Christ, at or after the Consecration thereof by any person whatsoever. And that the invocation or adoration of the Virgin Mary or any other Saint, and the Sacrifice of the Mass as they are now used in Church of Rome are Superstitious and Idolatrous. And We do solemnly in the presence of God profess, testify, and declare, that We do make this Declaration and every part thereof in the plain and ordinary Sense of the words read unto us as they are Commonly understood by English protestants, without any Evasion, Equivocation, or Mental reservation whatsoever, and without any Dispensation already granted us for this purpose by the Pope or any other authority or Person whatsoever, or without any hope of any such dispensation from any Person or authority whatsoever, or without thinking that We are or can be acquitted before God or Man, or absolved of this Declaration or any part thereof, although the Pope or any other Person or Persons or Power whatsoever should Dispense with or Annull the same, or Declare that it was Null and void from the beginning.[13]

After all this swearing was accomplished, no other business was undertaken.

Almost a month later, on August 9, 1708, the parishioners unanimously elected the Rev. Richard Marsden as the first rector of Christ Church. The incomplete vestry met the same day, chose Otho Russell as "Clarke" and sexton, and ordered an election on August 22 for choosing vestrymen in place of Captain Motte and Major Boone, at which time John Hale and Nathaniel Loughton were elected. The wardens, David Maybank and Henry Gill, were not sworn in until October 13.

Little is known of the members of this first vestry, but perhaps most of them were hardy adventurers who had crossed the ocean to make new homes in America. Warden David Maybank was a house carpenter. He married Susannah Wigfall and died about 1725. His will indicates that he had prospered, for he left his widow and children well provided for.[14] Warden Henry Gill died in 1720; his son Henry died the following year; and, with the marriage of Jean Gill, the name disappeared from the parish register.

Vestryman Thomas Barton, a member of the Assembly and a Church Commissioner, later became secretary of the Board of Commissioners of the Indian Trade and was its first storekeeper.[15] William Capers was a captain of militia, and between 1694 and 1703 he had received warrants for 1,450 acres of land, all apparently in Christ Church Parish. His second warrant, for 400 acres, was for the arrival rights of his eight Negro slaves, so he was a man of means. John Simes married Mary, daughter of Captain Capers, and owned a plantation of 500 acres called Lebanon, which had formerly belonged to Captain Capers.[16] Richard Fairchild, John Hale, and Nathaniel Loughton had warrants for lands on the Wando River in 1703 and 1704 and apparently were neighbors.[17] Nothing is known of Leonard Hickman, but members of the Hickman family in the parish today still bear the name Leonard.

The rector, Richard Marsden, a fine looking man about six feet tall, still in his thirties, and by the Church Act also a member of the vestry, was a "fugitive clergyman" who had been forced to abandon his church in Maryland in such haste that he left his wife and children behind him. Upon his arrival in Charleston, he claimed that he had been sent by the Bishop of London to take the place of the contentious Mr. Marston at St. Philip's Church.[18]

So plausible was Mr. Marsden's story, and so attractive was he himself, that he "was received and Caressed as one directly sent to them from heaven. Thus he continued the Darling of the People" of Charleston, who elected him rector of St. Philip's. When Commissary Gideon Johnston arrived with credentials from the Bishop of London, he had to bring pressure for four long months before he could induce Mr. Marsden to give up St. Philip's. Mr. Marsden then crossed Charleston Harbor to Christ Church Parish and was unanimously elected its first rector. His popularity here appears to have been as great as it had been in Charleston, for his new parishioners voluntarily contributed £90 extra to his official salary.[19] Although there was yet no glebe or parsonage, he was joined by his wife, children, and his wife's brother.

Near the close of this eventful year of 1708, the boundaries of Christ Church Parish were defined as the Wando River, Awendaw Creek, and the sea, which enclosed a narrow strip of 57,580 acres near the middle of the South Carolina coast. The parish was almost an island, for the headwaters of the Wando River and Awendaw Creek lay in adjacent swamps. The only artificial boundary was a line "drawn from the Cowpen of Captain Robert Daniel, on the swamp of the head of Wando river . . . to the cowpen of Joseph Wigfall" at the head of Awendaw Creek.[20]

This Captain Robert Daniel, a soldier and a sea captain, was "a brave man who had long served King William in his Wars both by Land and Sea." He had come to Carolina from the island of Barbados, and he was destined to serve as governor of Carolina in the years 1716 and 1717.[21] His plantation, Daniel's Island in the Wando River, still bears his name.

Less is known of Joseph Wigfall. He and his brother-in-law David Maybank had warrants for 500 acres each at the head of Awendaw Creek in 1704, but Maybank appers to have resided on his 200-acre grant on Hobcaw Creek of Wando River, while Wigfall raised cattle in the canebrakes of their combined 1,000 acres on Awendaw Creek.[22]

Lands on the waters surrounding the parish were in great demand in these early days, for without roads, travel was necessarily by boat. Among other settlers who had warrants for lands on Awendaw Creek was the governor, Sir Nathaniel Johnson, whose plantations of 1,700 acres near the coast were called Salt Hope and Salt Ponds; and later his additional 12,000 acres was Sewee Barony.[23] Other early grantees on Awendaw Creek were Robert Johnson, John Collins, and John Barksdale. Among Barksdale's warrants was one for 2,000 acres next to the Governor's barony. When he arrived in 1695, he brought his wife Sarah, their children (Charles, Thomas, John, and Mary), five white servants, and three slaves. Evidently he was a man of some means.[24] Several of his descendants served as vestrymen, and his great-great-grandson, Thomas Barksdale, gave notable service for many years as church treasurer. Another early settler whose descendants were to be identified with Christ Church was John Hamlin, who, before 1703, had lands on Copahee Sound,[25] where the Hamlin family still owns part of the same lands.

The Rev. Mr. Marsden's tenure at Christ Church was brief, and at the last meeting of the first vestry, January 9, 1709, the day that John Hale took the oaths as vestryman, Mr. Marsden announced that an inheritance from an uncle required his immediate "going for England." With a year's leave of absence to settle his estate, he again departed in haste, leaving his wife, three children, and brother-in-law, as well as many debts. The brother-in-law died soon after, heartbroken, it was said, from the losses he had sustained by having gone on Mr. Marsden's bond in Maryland. The unhappy wife, Mrs. Margaret Marsden, died a short time later, "overwhelmed with an unsupportable grief." The orphaned children were dispersed among the neighbors.[26] Mr. Marsden never returned, and two years later he was in Barbados. "God send that he may deal more honestly with the Merchants there," wrote Dr. LeJau of St. James, Goose Creek, "than he did here. I believe that the itching of trading which he does not understand has been the Cause of his misfortunes; for in the main he is a Sober Man and has an Art of Pleasing the Common People." [27]

During two years after Mr. Marsden's departure, on appeal from the vestry, Commissary Johnston and the neighboring clergy, Robert Maule, John LePierre, and Thomas Hasell held services alternately once a month. A grant of £30 a year from the Assembly was distributed among them as fees for their work at Christ Church.

Some of the Christ Church congregation, however, went to hear a Scotch preacher, the Rev. Mr. Pollock, described by the Commissary as "a most rigid and violent Presbyterian teacher," [28] who held services at Wando Neck, the narrowest part of the Parish between the Wando River and Sewee Bay. In that locality, a group of fifty-one Dissenters from New England, in 1696, after shipwreck on the North Carolina coast, had been settled by Governor Blake. As their homes were widely scattered, in 1699 they had built two meeting houses, one on Wando Neck and the other across the river. Their first pastor, the Rev. Hugh Adams, a "flighty youngster," had left them after two years, with half of his salary still unpaid.[29] The meeting house on Wando Neck became Wappetaw Independent Congregational Church and was destined in later years to share its pastor with Christ Church.

Although Christ Church was without a rector for three years after the exit of its first rector, vestrymen and wardens were elected in 1709 and in 1711; but no parish business was recorded for the first two years, and apparently no election was held in 1710.

The vestrymen and wardens of 1711 did not meet until September of that year, when they qualified as required by law, and then proceeded to draft an interesting letter to the Society for the Propagation of the Gospel in Foreign Parts, relating to their experiences with Mr. Marston and Mr. Marsden, and begging that the Society would send them as minister, "a Person of a Pious, Sober, and Virtuous Life and a good preacher."

Then they prepared for the Church Commissioners a detailed estimate of what would be needed to finish the church and build the parsonage. Among the various items for the church were a desk, a pulpit and sounding board, £30; two small lights for the pulpit, £1; to altering and arching the windows, with glazing and hardware,

£12; to railing in the communion table, £8; to paling in the churchyard, £9; altogether, including labor and other materials, a total of £110. For the parsonage, the estimate amounted to a little more than £115. A grant of these funds from the public treasury, and some private subscriptions, enabled the vestry to proceed with the work on the church.

This was timely, for in March 1712, the Rev. Gilbert Jones and his family arrived from England. By permission of Commissary Johnston, the vestry invited Mr. Jones to supply their vacant parish as curate until the arrival of the Society's missionary, who was daily expected. As there was no parsonage yet, the vestry wrote Mr. Jones, "we have given Col. George Logan orders to give you and Spouse invitation which will be to his House where you will receive a hearty welcome."

Col. Logan's hospitality was no doubt enjoyable, for he was an enterprising Scotchman of some means and importance. He is said to have come from Aberdeen in 1690, as colonel of a British garrison in Charleston. Ten years later, as public receiver of the province, he was accused by Edmund Randolph, collector of customs, of having conspired to seize and condemn ships so as to buy them at half their value. During the French and Spanish invasion in 1706, when again public receiver, he advanced his personal funds to repel the enemy. Later he was to become a commissioner of the free school, a member of the Council, a commissioner to regulate Indian trade, an assistant judge to try pirates, and speaker of the Commons House of Assembly.[30]

Soon after Mr. Jones arrived, the vestry with funds from the Assembly purchased a glebe of a hundred acres four miles from the church, and agreed with "David

Maybank to finish the Parsonage House for £35 all Carpenters work." A survey later showed the glebe to contain one hundred and sixteen acres. Mr. Jones appears to have been pleased with the parsonage, and described it as a good timber house, thirty-five feet long and eighteen feet wide, with a good kitchen, which was a separate building as was then customary, and twelve acres of cleared land.[31] This last was essential to supply vegetables for his family and forage for his horse.

After a long wait of many months, and no missionary having come from the Society for Christ Church, the parishioners elected Mr. Jones rector on December 10, 1712, a date set by the Church Commissioners. But his anxieties were not yet ended, for early in the new year the Rev. Nathaniel Osborn landed in Charleston as the missionary duly appointed by the Society for Christ Church. Mr. Jones' parishioners, however, were greatly pleased with him and did not want a change. It was a delicate situation, for Mr. Jones greatly needed the salary which the Society would supply if he were appointed missionary. Both he and the Commissary had to be careful not to give any offense. So Mr. Osborn was sent to the vacant St. Bartholomew's Parish; and, as the Commissary was returning to England on the same ship that had brought Mr. Osborn, he undertook to make full explanations to the Society when he reached London. The outcome was happy for all concerned. Mr. Jones was appointed the Society's missionary to Christ Church and received the Society's annual £50 in addition to the £100 he received from the province.

He described his parish as thirty-six miles in length from George Haddrell's plantation on Charleston Harbor to Joseph Wigfall's cowpen at the head of Awendaw

Creek, and seven miles in width from George Logan's plantation on Wando River to Jonathan Perry's plantation on the coast.[32] This area of two hundred and fifty-two square miles was sparsely settled and practically without roads—a formidable assignment!

But the Rev. Mr. Jones, a devout churchman and a faithful pastor, labored successfully in his parish, despite poverty, the scourge of malaria, and two serious upheavals in the province, which plagued the years of his rectorate.

In the spring of 1715, only four years after his arrival, the terrible Yemassee Indian War suddenly erupted, and so many tribes joined in the conspiracy that the total destruction of the colony seemed certain. White men who escaped the unexpected massacre fled with their families into the protecting walls of Charleston.

Christ Church Parish was untouched, for it was protected by the surrounding waters, it had only a few "tame" Indians, some of whom were slaves, and it was not in the path of the savages. But when the news of the massacre came, the frightened people abandoned their homes and took refuge with their rector; and for three terrible weeks the Rev. Gilbert Jones had more than a hundred people at his house.[33]

The mass of refugees in Charleston, and the resultant scarcity of supplies of every kind, caused prices to rise fantastically, and Mr. Jones like many others was soon deep in debt. All through the long hot summer, the women and children were crowded into the little town, and the men went forth with Governor Craven to fight the savages. By the end of the year most people had returned to their homes, but security was not fully restored until

1717. When Mr. Jones returned home, he found the parsonage intact, but he had lost his invaluable horse.[34]

For the period of the Yemassee War, in mute witness to the troubled times, only three entries appear on the minutes of Christ Church vestry. One of these, in 1716, was an agreement that Col. George Logan should get a warrant to run out the land belonging to the schoolhouse at Bermuda Town for the use of the parish. He was successful, and Christ Church acquired title to the schoolhouse and forty-five acres of land, which Mr. Jones desccribed as "being upon a Neck of Land commonly called Barmudas Town." [35] The "Seawee Broad Path" and a series of paths connected Governor Sir Nathaniel Johnson's lands on Sewee Bay with Bermuda Town,[36] which then must have been something of a community, since it had a schoolhouse. The Rev. Edward Marston had probably preached and perhaps taught in that schoolhouse for fully three years after leaving Charleston, but he had left the province in 1712. Perhaps the community had been depleted by the Indian war, and the schoolhouse was no longer in use.

During these years Mr. Jones suffered several severe illnesses, but worked hard at his parochial duties, holding services in Christ Church and also officiating regularly in the upper part of the parish above the Dissenters' meeting house on Wando Neck. He preached to few Dissenters, for he reported in the autumn of 1716 that of "105 house-keepers" in the parish, only one Quaker dissenter and three "Independent" families were living within a radius of eight miles of his parish church. Since his arrival, he had baptized 136 children and 7 adults, of whom 3 had been of the "Anabaptistical persuasion." His annual salary of £100 from the public, payable in two installments, at Ladyday and Michaelmas, "is worth no more than £12:10." He had no presents except £25 the previous Christmas, which the Assembly had given him and some others of the clergy. His "parishioners are generally poor, having nothing but what they labor for themselves. Therefore I have always declined any contributions, least I should become chargeable, and by that means they think their religion too dear, and consequently forsake it." [37]

Most of the Christ Church parishioners seem to have been small farmers and mechanics. Their free-ranging stock and the abundant wild game supplied meat, and they sent some hides and deer skins to Charleston whence these were shipped overseas. From the great heaps of shells left from immemorial feasts by the Indians along the creeks they burned tons of lime and made mortar, whitewash, and crude bricks for their own use, but some lime was sent on periaugers to the growing town of Charleston. They also made bricks from the scattered deposits of clay. The forest products, turpentine, rosin, tar, and lumber, were also marketable. But there was very little money in circulation. As Mr. Jones wrote to the Society, his salary was paid in money of this country, "which are bills of credit." [38]

Like all missionaries, Mr. Jones was deeply interested in the spiritual welfare of the "Heathen Slaves," and earnestly desired to convert them to the Christian faith, but the difficulties in his way were great. Most of the slaves, except a few Indians, were native Africans, savages who did not yet understand the English language. The plantations were remote and widely separated, so it was impracticable for him to reach the Negroes or to assemble them for instruction. Moreover, some slave owners were unwilling to release their Negroes from work

ROOM IN THE PARSONAGE OF 1769

Courtesy of the Charleston Museum

THE VESTRY HOUSE

THE PARISH HOUSE OF CHRIST CHURCH

to attend his classes. "Too eager a pursuit after wealth,"
wrote Mr. Jones, "I perceive to be the grand obstacle to
this as well as to all other good works."[39]

The Yemassee War had interrupted the work of com-
pleting Christ Church, which was already in need of repairs. A subscription list, therefore, was circulated and
Mr. Jones generously donated £205, which he had received for acting as clerk and register, to be used for repairs and for ceiling the church.[40]

In the spring of 1717, St. Andrew's Parish Church, on
Ashley River, became vacant. When the clergy held their
regular meeting in Charleston that year, they agreed that
until the vacancy was filled, Mr. Jones, Dr. Francis Le-
Jau, and the Rev. William Tredwell Bull would officiate
there alternately, every other Sunday, by which plan each
minister would be absent from his own church only once
in six weeks.[41]

For the Rev. Mr. Jones, this presented the problem of
traveling from his parsonage ten miles to a ferry, crossing
a river "four miles over," and then another ride to reach
St. Andrew's Church. Such a trip was not only expensive,
"but difficult and very dangerous." Moreover, his health
was so impaired by the frequent sicknesses he had suffered during the five years since his arrival that he was
"not able as formerly to undergo fatigues and the in-
conveniences of the weather." He therefore humbly requested the Society to permit him to remove to St. Andrew's Parish.[42]

Perhaps in expectation of receiving this permission,
Mr. Jones delivered to Church Warden Thomas Barksdale certain items of Christ Church property and received this receipt:

March 4, 1717/18

Rec'd then of the Reverend Gilbert Jones One silver
Chalice, one table Cloth and one Napkin, all belonging to the Communion table of this Parish, and one
large Common Prayer book, being the gift of Abel
Kettleby, Esquire, and the works of Dr. John Forbes
of Corf, belonging to the Library of this parish.
I say received by me

                              Thos Barksdale
    Witnesses present

    Wm Capers
    Jno Hartman

On the same day Mr. Barksdale received from Mr.
Jones £7 and half a crown, the remainder of the sacrament money in his hands.

But Mr. Jones was not transferred to St. Andrew's,
and in May of that year we find him among the vestrymen signing an order to the church wardens to agree with
workmen to repair the church windows, to rail the communion table, to make a pulpit, "and to buy Necessaries
of all sorts for the same."

It should be noted that throughout the rectorate of
Mr. Jones and later, a communion table was used instead
of an altar. This was customary in the colonial churches
of South Carolina and the practice dates from the time
of the Reformation in England. John Hooper, Bishop of
Gloucester, a leader of the movement, in a sermon before King Henry VIII, said: "the magistrate would do
well to turn the altars into tables, according to the first
institution of Christ; that by this means the people would
be cured of a false impression which they had, of a sacrifice to be done on the altars." Bishop Ridley, in obedience to the order of the king in council, replaced the al-

tars in his diocese with tables; but two bishops who dis-
obeyed were deposed and imprisoned.[43]

A letter from Mr. Jones to the Society in May 1719 [44]
tells of a curious and distressing affair in his congregation. A young man of Christ Church Parish applied to
the rector to be married to his own aunt, his mother's
sister. As such a marriage was prohibited by law, Mr.
Jones refused and explained why he could not. But the
couple lived together as man and wife, and the day after
their first child was born, they were married by a Rev.
Mr. Wye, "whose character," said Mr. Jones, "is very
well known to the Honourable Society," but who nevertheless, "still continues at St. Philip's" in Charleston.
"Many are much Scandalized at this Wedding," went
on Mr. Jones, "and if there be not some Severe and
speedy resentment shewed against such an enormity, I
cannot guess what he will not dare to committ."

At the next quarter court of general sessions, Mr. Jones
presented Mr. Wye and the guilty couple under a law
of the province which would impose a fine of £100 upon
the minister and £50 upon the contracting parties. He
hoped to have the statute fully executed, if Chief Justice
Trott, who was "very intimate with Mr. Wye," did not
"screen him from Justice."

As Mr. Jones did not reveal the names of the young
people involved in this scandal, the end of the story cannot now be traced.

It was in this same year, only two years after the final
phase of the Yemassee War, that South Carolina suffered a great political upheaval. Many Carolinians were
dissatisfied with the rule of the Lords Proprietors, despite the vast sums those noble gentlemen had spent in
bringing settlers to the province and in assisting them

with tools and lands to begin life in the wilderness. One of the chief grievances was that the Proprietors could not give the necessary military protection from hostile neighbors. Edmund Randolph, the king's collector of customs, is said to have begun the agitation. Be that as it may, a successful revolution ended the rule of the Proprietors, and South Carolina became a royal province under the Crown. The records of Christ Church do not reflect the change, and perhaps few of the parishioners felt much interest.

But their rector was uneasy, and on February 10, 1720, he wrote to the Society, requesting leave to return to Britain for the recovery of his health: "the continuance of my indisposition and the present confused and Unhappy State of this Province and the apprehension we are under of a Spanish Evasion from the Havana oblige me to renew my humble request . . . which I hope they will be pleased to grant when they have considered that I have been in this province upwards of Eight Years and now labour under so ill a State of health, that I am not able to discharge my Duty with that Constancy and Chearfullness wherewith I have done it hitherto and which I would by Gods grace Continue to do if my health permitted." [45]

He also reported having baptized fifteen more children and three slaves and that the number of communicants the past Christmas Day was seventeen.

Although the Rev. Mr. Jones was diligent in his parochial duties and served as clerk and register, his burials, marriages, and baptisms are not found among the extant records of Christ Church. The one baptism which records his name was that of George Paddon Bond, which apparently was added in 1744, when a number of other records of the family were entered upon the church register. Evidently Mr. Jones kept his registrations in a separate book which is no longer in the parish.

Eventually he received permission to return to his homeland. As one of his last good deeds before sailing for England, he prepared for the royal governor, Francis Nicholson, a devout churchman, a report dated June 8, 1721, on "The present state of the Parish of Christ Church."[46] This document has preserved much of the early history of the parish which is found in this chapter. From it we learn that there were then 107 families living in the Parish, comprising about 400 persons, and that there were 637 slaves; also, that the library of books given to the parish by Governor Nicholson had been delivered by Mr. Marsden to Thomas Barton, from whom only one volume could ever be recovered.

The explanation of Mr. Barton's negligence perhaps is found in the fact that he was elected secretary of the Board of Commissioners of Indian Trade in July 1711, and thereafter may have lived in Charleston. In 1712 the wardens of Christ Church were never able to have him at a meeting to explain his accounts with the church, although they made repeated efforts; and they noted upon the minutes that the deeds for the parsonage land were also wanting.[47] Thomas Barton's son John was baptized in St. Philip's, Charleston, in February 1712. Eventually, Thomas returned to Christ Church Parish, where he was buried in 1732.

The successor to Mr. Jones was the Rev. Benjamin Pownall, who came as a missionary from the Society in November 1722, and was elected rector by the parishioners the following month. Because of the inconvenient location of the church for the people on Wando Neck, the vestry agreed that Mr. Pownall should continue Mr. Jones' work there and preach every third Sunday at the home of George Benison.

Mr. Pownall remained only two years. When he returned to England in 1724 because of his private affairs, the population of the parish had increased to 470 freemen and more than 700 slaves. The parishioners were described as "sober, industrious and regular attendants on public worship," but although the Christ Church congregation was so dutiful, only thirty communicants were reported.[48]

The question of assessing property owners in the parish seems to have been considered by the vestry for the first time at the April meeting in 1724 and was carried in the negative.

The parish church was now only sixteen years old, but it was described as being in a ruinous condition. John White offered to do necessary repairs for £50, if the vestry would supply 6,000 four-penny nails. Governor Nicholson contributed £20 towards the work. But instead of repairs for the little church, it was decided that a new and larger church should be built. The Assembly voted a grant of £600 which the vestry drew an order for in June 1724. As this was insufficient, the vestry petitioned for more funds.

But before further action was taken, the small timber church, with its arched windows and paling fence, was accidentally destroyed by fire, February 13, 1725, perhaps from a fire in the surrounding woods, which in those days were regularly burned off at that season to remove the underbrush and let grass grow for the cattle.

TWO

THE BRICK CHURCH

The burning of the first Christ Church speeded the plans for the new church, and on the assurance of provision in the next year's appropriations for an additional grant of £400 towards "compleating the new Church to be built in Christ Church Parish,"[1] the vestry resolved that two vestrymen should serve with the two church wardens to handle all funds and to oversee construction of "the new Brick Church." Accordingly Thomas Boone and George Benison, vestrymen, and Alexander Parris, Jr., and Thomas Barton, Jr., church wardens, signed a surety bond of £2,000 for their faithful performance of duty.

The summer following the destruction of the little wooden church, the vestry accepted the offer of the Rev. John Warden to serve as supply until the Society should send a missionary. He preached for the first time on August 15, 1725, but the records do not reveal where he officiated. Unhappily, he died and was buried the following November.

Construction of the brick church began promptly, and John Metheringham, the builder, in the spring of 1726 received £500, and other workmen £400 in several payments for the work. Apparently the new building was used for church services before it was completed, for the Rev. Thomas Morritt, the next supply minister, "first preached in the Parish Church" on April 30, 1726. He was transferred to Prince George's church, and the Rev. Bryan Hunt was next to officiate.

In the autumn of 1726, Christ Church became heir to its first legacy. Patrick Logan, a blind, unmarried son of Col. George Logan, had been serving as clerk, sexton, and register of the church, but in association with Anthony White, because of his handicap. By his will, made in October, shortly before his death, Patrick Logan bequeathed to the church all of his silver, to be delivered to the vestry within one month of his death, and £50 current money, to be paid within two years.[2]

The following month, the vestry sent a letter to the Rev. Gilbert Jones by a lady departing for London, asking him for £40 "he had of the Parish upon his going off the Country," to be delivered to the lady to dispose of "in particulars for the Church."

The following spring, on March 1, 1727, the Rev. John Winteley arrived with credentials from the Society, and four days later he began to officiate.

The vestry now made an agreement with William Elliott to plaster and roughcast the exterior of the church for £55. Although the interior of the church was still unfinished, the new building was solemnly dedicated on March 28, 1727, receiving at that time a large Bible and a book of common prayer from the Society.

At the meeting of the parishioners on Easter Monday, April 3, 1727, Thomas Boone, George Benison, George Logan, George Haddrell, and John White were elected vestrymen; and John Metheringham and Benjamin Law, church wardens. No rector was chosen because the Church Commissioners did not authorize an election for that purpose until November 14, 1727. At that time, for reasons now unknown, Mr. Winteley was not elected. The

Society evidently approved of the vote, for it dissolved his connection with the parish. He ceased to officiate on January 21, 1728, although the vestry did not give him a final discharge until October, and he left the province in 1729.

Christ Church suffered another loss when on February 23, 1728, the schoolhouse at Bermuda was burned to the ground. In April the vestry agreed that a new schoolhouse should be erected on the same site, but whether this was ever done, and who were the schoolmasters, the records do not reveal.

Probably there were no funds for building the schoolhouse, for work on the new brick church was not yet completely paid for. John Metheringham had received an order for £120 in April 1727, as part of his last payment. The parishioners who had promised to contribute were slow in paying, and the vestry was having trouble in collecting subscriptions. In October the vestry met and advertised that all who were indebted by subscription were desired to pay forthwith, or else they would be proceeded against according to law; also, that on the first day of November, the pews of the church would be disposed of for money to defray the charges of finishing the church. Thomas Barton, Jr., settled his account in full, and like-wise Thomas Boone, Esquire, but apparently no one else In June 1728, the vestry drew an order on Jacob Bond, justice of the peace, to issue warrants against persons who had not yet paid their subscriptions towards the rough-casting of the new church. A year later, the vestry was still threatening the defaulters.

At the October session of the vestry in 1728, letters were written to Commissary Garden, to the Bishop of

London, and to the Society. To the former faithful rector, the Rev. Gilbert Jones, went this letter:

> Revd Sir
>
> We the Vestry and Wardens . . . take the freedom to acquaint you of our misfortune of having our Church burnt, which obliged us to build a new Brick Church, therefore we desire the favour of you to send us out of the Money which you received belonging to the Parish, a Cushion and Pulpit Cloth if the Money will afford it, but in case it will not, then be pleased to send what you may think convenient for the said Church.

The year 1729 passed with Christ Church lacking the services of a rector. But vestrymen and wardens were duly elected. They made an estimate of the amount needed for relief of the poor; wrote letters to the Commissary, the Bishop, and the Society, with affidavits against Mr. Winteley; viewed the parsonage and signed an agreement with John Metheringham for its repairs; found a home for an illegitimate child; and assessed the parishioners for the relief of the poor, fixing the rate at two shillings per head for slaves, and twelve pence per acre for lands.

On Christmas day, the Rev. Edward Dyson began to officiate as supply minister until a missionary should be sent by the Society; he served, with two omissions, until July 26, 1730, when the Rev. John Fulton arrived.

In a letter to the Society the following December,[3] Mr. Fulton reported that he had been joyfully received, and the church, which had "neither door, Pulpit, Pavement, chancel or anything in order," could "scarce contain the Number of both Churchmen and Dissenters that came thither." He also noted that the people of the parish were very poor and that all the churchmen lived within ten miles of the church except three families at the upper end of the parish near Awendaw, who attended services only occasionally; altogether there were fifty-three families, of whom twenty were Dissenters and three were free Indians.

The great number of Negro slaves, he continued, sometimes made insurrections, so that "the People are forced to come to Church with Guns loaded," and conversion of the Negroes to Christianity was "found impracticable . . . by reason of the bad lives of those who have been baptized." Carrying loaded guns to church had long been required by law in the province.[4]

As usual, malaria was taking its toll, and according to Mr. Fulton, at the last annual meeting of the clergy, only the Commissary and four ministers attended, the rest being ill "with the fever and Ague which Raged Vehemently in this Province all this Summer."

To relieve the congestion in the church, the vestry and the parishioners held a meeting and decided to alter all the pews to make them longer and narrower, and then to sell them when finished, except that Captain Boone should "have his Choice of the said pews Gratis." Charvil Wingood, a "professional House carpenter," did the work and made new doors for the church for £60.

There was no door then apparently at the west end of the church, nor any center aisle, as at present, with long benches on either side. Instead, Christ Church had two doors, one at the center of the north wall, and other door opposite at the center of the south wall. In the customary plan of that day, the pews probably were in the form of squares or oblongs, built in pairs through the middle of the church, each pew opening upon either the north aisle along the north wall, or the south aisle along the south wall.

In April 1732, the pews, after being advertised, were sold to the following parishioners:

North aisle,
No. 1, Charvil Wingood,   value £15
No. 2, Richard Fowler,   value £25
No. 3, Capt. George Benison,   value £25
No. 4, Capt. Thomas Boone,   value £25, *gratis*
No. 5, Capt. George Logan,   value £25
No. 6, Joseph Law and
       Thomas Barton, Jr.,   value £25
No. 7, Joshua Wilks,   value £25
No. 8, Catherine Severance,   value £20
No. 9, Robert Clemmons and
       James Allen,   value £15
South aisle,
No. 1, John White,   value £15
No. 2, Capt. Hugh Hext,   value £25
No. 3, George Haddrell,   value £25
No. 4, Clergy
No. 5, Andrew Quelch,   value £25
No. 6, John Metheringham,   value £25
No. 7, William Cook,   value £25

The south aisle had only seven pews, probably because the pulpit was on that side. All of the pews were paid for in full, and the money was received by the warden, George Haddrell. A month later, the wardens and vestrymen met with the purchasers and signed the titles to the pews.

By August 1732, the congregation had grown too large for the church, and Jacob Bond and his family had nowhere to sit. So he petitioned the vestry to close either the north door or the south door, and place a pew there for him. The vestry, however, decided it would be better "that there be an addition made to the church." The records do not reveal whether this was done, but possibly the money received from the sale of pews may have been used to add the chancel at this time.[5]

Although the rectorate of Mr. Fulton had gone well during the two years since his arrival, a change was now at hand. Mr. Fulton was taken sick and ceased to officiate from July 21 until August 20, 1732. In late October he was again ill and held no services until November 21. His parishioners believed that these illnesses were caused not by malaria but by his intemperance. Mr. Fulton was tried in the Commissary's court on this charge and suspended. His name appears on the records of Christ Church for the last time as rector on March 26, 1733, although his salary was paid by the wardens until September of that year. His annual salary of £500 currency was then worth about £70 sterling. His connection with Christ Church was dissolved by the Society, and apparently he left the province in 1734.

Christ Church seems to have remained closed until June 2, 1734, when the Rev. Laurence O'Neale became substitute minister until the Society could be heard from. He served until February 1735, when the Rev. John Fullerton arrived as missionary.

The parishioners of Christ Church were highly pleased with Mr. Fullerton, and Mrs. Susannah Haddrell presented him with a surplice. The vestry addressed her their thanks and "agreed that a good substantial Chest be made to place the said Surplice and particular things in the Church."

The name of Mr. Fullerton appears but once with those of the vestry, when at the April meeting in 1735 he is listed among those present as "Clark." To the grief of his congregation he did not live to be elected rector, for he was taken suddenly ill, and in September of that year, a month when malaria is usually at its worst, he "departed this Life much lamented by his Parishioners."

After the death of Mr. Fullerton, various visiting clergymen held occasional services.

A new face appeared among the vestrymen of Christ Church when Andrew Rutledge was elected on Easter Monday in 1736. He was a lawyer from Ireland who had recently married Sarah Boone Hext, widow of Hugh Hext, and a daughter of John Boone. Mr. Rutledge was then residing with his wife about two miles from the church on a plantation which her former husband had bequeathed to her for life. In the autumn of this year, Andrew Rutledge was one of the members of the Assembly, elected to represent Christ Church Parish.

The Society in 1736 appointed the Rev. Thomas Morritt as missionary to Christ Church. But the vestry had heard some stories concerning Mr. Morritt's character when he was rector of Prince Frederick's Parish and therefore felt unwilling to accept him. After an odd exchange of letters with the vestry, Mr. Morritt wrote the Society early in 1737 that he had "enjoyed such a bad state of health for this two years past and upwards" that he planned to tour the adjacent colonies for recovery, and, if benefited, he would return to England; he therefore had requested the Christ Church vestry to apply for another missionary.

Visiting ministers, meanwhile, continued to hold occasional services only through February, and the church was closed during the spring and summer of 1737. Early in October the parishioners appointed Stephen Hartley, a schoolmaster and register of the parish, "to read on Sunday or other Holy days the Morning and Evening Prayers, with a Sermon after Morning Service and to continue" until the Society should fill the vacancy with a missionary. Stephen Hartley, therefore, is to be remembered as the first lay reader of Christ Church.

Some of the vestrymen apparently became lax in attending vestry meetings during these months, and at the April session in 1738, the vestry agreed that a fine of twenty shillings would be imposed upon any vestryman, warden, clergyman, "or other person so officiating" who should "omit giving his or their attendance" at the appointed place of meeting for the transaction of parish business. A margin of only fifteen minutes after the appointed hour was allowed for punctuality. The appointed place of meeting then was the vestry house in the churchyard, and it was in the vestry house that the parishioners had met when they elected Andrew Rutledge a vestryman.

Although the location of Christ Church, geographically, was not central, it was the center of population, especially for members of the church, and hence it was the most convenient place for the transaction of parish business.

The vestry met near the end of October 1738 and joyfully received from the recently arrived Rev. Robert Small a letter from the Society accrediting him as a missionary to Christ Church. His testimonials showed that he had been ordained deacon on February 26, 1737, and priest on April 16, 1738, by the Bishop of London; and on the following May 15, he had been licensed for work in South Carolina. Evidently Mr. Small had had a long voyage to the new world, for he did not lay his papers before Commissary Garden in Charleston until mid October.[6]

One of the early ministerial acts of Mr. Small was to officiate on Christmas day 1738 at the marriage of Dr. John Rutledge, younger brother of Andrew Rutledge, to Sarah Hext, only child and heiress of Mrs. Andrew Rutledge and her first husband, Hugh Hext. The bride was only fourteen years old, not an unusual age for marriage at that time.

The parsonage having now fallen into very poor condition, the vestry raised £300 from the parishioners by subscription, and requested Andrew Rutledge to draft a petition to the Assembly for aiding in defraying the cost of a new parsonage. With the petition was a statement from John Thomas Capers, John Hollybush, and Charvil Wingood, "professed House Carpenters," that they had found the lower timbers, windows, frames, and shingles of the parsonage so rotten that repairs would cost almost as much as a new building. The petition set forth that the parsonage house "is in so decayed and ruinous a Condition as to be past any repair and very unsafe to dwell in," and the sum raised by subscription "falls very short of the sum necessary." In February 1739, the Assembly granted £400 for the new parsonage.[7]

The vestry's plan for the new parsonage specified that it should be thirty-two feet in length by twenty-two feet wide, of two stories, the first being ten feet high, and the second eight feet. The plan also called for a cellar, but this later was omitted. Captain George Benison and Charvil Wingood, vestrymen, and John Hollybush, church warden, were named as a committee to make arrangements for the sawing of the necessary timbers and boards— which then had to be done entirely by hand, a truly formi-

CHRIST CHURCH, ABOUT 1900

HADDRELL'S POINT
By Charles Fraser
Aquatint from *The Analectic Magazine*, X (August 1817)

GARDEN IN MOUNT PLEASANT
from *Scribner's Monthly*, VIII (June 1874), 131

dable task! The committee also was to agree with the builder to erect the parsonage and a kitchen.

Unhappily, the Rev. Mr. Small did not live to see the new parsonage. Like his predecessor, Mr. Fullerton, he apparently fell victim to malaria, and died on September 28, 1739.

Among other deaths that fall was that of George Haddrell, who had been serving Christ Church as vestryman and as warden for more than twenty years. He was buried near the northwest corner of Christ Church. His widow, Susannah, survived him many years. His plantation on Charleston Harbor was known as Haddrell's Point until it was absorbed into the village of Mount Pleasant after the Revolutionary War.

On Easter Monday, April 7, 1740, the parishioners elected as vestrymen: Andrew Rutledge, for the fifth time; Jacob Bond, Thomas Boone, and George Benison, who had already given many years of service; and Robert Brewton, James White, and William Pinckney, who were new members. The church wardens were Andrew Quelch, who had served many times, and Stephen Hartley, the schoolmaster who had previously been the efficient register, clerk, and sexton, as well as the first lay reader.

What is known of these men indicates that persons of somewhat greater importance were then appearing among the mechanics and small farmers of Christ Church Parish.

Of James White nothing is known except what appears upon the church register, and the fact that when re-elected thereafter, he was always given the title of Doctor.

Jacob Bond, born in Cornwall, England, in 1695, and a seafaring man in his youth, had married David Maybank's daughter Susannah at the time of the Yemassee

War and settled down as a rather extensive planter on
Hobcaw plantation, two hundred acres of which was the
Maybank homestead which his wife had inherited from
her father. Mr. Bond was a justice of the peace, an important official then, and also had served many times in
the Assembly.[8]

Robert Brewton, born in 1698, had been a church warden of St. Philip's, Charleston, had represented St.
Philip's Parish in the Assembly, and had been powder receiver of the province. At least one of the notable houses
he had owned in Charleston is still standing on Church
Street. Later, he resided in Christ Church Parish and
represented that Parish in the Assembly.[9]

William Pinckney married Robert Brewton's daughter
Ruth and also resided in the Parish. Born in 1704, he was
the youngest brother of Charles Pinckney, Speaker of the
Commons House and for a brief time Chief Justice of the
province. William Pinckney also served in public life, as
a major of militia, deputy secretary of the province, commissioner in equity, and commissary general. The first fire
insurance company in America was organized in his
Charleston office.[10] His son, Col. Charles Pinckney, purchased Snee Farm in 1754, and in turn, his son and name-
sake was destined in later times to win national fame as a
framer of the federal constitution.

Christ Church remained without a minister until May
24, 1740, when the Rev. John Holmes came into the
parish on his way to Charleston and was invited to preach.
He pleased the vestry and the congregation so well that
they requested him to remain "to officiate as a Minister
of the Church of England." At a vestry meeting held a
month later, it was agreed that Mr. Holmes should be
paid the regular public salary, and that an effort would

be made to procure for him the Society's appointment as missionary; but if the effort should not be successful, then the vestry would oblige itself to raise enough by sub-scription to make his total annual salary amount to £80 sterling.

The arrangement with Mr. Holmes did not continue long, for the Rev. Levi Durand arrived from the Society and began his ministerial duties on November 16, 1740. With Mr. Durand came his young wife Charlotta. Al-though his name appears of French origin, Mr. Durand had been born in London in 1708, the year that Christ Church had elected its first rector, and he had been or-dained deacon in 1738, and priest in 1739, by the Arch-bishop of Dublin.[11] Apparently he was now serving his first charge.

At the last meeting of the vestry, in January 1741, some interesting but not altogether clear decisions were made. The first was that the Assembly should be pe-titioned for permission to sell the schoolhouse lands at Bermuda Town, forty-five acres, for the benefit of the church and the new parsonage. Second, it was agreed that both the north and the south doors of the church should be made into windows, and the resultant space used for pews for members of the church who had none; "that moving benches may be placed at the North door; and a pannell'd front agreeably to the rest of the Church work." As noth-ing is said about cutting down a window into a door, and movable seats were to be placed at the north door, that door must have been allowed to remain open. The third decision was that "Mr. Ford" should have half of the pew where "Mr. Spencer sits" and pay £25 for the seat and £15 pounds "to pale the churchyard."

The Rev. Levi Durand was unanimously elected rector of Christ Church on February 23, 1741.

At the Easter Monday election for vestrymen and wardens, the only changes were made in the wardens, the Rev. John Holmes and Mr. John Atkin [12] being chosen.

When the great task of preparing materials for the new parsonage was completed, the vestry met at the glebe on July 7, 1741, "according to appointment, and had the Parsonage House raised."

How soon Mr. Durand and his young wife moved into the new parsonage is not known, for no minutes of the vestry exist for the period between the day that the parsonage was raised and the Easter Monday election on March 26, 1744. At that election, Robert Gibbes replaced William Pinckney, whose office in Charlestion necessitated his residence there. The wardens were George Logan, Jr., and George Paddon Bond, a son of Jacob Bond. Perhaps Robert Gibbes was then residing at Haddrell's Point, for in 1741 he married Elizabeth, daughter of George and Susannah Haddrell.

Christ Church in those days did not have a wooden floor but was paved directly on the ground as in the old churches of England. When Mrs. Andrew Rutledge, Sarah Boone, died in the autumn of 1743, she was buried beneath her own pew in the church.

In April 1744 Mr. Durand wrote the Society that the Dissenters were coming as usual to Christ Church, and that one of them, William Hendrick, Esq., had given sixteen shillings, sterling, towards repairing the pews; also, the church had recently been glazed and painted. At this time the Dissenters had been without a pastor at Wappetaw Church ever since the death of the Rev. Job. Parker in 1735, and almost all of that congregation were attending Christ Church. Mr. Durand's postscript further revealed that "This Place is more infested with free-thinkers than it is with Enthusiasts." [13]

The first son of the Rev. and Mrs. Durand was born in the autumn of 1744 and was baptized with his father's name. But two days later, Mrs. Charlotta Durand was buried in the chancel of Christ Church under the altar. Recorded upon the church register with the entry is a quotation in Latin from Virgil, which in translation reads: "A rest unbroken and an iron sleep oppress her eyes; her light is quenched in endless night." Her little son survived until May 16, 1745, two days after Mr. Durand's marriage to Susannah, daughter of Thomas and Mary Boone. Tragedy again struck the Durand family, when, near the end of August, little Susannah, daughter of the rector and Charlotta, died.

Malaria prevailed throughout the parish except upon the open coast, where the deadly anopheles of the inland swamps was replaced by the harmless mosquitoes of the salt marshes. The parsonage was adjacent to swamps, at least one of which is said to be below sea level, and to this day has never been drained.

Mr. Durand was conscientious in performance of his duties and catechised the children of the parish in Lent, but he was not happy. He had no financial anxieties, apparently, for he had inherited an estate in England. But his ministerial work was heavy, and, in addition to his family afflictions, he suffered severely from sciatica; and although he was now married to a native of the parish, he did not think well of his neighbors. On April 23, 1747, he wrote to the Society:[14]

A contented mind is the greatest Blessing a man can enjoy in this World, but this I shall never possess

while I live in this Province, where Infidelity, Pro-
faneness, Heresy, Blasphemy and the most offensive
Breaches of Common Morality have scarce ever appeared with more Insolence; and tho for these things
the Lord does yearly visit, sending Pestilential Dis-
eases amongst Men and Beasts, which yearly sweep
away Numbers of Both, yet none Regard these
things, but as tho' nothing were the matter, Sad
Omen! We eat, We drink, we Play, and shall continue so to do, till everlasting Flames surprise us; I
may well say with the Royal Psalmist, Woe is me,
that I'm constrained to dwell with Mesech &c but I
shall endeavour to content myself with that Province
God has allotted me in one of the dark corners of the
World, even tho' amidst a perverse and Crooked
Generation.

Mr. Durand made it a practice to send each of his
letters in six copies by six different ships, but very few
of his letters seem ever to have reached the Society.

In his dark corner of the world, Mr. Durand was not
the sole laborer. In 1748 a new minister appeared at the
Independent Church on Wando Neck, the Rev. Joachim
Zubly, a native of Switzerland and only twenty-four years
old. Mr. Durand was not cheered by this and on February
20, 1749, he gloomily wrote to the Society:[15]

My Congregation is diminished by the Deaths of
Some of the old Standards and by the going away of
others out of the Parish, as the Land of this Parish
is almost worn out, it being one of the first Settled
Parishes of the Country Parishes in this Province—
I can't say but that there are still numbers of in-
habitants in the Parish, but the Major Part are
Dissenters which used constantly to frequent the
Church till the Coming of One Mr. Zubley, a
Whitfieldian Preacher, amongst them, which for the
present thin's my Church; but I believe this will not

hold long, as his People never could be contented long with any minister they have had Since my time here; Notwithstanding this Discouragement I continue the Duties of my Function with great Alacrity.

For reasons now unknown, Mr. Durand gave up the parsonage as his residence about this time, and in January 1749, Henry Varnor, warden of Christ Church for three years past, was advertising in the *South Carolina Gazette* that he had removed to the parsonage and opened a school. His subjects were reading, writing, arithmetic, accounting. The venture must have been unsuccessful, for the following December Mr. Durand was advertising for rent, "the parsonage of Christ-Church Parish, a commodious two-story house, pleasantly situated, having therein a large hall and six bed-chambers, 3 of which have fire-places: This house will suit a school master, which is very much wanted in this Parish, there being a great number of children in it." [16]

In April 1750, Henry Varnor was operating Hobcaw ferry across the harbor to Charleston, offering the public good entertainment and safe and speedy carriage.[17]

Much of the vestry's work this year was concerned with relief of the poor and assessments of the "poor Tax." Mr. Durand took an active part in settling the estate of John Gibbens, which seems to have been quite involved, and a special subscription of almost £90 was collected for the Widow Gibbens. Mr. Durand also officiated once every three months at St. James' Church, Goose Creek, twenty-three miles from his residence, because of a vacancy at that church.

Among the "old Standards" of Christ Church who died in 1750 was Dr. John Rutledge, whose death occurred on Christmas day, the twelfth anniversary of his marriage to young Sarah Hext. Two days later, he was buried at St. Philip's, Charleston, although he then had been for five years a vestryman of Christ Church. Both he and his brother Andrew had represented the parish in the Assembly. His widow, then twenty-six years of age, was left as executrix of a large estate in addition to her great task of rearing and educating their seven children.[18]

Despite the many losses in the congregation of Christ Church, there were then sixty communicants enrolled. Among them were named John and Edmund Atkin,[19] Charleston merchants. This seems to have been the most flourishing era of Christ Church.

Along with the increase of church business there had come a need for a better vestry house in which the business could be conducted. In the spring of 1751, the vestry made an agreement with James McCraw to supply the bricks for the new building, which was to be twenty-two feet long by fourteen feet wide, with one door and three windows. John Holmes was to cart the bricks to the site in the churchyard, Archiband McDowell was to lay the bricks, and Thomas Hamlin, Jr., was engaged for the "Wooden work." The total cost was almost £176.

This same year the last recorded skirmish with Indians in the parish took place, when a flying party of northern Indians was defeated by the Christ Church Parish militia under Captain George Paddon Bond "near the seaside, about two miles from the parish-church."[20] This may have been on a portion of Thomas Barksdale's plantation, then called Youghal, but now called Porcher's Bluff.

Mr. Durand had now made up his mind to leave Christ Church, and in November 1751, after almost eleven years of service which seems to have brought him very little happiness, he informed the vestry that he would leave to officiate in the Parish of St. John's, Berkeley. The vestry wrote letters to the Society and to the Bishop of London, asking for a missionary in Mr. Durand's place; and they agreed to let Maurice Delany "live in the Parsonage House during their pleasure." In March 1752, the vestry received from Mr. Durand the silver chalice, one tablecloth, one napkin, and one surplice, all belonging to Christ Church; also, a catalog of the books received by him from the Society in place of the library which had never been recovered (except one book) after Mr. Marston delivered it to Thomas Barton more than forty years before. On the same day, March 30, 1752, was recorded a receipt to Dr. Durand for £20 which he then paid to John Metheringham, Jr., for serving as clerk, register, and sexton during the past year. As election of church officers was being held that day, the vestry agreed with Metheringham to continue his three offices at the same salary. He was regularly reappointed each year until his resignation five years later.[21]

No services were held in Christ Church until the following December, when the Rev. Bartholomew Zauberbuhler, a Lutheran minister, held one service, and Commissary Garden another.

The Society promised to send another missionary to Christ Church "as soon as it should appear that some things then amiss in that Parish were rectified." [22] Whatever was amiss seems not to have been rectified, and the church remained without a rector for more than six years. During that time the congregation was held together by a succession of eight visiting ministers, including the Commissary, who held thirty-nine services.

Despite the long vacancy, the regular elections for vestrymen and wardens were held on each Easter Monday, and parish business was transacted. In May 1755 the vestry had John Metheringham, Jr., make a survey of the church and estimate the cost of repairs, after which the vestry met at the home of Thomas Phillips near the church, signed an agreement with Richard I'On to supply 10,000 shingles, 18 inches in length, at £5.5 a thousand, and agreed to have the church repaired inside and out. Each member also signed the contractor's agreement:

> I, George Gardner, do positively agree to do the above work for One hundred and fifty pounds, and to be done in a workmanlike manner, of which the Vestry shall be a judge off, before the payment of the Money for the said work.
> I promise to begin as soon as the Materials are ready.
>
> George Gardner

Wm Boone		
Robt Dorrill		
Richd Tookerman	Vestry Men	
Thos Whiteside		
Thomas Phillips		G. Paddon Bond,
James White		Church Warden

The British governor of Nova Scotia about this time sent into South Carolina, without warning, almost a thousand French Acadians. The Assembly provided funds for their necessities, and some of the unfortunates made a living by working on the fortifications of the province. The next year, the 645 Acadians still unemployed were distributed among the parishes to be sold by the vestrymen and church wardens as indentured servants, the men for terms of three years, and the children for longer. The quota for Christ Church Parish was received on July 25, 1756, by the vestrymen and wardens, "to remain Three months, at Ten shillings per week each head so received which allowance is to continue to those that are not taken away by private persons." Many of the Acadians returned to Charleston, but they could not speak English and were not easily absorbed into the population, and seven years later some of them were sent to Haiti. A few families, however, remained in South Carolina, and eventually became citizens.[23]

Although he was not a missionary from the Society, the Rev. Wingood Serjeant, in the spring of 1758, was elected rector of Christ Church. Ordained to the priesthood in December 1756 by the Bishop of Rochester, England, Mr. Serjeant had served briefly as assistant minister at St. Philip's, Charleston. His name appears on the minutes of the Christ Church vestry only at the meeting of October 14, 1758, when he was present as a vestryman and received an order for a half year's salary and £150 for a year's house rent. In 1759 he went to St. George's as rector.[24]

The Society decided in 1759 that the Church of England was sufficiently strong in South Carolina to need no further aid and voted to provide no missionaries in future for vacant cures. The Rev. Levi Durand was the last missionary sent to Christ Church by the Society for the Propagation of the Gospel in Foreign Parts. Indeed, the Society's missionaries in the parishes of South Carolina had done their work so well that the Church of England was more firmly established in that province than in any other British colony in North America.

Meanwhile, the population of Christ Church was slowly growing, especially in the area next to Charleston. Jacob Motte, public treasurer of South Carolina for many years and son of John Abraham Motte, had acquired property in the sand hills overlooking Charleston Harbor.

He also owned several plantations in other parts of the province, to each of which he gave a name, and the home on the sand hills in Christ Church Parish he called Mount Pleasant. In 1759, Mr. Motte was elected to the vestry of Christ Church, and four years later he presented the church with a heavy silver paten for the communion service. Some years earlier he had given the church a large prayer book for the use of the parish clerk, who led the responses in the church services.

After Mr. Serjeant's transfer to St. Philip's, the Christ Church vestry agreed to meet the following May to consult on sending for a minister. But it proved to be slow work, and not until September 1762 did the Rev. Samuel Drake become rector. Although but recently arrived in the province, and faced with some trying conditions, Mr. Drake seems to have worked harmoniously in his charge. The "commodious two-story" parsonage which had been built in 1741 was now so decayed as to be "ruinous and uninhabitable," so the vestry circulated a subscription list to raise money for an annual rent paid by Mr. Drake for a "tenement" in the parish. Later, he rented a house in Charleston and subscriptions for rent payments were continued throughout his rectorate.

When the clergy of the province held their annual meeting in Charleston in April 1763, Mr. Drake was chosen to preach the sermon. His name disappears from the Christ Church register after June 1765, and he returned to England, but apparently with some expectation of coming back to South Carolina.

On a mid-July day that summer, an interesting visitor made a brief visit to the parish, John Bartram, a Quaker naturalist from Philadelphia, who was returning from a trip to Florida. Before leaving Charleston that morning with William Hopton, register of deeds at the state house in Charleston, who owned a plantation on the Wando River, John Bartram had carefully recorded that the temperature was eighty-five degrees. He spent that night on the plantation, which Hopton facetiously called "Starvegut Hall," in the brick house on the river opposite the village of Cainhoy. Together, Hopton and Bartram walked over the plantation to see the rice ground and the numerous salt marshes, but the botanist was too much interested in the varieties of palmettoes to record any other details of his visit.[25]

Early the next year, the Christ Church vestry received a letter of introduction from the Rev. Samuel Drake, dated January 1, 1766, from Mount St. John, Yorkshire, England, saying:

> as I shall not immediately return to Carolina, I have persuaded a clergyman to supply my place amongst you. The revd. Mr. Lonsdale, the bearer, is a person whom I wou'd recommend, and I hope he will please you in every respect. He is my old schoolfellow and has a large family, whom I recommend to your protection. I make no doubt but you will assist him in every respect which his occasions and your kindness will approve. He hath a desire for planting; so your prudence will easily suppose him to want a house and land; but I would not presume to direct you in such an affair.

As this letter is in the files of Christ Church, the Rev. Mr. Lonsdale evidently delivered it to the vestry, but nothing further is known of him or his large family.

A real estate project was launched in the parish in the spring of that year, when Jonathan Scott, an Englishman, advertised in the *Gazette*[26] that he had purchased a tract of land between Jacob Motte's country seat, Mount Pleasant, and the estate of the late George Haddrell, then called Haddrell's Point. Scott announced that he would lay out lots of about one acre each, fronting on Charleston Harbor, "for the Use and Convenience of Gentlemen in Town and Country." His lots were disposed of readily, for they were in a beautiful and healthful location, and thus the first real village in the parish was begun, the present town of Mount Pleasant, which eventually included and took the name of Jacob Motte's property. Jonathan Scott also donated fifty acres of woodland as a Common for the people of the village to get firewood.

After the departure of the Rev. Mr. Drake and Mr. Lonsdale, Christ Church was served by the neighboring clergy. Among these were the Rev. Joseph D. Wilton, assistant at St. Philip's, Charleston, who died in 1767; the Rev. James Crallan, who succeeded him and who in 1768 on his return voyage to England threw himself into the sea and was drowned; and the Rev. Charles Martyn, a diligent divine who long served St. Andrew's Parish and had voluntarily reliquished his salary from the Society because his salary from South Carolina was ample.[27]

In the summer of 1769, the vestry of Christ Church made an agreement with the Rev. Thomas Panting, headmaster of the Free School, Charleston, to hold services at the church every second Sunday for twelve months. But on February 22, 1770, Mr. Panting resigned in this fiery letter to the vestry:

> Gentlemen,
>
> Without giving any notice to the Gentlemen of the Vestry, or me, I am informed that Mr. Andrew Hibben has been pleased to engage your Parish Church for Sunday next, and that the Minister of

the Dissenting Congregation had such timely Notice sent to him, that he publickly signified it to his
Congregation on Sunday last.

If the Gentlemen of the Vestry think no Civility
due to them on such an Occasion, or to myself, as
engaged by them, it seems natural to me to conjec-
ture that Mr. Hibben may on the same Presumption
at any time dispose of the Church.

I look upon this Behavior as so gross an Insult to
the Established Church, and to the Vestry of the
Parish of Christ Church that for the future I do
not intend to do the Service in any Church whose
Vestry can submit to such an Indignity. If the Gentlemen of the Vestry of the Parish of Christ Church
can give their Approbation of Mr. Hibbins his Con-
duct, I send this to acquaint them that I am and will
be no longer Mr. Hibbins or

Their Humble Servant,

Thos Panting [28]

Andrew Hibben, who had so upset Mr. Panting, was
a young silversmith who had arrived in Charleston in
1763 from Kent, England, with the celebrated evangelist, the Rev. George Whitefield. Hibben's advertisements
in the *Gazette* show that in October 1764 he had a jewelry and watchmaking shop in Elliott Street, Charleston, and in January 1765 he removed to the "Sign of
the Dial" on Broad Street. After his marriage a year
later to Elizabeth (Barksdale), well-to-do young widow
of John Sauseau Wingood of Christ Church Parish,
Hibben gave up his Charleston business and became a
planter. On his many journeys through the province,
Whitefield is said to have visited Hibben at his plantation, Seaside, near Christ Church, and on these occasions
tradition has it that the walls of Christ Church "more

than once resounded to the eloquence of Whitefield."
Mr. Whitefield was in the vicinity during this period,
and it seems not unlikely that Mr. Panting's outburst
was caused by news that Andrew Hibben had engaged
Christ Church for a service by Mr. Whitefield.[29] The
evangelist left Charleston on March 5, 1770, having
"preached here to crowded Audiences almost every Day
since his Arrival." [30]

The lack of a dwelling on the glebe was a costly and
troublesome situation, and the vestry now proceeded to
draw up specifications for a new house and outbuildings.
In December 1769 an estimate was submitted by Samuel
McCorkell and Jonathan Hood to build a house of yellow pine on a brick foundation, 34 feet by 24 feet, with
two chimneys; the lower story 10 feet high, with a hall,
a parlor, and one room; the upper story 8 feet high, with
four rooms; to be lathed, plastered, glazed, and painted;
with a pitched roof, shingled with seasoned cypress;
paneled doors and windows, and "one Beaufeat"; two
piazzas 8 feet wide; complete for £2,830.[31]

There is no available information on the construction of
this house, but apparently it was built with some alterations. The house which stood on the site until after the
first World War faced the south with a piazza the length
of the front, from which a door opened upon a large living room, the "hall" of the specifications. This had a paneled wainscoting around three sides, and the entire interior
chimney wall was paneled to the cornice. In the northeast corner was a beautifully constructed china closet, the
"Beaufeat" of the specifications. On the right of the high
mantel over the large fireplace was another closet concealed in the paneling. A door to the right of the chimney opened from the living room into an east room which

ST. ANDREW'S CHAPEL

(the first building, now extensively renovated)

St. Andrew's Chapel.

(the second building)

may have been the "parlor" or the master bedroom. Another door on the north wall opened from the living room upon a stair hall at the rear, upon which a north window of the living room opened. Upstairs were three bedrooms. The entire house was lathed and plastered. The principal change from the original plan was the one interior chimney instead of two.[32]

As the Rev. Charles Martyn returned to England about this time, the vestry asked him to engage a minister for Christ Church. In his reply, dated from London, March 15, 1771, Mr. Martyn wrote:

> The Bearer of this is the Revd. Mr. Hinde, whom I have engaged as Minister of your Parish, in consequence of the Letter which you sent me for that Purpose. Mr. Hinde was educated, and graduated as Master of Arts at Jesus College in Cambridge: and he hath been in holy orders for some years past, during which he hath acquitted Himself with a good character and much Reputation in his function, as his Testimonials fully ascertained. He hath given me the strongest Assurances that he will continue in your Parish and not quit it for any other; and therefore I flatter myself that you will pay Him the usual compliment of defraying the expense of his Passage to Carolina.

Perhaps it was on this prospect of a resident minister that the vestry came to this undated agreement:

> The Vestry and Wardens of Christ Church having settled a regular minister in their Parish, and their funds not being adequate from their annual income to provide the necessary comforts and conveniences for the Rector and his family—have resolved to raise by Subscription a sum sufficient to purchase a

family of Servants for the Parsonage and Glebe land.

They therefore respectfully invite and Solicit the friends and Members of the Church and the parishioners of Christ Church generally, to aid them in promoting a design which they believe will be beneficial to the welfare and increase of christianity in this their parish.

The subscription list was circulated from early 1771 into February 1772, and from twenty-seven contributors [33] more than £400 was raised for the "purchasing of a negro or negroes to be appropriated to the perpetual use of the Minister of this Parish." Among the subscribers was Thomas Lynch, Jr., who was destined a few years later to sign the Declaration of Independence of the thirteen American states.

The Rev. John Hinde duly arrived in Christ Church Parish and delivered his letter of introduction to the vestry. In July 1771, as "Minister of this Parish" he baptized a daughter of Joseph and Hannah Cook; three days later he officiated at the funeral of Mrs. Plowden Weston; and at the close of that week he baptized Daniel Jones. Except for a draft signed by him on December 27, 1771, upon John Sandford Dart, church warden, there is no further mention of the Rev. John Hinde.

Early in 1772, the Rev. Henry Purcell became rector of Christ Church. Born in Hereford, he was graduated from Oxford in 1763 and arrived in Carolina in 1769. After a brief experience as assistant minister at St. Philip's, Charleston, he had been rector of St. George's, Dorchester. Only thirty years old when he came to Christ Church, Mr. Purcell was an interesting personality and a true musician,[34] but his talents as a composer and a choir master probably found small chance for expression in his country parish. Nevertheless, he remained until six years later when he went to St. Michael's, Charleston.

Throughout the rectorate of Mr. Purcell, the rumblings of the approaching Revolution were steadily moving to a climax, and he, although so recently arrived from England, ardently embraced the American cause.

Not long before the outbreak of hostilities, the Rev. Charles Woodmason sent to London a comprehensive report on the state of the Anglican churches in the Carolinas and Georgia. His report was based on his survey, but apparently he only glanced at Christ Church in passing, for he dismissed it in one line: "Christ Church Is a pretty Brick Building—but very plain." [35] There is no mention of a cupola in the minutes of the vestry during the period of the establishment, and this fact along with Woodmason's comment suggests that then there was no cupola.

A noteworthy event of the year 1775 for Christ Church was the death on September 21 of Mrs. Elizabeth Fleming, who two days later was buried in the churchyard. As Elizabeth James, she had married Maurice Fleming, August 12, 1744, and was now a widow. She bequeathed the bulk of her estate to the parish: "two hundred Pounds to be kept at use for the Parish Church" and all the rest of her estate, after payment of debts, "to be sold and the money to be put at use for to build a School in this Parish for the Good of the Poor as my Executors shall see fit." Her executors were Jonathan Dorrill, Andrew Hibben, and Thomas Barksdale. The total legacy amounted to almost £2,344 currency.

South Carolina made her own declaration of independence from the mother country on March 10, 1776, and wrote her first state constitution. In May of that year, Mr. Purcell was appointed chaplain of Col. William Moultrie's regiment, but he continued to officiate at Christ Church. When the British fleet attacked Charleston on June 28, a company of Christ Church Parish militia under command of Captain Arnoldus Vanderhorst of White Hall plantation was stationed at Haddrell's Point.[36] The amazing victory of the Carolinians that day won peace for their state for several years. When the Declaration of Independence for the American colonies was signed in Philadelphia on July 4, among the signers were two men who had roots in Christ Church Parish, Edward Rutledge and Thomas Lynch, Jr.

Thomas Lynch, Jr., was the only son of a wealthy family which had owned large tracts of land in the province for three generations. In Christ Church Parish, Lynch Grove, a plantation of more than seven hundred acres, was on Wando Neck; and Thomas Lynch, the elder, owned an 817-acre tract on Wacandaw Creek of Wando River, on which as late as 1755 was the railed-in burying ground of his father, Jonah Lynch.[37] Both Thomas Lynch, the elder, and Thomas Lynch, Jr., were members of the Continental Congress which adopted the Declaration of Independence of the original thirteen states.

The Rev. Mr. Purcell was appointed deputy judge-advocate general in 1778 for South Carolina and Georgia. He resigned from Christ Church, and once more its doors were closed.

Another blow fell that year. South Carolina's legislature framed its second state constitution, and to the joy of the Dissenters, the Church of England was dis-established. "The Christian Protestant religion" was declared

to be "the established religion of this State," and "all
denominations of Christian protestants in this State, de-
meaning themselves peaceably," were to "enjoy equal religious and civil privileges." [38] As there was not yet a
bishop in America, and no organization of Episcopal
churches, Christ Church, without a rector, was destined
to remain for almost a generation as a lone sheep without a shepherd.

When Charleston was surrendered to the British in
May 1780 and the state was overrun by the enemy, General Moultrie and other Continental officers were paroled
to barracks at Haddrell's Point. By the terms of their
parole, they were restricted to an area within six miles
of the barracks—perhaps because six miles was the distance to the parish church.

After the surrender, the British legion under the re-
doubtable Col. Banastre Tarleton took post at the narrowest part of the parish on Wando Neck and made barracks in Wappetaw Church, a strategic point for patrolling
traffic between Charleston, Georgetown, and points north-
ward. The Rev. Mr. Atkins, pastor of Wappetaw Church,
is said to have been murdered in his parsonage by his
slaves at the instigation of the British,[39] who especially
disliked Dissenters as leaders of rebellion.

Despite disestablishment of the church and although
Christ Church Parish was occupied by British troops, on
Easter Monday, April 16, 1781, the parishioners met at
the church as usual for the annual election of church officers. For wardens they chose Jonathan Scott and Andrew Hibben, and as vestrymen, George Paddon Bond,
William Bennett, Thomas Whitesides, Jen Dorrill, Peter Croft, John Boone, and James Dewar.

During the year 1781 the fortunes of war began to brighten for the American cause. After the victories of the South Carolina partisans and the surrender of Cornwallis, the British realized that they had lost the war, and in December 1782, they evacuated Charleston and sailed away to the West Indies. Before leaving, they burned Wappetaw Church and the home of an officer [40] of Christ Church in which books, vestments, and some of the church silver in his charge were consumed. This act of vandalism probably accounts for some of the gap of thirty-eight years, 1759-1797, in minutes of the Christ Church vestry.

Evidently the British realized that in Christ Church Parish there was little difference between Dissenter and Anglican, for they also burned both Christ Church and the vestry house.

CHRIST CHURCH OF THE
PROTESTANT EPISCOPAL CHURCH

THREE

A SECOND RESURGENCE FROM ASHES

After the cruel war for independence from Great Britain, the blackened ruins of Christ Church remained beside the Georgetown-Charleston road, reminding all who passed of the hatefulness of war. Since the disestablishment, the parishioners could no longer look to the public treasury of South Carolina for funds to rebuild their church, nor was there as yet any organized Protestant Episcopal Church in America to which they could appeal for aid. Many members of the old congregation of Christ Church had died during the late war, and those who remained had been impoverished by destructive losses. The outlook for the continued existence of the church was indeed dark. But the darkest hour proved to be just before the dawn.

After the treaty of peace with Great Britain was ratified, a convention of clergy and lay delegates from the surviving Protestant Episcopal churches in the United States met in New York early in October 1784. Here plans were made for organizing a General Convention of delegates from churches in all the states to meet in Philadelphia. The following month the first bishop of the church in America, Samuel Seabury of Connecticut, was consecrated in Scotland.

In South Carolina at this time there was neither a bishop nor a diocese, but in May and July 1785, delegates from South Carolina churches met in conventions in

Charleston. The ruins of Christ Church sent no delegates, but her former rector, the Rev. Henry Purcell,
and two of her parishioners, Charles Pinckney of Snee
Farm, and Jacob Read, who had been born at Hobcaw,
were elected as delegates to the General Convention to be
held in Philadelphia.

The following year when a convention of South Carolina churches met in Charleston, John Sandford Dart,
son-in-law of Jacob Motte, represented Christ Church
and signed a tentative church constitution which had been
framed by the Convention.[1]

Thus slowly but surely the Protestant Episcopal Church
in South Carolina began to revive from the paralyzing
but beneficent blow of disestablishment.

The following year the surviving members of Christ
Church petitioned the legislature to incorporate the vestry and received a charter.[2]

After the Easter Monday elections, the vestry sent to
the *Gazette* this advertisement:

Christ Church Parish, April 24, 1787

Whereas the Vestry and Church Wardens of the
Episcopal Church in the parish of Christ Church,
have resolved to rebuild the said Church and Vestry House, as speedily as possible, therefore Public
Notice is hereby given, to any person or persons,
that are inclinable to undertake the rebuilding of
the same, that they do give in their proposals in
writing, sealed up and directed to the Vestry and
Church Wardens of said Church, and to be left with
John Sandford Dart, Esq., in Charleston, on or before Monday the fourth day of June next.

Stephen Townshend, ⎫ *Church Wardens*
Paul Pritchard, ⎭

Below it were also advertised the parsonage and glebe lands for let on lease for one, two, or three years.[3]

The legacy of Mrs. Elizabeth Fleming, meanwhile, was not forgotten, and in July of that summer Thomas Barksdale, executor of her will, delivered to the vestry "£48, 11, 5, being in full for £200" currency, with ten years' interest.

The state charter which incorporated the vestry empowered the church wardens and vestrymen to have the "church completely rebuilt or repaired." As the solid brick walls of both the church and the vestry house had survived the fire, the vestry decided to restore the roofs and other wooden accessories. The work was begun on June 17, 1787, and was completed on June 23, 1788. Pews and a pulpit were installed, and the total cost was £130.10.7.[4] Once more the old church was ready to serve the parishioners. But three years later, when George Washington on May 2, 1791, passed by and breakfasted at Snee Farm, the church had not yet been reopened.

A subscription to defray the cost of rebuilding had failed to raise sufficient funds, so on St. Valentine's Day 1788, a dozen of the well-to-do members of the congregation pledged an additional £119.7.4. Paul Pritchard, church warden, kept an itemized account of the work and paid the bills, but ten years later the church still owed him £58.3.1, plus interest.

The problem of finding a rector still remained. Ministers were no longer being sent from London, and as yet no seminary and no bishop were in South Carolina to train and to ordain young men to the ministry. And if a minister should be found, his salary no longer would be paid by the government, and the congregation was too poor to support him. In the general dearth of both clergy and funds, Christ Church had no minister for almost another ten years.

Other denominations in the parish, however, were stirring. When Bishop Francis Asbury had journed through the parish in 1786 on his way to Charleston, he had noted in his diary on January 10 that when he rode past Wappetaw "It was no small comfort to me to see a very good frame prepared for the erection of a meeting-house for us, on that very road along which, last year, we had gone pensive and distressed, without a friend to entertain us." [5] This old Methodist Church, twelve miles from Mount Pleasant, has now disappeared, but four tombstones survive in its overgrown cemetery.

The Congregational church at Wappetaw also had been revived and incorporated in 1786.[6] Two years later, the members, having rebuilt their church, chose as their pastor the Rev. Daniel McCalla. This interesting man, a native of Pennsylvania and a graduate of the College of New Jersey, had studied both medicine and theology and had mastered several modern languages as well as the classics.[7]

Deeply interested in the cause of American independence, Mr. McCalla had been commissioned during the Revolution as an army chaplain. Later he had opened an academy in Virginia, where he was popular both as a teacher and a preacher. "Mr. McCalla was eminently a social man and perhaps not always discreet. He mingled in scenes of conviviality more than was pleasant to those who looked upon these things with severity. Finding himself the subject of censure, he left the position he occupied and became the minister of the church of Wappetaw, in 1788." [8]

There Mr. McCalla served most acceptably, and at least one of his devoted congregation attended communion services by riding horseback to Wappetaw from forty miles away in St. Stephen's Parish.[9] Mr. McCalla was admired and respected among the people of Christ Church Parish generally.

A long-felt need of the Protestant Episcopal Church in South Carolina was met in September 1795 when the Rev. Robert Smith of Charleston was consecrated in Philadelphia as the first bishop of South Carolina. But unfortunately, he lived only six more years; and, of the five young men whom he ordained to the ministry, two died young and two left the state.[10] So the dearth of clergymen continued, and Christ Church remained without a rector.

The members of Christ Church, however, devised a plan for reopening their church.

In April 1797, they met as usual to elect church officers, but, probably for lack of a quorum, adjourned until the first day of May. On the appointed day they again met at the church and unanimously elected Stephen Townshend and Richard Fowler, church wardens; Charles Pinckney, William Gowdy, Robert Henderson, William Bennett, William Dorrell, Moses Whitesides, and Charles James Air, vestrymen. The vestry and the church members then met together and passed these resolutions: *first*, that funds should be raised by taxing each pew £3 a year, payable quarterly; *second*, that Mr. McCalla should be invited to preach at Christ Church on the first Sabbath in each month; *third*, that Mr. McCalla "be permitted to use his form and mode of worship in this Church and that the doors thereof be always open to him; *fourth*, that he be paid £50 annually, payable semiannually.

Letters were then written to the Rev. Mr. McCalla and to his congregation, saying that "having been long without the comfortable doctrine of the Gospel," they felt a desire "of sharing the felicity of having the gospel preached among the inhabitants of this part of the parish," and requested concurrence in these proposals.

In anticipation of success in reopening the church, another letter was written to Col. Arnoldus Vanderhorst asking that he transmit to the vestry "certain Books and Papers belonging to the Episcopal Church in this Parish."

As the church was now out of order, it was unanimously agreed that the wardens be vested with full power to contract for the work of repairs; and, as a possible source of funds, they were authorized to lease the glebe land.

The letters to Dr. McCalla and his congregation brought favorable replies, and once more Christ Church began to revive.

The leasing of the glebe proved to be more difficult, for one William Cook was in possession of the parsonage, and he refused to vacate or to pay rent. The wardens were therefore vested with full power to issue a warrant of distress against him, but it was not until three years later that they collected even a fraction of the amount due. A part of this was applied to the debt so long owed to Paul Pritchard for the rebuilding of the church, a debt on which the vestry refused to pay any interest. The rest of the payment was loaned at interest.

Dr. McCalla was so well received by the Christ Church congregation that the vestry every year unanimously renewed their invitation that he continue, and he was requested to administer the sacrament of holy communion "in any manner he may think proper."

At the request of Wappetaw, the vestry in April 1802 agreed to pay £83. 6. 3 a year for Dr. McCalla's services. But the Christ Church congregation refused to sup-

port the increase, and in February 1805, the vestry notified the Wappetaw congregation that it was no longer
possible to pay this quota. At a joint meeting with a
Wappetaw committee to consider the question, the vestry
unanimously resolved that all money received from pew
rents, "be the same more or less," should be given to
Dr. McCalla for his services. On this basis thereafter the
usual unanimous invitation was issued each year and Dr.
McCalla continued his services.

During all the years since the Revolution, Christ
Church had been an isolated and independent entity, and
in organization it was as truly a "congregational" church
as Wappetaw, for Christ Church also was under the sole
control of its own congregation and the men who represented the congregation on the vestry. Christ Church had
taken no part in the annual church conventions in Charleston until the seventh in 1789, when John Sandford Dart
was a lay delegate. The name of Bishop Smith is not even
mentioned on the existing records of Christ Church. After
the death of Bishop Smith in 1801, the Rev. Edward
Jenkins of St. Philip's, Charleston, was chosen bishop in
1804, but he declined because of his age, and for eleven
years after the death of Bishop Smith, South Carolina had
no bishop. The Protestant Episcopal Church in this state
seemed perilously close to extinction.

In these years of congregational isolation, when few
churches had a rector to preside at meetings of the vestries,
a new church officer was evolved, the "chairman of the
vestry." This chairman was not necessarily the senior
warden, but was usually the most energetic and devoted
member of the vestry, and was chosen by the members of
that body. Sometimes the chairmanship was conferred
upon the secretary.

The chairman of the Christ Church vestry in 1804 was Clement Lampriere Prince, who came of a family of ferry owners, and operated Prince's Ferry across the Cooper River to Charleston in rivalry with Hibben's Ferry from Shem Creek.[11] While chairman of the vestry, he brought up the question of Mrs. Elizabeth Fleming's bequest of £2344. 10. which she had directed was to be used for the education of the poor children of Christ Church Parish; and it was agreed that he, John Glen, and Benjamin Joy should be a committee to consult the executors of her will as to the status of the bequest. The upshot was that a board of eight trustees was incorporated in 1809 to receive the legacy: Samuel Warren, James Hibben, William Scott, Nicholas Venning, Elias Whilden, George Barksdale, Moses Whitesides, and David Ramsay. As soon as they received the legacy, the trustees proceeded to build an academy in the village of Mount Pleasant. Two years later the trustees were authorized by law to raise funds for completion of the academy by means of a lottery.[12]

The charter which incorporated the trustees followed the instructions of Mrs. Fleming's will and directed that the trustees build a school "for the sole purpose of educating the poor children of Christ Church Parish." But the Mount Pleasant Academy became the village school for all the children of that community, and eventually it was merged into the public school system.

After the Easter Monday election on April 3, 1809, the vestry met and resolved that "Episcopal Ministers be invited by the Vestry to perform divine services whenever it is agreeable to them" and that "the wardens be instructed to make the immediate necessary repairs for the reception of the Minister and congregation." These were

BOONE HALL.

Courtesy of Mr. and Mrs. Harris McRae

SNEE FARM

Courtesy of "The News and Courier"

timely decisions, for three days later the Rev. Dr. Daniel McCalla, at the age of sixty years, died at The Grove plantation on Sewee Bay,[13] after twenty-one years of service at Wappetaw, twelve years of which were shared with Christ Church.

For ten of those twelve years, 1797-1807, Charles Pinckney of Snee Farm was annually elected to the Christ Church vestry. Since he was then successively occupied with duties as governor of the state, as United States senator, and as United States minister to Spain, it must be assumed that these elections were purely honorary, a recognition of the most distinguished citizen of the parish. Only in 1807 did he qualify as a vestryman, but there is no other mention of his having been at a vestry meeting.

William Hort, a methodical and dependable businessman, became chairman of the vestry in 1810. Born and reared in Barbados, he had come to Charleston in 1770, and two years later had married Alice Gibbes, a native of Christ Church Parish. When he acquired lands at Haddrell's Point, characteristically he marked the boundaries with massive brick pillars.[14]

At the first vestry meeting over which Mr. Hort presided, the church wardens were instructed to call upon Mrs. Henderson, widow of a former warden, for the surplice and the communion silver. The repair of the pulpit was placed in charge of Clement L. Prince.

At the same meeting appeared the Rev. Dr. J. L. Witherspoon, son-in-law of Dr. McCalla, with a claim against Christ Church for £272. 9. 11, which he said was due and unpaid to Dr. McCalla's estate. After a great searching of the records, the vestry at the next meeting agreed to settle the claim by assigning to Dr. Witherspoon sundry debts and unpaid dues for pew rents. But a year later Dr. Witherspoon reported a deficit still due on the claim, and, as he received no satisfaction, he placed the claim with his attorneys and filed suit against the vestry in the court of equity. Apparently the vestry regarded the claim as settled, regardless of whether or not Dr. Witherspoon could collect the debts assigned to him. At any rate the suit dragged along for many years, and seven years later the vestry paid £100 to each of their defense lawyers. The last mention of the suit was in 1821, when the vestry's solicitor advised taking the suit to the court of appeals.

When the Twenty-Third Convention of the church met in Charleston in 1810, Christ Church was among the fourteen country parishes which sent no delegates.[15] Not yet was there a bishop to organize and bring life to the diocese.

But in the summer of that year, the Protestant Episcopal Society for the Advancement of Christianity in South Carolina was founded, an organization with aims very similar to the venerable English Society for the Propagation of the Gospel in Foreign Parts, and destined to become equally successful in realizing those aims. The three objectives of the Episcopal Advancement Society were first, to distribute Bibles, prayer books, and other religious works; second, to educate young men for the ministry; and third, to send missionaries to every part of South Carolina where they were needed. Annual dues for members were set at $5, and life memberships at $50. At the first annual meeting, 234 regular members and 10 life members were reported.[16]

The Rev. James Dewar Simons, the young rector of St. Philip's, Charleston, and a trustee of the Episcopal Advancement Society, took an active interest in Christ Church, and whenever possible, he or his assistant rector, the Rev. Christopher Edwards Gadsden, officiated at Christ Church. At Mr. Simons' suggestion, the Christ Church vestry agreed that the congregation should meet at the church every other Sunday, weather permitting, and the service should be gone through. If no minister could be present, then the service and a sermon should be "read by some of the Lay-Gentlemen of the Parish."

Such an occasion arose when in December 1810, the Rev. Mr. Simons became ill and Mr. Gadsden had to officiate at St. Philip's instead of Christ Church. Fore-warned of this by Mr. Simons, one of the panic-stricken vestrymen wrote to another that he would cooperate with his bretheren to promote the desired purpose, but

> I have never read nor spoke in Public to any As-semblage of persons, consequently shall be embar-rassed—but looking to you in an especial manner to aid in the business—will conclude that both of us be provided on Sunday next for the occasion—and when we are assembled, take the sense of the Vestry and them present, how to proceed, or in what manner to perform, divide or allot the duty. . . .[17]

When the congregation was consulted, however, Mr. Simons' suggestion was not accepted.

The vestry was now inspired to go forward with re-pairs to the church and the glebe buildings. The cupola which had been erected on the church when the ruins were re-roofed in 1786 was in bad condition, and the vestry had it taken down. Perhaps it was not replaced, for the work-men were ordered to repair "the roof underneath the same, removing the Ridge board and making one compleat the full length of the building."

Among the numerous other specifications were two "pair of Double or half panel doors," each with three pairs of hinges. One double door was to be secured on the inside by an iron bar across it, set into large iron staples on each side; the other was to have a twelve-inch lock. Since two doors are mentioned, it is evident that the north doorway had not yet been closed up into a window as it is at present.

Another and rather odd specification was for a semicircular table in the chancel for an altar, and two semicircular benches, one on each side of it. The intended use for these benches was not given. Were they for communicants at the Lord's supper?

At the annual Diocesan Convention in 1812, the year of the outbreak of the second war with Great Britain, the Rev. Dr. Theodore Dehon was elected the second bishop of South Carolina. Once more there was promise of new life for the Protestant Episcopal Church.

During the War of 1812, however, the minutes of the vestry show Christ Church at a low ebb. Vestrymen were summoned but failed to meet. Perhaps the vestry had given up all hope of ever having a resident minister, for on September 13, 1813, the church wardens and vestrymen sold the parsonage and glebe land, 116 acres, to Dr. Daniel Legare for $1154.28.[18] He merged the property into his adjoining Elm Grove plantation, and apparently he made the parsonage his plantation residence. In getting together the vestrymen to sign the title deed for the transfer of the glebe, Mr. Hort mentioned that the Rev. Dr. Warren would be at Mr. A. H. McGillivray's on Shem Creek, and would "probably offer divine service in the Neighborhood—the villagers are pleased with him, which is in favor of Episcopacy."

Three years later, on Easter Monday, March 27, 1815, Bishop Dehon officiated at the first confirmation service ever recorded in Christ Church, and "Confirmed in Baptism Sarah Scott Geyer, Sarah Rutledge Hort, and Susannah Gibbes Hort."

Another notable service occurred the following month, on Thursday, April 15, 1815, when the first Thanksgiving service in the church was held, "This being the day appointed by Congress for Thanksgiving" for the return of peace after the War of 1812. The Rev. Maurice Harvey Lance officiated. In July the vestry asked Mr. Lance to officiate for the remainder of the summer, but he declined.

The fostering aid of St. Philip's rectors continued through these and the ensuing years to supply services for Christ Church, with a different minister officiating at each service. In addition to the Rev. Mr. Gadsden and Bishop Dehon, the ministers who came were a Rev. Mr. Darnielle, John Barnwell, William Percy, Joseph Warren, John Jacob Tschudy, Maurice H. Lance, Thomas D. Frost, Andrew Fowler, Albert A. Muller, Allston Gibbes, Henry Gibbes, and John White Chanler.

A letter from Mr. Gadsden in March 1816, announcing a service on the 31st instant, shows what was expected of these earnest men: "one of our Clergy will if agreeable to your parishioners hold divine service in your Church, catechize the children if there be any, baptize such as may be prepared for that sacrament, and administer the Lord's supper."

There was no election of Christ Church officers on Easter Monday that year, and despite advertisements, no election was held in May. On Friday, May 10, Bishop Dehon "preached to 13 White females no white Males attended." Near the end of June the wardens and vestrymen were elected, and at their first business meeting William Hort, who had been a member the preceding six years, was chosen chairman. He seems to have been given also the duties of secretary and treasurer, and carried on his triple functions for many years.

While Christ Church seemed near to extinction, Episcopalians in another part of the parish were planning for a place of public worship nearer to them than the old parish church. On Sullivans Island, a popular summer resort, subscribers led by Bishop Dehon purchased in 1817 a large brick building on the island which had been erected for a lazaretto, and remodeled it for a church. Tragically, Bishop Dehon died in August that summer of yellow fever.

In August 1818, when the trustees of the Society for the Advancement of Christianity made a report on the thirty-three congregations of the diocese, they listed Sullivans Island and Christ Church among the ten "which are properly to be considered the destitute Churches of the Diocese" and "not competent to support a Minister under any arrangement as yet suggested." As the funds of the Society were inadequate to give support to all, the trustees suggested that the Sullivans Island vestry unite with the Christ Church vestry, and promised that the Society would contribute $500 annually for three years to the support of a minister to serve the two congregations.

Christ Church appointed a committee to confer with a committee from Sullivans Island and to write to the trustees of the Society "Acceptance of their Benevolent proposition."

But matters moved slowly. In June 1819 Bishop Bowen consecrated the remodeled lazaretto as Grace Church. In October the Society notified Christ Church that the

entire sum intended for Grace Church and Christ Church
jointly would be allotted to Christ Church. In November
members of the Christ Church committee reported that
no conference had been held with the Grace Church committee, but in conversation they "understood that a Union
of the two Vestries was declined by the Vestry of Sullivan's Island." This proved to be correct, and in 1820 the
Grace Church vestry was incorporated.[19]

FOUR

THE FIRST RECTOR OF THE AMERICAN CHURCH

The assurance of $500 from the Episcopal Advancement Society made it possible for Christ Church once more to become active, and the vestry elected the Rev. Albert Arney Muller, a young Charlestonian who had been ordained deacon in 1817 by Bishop Dehon, and priest in 1818 by Bishop William White of Pennsylvania. Although Mr. Muller declined the call, he reconsidered when the vestry agreed that his salary should be retroactive to the preceding November; and on January 1, 1821, he accepted as rector with the understanding "that a house would be procured and rendered comfortable" for his family.[1]

Mr. Muller thus became the first rector of the old parish church under the American Church, and the first in the forty-two years since the resignation of the Rev. Henry Purcell during the Revolution. He must also be regarded as a missionary of the Episcopal Advancement Society. The communicants of Christ Church then were 12 whites and 40 Negroes.

As Mr. Muller made it clear in his numerous letters to William Hort, chairman of the vestry, that he was in desperate financial straits, the vestry immediately advanced him $200, and he made his plans to stay at Mr. Pritchard's in the parish until a parsonage could be made ready.

[76]

On January 17, 1820, with Mr. Muller's approval, the vestry purchased from James Mitchell and his wife Rebecca a small house near Mount Pleasant, with sixty-five acres of land, formerly owned by James Scott.[2] As it bordered upon Hobcaw and Belvue plantations, it probably was on the Mathis Ferry Road.

Almost daily letters from Mr. Muller to the good old chairman of the vestry urged assistance for his varied and pressing needs—axes to cut timber, carts to haul lumber and shingles for repairs to the parsonage,[3] carpenters to make repairs, hay for his horse, laborers to build a garden fence, nails, staples, panes of glass; and, always, his ever desperate need for money. In February he was asking that the aid from the Society be advanced to him at once.[4] The vestry agreed that on receipt of the Society's funds, if any balance remained after paying for materials, workmen, and the sum due on the note for the new glebe, then $280 would be advanced to Mr. Muller. A bill rendered by Mr. Muller for reimbursement of sums he had paid for repairs includes an item of two gallons of rum for the carpenters.

As the planters then removed from their plantations during the summer because of malaria, Christ Church was closed until autumn. In June of his first summer, Mr. Muller wrote William Hort from Moultrieville, Sullivans Island,[5] that he was almost penniless and would have to borrow from friends to enable him to go to market, unless he should receive some money due him from a previous rectorate; also, he was trying to get a loan of $100. In July he wrote again from Moultrieville, reproaching the vestry for the slow repairs on the parsonage:

How gentlemen, shall I in obedience to the injunction of the Apostle "give attendance to reading and study," when I can hardly turn around to partake of my meals, or find room to sleep in the small rooms of the Parsonage. How can I discharge my duties to the Church, if I am not comfortable in my family.

In August Mr. Muller wrote again from Moultrieville, this time to ask that a building committee be appointed, suggesting James Gregorie and John Whitesides as members. On the same day the vestry met and resolved that Jacob Bond I'On, James Gregorie, and the wardens should "adopt the best plan in their Judgment with as little expence as possible [for] having an addition to one end of the Parsonage as the Rector shall prefer." In November Mr. Gregorie had procured two carpenters from Dr. Read and was sending one of his own to meet with the vestry at the parsonage. The next month Mr. Muller reported that the frame of the storehouse was completed —and his need for immediate supplies for his family and an advance of funds was urgent. But the vestry held no more meetings for the ensuing nine months and apparently little was accomplished.

The Episcopal Advancement Society continued its aid in 1821, but the new year brought little comfort to Mr. Muller. He needed a new kitchen, a stable for his horse, back steps for the parsonage—and the storeroom for his groceries had not been completed. In April he wrote that the carpenters who had been working on the storeroom for two weeks had eaten him out of house and home— would Mr. Hort procure from his Charleston factors a barrel of rice for the rector's family?

When the vestry finally convened in May, William Hort, the hard-pressed chairman, offered the opinion that the three officers of chairman, secretary, and treasurer, which he so long had been carrying, "were incompatible to be vested in one Person," and further as he was "advanced in Years and declining in health," he asked to be relieved from the trust. He then recommended that a Committee of Accounts be appointed to examine his financial records and report thereon. The vestry promptly elected him once more as chairman; Thomas Barksdale as secretary and treasurer, and a member of the Committee of Accounts; and Arnoldus Vanderhorst, Paul Weston, and Thomas Barksdale as delegates to the Convention.

This Thomas Barksdale was the third of that name to serve on the Christ Church vestry, and he was destined to prove himself one of the most efficient and devoted officers the church ever had.[6]

Mr. Muller now removed his family to town, and for the next six months the vestry paid a caretaker to stay at the parsonage. Despairing of ever making it comfortable, Mr. Muller in June suggested that it be sold, and a small house be built in the village of Mount Pleasant.

At this period in the history of the church in South Carolina, both rectors and vestries were agreed that a rector's functions were strictly spiritual, and a vestry had exclusive control of the temporal affairs of the church. In July 1821, when invited to meet with the Christ Church vestry in Charleston, Mr. Muller wrote:

> I received your polite invitation to attend a meeting of the Vestry and Wardens on Thursday morning at St. Michael's Church . . .
> As I feel a delicacy in meeting the vestry, and it's not usual in *modern times* for a clergyman to be with such a body, I must decline your respectful invitation.

Several of the vestrymen had offices in Charleston, and it was not unusual for them to meet there when convenient. At this July meeting, it was resolved that Mr. Muller's salary should be paid quarterly.

But this did little to relieve Mr. Muller, for in August he was writing William Hort:

> Miserable and poor indeed is the state of a dependent clergyman. . . . I am disposed to attach all the blame to Whitesides, who is a miserable creature, and more fit for a tavern keeper, than Warden to a respectable body of men. I hope the vestry will make a more judicious choice hereafter in appointing such a man as one of a Committee.

In September Mr. Muller wrote that he had determined to reside at the parsonage the ensuing winter, but in October 1821, he was at 131 Queen Street, Charleston, where two vestrymen wrote him that they would agree to whatever repairs were sanctioned by the chairman. At the end of the month his wants were pressing, and he was pleading for $250 to enable him to move his family and procure some necessaries for their use.

1n 1822, the Episcopal Advancement Society again appropriated $500 for the missionary to Christ Church, with the proviso that he should officiate alternately in some other place than the parish church, the time and place to be designated by the Bishop.

Mr. Muller's financial crises continued, however, and in January he wrote that he was going to town in time for the Epiphany, but would go penniless unless Mr. Hort would permit him to have something in his pocket. In April Mr. Hort advanced him $160,[7] perhaps because Mr.

Muller was moving his family, for once more the vestry had to find a caretaker for the parsonage.

At this time cotton was the staple crop of Christ Church Parish, and although prices had been good after the War of 1812, a decline had now set in and it was selling for only half of the former price. Christ Church had a small endowment which had been slowly growing ever since Mrs. Elizabeth Fleming's bequest had been received. In September 1817 John Geyer and Daniel Joy had reported a balance on hand of $2,680.70, and by 1822, this had increased to $2,975.34. This money, however, was on loan at seven per cent interest and was unavailable for current expenses. The low prices of cotton and the status of the endowment help to explain Mr. Muller's difficulties in obtaining money from his parish.

In October 1822, the trustees of the Episcopal Advancement Society notified Mr. Barksdale, treasurer of Christ Church, that $500 would again be granted for the ensuing year, and further, that the Society would also give an additional amount equal to whatever sum should be raised by the vestry up to $500. Mr. Muller accepted the rectorate for another year, but apparently he did not return to the parsonage, for on December 2, 1822, the trustees of the Society passed a resolution that the secretary

> address a letter to the Rev. Mr. Muller, stating respectfully as the opinion of this Board that the duties of a Missionary of this Society cannot be adequately or efficiently discharged by one not residing at the scene of his duties: and suggesting the propriety of making such arrangements as will enable him to reside in his Parish, during the winter and spring, and also, if a healthy situation can be procured, in the Summer.

In March 1823, Mr. Muller notified William Hort of his intention to relinquish the church at the end of the year.

Treasurer Thomas Barksdale, meanwhile, was receiving bills for materials and services at the parsonage which had been authorized by Mr. Muller but not by the vestry. Mr. Barksdale's report brusquely records that there was "no authority given Mr. Muller by the Vestry to put up a Carriage House to cost $100 as per Mr. Bonneau's Bill; that the charge is illegal . . . if Mr. Muller had this work done on his own account let him pay for it." The bills for materials Mr. Barksdale also refused to pay. In July he discovered that two members of the vestry, without consultation with other members, had given Mr. Muller an order on the Episcopal Advancement Society for $200, and as this money was not due until November, Mr. Muller had discounted the order at a bank.

Without waiting for the end of the year, Mr. Muller went to Pennsylvania seeking another church and left his family in great need. The vestrymen were greatly disturbed by the distress of Mrs. Muller, but Mr. Barksdale felt that in view of Mr. Muller's debt to the church, only twenty dollars should be advanced to the lady, and he would send her what necessaries he could spare from his plantation; the "funds of the church I hold sacred," he wrote to William Hort.

In September, Mr. Muller having settled at Bristol, near Philadelphia, sent for his family, and it is to be hoped that his financial troubles were ended.

Bishop Bowen and the clergy of Charleston once more came to the rescue of Christ Church and offered to officiate alternately on the second Sunday in every month. But when the Rev. Andrew Fowler came in December, it was a rainy day and he found no congregation. The same happened again for the Rev. Christian Hanckel's appointment in February. But on the first Sunday in December 1824, the Rev. Mr. Fowler succeeded in holding the first service of the season, and the next day the vestry got together a quorum for a business meeting at St. Philip's.

The following Sunday, the Rev. Francis Huger Rutledge held service at Christ Church, and thereafter he officiated regularly as deacon in charge. This young man, a son of Hugh and Mary Rutledge, had his ancestral roots in the parish. He had been ordained to the diaconate by Bishop Bowen on May 9, 1823, in Prince George's Church, Winyah. The Christ Church vestry now appealed once again to the Advancement Society for aid and received a grant of $200. In 1825, Mr. Rutledge became rector of Christ Church.

In the spring of the same year, the vestry sold the parsonage and glebe which had caused so much trouble for $500 to Nicholas Venning, Jr., whose plantation, Belvue, it adjoined.

It was during 1826 that some of the most dependable members of the Christ Church congregation were organized into an auxiliary of the Episcopal Advancement Society.[8] Mr. Rutledge's report shows an attendance then of from 30 to 40 persons at his services, and he held a second service for as many Negroes, to whom he gave a course of instruction adapted to their condition. Occasionally he held a third service in the Village of Mount Pleasant, "where a small, but respectable audience attended."

In 1826, probably during the summer season, Mr. Rutledge became rector of Grace Church, Sullivans Island,

and soon his work there was combined with the rectorship of St. Thomas and St. Dennis, near Cainhoy.[9]

In the fall of 1826, the vestry's annual appeal to the Advancement Society expressed a hope that with continued aid a minister's salary might be made up from pew rents, and the church again opened, otherwise it would be closed and the congregation "will have to worship, some at the Independent, and others at the Methodist Church in the Parish." But this dispersal of the congregation did not occur. In 1827 the Rev. Philip Gadsden came and served for one year as deacon in charge. No meetings of the vestry were held that year because of no quorum, and nothing is on record regarding Mr. Gadsden's labors.

FIVE

A GREAT MISSIONARY AND HIS CHAPEL

A new era of stability came to Christ Church in 1828 with the election of the Rev. Andrew Fowler as rector.[1] Described by Bishop Thomas as "one of the greatest missionaries of that century in the American Church," Mr. Fowler had been born in 1759 in Guilford, Connecticut, the son of a Presbyterian father and a Congregationalist mother. After acquiring two degrees from Yale, he entered the ministry. He came to South Carolina in 1807 to become rector of St. Bartholomew's Parish. Later, as the first missionary of the Episcopal Advancement Society, among other charges, he revived Grace Church, Camden; St. David's, Cheraw; and founded Trinity Church, Columbia, as well as a church each in North Carolina and Florida. While rector of the church on Edisto Island, he presented on March 20, 1813, the first class ever confirmed in South Carolina.[2]

Now at the age of sixty-nine years, he bought a home on Whilden Street in the village of Mount Pleasant[3] and settled down for what was to be, up to that time, the longest rectorate of Christ Church since its founding. It was indeed fortunate that Mr. Fowler had some private means and that the Advancement Society was continuing its aid, for Mr. Barksdale wrote to the secretary of the Society on January 18, 1828, that for the winter and spring months Christ Church would be able to allow him about $150.

[85]

Perhaps the greatest discouragement faced by Mr. Fowler in his new charge was the fact that the vestry had not met in two years. A severe blow fell when the Episcopal Advancement Society notified him after the Convention of 1828 that he would be granted only $100 aid. In his report to the Convention in 1829, he said that the congregation was greatly diminished by the death of many of the most respectable members, and the greater portion of the Negro members had either died or attached themselves to the Methodists.

His report in 1830 was equally gloomy, for he said he had found the Parish "in an expiring struggle, and it but a little better now. . . . I have always found it easier to gather a Congregation among entire strangers to our religion, than to attempt to resuscitate one in a Parish that has fallen off and degenerated from its pristine love of our doctrine and discipline." Another year had passed without a vestry meeting, but he was pleased with Mr. Barksdale's expert management of the church funds, which were steadily increasing. "It is a misfortune," Mr. Fowler continued, "that we have neither a glebe nor a parsonage. . . . A love to my Church, and a desire not to be idle, are the only inducements that have fixed me here."

At this time, divine services were held at Christ Church every Sunday from January to June for a congregation of some 40 persons, half of whom were Negroes, and in Mr. Fowler's own house in Mount Pleasant from June to Advent for a congregation of from 35 to 40, very few of whom were Negroes. Communicants, however, continued to be few, only 9 white and 25 Negroes. But the old rector found great comfort in the attentiveness and the hearty responsive reading of his congregations: "As it had pleased God to bestow on them the faculty of speech, so they were not ashamed to use that inestimable gift in his service." He also commented on the custom of silent prayer upon entering the church: "It was peculiarly delightful to see fathers, and children, come into our worshipping assemblies, and fall low on their knees to invoke the blessing of God upon the spiritual labours of the day."

At one of the rare meetings of the vestry, in October 1831, the treasurer was directed to pay to Mr. Fowler out of the first cash he received belonging to the church, $100 for the minister to purchase a horse and conveyance to enable him to attend at the parish church six miles from Mount Pleasant.

At the same meeting, the vestry reached another momentous decision. On motion of Treasurer Barksdale, it was unanimously agreed that:

> to establish a Church and a Minister for the Same, [it] is necessary that a Fund be created sufficient for the purpose, relying on aid from Societies and other similar resources being altogether uncertain and precarious. The Funds of Christ Church Parish Church is now inadicate to the comfortable support of a Minister; and unless it be nursed never will; and the sooner the work is commenced, the earlyer the desired object will be obtain'd of having a respectable and perminent Minister, be it therefore RESOLVED . . . that the Funds of the Christ Church Parish Church be not broken in upon or made use of for the purchase of any property whatever neither real nor Personal; but the Interest arising from the Said Fund be added to the Principall . . . untill the Interest shall Amount to One Thousand Dollars a year."

By the skillful handling of Mr. Barksdale, the funds of Christ Church in 1833 had increased to almost $8,000. The vestry could not have adhered to the above resolution if their rector had not been a man of some means. Mr. Fowler provided his own residence, and he was drawing more than half the support of himself and his family from his own resources.

With the true spirit of a missionary, Mr. Fowler had begun holding two services every Sunday at his dwelling from June to Advent, and this activity bore fruit. In February 1834 he reported:

> We have raised sufficient to build a small Chapel of Ease in the village of Mount Pleasant, in this Parish, which we shall begin to erect as soon as I can raise $250, to purchase a proper site.

A committee of gentlemen on October 15, 1833, attended a meeting of the Christ Church vestry at the home of the chairman, Dr. William Read, in Charleston, and stated that it was contemplated to build a church at the village near Haddrell's Point, and it was wished that the minister of the parish should preach there during the summer and sickly months, when most of the congregation resided there, and that the said new church should be governed by the vestry of the parish church.

The vestry of Christ Church, after some thought, consented, with this strongly worded condition:

> That it be clearly, fearly and fully understood that the Village Church in its connection with the aforesaid Parish Church do not nor shall not have any thing to do with the FUNDS of the said Parish Church 6 miles (Six) from the Village; that it has not, nor Shall not hereafter have any Claims, In-

terest, or demands whatsoever on the aforesaid Parish Church Funds, and . . . in case any intimation or proposition of the Fund of the Parish Church being appropriated in any way or at any time whatsoever for the benefit of the Village Church in any way or respect, that . . . the said Parish Church immediately withdraw from the said Village Church and have no further Connection or Communication with The Said Village Church.

Every member of the vestry who was present signed this resolution, except John Hamlin. As the new church was not an organization, there was no one who could sign for it and thus give the resolution the standing of a legal contract. Apparently there was no lawyer on the vestry to point out this fact, and Thomas Barksdale felt that the funds of Christ Church were fully protected.

Samuel Venning and John Hamlin were appointed to receive subscriptions for the village church, to be paid when collected to Dr. Robert S. Bailey. The committee to inspect the building when completed included William Lucas, Samuel Venning, and John M. Philips.

Finally, the vestry resolved that the new church to be built in the village should be called the "Chapel of Ease" of Christ Church, and that no minister officiating there should assign another minister to perform services in it without consulting and obtaining the approval of the vestry.

The term "chapel of ease" was well known in colonial South Carolina under the Established Church of England, and when any congregation felt that one was needed, a petition was presented to the General Assembly, and a chapel of ease was authorized by a special law. The old parishes of the Establishment were very large, and the roads were very bad, so often the parish church was not easily reached by all the communities of the parish. Sometimes a chapel was needed in the pineland or seashore settlements where the planters took their families in the summer, the "sickly season," to escape the ravages of malarial fever.

Dr. Dalcho says that under the ecclesiastical law of England, baptisms, burials, and the communion service were not performed in chapels of ease, but only in the parish church.[4] Chapels of ease did not have a rectory or an endowment. They were dependent upon the parish rector for divine services, and further to safeguard their dependence upon the mother church, the services of the great church festivals, Christmas, Easter, and Whitsunday, were required to be performed only in the parish church.

In St. Andrew's Parish, the people of James Island built a chapel in 1756, but they could not have services there until they petitioned, and the General Assembly made it a chapel of ease; the special law required the rector of St. Andrew's to hold a service at the chapel every fourth Sunday, "provided it did not happen upon Easter Sunday, Whit Sunday or Christmas day." A similar law was enacted for St. Paul's Parish, but a chapel at Wiltown was not built. Special laws for chapels of ease were passed for St. Andrew's, St. Helena's, and St. George's parishes.[5]

Under certain conditions, what was called a parochial chapel of ease was created by legislative act, which permitted all church services, including burials, baptisms, and the sacraments. In St. Bartholomew's Parish, which was very large and had no parish church, services were held alternately in two parochial chapels of ease. St. John's, Berkeley, had a parochial chapel at Strawberry Ferry, and

St. Thomas' Parish had one at Pompion Hill, both of which chapels have interesting cemeteries.[6]

All laws for chapels of ease were nullified in 1778 when the Anglican Church was disestablished in South Carolina, and after the Protestant Episcopal Church was organized it made no provision for these chapels. Bishop Gadsden later realized that there was a real need to be met when there were shifts of population from the old churches, and in 1843 he recommended that chapels of ease should be built and consecrated,[7] especially where there were seasonal shifts of population to the summer resorts. But the American Church has never provided for them and instead has met the need by organizing missions.

While subscriptions were being collected for the village chapel, the Christ Church vestry authorized the church treasurer, Thomas Barksdale, to contract for repairs and improvements to the old church, "it being in a state of Ruin except the Walls." Mr. Barksdale was always thorough in his undertakings, and his detailed, beautifully written accounts of the work on the church use the word "Rebuilding," a term which seems well chosen. The contract was let to P. H. Marchant. New rafters were put in the roof of the church, and both the church and vestry house were shingled with cypress, and the new roofs were painted. In the spring of 1835 a new cupola was erected, and the walls of both buildings were roughcast, with quoins at the corners to look like stone blocks.

The plans for the village chapel also were progressing. A lot on Whilden Street was purchased, and a building was erected 50 feet long and 30 feet wide. In August 1835 a committee appointed by the congregation of the chapel met there with the vestry of Christ Church and tendered the new building and grounds, which were accepted.

Thomas Barksdale, however, did not attend, for he regarded the chapel as "the village church," as unrelated to his beloved Christ Church as were the churches of Charleston.

Mr. Fowler, Richard Venning, and John Hamlin were appointed to call on Bishop Bowen and inform him that the chapel was ready for consecration. On September 29, 1835, it was duly consecrated with the name St. Andrew's Chapel. The reason for the name is now unknown. Perhaps it was because St. Andrew was a fisherman, but it would be pleasant to think that the name was in appreciation of the labors of the faithful old missionary who had founded it.

Mr. Fowler reported these events to the Convention the following February, and noted that "The Sunday School, to use a modern phrase, is well attended by the gentlemen I formerly mentioned," probably Dr. Robert S. Bailey, John Hamlin, and Elias W. Hort, who were the teachers.

At a vestry meeting on April 24, 1837, Mr. Barksdale's report showed that the funds of Christ Church had increased to $9,519.06, and the income from investments in 1836 had been $718.93. On motion of John Hamlin, the thanks of the vestrymen and wardens were voted to "Thomas Barksdale, Treasurer, for his care, attention, and addition to The Church Funds."

In October Mr. Barksdale reported that the interior of Christ Church also required repairs, and that funds for the work were available. He was authorized to advertise for estimates, and Joseph Maybank and Effingham Wagner were named to his committee to attend to the work. With his customary thoroughness, Mr. Barksdale continued with what proved to be a three-year program of complete renovation of his church. The floor was laid with new tiles.

Sashes were made for the windows, and new glass was put into windows "not Sashed or Glazed before." The pews were taken down and refitted. The window over the altar was cased. Last of all, Mr. Marchant was given a contract for a reading desk and a new pulpit to be modeled after the one in St. Peter's Church, Charleston, but to be reduced in size.

Much of the other work apparently was done by Mr. Barksdale's own plantation carpenters under his personal supervision. His carts did some of the hauling of materials, and they brought from the ferry the new pulpit. Then the church was painted, inside and out, upon which Mr. Barksdale commented "Never before painted." For the altar, reading resk, and pulpit, Jacob Bond I'On donated a handsome set of velvet hangings, which he asked Mrs. Barksdale to select, relying upon her good taste.

The plain little country church had indeed been transformed, and although the expenses had been heavy, all had been paid for in full out of the church funds.

To Mr. Barksdale's grief, some of the funds of Christ Church, £2,362 in insurance stocks, were lost when a great fire in Charleston on the night of April 27, 1838, destroyed a large part of the city and bankrupted the insurance companies. Money for the relief of sufferers was sent to Charleston from all parts of the nation. The Christ Church vestry applied to the city Council for a share to cover some of the church's loss, but received no reply. This loss made the vestry uneasy about the safety of other investments in stocks, and it was decided to sell 110 shares of bank stock. Fortunately, these shares sold at a premium amounting to $492.50, which offset a small part of the insurance stock loss. Again in August 1839, the vestry unanimously voted thanks to Mr. Barksdale "for his gratuitous Care, attention, improvement, and addition to The Church Funds" which he had nursed so long and successfully.

Enfeebled by the age of almost four score years, Mr. Fowler in the summer of 1839 traveled to the North to regain his health. The following February he attended the Convention as usual and reported: "I am happy . . . to say, the people have treated me with kindness and respect; and I thank God that I have never had any difficulties and contentions to arise among my brethren. I love and respect them." Apparently he had no resentment for the meager support he had received from his chapel and church: "The congregation being few in number, they can do little towards the decent and comfortable support of a Clergyman. We have no parsonage or glebe." He then paid tribute to the dedicated church treasurer: "Thomas Barksdale, Esq. is entitled to the gratitude of the parishioners, for his strict attention to the funds and temporalities of our Church; and it is to be hoped, that at the close of my ministry, a Clergyman will meet with reasonable living, as the funds are accumulating."

The old rector's report in 1842 sadly noted that only a dozen families were left in his congregation, "so many have died or removed from the Parish." During his absence the past summer, "Mr. Elias W. Hort was kind enough to read prayers and sermons in the Chapel." He closed with this announcement: "The first of June next, I expect to leave this Parish, as I can bear the burden of it no longer. I have now served the Church for 60 years, either as a Lay reader, or as a Clergyman; and I never had full support for myself and family but 3 years during that period, which was at Edisto Island."

At the age of eighty-three years, Mr. Fowler decided to return to his native New Haven, Connecticut, and late in May 1842, he requested the vestry to give him a certificate stating the number of years he had served, for it might be of service to him "in obtaining assistance from other Congregations." The vestry graciously certified that he had "been our Minister or Pastor Since the Year 1828; that this venerable and Esteemed Minister of Our Lord Christ Jesus has always been faithful to his Charge and Esteemed by his Congregation."

Jacob Bond I'On, chairman of the vestry, wished to call a vestry meeting to elect a new rector. But Mr. Barksdale wrote him that he "would object to having a Stated Minister this Winter, to keep him on a poor salary, and prevent The Church from having a proper Fund established and give it the means of supporting a Minister (a short time hence) comfortably. . . . the cloud of poverty and indigence has . . . long enough hung over our Church." As all the funds of the church were invested, he added "at present the Church has not a dollar of Cash nor will have any to pay a minister for Twelve months." His concluding sentence was characteristic of Mr. Barksdale. "As regards The Church, my only motive and hearts desire is to see our Church made independent."

So once more Christ Church became dependent upon visiting clergymen, and in the winter of 1842-1843 services were held by the Reverend Messrs. John H. Cornish, Charles P. Elliott, and Robert D. Schindler. But on April 2, 1843, the Rev. Andrew Fowler was back in the pulpit of Christ Church! Perhaps he had found the New England winters too severe, but whatever the reason, he had settled down in Charleston in time to attend the Convention there in February 1843. For the last time he made a report on Christ Church, showing no baptisms, no marriages, and no funerals. He also explained the reasons for his resignation: the Society had withdrawn its aid on the first of June, 1841; and at the close of the winter season, June 1, 1842, the congregation had contributed only $41 to his support; therefore "I was compelled to relinquish my station . . . after having served my cure to the best of my ability for the space of fifteen winters at the Mother church," and thirteen summer seasons at the village, for four of which he received no compensation. His closing sentence gives a surprising reason for his long tenure: "I would not have remained so long in this Parish, had it not been from the persuasion that some of my good friends would accuse me, as they had often done, of being so unstable that I could stay no where."

Mr. Fowler ended his days in Charleston at the age of ninety-one years and six months, and was buried in St. Michael's churchyard.

SIX

TWO CHANCERY SUITS ON BEHALF OF THE
CHAPEL

In the spring of 1843, the cupola which had been erected on Christ Church eight years earlier was taken down and made higher. This was destined to be Mr. Barksdale's last service to his ancestral church. The old members of the vestry with whom he had worked so many years were now dead, and he was in a minority of one, for the former members from the old church had been replaced by men from the village congregation of the chapel: Joseph Maybank, John Hamlin, Robert Venning, William Lucas, and Dr. Robert S. Bailey all dwelt in or very near the village and worshipped at St. Andrew's.

These vestrymen met in Mount Pleasant and elected the Rev. Edward Phillips to take charge of St. Andrew's Chapel for five months, ending November first. When the bill for his services was sent to Mr. Barksdale for payment, he endorsed it: "The Resolution of Paying Mr. Phillips $200 for officiating at another church than the Parish Church . . . being contrary to the Charter [1] . . . and unjust, I will not enter such an abominable Resolution in the Records."

When the vestry met in the village in July, it was agreed that Mr. Phillips should be invited to take charge of the parish church also. Mr. Barksdale did not attend that meeting, but he sent some resolutions which were

[97]

adopted: first, that no vestryman should borrow church funds; second, that no debtor to the church should be elected to the vestry, and "in particular, the Church Treasurer shall not be allowed to borrow any part of The Church Funds."

The following month, when Joseph Maybank, who was "considered a Chairman of the Vestry of the church at Mount Pleasant," sent Thomas Barksdale the title deed for the chapel lot, Mr. Barksdale returned it with a brief letter, saying, "I do not now nor never did consider myself a Vestry man of Mount Pleasant Church. The Title is defective, and when made correct, it had better be recorded."

At the annual election of church officers on Easter Monday 1844, Mr. Barksdale again was unanimously elected to the vestry. But when the vestry met to organize, his posts as secretary and treasurer were given to John Hamlin, who described himself as "of the Village of Mount Pleasant." The new treasurer was instructed to demand of Mr. Barksdale a full settlement of accounts and a transfer of all records, bonds, deeds, books, and other property in his custody as treasurer.

At the same meeting was announced the death of Dr. William Read, former chairman of the vestry, and a lifetime friend and staunch supporter of Mr. Barksdale. Effingham Wagner was elected chairman.

In reply to the demand for transfer of church property in his custody, Mr. Barksdale said that he was unwilling to comply until his own demand against the church for services and commissions was fully satisfied. He had served for twenty-four years as both secretary and treasurer as well as in other ways, and the vestry had made provision for commissions which he had never collected

Now, in a desperate hope of salvaging some of the endowment which he had so diligently nurtured with the hope of making Christ Church independent, he submitted a bill of $4,050! [2]

The vestry countered this surprising move by appointing a committee empowered to employ counsel and to use all legal means to compel compliance from Mr. Barksdale.

In an effort to avoid court action, John Hamlin, chairman of the committee, wrote Mr. Barksdale a long personal letter, in his beautiful handwriting, citing Scripture, especially "the Servant that took his Lord's money and laid it up in a Napkin"—which does not seem exactly applicable to the church servant who had increased the Christ Church funds more than fivefold.

Mr. Barksdale acknowledged the letter as a "Sermon," but, he said, "as I believe it was intended for my instruction and good, I receive it as such; I have read my Bible over and over again, and am acquainted with the . . . Scriptures which you quote." Then, alluding to the distance of six miles between the church and the chapel, he continued, "As regards my wishing to promote the Gospel of our blessed Savior only Six Miles, [the idea] must have originated with yourself, and I will retort . . . if the Parish church funds are to be distributed in Christian Charaty . . . why not extend that Christian Charity over Six Miles across the Water to some of the poor churches in the City . . . (The Village church has no more claim on the Parish church funds than St. Michael or St. Philips church)."

In this Mr. Barksdale was correct, for St. Andrew's Chapel in reality was a mission of Christ Church and should have had its own warden and vestry committee.

But these matters at that time had not been clearly defined, and the vestry which had been elected from the congregation of the chapel was the vestry of Christ Church in name, and the chapel had been accepted by the vestry of Christ Church as the "chapel of ease" of Christ Church, although the Episcopal Church in the United States has never provided for chapels of ease.

Mr. Barksdale's letter to Mr. Hamlin went on to express the hope that an ordained minister might be appointed to begin officiating at the parish church on the first of November. He also suggested that John Richard Fell, a young theological student of Charleston, who had been voluntarily serving as lay reader, should be paid "$125 for his services during the last Winter and Spring (I understand he will not accept anything; if not, I hope the Vestry will have the liberality to make him a present of that amount)." [3] And, he added, "I would bring to view of $100 being paid to The Revd. A. Fowler, the Venerable Pastor of the Parish for Twenty Years; who stands in need of the same; this will be true Christian Charaty."

In a postscript to this long letter, Mr. Barksdale wrote, "I will now conclude with one wish, that I continue in Friendship with you; for I see no cause [that] our differing in church matters should make it otherwise." His later endorsement on his draft of this letter was, "The above proposal relative to Mr. Fell and Mr. Fowler was treated with silence and [I] believe [was] never thought of."

Both Thomas Barksdale and John Hamlin were deeply religious men, and both sincerely desired to do what was right, but never were there two men more wide apart in their thinking.

Oakland Plantation, formerly Youghal

Hobcaw Plantation, about 1912

Mr. Barksdale was planting Youghal, a model plantation which had been in his family for a century, only two miles from the parish church with well-cultivated fields, neat white fences, and white buildings for every possible plantation need. His Negroes were comfortably quartered in a "street" of small houses near his dwelling, and there was a day nursery where the mothers left their children in care of an old woman called a "mauma" when they went to work. There were buildings for the ginhouse, carriage house, stables, and barns. His vegetable garden and his orchard were well kept and prolific. The grounds around his dwelling house were laid out with walks and flower beds, and a magnificent avenue of live oaks led from his house to the public road.

Mr. Hamlin, too, was a slaveholding planter whose ancestors had been among the earliest settlers of the parish, and he operated Seaside, which had formerly been owned by Andrew Hibben, near Mount Pleasant. But he had his own ideas on how to manage his Negroes, and instead of providing food and clothing for them as did his neighbors, he paid each family a weekly allowance of money with which to provide for its own needs. The result was that at best the money was spent wastefully, and at worst it was used for whiskey or gambled away in crap games. His Negroes, therefore, were hungry, ragged, and unable to do good work, and when he punished them for their blunders and "laziness," he acquired the name of being a hard master.[4]

As Mr. Barksdale and Mr. Hamlin could not agree on how church funds should be spent, and Mr. Barksdale retained the bonds until his bill should be paid, the vestry proceeded to bring suit against Mr. Barksdale in the city court of Charleston. This court had no jurisdiction in such a case, and through this error, a term of court was lost before a bill was filed in the court of chancery. By consent of both parties, the court ordered all the bonds and other property of the church to be placed in the custody of a master in chancery. Mr. Barksdale's detailed list of church investments in June 1846, showed a total of $13,987.80, but some of this was in insurance stock of no value.

Mr. Barksdale had been so long identified with Christ Church and its interests that he requested the law firm of Hunt, Petigru, and Memminger "to appear for the Church" of which he still felt that he was champion. But these lawyers had already been retained by the vestry. No longer was he an officer of the church, and the vestry that sued him was officially the vestry "of the Protestant Episcopal Church in Christ Church Parish." After a delay of the two terms of court, the vestry won a decree against Mr. Barksdale that funds of the church could legally be used to pay a minister who held services only in the chapel. He immediately appealed the case to the court of errors, but after some delay, the decree in chancery was upheld, and in 1848 the vestry took over all funds of Christ Church.

Mr. Barksdale in the autumn of that year sadly wrote to J. H. Read of his old association with Dr. William Read, "your Father being one of The Good old Vestry who aided me in rebuilding the Parish Church . . . (which was in ruins) and Increasing The Church Funds from $2000 . . . to $14,000."

Five years later, Mr. Barksdale's goal of a thousand dollars a year income from the church endowment was practically attained, for in August 1853 the revenue from the church investments for the preceding twelve

months was $999.50. He did not live to know this, for
in 1850 both he and Mr. Fowler had departed this life.
Mr. Barksdale's will reflected his deep hurt in the chancery decree against him, for he said that should any of
his property be sold for division, "it is my particular will
and desire that it not be sold by any master or commissioner in Equity and that they have no concern whatever with my estate."

While the chancery suit was in progress, Mr. Fell, the
young lay reader, had been ordained and on December
15, 1844, had taken charge of the parish as missionary.
At the ensuing annual Convention he reported 15 white
communicants and 7 Negro; 54 white non-communicants
and 40 Negro; that the Christmas festival had been celebrated for the first time in many years; and the Sunday
School during the summer at St. Andrew's had as its
"pious Superintendent, Mr. John Hamlin."

The Rev. Pierre Teller Babbitt reported at the Convention of 1846 as missionary for Christ Church and other
parishes. But Mr. Fell still served, and in November
of that year the vestry invited him to assume the rectorship. He married Sarah, daughter of John Hamlin, and
settled in Mount Pleasant for the remainder of his life.

Mr. Fell was deeply interested in his work among the
Negroes of the parish. In his report to the Convention
of 1848 he said, "The Vestry have displayed a feeling
of interest in the religious welfare of the negroes, by ap-
propriating to their use certain pews in the Church. Previously, the only accommodation for them consisted of
a few benches in the [a]isles, and the dimensions of the
edifice being small but a very limited number were able
to gain admittance." When the church was closed during
the summer months, and "the Rector was removed from

this portion of his flock, he still ministered to them by holding occasional services on Sunday in the country." At Mr. Fell's request, Bishop Gadsden in 1848 appointed Edwin A. Wagner as lay reader to help with the religious instruction of the Negroes. There were two drawbacks to the work, however, mentioned by Mr. Fell; first, the Negroes' preference for other denominations; and second, the fact that no chapels had been built for them.

The vestry at a meeting in May 1848 decided upon "sundry alterations of the Parish Church" interior arrangement, but what they were is not revealed. Apparently nothing was done, for in his report to the Convention in 1851, Mr. Fell said that the vestrymen at their own expense and with aid from the congregation had determined to make changes in the interior arrangements of the parish church. He also mentioned the gift from Miss M. R. Simons of a Bible and prayer book for desk service as a Christmas offering.

In the summer of 1855 the congregation of the chapel petitioned the vestry to appropriate funds from the Christ Church endowment for the erection of a new and larger chapel in Mount Pleasant. Some members of the vestry doubted that such use of the endowment would be legal, so the matter was referred to Henry D. Lesesne, an able lawyer of Charleston. He gave his opinion that under the church charter, the vestry was not authorized to use any funds of Christ Church for erecting a chapel. At an adjourned meeting of the vestry in September, Mr. Lesesne's opinion was read, and the vestry unanimously agreed that it was not legally authorized to use any of the church funds for building a new chapel.

The promoters of a new chapel, however, were not satisfied, and at a meeting of the vestry at the church in

December, the matter was reconsidered. An opinion from James Louis Petigru was read, in which a distinction was drawn between funds derived from the legacy of Mrs. Elizabeth Fleming and funds from other sources. The funds from the legacy, he said, were exclusively for the use of Christ Church; other funds could be used at the vestry's discretion. Mr. John Hamlin then offered four resolutions: first, that it was the duty of the vestry to erect a larger chapel; second, that the vestry appoint a building committee to get plans and estimates; third, that the vestry appoint a committee to solicit subscriptions; fourth, that if subscriptions proved to be insufficient, then the vestry should draw on the treasurer for the balance necessary to complete the new chapel. After some discussion, these were adopted.

To quiet all doubts as to the legality of these proceedings, the vestry unanimously approved the motion of George F. Kinloch that a suit be instituted by Henry D. Lesesne on behalf of the "doubting members" to restrain the vestry from using church funds for a new chapel in Mount Pleasant.

Mr. Lesesne accordingly filed in the chancery court of Charleston District a bill against the vestry and wardens of the Episcopal Church in the Parish of Christ Church. A paragraph of the bill set forth that since the time that the old chapel was built:

> Mount Pleasant has undergone a great change. In place of being a small isolated Village, with a few straggling houses, the summer resort of the neighboring farmers, it is now intimately connected with the City of Charleston, by a Steam Boat Ferry; handsome dwellings have sprung up, a fine Hotel, and Shops and Factories have been established, it is

an incorporated town with its municipal government, and from its salubrious climate and other advantages, has attracted to it a population of considerable size and wealth. That with the exception of two . . ., all the members of the Vestry reside there during the summer, and one of the members has sold his property in the Country and resides there all the year. That the Church chapel is an humble building not in keeping with the present flourishing condition of the town and moreover is too small for the accommodation of the Episcopal Inhabitants. And instead of building one to suit their views, with their own means, they have applied to the Vestry to use the funds of the Parish Church for that purpose.

On June 25, 1856, Chancellor George W. Dargan handed down his decree, which closed with:

It is evident that the building of a Church or Chapel in the Town of Mount Pleasant, is not one of the objects for which this Vestry may use their fund, as those objects have been explained above. It is therefore ordered that the Defendants, The Vestry and Church Wardens of the Episcopal Church in the Parish of Christ Church, be perpetually enjoined from using the fund in their hands, or any part thereof, for or towards the building of a Church or Chapel in the town of Mount Pleasant. Costs to be paid by the Defendants.[5]

The Rev. Mr. Fell was deeply interested in everything connected with these matters, but from early June until late September he had been unable to perform his parochial duties, partly because of "severe affliction" in his family, and partly by his absence at the North for his own health. During these months, the Rev. David McElheran officiated in the chapel. Born in Liverpool in 1801, he had commanded vessels sailing between England and the East Indies until he came to America and entered the ministry. He was ordained deacon by Bishop Bowen in 1831, and two years later to the priesthood in St. Philip's. He then became rector of St. Helena's on St. Helena Island until he retired in 1856 and came to live in Mount Pleasant. There he bought a house and lot from John Hamlin on part of his bucket factory property on Factory Street, which has recently been renamed Live Oak Drive.

After Mr. Fell's return home, Mr. McElheran continued to hold services every Sunday morning during the winter at the chapel in Mount Pleasant, and thus Mr. Fell had more time to instruct the Negroes when he held services at the parish church. Mr. Fell noted in his report that a pious lady of Mr. McElheran's household, aided by several young persons, gave instruction to both white and colored children in Mount Pleasant.

Although Chancellor Dargan's decree had forever prohibited the use of any funds of Christ Church for the erection of a chapel in Mount Pleasant, John Hamlin and the vestrymen who agreed with him were not deterred, and they appealed to the court of appeals, chancery, which, in January 1857, decreed that the vestry did have the right so to apply the endowment of Christ Church.

At a meeting in March 1857, the vestry rescinded its resolution of 1833, which forbade the use of church funds for the chapel. Plans for the new chapel drawn by Edward Brickell White, a distinguished architect of Charleston, were accepted, and the contract for its construction was given to James M. Curtis, whose bid of $4,500 was below that of P. M. Hamlin by $2,000. The building committee was authorized to employ an architect to supervise the construction. Some changes in specifications were found to be advantageous, and when the new chapel was completed in December 1857, the total cost had reached about $5,700. Mr. Curtis received an extra $270.

On Christmas Day 1857, services were conducted for the first time in the new St. Andrew's Chapel. But strange to say, neither the rector nor the vestry had been consulted or had given consent. Deeply hurt, the Rev. Mr. Fell immediately submitted his letter of resignation. The vestry, however, mended matters by sending him copies of a series of resolutions which had been approved in a meeting on January 5, 1858:

1 That we disapprove of the action referred to . . .
2 That we deeply sympathize with the Rev. Mr. Fell (Our Rector) in the trying and painful position in which he is placed, and that he still has our Warm attachment and unabated confidence.
3 That the Chairman be requested to furnish Mr. Fell with a copy of these resolutions; and at the same time express to him our anxious desire that he withdraw his letter of resignation.

At the same meeting the vestry considered a petition of St. Andrew's congregation that permanent provision be made for regular services at the chapel during the winter months, and the rector was requested to invite Mr. McElheran to continue officiating at the chapel during Mr. Fell's impending absence, trusting that financial arrangements might be made before long. Later, Mr. McElheran was elected as assistant minister in charge of the chapel services, the vestry assuring him that the amount of labor to be performed would be entirely at his discretion, for like Mr. Fell, Mr. McElheran was in frail health.

Early in April 1858, the vestry held an evening meeting at the Council Chamber in Mount Pleasant and granted the petition of the congregation of the chapel that a poll be opened in the village as well as at the parish church for the Easter Monday election of officers, allowing qualified persons who were not able to vote in person to vote by proxy.

The annual report of the treasurer was read, showing the total endowment remaining to Christ Church as $9,258.39, yielding an income of $660.93. This was far from enough to pay two ministers, but it was hoped that sales and rentals of pews in the new chapel would make up the deficiency.

When the second St. Andrew's Chapel was consecrated by Bishop Davis on May 11, 1858, the Rev. Mr. Fell was absent, for once more he had sought a restoration of health by traveling to the North. He and Mr. McElheran despite their handicaps continued to serve the church and the chapel as long as they were able.

The first St. Andrew's Chapel was sold to the Masons of Mount Pleasant and is still the headquarters of Etiwan Lodge.

SEVEN

CATASTROPHES AND ABANDONMENT

The coming of the steam ferry, the resultant growth of the village of Mount Pleasant, and the erection of the second St. Andrew's Chapel were not the only changes in the parish since the days of Thomas Barksdale and the vestry that had worked with him for the endowment of Christ Church. Indeed, Mr. Barksdale's own plantation, Youghal, was now owned by a stranger and had a new name, for in January 1859, his son-in-law, James Macbeth, having renamed it Oakland, sold it to Philip Edward Porcher of St. Stephen's Parish. At the Easter Monday election in 1860, Mr. Porcher was elected a vestryman of Christ Church.

Another change was that vestry meetings ceased to be held at Christ Church, and in the minutes St. Andrew's Chapel was usually referred to as "the church."

But the great changes came in the events which soon engulfed the entire South in the tragic War of Secession, bringing death, destruction, and actual hunger to its people.

The Rev. Mr. Fell had not regained his health, and in April 1860 the vestry gave him leave of absence and raised $100 to help defray his traveling expenses, but in July he sent a letter of resignation which was regretfully accepted. In January 1861, the vestry not having been able to fill the vacancy, he resumed volunteer services at Christ Church and continued his work among the Negroes.

He felt encouraged in officiating at the church because of the attendance of a company of Confederate soldiers from Sumter District who were encamped nearby. The following winter he had to discontinue these services for want of a horse. Mr. McElheran continued to serve the chapel every Sunday, with an occasional service from Mr. Fell, until most of the villagers fled from the federal bombardment and took refuge in the upper part of the state. His report to the Dioscesan Convention at Spartanburg in May 1864, noted that St. Andrew's Chapel had been closed for regular services on the first of October 1863.

An address of Bishop Davis has recorded that on January 29, 1865, at Mount Pleasant, he "preached in the forenoon and confirmed two white persons, one of them belonging to the Marion Artillery. In the afternoon I rode over to Sullivan's Island in an ambulance, and was present at a service in Major Blanding's quarters, a gratifying number of troops" attending.

Mount Pleasant was not damaged by the guns of the enemy, and Christ Church was completely out of range.[1] But Grace Church on Sullivans Island fell an early victim to the federal bombardment, and when the Union soldiers established batteries on Morris Island, cannon balls riddled the roof and floor, setting fire to the woodwork. The brick walls stood for some years, but the church was never rebuilt.

After the bloody fighting ended, General Daniel E. Sickles, in September 1865, was placed in charge of conquered South Carolina. Ferdinand Gregorie, intendant of Mount Pleasant and warden of Christ Church, had to "surrender" the village to the General, who made his headquarters in Charleston. Negro troops were stationed in Christ Church Parish, supposedly to keep order. A company of Negro cavalry used Christ Church as a stable, and the church was wrecked. Doors, windows, pews, and pulpit were burned in camp fires; and it is said that the tablets of the Lord's prayer and the ten commandments on the walls beside the chancel were torn down and were seen by a horrified parishioner as part of a pig sty.

The four walls and a roof were all that remained of Christ Church. Open to stray cattle, owls, and bats, the ruins became a favorite haunt of a harmless lunatic from Mount Pleasant, who frequented the place, endlessly muttering to himself, "A million a minute! A million a minute!"

In January 1866 two white families [2] returned to their plantation homes in the parish, but in the chaotic conditions of the time, they were regarded by their friends as foolhardy, for ruin was on every side, and most of the planters preferred to remain in their summer homes in Mount Pleasant.

St. Andrew's Chapel was reopened in February 1866, with the young Rev. Thomas F. Gadsden as deacon in charge. In May of the following year, he reported at the Convention that the chapel was the only place of public worship then open in the village, and hence there was a large number of irregular attendants at his services. At the Easter Monday election of church officers in April 1867, Dr. Edward M. Royall, a devout Baptist, was elected a vestryman.

Early in the year, a Negro minister applied to Mr. Gadsden for the loan of Christ Church, but the vestry agreed that such a loan would be inexpedient.

The vestry was now anxiously attempting to salvage something from the Christ Church endowment, of which

$4,000 had been invested in Confederate stock and bonds. The remainder was in bank shares, City of Charleston six per cent "stock," some bonds from individuals, and a bond from Etiwan Masonic Lodge, $333.33, for the purchase of the first St. Andrew's Chapel as lodge headquarters. The actual value was very little.

In St. Andrew's Chapel on Thursday morning, January 23, 1868, Mr. Gadsden was ordained to the order of priest by Bishop Davis, and shortly after, he became rector. Assisted by Mr. Fell when health permitted, Mr. Gadsden diligently continued his work among the freedmen, holding services on the plantations and teaching their children in Sunday Schools.

Mr. Fell died on September 20, 1868, in the fifty-first year of his age, having served, like Mr. Fowler, a rectorate of fourteen years and several more as a volunteer. He was buried in Christ Church cemetery by the side of his children who had preceded him, midway of the south wall of the church.

In January 1869, the vestry notified Mr. Gadsden that "the impoverished condition of the Parish and the low state of the funds of the church" rendered it impossible to support a rector, and he reluctantly accepted a dissolution of that relationship, promising to state the need of the parish to the Bishop "in hopes he may include it in Missionary arrangement." He also generously cancelled the debt for salary owing to him and offered to hold services as long as he continued to reside in Mount Pleasant, saying he considered himself "sufficiently compensated by the kindness of the congregation."

When the news of Mr. Gadsden's release became known, William H. Johnson, principal of the Mount Pleasant Academy, carried around a subscription list and raised $439 in pledges. As the interest from the endowment bonds would amount to $139, the vestry decided to offer Mr. Gadsden $500 a year, to be paid semi-annually; and, as he had been asked to be missionary at St. James', Santee, he would be allowed to officiate there one Sunday a month. Mr. Gadsden accepted this offer and made arrangements to spend one week in each month at his new charge.

He also arranged for lay readings in each parish on the Sunday when he should be absent. In St. James' Parish he officiated at the "River settlement" in the winter, and at McClellanville in the summer. His report on his first year says of this work, "The people, still clinging tenaciously to the Church of their fathers, welcomed even with tears of gratitude the restoration of religious services, of which they had been deprived for about ten years."

Mr. Gadsden gave new proof of his devotion to his first charge when, in April 1859, he offered to transfer to Christ Church as a parsonage a house which had been bought in his name from Dr. J. E. Dawson, chairman of the vestry. This house, on a high brick basement, had four stories, including the ground floor and attic, with two rooms on each floor, and stood on a large lot at Amen Corner, the junction of Bennett and Morrison streets in Mount Pleasant. Mr. Gadsden offered to pay $900 [3] (of which $130 had been borrowed and must be repaid), as the first installment on the purchase price of $1800, the remainder to be paid by the vestry in one year with interest. His generous offer was gratefully accepted. Eventually, the vestry paid the remaining debt in 1872 by selling the City and Bank securities from the endowment of Christ Church, and the Dawson house became the parsonage of

Christ Church until it was accidentally burned in the next century.

The darkest days of Reconstruction were now in progress. Federal troops still occupied South Carolina, and poverty was the general lot of its people. So poor were the members of Mr. Gadsden's congregation that the vestry in 1870 informed him that a salary of $400 a year, and the parsonage rent free, was "the utmost that the Vestry could do this year." In the autumn the vestry went further and requested him to discontinue the ancient practice of collecting alms from the whole congregation on Communion Sundays. Three years later the good rector's annual salary was reduced to $300, and all too frequently even this meagre stipend was not paid promptly. As he said of his flock, "There is here a nucleus of Episcopal families which is the steadfast element of the Parish. But our work is largely that of a Missionary in Mount Pleasant, . . . preaching the Gospel to the poor."

Mr. Gadsden suffered illness and sorrow as well as poverty. When his little son died and was buried near the chancel of St. Andrew's Chapel, the vestry voted that a plot fifteen feet square should be reserved for the rector's family, provided the town authorities gave permission. The vestry also gave him a leave of absence "without any diminution of his salary." He noted in his report to the Convention in 1872 his travel expenses of $80.95.

Apparently through negligence, as well as poverty, taxes were not paid on the parsonage,[4] and the vestry requested the ladies of the congregation to give an "Entertainment" to raise money to rescue it, and the rector to take up two collections for the same purpose.

At some time during these years of gloom, the vestry house at Christ Church was burned, ignited probably from a woods fire. Only the chimney and the crumbling walls remained, and gradually many of the loose bricks found a place in the chimneys of neighboring cabins.

Meanwhile, the plantation families sadly missed the services in Christ Church. As Mr. Gadsden noted, "Our Parishioners in the country have long cherished the desire of having the old Parish church restored and reopened for Divine Worship." In August 1873, the vestry appointed a committee to report what was needed, and agreed that Mr. Gadsden should take up a collection on one Sunday in the month to be appropriated to the repairs.

After service on March 8, 1874, a meeting of the congregation was held in the chapel to consider further means of raising the necessary funds. At the ensuing vestry meeting, George F. Kinloch, L. A. McCants, and Philip G. Porcher were named as a committee to attend to the work. On motion of Edward O. Hall, it was agreed that whatever money should be collected was to be used as far as it would go, but first for repairing the doors and windows. The roof also needed work, and it was planned to put in a wooden floor, the old tile floor having been destroyed. Not less than $500 was estimated for all the work, inside and out. In the fall, it was hoped, a few pews might be put in and the church reopened for the ten families who would worship there. The Ladies' Sewing Society contributed $28.65, and the congregation of St. James, Santee, donated $10.00, but apparently no record remains of the other contributions.

On the Sunday after Christmas, December 27, 1874, for the first time in its long history, Christ Church was consecrated by Bishop William Bell White Howe, "for

SEASIDE PLANTATION

Courtesy of Mr. and Mrs. J. C. Long

CHRIST CHURCH, 1961
Rear view showing new additions

the sole use of the Episcopal Congregation . . . to be by them separated henceforth from all unhallowed, ordinary, and Common uses, and dedicated to the service of Almighty God, for reading and preaching His Holy Word, for Celebrating His Holy Sacraments, for offering to His Glorious Majesty the sacrifice of prayer and thanksgiving, for blessing His people in His Name, and for the performance of all other Holy Offices."

Three years later the vestry received $400 from the trustees of a fund bequeathed by Thomas C. Moore of Plainfield, New Jersey, for southern churches which had been damaged during the late war. After a survey of the further needs of the church and of the chapel, $187 was allocated for the church and $208 for the chapel. Ferdinand Gregorie, a member of the vestry, was given the contract for the entire work on the church.[5] The chapel had not been injured during the war, but in the twenty years since its erection, it had become shabby and needed paint, new steps, and complete repairs to the side porch which served as a belfry.

At the Dioscesan Convention in 1876 Mr. Gadsden noted in his report the death on July 17, 1876, of the Rev. David McElheran, who, despite the infirmities of ill health, had for so long gratuitously served St. Andrew's Chapel. He was buried in the cemetery of Christ Church very near the chancel. To the end of his days he had kept around him mementoes of his youthful voyages to the far east.[6]

"The re-opening of Christ Church," Mr. Gadsden's report continued, "has been a real comfort to the families in the country." As transportation was then very difficult for the planters, he sometimes held services for them in private homes, as well as in the two churches and two chapels of his two parishes. "During the trying years since the war," he went on, "our people have, in many cases, borne their troubles well. They have done what they could."

The year 1876 was destined to show what the people of South Carolina could do, for the Red Shirt campaign that year restored the government of the state to its citizens, and on April 10, 1877, federal troops were finally withdrawn—twelve long years after the surrender of Lee at Appomattox!

Because of the poor health of himself and his family that memorable summer, Mr. Gadsden had leave of absence in July and August; and in September he submitted his resignation, not to be effective until November. This was a painful blow to his congregation, and the vestry unanimously adopted a preamble and four resolutions expressing the general sorrow in the loss of "a Guide we may never replace."

On November 1, 1877, Mr. Gadsden took leave of his congregation which he had served so well and went to continue his ministerial labors at Grace Church, Anderson.[7]

His successor, the Rev. George Waldo Stickney, took charge of Christ Church Parish in January 1878, not as the rector but as a missionary. He had come into the diocese in 1874 and had served briefly on Edisto Island, in Marion, and at Florence.

After years of discussion, the vestry now finally foreclosed the mortgage on a house in Mount Pleasant which a former vestryman had given as security for a loan of $1,000 from the Christ Church endowment. The cash received from sale of the house "was all consumed in the expenses of the suit except $20.50," which was used by the vestry for incidental expenses. The credit proceeds of the sale consisted of two 7 per cent notes for $175 each, secured by a new mortgage on the property. This was all that remained of the endowment [8] which Thomas Barksdale had so painstakingly accumulated for Christ Church.

As the successor of the greatly beloved Mr. Gadsden, Mr. Stickney was at some disadvantage, especially when he tried to introduce innovations. Early in his ministry, the vestry instructed the secretary to inform him "that the trinity decorations and symbol in the Chancel are not in accordance with the views of the Vestry and Congregation; and to request him to have them removed." At the next meeting, it was agreed to inform him that the vestry would be unable to recall him at the expiration of his current engagement. He then offered to give one service a month from the first of October in return for the offering of that day, the use of the rectory, and the appropriation from the Board of Missions. The vestry accepted with the proviso that the agreement should terminate on January 1, 1879.

A committee was then named to solicit pledges and to ascertain the wishes of the congregation in regard to electing Mr. Stickney for another year. Only $50 was pledged, and the congregation was divided in opinion. It was then agreed that Mr. Stickney should be invited to officiate two Sundays a month for the first six months of 1879.

Early in that year the vestry consulted with the vestry of St. Thomas and St. Dennis on a plan to bring back Mr. Gadsden to serve the two parishes, but this failed, and Mr. Stickney was invited to continue on a month-to-month tenure.

In the spring of 1880, Mr. Stickney asked the vestry for an increase of salary and also to be termed "Rector." In reply, he was notified that after May 16 his services would no longer be required. The following week the vestry requested Mr. Gadsden to "renew his rectorship of our Church." But Mr. Gadsden declined.

At the Convention in 1880, Mr. Stickney reported that he had conducted services in the parish church "with greater regularity and satisfaction on one Sunday [in each month?] during the Winter," and that the interior of Christ Church had been improved in comfort and propriety. In addition, he had assisted in services outside of the parish forty-one times, for which he received $99.25.

In the autumn the vestry arranged with the vestry of St. Thomas and St. Dennis to have the services of the rector, the Rev. Robert F. Clute, as missionary for one Sunday each month. He alternated with Mr. Stickney, however, who officiated April to July, and Mr. Clute, January to April, and October to January. The next year, Mr. Clute reported at the Convention, "The people are poor and cannot give much. The resident churchmen attend well." He continued to serve as missionary in the parish until, in April 1883, the Rev. J. Mercier Green became rector on a part-time basis.

Mr. Green had been ordained deacon by Bishop Davis in 1857 at the Church of the Cross, Bluffton. During the war years he helped to keep open the churches of Charleston and assisted in Cheraw. He was rector of St. John's, Charleston, from 1878 until he resigned in 1880 to become superintendent of the city public schools. Later he took charge of St. John's, Florence.

As rector of Christ Church Parish, he officiated two Sundays a month and whenever there was a fifth Sunday.

As minister of the John's Island church, he officiated there two Sundays a month. During the winter, he held one service a month at Christ Church. St. Andrew's Chapel was open every Sunday, for when Mr. Green was absent the lay reader, A. T. Broughton, supplied.

Mr. Green entered upon his duties as rector on May 13, 1883, and in July he attended the first meeting of the vestry which had been elected the preceding Easter Monday. The reason for his presence is not revealed in the minutes, but it should be noted that this was the first time a rector of Christ Church had met with the vestry since the disestablishment of the Church of England more than a hundred years ago. At this meeting Warden Edward O. Hall was elected chairman and treasurer, and Theodore S. Gaillard, secretary.

Mr. Green resided in Mount Pleasant until the following November, when he removed to Charleston to be in easy reach of both his churches.

At the Convention in 1884, Mr. Green reported that there were seventy-five communicants in his two parishes. "This last year," he continued, "has been a hard one on the planters, but its losses and discouragements have not abated the interest which is manifest in the church." Attendance at Christ Church during the winter monthly services was very good, considering the sparseness of the population: "The few, however, residing in the immediate vicinity, take a deep interest in the church, and as many at Mt. Pleasant as can obtain vehicles come out to the services." Also, through the exertions of Mrs. Philip Edward Porcher, of Oakland plantation, and the Ladies' Sewing Society of her neighborhood, "a handsome white marble font has been purchased and placed in the chancel of the Parish Church."

The next year, the unfortunate planters suffered the loss of their crops when the area was devastated by the tropical hurricane of August 25, 1885. One year later, a new disaster struck terror and despair when a series of earthquakes began on August 31, 1886, and demolished much of the city of Charleston. Christ Church, the chapel, and the rectory suffered some damage. Relief donations came from far and wide, and Bishop Howe awarded to the vestry of Christ Church $500 from this earthquake fund for repairs.

At some time during these years of disaster, the monthly winter services at Christ Church ceased. No mention of this appears upon the minutes of the vestry nor upon the annual reports of the Rev. Mr. Green to the Dioscesan Convention, but on February 16, 1886, the vestry agreed that "the Melodeon now in the Church be loaned to Miss May Ferguson until it be needed by the Church." Miss Ferguson was the organist at the chapel, and the removal of the melodeon ⁹ would seem to indicate that services at the church had been discontinued.

This year also saw the beginning of a new Episcopal church on Sullivans Island, when William G. Mazyck as lay leader began to hold services in the Presbyterian Church. Six years later, a beautiful granite church was completed, which was consecrated on September 12, 1895, as the Chapel of the Holy Cross. Eventually, this lovely building was sold to the federal government, and in June 1907 the cornerstone of the present Holy Cross was laid on another site nearer the eastern end of the island.

The last mention of services at Christ Church was in the Rev. Mr. Green's report to the Convention in 1884. Whatever may have been the date when they ceased, he was the last rector to officiate there with any regularity for about thirty years. During the years of abandonment the public road gradually encroached upon the churchyard, and George Haddrell's tombstone at the northwest corner of the church was destroyed by traffic. Even the corner of the church was battered by passing vehicles and defaced.

Mr. Green resigned, effective in October 1890, but continued his work on Johns Island. There only five years later he suffered a stroke in the pulpit and died the same day.

Once more the thoughts of the Christ Church vestry turned to the beloved Rev. Thomas F. Gadsden, and the chairman was requested to endeavor to secure him for two services a month. But this proved to be impossible, and in October 1891, the Rev. Phineas Duryea, rector of St. James, Santee, accepted as rector, to officiate at St. Andrew's Chapel two Sundays a month. On the Sundays when the rector was in McClellanville, Mr. E. O. Hall kept St. Andrew's open as lay reader. Mr. Duryea resigned in September 1892, and was succeeded briefly by the Rev. Herbert Munson Jarvis, who had recently come into the Diocese. In August 1893, the vestry requested his resignation.

On the last Sunday in that month, August 27, 1893, the parish was again devastated by a tropical hurricane and a tidal wave which destroyed both life and property.

The parish was without a rector after Mr. Jarvis' release until December 2, 1894, when, in conjunction with St. John's, Berkeley, the Rev. Jacob Schantz Hartzell took charge, to give two services a month at the chapel.

Mr. Hartzell was a native of Allentown, Pennsylvania, and had been graduated from the Philadelphia Divinity School. After serving churches in New Jersey and Pennsylvania, he had assisted the rector of Holy Comforter in

Sumter for some four years before coming to Mount Pleasant. He proved to be not only a diligent rector but also a writer and editor of religious publications.[10]

Soon after his arrival, an interesting change took place in the organization of the vestry. At the meeting on April 19, 1895, a chairman and a secretary-treasurer were elected as usual and other business was transacted: "The Matter of the Rector presiding at the Vestry Meetings was then brought up, and after those portions of the Cannons of the Church touching upon the Subject were read . . . it was decided to request Our Rector to be present and preside at the Vestry Meetings Whenever it was convenient for him to do so." In May the time for the regular monthly meeting was changed from the second to the third Sunday so that the rector might be present. Mr. Hartzell was married to Miss Gertrude Waddell of Cheraw in June, and he did not appear at the vestry meeting until August. Later, he served also as secretary.

After seven years of faithful service, Mr. Hartzell, having received an offer at a material increase in salary and in a more favorable climate, submitted his resignation, effective immediately. On April 14, 1901, it was accepted. But both he and his wife were held in high regard by his congregation, and on May 5 the vestry reconsidered and decided against releasing him. More than a year later his second letter of resignation was read and "received as information." But in September 1902 it was reluctantly accepted, and resolutions of regret were unanimously adopted.

At a meeting of the chapel's congregation it was decided to call the Rev. William E. Callender, and on April 8, 1903, he was officially welcomed at his first meeting with the vestry. In July the next year it was agreed that he should accept a call from Johns Island church to officiate there two Sundays a month and reside at Rockville. In June 1905, his resignation was accepted with regret. Four years later he was transferred to another diocese.

During the intervening years before another rector was secured, the chapel had occasional services from the Rev. Mr. Wood of Charleston.

In November 1905, the vestry became deeply concerned over the prospect of obtaining reimbursement from the United States for the damages inflicted upon Christ Church when it was occupied by Negro troops just after the War of Secession. The matter was placed in the hands of W. St. Julien Jervey, a Charleston attorney who represented a law firm in Washington. The lawyers' fee was to be one-third of whatever sum might be collected, and nothing if not successful. A committee of the vestry located some twenty persons whose affidavits would be valuable in establishing the claim, and the lawyers were to send a man to obtain the affidavits. Philip G. Porcher, one of the vestrymen, paid the expenses of a trip to Washington by Mr. Jervey; and a claim for about $2,000 was submitted.

On the morning of Saturday, August 3, 1907, the tall rectory at Amen Corner, which had been secured through the generosity of the Rev. Mr. Gadsden, caught fire and was burned to the ground. The insurance amounted to $1,500, so the vestry immediately appointed a building committee to make plans for erecting a bungalow on the rear of the rectory lot. The only bid received was for $2,218.75, and it was accepted.

On March 1, 1908, the Rev. Charles William Boyd was called to the parish, and in May he presided at a meeting of the congregation. The financial statement presented at this meeting showed a thousand dollars debt upon the rectory. For this reason, the vestry applied to the Secretary of State, Columbia, for an amendment to the church charter to enable the vestry to borrow.

Mr. Boyd was reputed to be "a deep thinker," and "noted for his fine sermons." [11] When he decided to leave, his resignation, effective December 1, 1909, was accepted with "profound regret."

On recommendation of Bishop Guerry, the vestry issued a call to the Rev. James William Sparks, then at St. Helena's, Beaufort, offering him $600 a year and the new rectory, with the request that he should "preach two whole Sundays in each month" and, if possible, give the chapel a service every Sunday. Mr. Sparks accepted.

Born in Wales, educated and ordained in Great Britain, Mr. Sparks was a typical English cleric and made some good friends in his congregation. But when the hot days of summer came, his family declared that the new rectory was too warm for human endurance and refused to live in it. One thing led to another, and eventually Mr. Sparks was transferred to Cainhoy.

The next rector, the Rev. Dr. Percival Hanahan Whaley, a scholarly man, came on April 15, 1912, from Trinity, Edisto Island. Earlier he had had large congregations in Connecticut and Florida. A native of Edisto Island, where he was born May 17, 1853, he proved to be congenial with the members of his new charge and immediately won their affection. Having a deep interest in history, he made a search for the old records of Christ Church, the location of which had been unknown for some time. His efforts were rewarded, and he found the oldest records on the floor under a cabinet at the chapel. At his suggestion, the vestry bought a safe in which to keep them.

EIGHT

A WOMAN'S CONGREGATION AND CHURCH BENEFACTIONS

During the decades that Christ Church was without regular services, a potential congregation was being held together by Mrs. Philip Edward Porcher of Oakland plantation. This godly woman had grown up at Ballsdam, an isolated plantation in St. Stephen's Parish, where it was difficult and often impossible to enjoy services at the parish church on Sundays. In her father's home, family worship was customary. When she married a planter, she continued having family prayers every evening and always read to her children on Sundays. During the war years, when her husband was in the Confederate army, she and the children lived with her father at Ballsdam. When the family returned to Oakland in 1866, Christ Church was a ruin. With only one mule on the plantation, it was impossible to attend Mr. Gadsden's services at the chapel. So she read for her family and friends the prayers for morning service from the prayer book, including the *Te Deum* and the proper psalms for the day and the first and second lessons from the Bible. The children were taught the catechism. After Christ Church was repaired and opened for monthly winter services in 1874, she continued her home readings on the Sundays when there were no services at the church.

As an experiment in 1876 she persuaded her husband to build a log house at Porcher's Bluff on his plantation, to spend the summer there instead of removing to Mount Pleasant. The family enjoyed as good health there as in Mount Pleasant, and thenceforth the summers were spent at Porcher's Bluff. Her son built his house there, and Mrs. Porcher's little congregation then included her grandchildren. To attend services at that season in Mount Pleasant was impossible, as the nine miles of road was a deep sand bed which the farm animals could take only at a walk.

When her son-in-law, Ferdinand Gregorie,[1] rented Oakland in 1894 to plant and his family came to live there, Mrs. Porcher was enabled to add the singing of hymns to her Sunday readings. Later, when the Elias Whilden family came to an adjoining plantation, the little congregation further grew. In 1906, the Isaac Auld family came to join the group. Eventually, Mrs. Porcher's great-grandchildren were among the family and neighbors at her services. When a Presbyterian friend gave her a subscription to *The Christian Herald*, she added to her readings the interesting sermons of the Rev. Dr. Talmadge. During the summer months her services were held at Porcher's Bluff and in the other months at Oakland.

Christ Church, however, was not forgotten, and sometimes an annual service by the Bishop or the rector from Mount Pleasant was held there in the autumn. Then Mrs. Porcher, her daughters, and grandchildren, armed with brooms, rakes, and hoes, would repair to the church and make it ready for the service. A litany service there by Bishop Capers is one of the most vivid early memories of this writer.

Dr. Whaley was deeply impressed by Mrs. Porcher's work, and he asked her to write an account of it to be used in the history of the diocese, which he, as the official historiographer, planned to write. She was too modest, however, to comply.[2]

After more than fifty years of her services, she grew old and feeble, but her work was not lost, for Dr. Whaley arranged to hold regular services at Porcher's Bluff on the afternoons of the first and third Sundays from June 1 through October; and during the other months he held a monthly morning service at Christ Church. He also made a great effort to induce the St. Andrew's congregation to attend the services at Christ Church, and the Christ Church congregation to attend the services at St. Andrew's, but this met with little success.

At Porcher's Bluff, Mr. Isaac Auld, a devout Presbyterian, was now in charge of the Sunday School.

Meanwhile, because of leaks before the tin roof was installed on the church, the plastering had become unsafe. With enthusiasm the Porcher's Bluff congregation undertook the repairs, and Dr. Whaley said he would approach the Bishop for help. Also, under President Wilson's Democratic administration, there was now some prospect that the long pending claim for war damages might be paid.

When the plastered ceiling was removed, a most interesting system of beams, braces, and trusses was revealed, and a member of the congregation suggested that these should remain uncovered. But the suggestion met with no favor, and a ceiling of pine boards was installed by a ship carpenter. When the repairs were completed, the congregation bought a small organ. Dr. Whaley reopened the church with a beautiful service and delivered an historical sermon compiled from the church records. His Easter letter in 1915 closed with the words, "The love of my parishioners is my greatest blessing." He had indeed won their love.

As expected, the claim for war damages to Christ Church was finally settled, and at the vestry meeting in Mount Pleasant on August 15, 1915, Warden William J. Edmonston announced that he had in his possession a check from Washington for $1,160.60, payable to the wardens and vestrymen. The vestry agreed that $500 should be used to pay half the mortgage on the rectory and that outstanding debts contracted for the operation of the chapel should be settled. Only $60 was allocated to Christ Church for repairs. A committee was then appointed to get prices for the erection of a fence around the cemetery of Christ Church.

These decisions were deeply disappointing to the congregation of Christ Church, who had assumed that since the damages had been suffered by that church, the money would be used for its benefit. Members of that congregation therefore drew up and unanimously signed a petition to the vestry asking for a separation from St. Andrew's Chapel. Bishop Guerry met at the church with the congregation and heard the reasons for desiring the separation. He then met with the vestry and found that the majority of its members were unalterably opposed to a separation. Without their consent and a formal request from the "Vestry of Christ Church," a separation was canonically impossible.

The Bishop, however, worked out an agreement that the congregation of Christ Church should elect three members of the vestry, that Christ Church should contribute annually $203 to the support of the rector, and that one morning service and one afternoon service should be held each month at the parish church. Except for changes in the amount of money to be paid by Christ

Church, this agreement remained in effect for thirty-nine years.[3]

To the grief of both congregations, Dr. Whaley died unexpectedly on September 2, 1915.

The Sunday School at Porcher's Bluff was transferred to Christ Church on September 25, 1915, Mr. Auld remaining in charge. Mrs. Auld played the organ and taught the infant class.

In October the vestry issued a call to the Rev. Sanders R. Guignard, a native of Columbia, then in charge of St. John's, Florence.

Mr. Guignard and his family arrived early in 1916, and he presided at the February meeting of the vestry. When the question of paying the lawyers' fee for the war damage claim was put to a vote, four members voted for a compromise, and four voted to pay nothing. The matter was then referred to Mr. Rutledge Rivers, a lawyer of Charleston, whose decision would be accepted.

On the third Sunday in November 1916, after service, the vestry met at Christ Church, apparently for the first time since March 26, 1857, an interval of fifty-nine years and six months. At this meeting it was agreed that the erection of a fence around the churchyard should be deferred because of the high price of wire.[4] Also, Mr. Guignard was authorized to sell the rectory and the entire lot for $2,750. But not until 1920 was it sold, when H. L. Wacker bought the property for $3,000.

Meanwhile, the congregation of Christ Church was still disturbed about the subordination of Christ Church to the chapel and sent a petition to Bishop Guerry asking for a separation. The Bishop referred it to the vestry, which drew up a counter petition and sent it to the Bishop. There the matter rested for many years.

After the death of Mrs. Philip Edward Porcher in the summer of 1917, her descendants planned for a stained glass window to her memory in the chancel of Christ Church. Before this was accomplished, James Palmer Porcher, her son, came home from New York, where most of his life had been spent, to live at Porcher's Bluff. He brought with him the window which is now above the altar and dedicated it to his father and mother.

Mr. Guignard officiated not only at the chapel and the church, but also from time to time at Holy Cross Chapel, Sullivans Island, and later also at St. James', McClellanville. After five years of faithful service, he resigned to accept a church at Lincolnton, North Carolina.

On recommendation of the Bishop, the Rev. William Bee Sams was called from Cordele, Georgia, as rector in June 1921, and in December he was settled in a rented house on the Mount Pleasant waterfront. Born in Bamberg in 1875, Mr. Sams had served churches in South Carolina, Texas, Alabama, and Georgia. He was very happy in his new charge and was destined to enjoy there the longest rectorate in the history of the parish. He also officiated regularly at St. James', McClellanville.

In December 1923, John F. Maybank [5] of Charleston expressed a desire to erect a suitable fence around the churchyard of Christ Church and to put the church in complete repair. He also said that if the vestry would keep as a permanent fund the $502 already allotted from the war damage payment for the erection of a fence, he would add to it enough to raise the amount to $1,000, the interest on which should be used to keep the churchyard in order. The vestry agreed to place $500 in a permanent fund, and Mr. Maybank gave $500. This was invested in a bond paying 5 per cent, and for many years the revenue was adequate.

As soon as the highway was relocated outside of the churchyard, a sturdy fence selected and donated by Mr. Maybank was erected at a cost of $1,686.45.[6] The church repairs were extensive. All the roughcast done in 1835 by Mr. Barksdale was scraped from the exterior walls and replaced by a cement plaster, but without the ornamental quoins at the corners. The interior walls were replastered, and the key-stoned wooden arch which framed the chancel was discarded. The eaves of the roof were extended with a boxing, as was then in vogue, and all woodwork was repaired where necessary and painted. The church doors were shortened so as to open on the raised wooden floor, and outside steps were installed. The ornamental pinnacle of the cupola was replaced by a substantial metal-covered cross. The total cost to Mr. Maybank was almost $5,000. In appreciation of his generosity, the vestry unanimously elected him an honorary life member—an action without precedent, but Bishop Guerry approved.[7]

The secretary of the vestry, Mr. J. Oswald Freeman, felt a deep interest in Mr. Maybank's gifts to Christ Church, and when all repairs had been completed, he compiled and presented a handsome bronze tablet beside the door of the church, commemorating some of the events in its long existence.

The year 1924 brought another gift to Christ Church when Mr. Sams received from the American Church Building Fund a check for $500 to be used to complete the purchase of a rectory. The vestry then bought from Mrs. Annie S. Hall her home on Bennett Street for $2,800. This is still the rectory.

Another substantial gift came from an unexpected source when, in April 1924, Miss Harriet Adelle Pearce of Mount Pleasant died and was buried in her family plot at Christ Church. She had bequeathed her house and lot on Bennett Street to the vestrymen and church wardens of the Episcopal Church in Christ Church Parish. In October of the following year this property was sold to J. S. McKnight for $2,000 in cash, which was deposited in the Carolina Savings Bank in the name of St. Andrew's Chapel. From this fund extensive repairs and improvements were made to the chapel and the rectory.

In January 1925, Mr. Sams resigned to accept a call to the Church of the Redeemer, Orangeburg. The vestry was dismayed and after a long and serious discussion agreed that he must not go. With the financial aid of the Bishop, a small increase of salary was arranged and Mr. Sams stayed.

In 1929, an event occurred which eventually was to affect the parish profoundly and change it from an isolated plantation area into a thickly populated region whose residents commute to businesses elsewhere. A spectacular steel and concrete bridge was completed across Charleston Harbor, linking the parish with the city. Unhappily, the year closed with events which signalled the beginning of a worldwide calamity, the great depression of the 1930's.

When this disaster was reflected in the church finances, Mr. Sams asked the vestry to reduce his salary from $73 a month to $60, beginning with the year 1933. By the end of the year even this small stipend was in arrears, but Mr. Sams remained with his congregations and shared their privations.

When conditions began to improve, the Woman's Auxiliary of Christ Church decided in 1938 that the ruins of the old vestry house in the churchyard should be restored for a much needed Sunday School. Mrs. Philip G. Porcher,[8] chairman, and her committee wrote letters to friends and former members of the congregation and received a number of donations. In July a lawn party was held at Porcher's Bluff and in December an oyster roast, both of which added to the fund for restoration, and altogether $300 was raised.

Albert Simons, well-known architect of Charleston, donated a plan which included two additional rooms, but the cost was too great, and it was decided to rebuild on the remains of the original walls. Timbers for the roof were sawed on Oakland plantation by the R. J. Herrin Lumber Company and were hewn with a broadaxe to resemble colonial work. C. M. Trott of Charleston ordered planks for the floor and the sheathing of the roof in the dimensions of the originals. Old bricks were donated from a wrecked building in Charleston and were hauled to the site by S. E. Baitery. Sand for the masonry was given by Thomas A. Stone from the dredging of a creek on Boone Hall. Most of the labor of rebuilding was done by Philip G. Porcher[9] of Stratton Place. Furnishings for the Sunday School were also products of volunteer workmanship. Thus by community effort, the restoration was achieved within the limits of the small sum available, and in September 1939, the vestry house was dedicated to its new functions by Bishop Thomas.

During the depression years, Mount Pleasant acquired, with federal aid, waterworks and a sewer system. These improvements and the convenience of the bridge across the harbor soon attracted a great increase of population, the congregation of St. Andrew's Chapel grew, and more funds for improvements became available. In 1942 the chapel acquired a fine memorial organ; in 1945 a modern heating system was installed and $5,000 was raised to build a parish house.

Christ Church contributed what it could to the parish house, but its congregation was not increasing, and indeed could not, with only two services a month, one in the morning and one in the afternoon. The old church found a new friend, however, and in December 1942, Mrs. Anna Corcoran Ewing of Snee Farm presented it with a deed of gift for 1.8 acres of woodland adjoining the churchyard for cemetery purposes.

Mr. Sams was now eighty years old and not in good health. After a rectorate of twenty-five years, he resigned in August 1945, and retired to a small house he had purchased in Mount Pleasant.

In September 1946, the Rev. Llewellyn B. Catlin came from a church in Kentucky as rector. Two years later a parish house was completed on the chapel lot and further stimulated the growth of the chapel's congregation. Indeed the congregation was now so large that the rector needed secretarial aid. At first this was supplied by Mrs. B. L. Greenway as a volunteer, but later she was paid on an hourly basis and now is a fulltime employee.

Early in 1952 the vestry began to take steps for the sale of the old subscription list which had been circulated in the parish in 1771 to obtain funds for the purchase of a slave for the rector of Christ Church. As the signature of Thomas Lynch, Jr., a signer of the Declaration of Independence, appears on this document, it had a commercial value. Letters were written to various dealers in New York, and a photostat to one who evidenced an interest, brought him down to see the original and to offer a client.

At the annual meeting of the congregation in Mount Pleasant on January 12, 1953, the vote on selling the document was 38 in favor and 11 opposed. Through the agent, an offer of $4,500 from Dr. Frederick M. Dearborn of New York was accepted. Philip G. Porcher, representing Christ Church, and Joseph G. Hollowell, representing the chapel, went to New York to deliver the document and receive the payment. Of this sum the chapel received $2,250. Christ Church received $1,890, because the church paid the agent's fee, $250, and the expenses of the chapel's representative, $110. The church paid nothing for Mr. Porcher because he also transacted business for his company, which paid his expenses.

After the sale of the old document, Mr. Porcher received a letter from Dr. Dearborn enclosing a check for $1,500 for Christ Church, to be used, he said, for some specific object, such as an organ, which would cost $2,600, the balance to be made up from other funds. His gift was to be a memorial to his late wife, Anna Gayle Dearborn, who was born in Mobile, September 6, 1889, and died in Keene, New Hampshire, August 1, 1941. They had been married in Christ Church, Nashville, in 1910, by a South Carolinian, the Rev. Henry Judah Mikell, who later became Bishop of Atlanta.

With Dr. Dearborn's gift and some other memorial contributions, an electric organ was installed in Christ Church, bearing a small brass plaque engraved with the names of:

Anna Gayle Dearborn, Harriet Maybank Royall, Leila Laurence Stack, Philip Porcher Gregorie, Maria Porcher

Wayne, Mary Frampton Freeman, Agnes Ashley Auld, Thomas and Anna Corcoran Ewing, Francis Augustus Wayne, Osgood Darby Hamlin, Robert Clark, Harvey Cuthbert Heyward, Arthur Davenport Wall, Camilla Lavinia Porcher, Edith Elise Ware, The Rev. John Richard Fell, Thomas G. McCants.

Miss Clara A. Langley of Porcher's Bluff, who long had struggled with the old discarded organ, continued her services as volunteer organist until two years later when compelled by failing health to resign.

At the same meeting of the congregation which voted to sell the Christ Church document signed by Thomas Lynch, Jr., another important resolution was approved authorizing the vestry to give burial lots at Christ Church free of charge to all members of the chapel upon request until April 1, 1953, after which date lots would be sold at $100 to Episcopalians and $200 to others. The vote was 37 in favor, 7 opposed. As a result of this vote, practically all remaining space in the old churchyard was deeded to lot holders.

NINE

REBIRTH IN OLD AGE

Early in 1954, the vestrymen representing St. Andrew's Chapel requested Christ Church to yield its monthly morning service to the chapel and accept instead another afternoon service.

A meeting of the Christ Church congregation to consider this proposal was held at Oakland plantation on the evening of March 8 with 22 members present. Mr. Catlin presided, and both wardens from Mount Pleasant attended to present the views of the chapel. They stated that the chapel's congregation was large and rapidly increasing and the congregation of Christ Church was not, therefore it was more important to have all the morning services at the chapel. The members of Christ Church, however, felt that the monthly communion service was vital to the life of the church. They also desired a morning service every Sunday at a regular hour, perhaps with a lay reader for three Sundays and a minister once a month for the communion service.

After Mr. Catlin and the wardens left, the meeting was continued by Christ Church members, Mrs. Ferdinand Gregorie presiding, and it was unanimously agreed that a separation of the church from the chapel was the only solution to the problem.

At a special meeting of the vestry on March 14, Ferdinand Gregorie, Jr.,[1] presented the proposals of the Christ Church congregation.

As the vestrymen who had opposed separation in 1915 were now dead or had been replaced by young men who were quite willing for the separation, it was agreed that each congregation should elect representatives to take the matter to Bishop Carruthers.

It was realized, however, that as there were only eight men among the thirty communicants of the small congregation, the church could be only a mission, but it was hoped that the sale of lots from Mrs. Ewing's addition to the cemetery would aid in financing it, and, with regular morning services, the congregation would increase and the parish status might eventually be recovered.

Plans for the separation were harmoniously worked out with Bishop Carruthers by representatives of the two congregations [2] and were unanimously approved at a special congregational meeting in Mount Pleasant on April 22. At the Diocesan Convention in May 1954, St. Andrew's Chapel was recognized as a parish and Christ Church became an organized mission.

Bishop Carruthers appointed as the vestry committee of Christ Church Ferdinand Gregorie, Jr., Philip G. Porcher, I. Dennis Auld, I. Dennis Auld, Jr., and J. Seabrook Auld, who had been chosen by the Christ Church congregation at a special meeting at Stratton Place on April 27.

St. Andrew's then delivered to Christ Church the remaining records prior to 1835, retaining all since that date, and also returned the old silver marked with the name of Christ Church. The church gave to St. Andrew's deeds to the rectory, the parish house, and to St. Andrew's building itself, built by Christ Church in 1857 after many years of litigation. Thus, hallowed by vicissitudes of almost two and a half centuries, Christ Church was reborn, possessing only a cemetery and a small but devoted and enthusiastic congregation.

Bishop Carruthers arranged for the Rev. Roderick J. Hobart to take charge of Christ Church mission and give the monthly communion service and for Mr. Maurice John Bywater, a theological student then teaching in St. Andrew's Parish, to hold the other morning services as lay reader.[3] Mr. Bywater later became priest in charge of the mission, and also of Holy Cross, Sullivans Island.

As one of its first projects, the Christ Church congregation cleared the wooded growth [4] from the land given by Mrs. Ewing and enclosed it with the cemetery at a cost of $884.61. The wire and metal posts were donated by Allan P. Sloan, junior warden of St. Andrew's.

In 1955, for the first time, the church acquired a bell, donated by Floyd Edward Bliven of Erie, Pennsylvania, a friend of the Misses Langley of Porcher's Bluff. The bell was one of a pair on the first oil-electric locomotive, built in Erie in 1929, and operated on Eleventh Avenue, New York City, in the afternoons "with a cowboy on a horse riding ahead of the locomotive with a red flag waving to trucks and other traffic to get off the tracks." After the locomotive was returned to Erie and junked, the other bell went to "an Episcopal Church in Winnepeg, Canada." [5] Funds for the wrought iron belfry at Christ Church were a gift from Julius W. Nicholes, and it was designed by Richard Millar of Charleston.

At a cost of some $5,556, the congregation in 1957 completed and furnished a well-planned parish house,[6] which was dedicated by Bishop Carruthers on Easter Sunday. This is now used regularly by the Sunday School and is available for congregational meetings and other church activities. With some financial aid from Mrs. John

C. Sheridan, Jr., formerly of this parish, a gas heating system was installed in the church at a cost of $852.76.

In June 1958, Philip Gendron Porcher, Jr.,[7] was ordained to the diaconate in Christ Church by Bishop Carruthers, the first ordination there in the long history of the church.

Christ Church received a check for $4,000 from Miss Catherine P. Langley of Porcher's Bluff in May 1959 to be used in adding two small rooms to the church, one on each side of the chancel. For many years Miss Langley and other devoted women of Christ Church had done the work of cleaning and preparing the church for each service, polishing the sacred vessels, caring for and adorning the altar and other furnishings with the appropriate hangings. All equipment and materials for these tasks, as well as the choir robes, were kept in the vestry house, and the going back and forth from the church to the vestry added much to the effort of performing the tasks. Miss Langley, therefore, wished to lessen the labor by building a sacristy on the north of the chancel and a rector's room on the south side. The Vestry Committee is considering the plan.[8]

Mr. Bywater accepted a call to Florida and departed in July 1959. Four members of the Vestry Committee, Philip G. Porcher, Francis P. Porcher, Paul A. Foster, and Francis A. Wayne, Jr., volunteered to serve as lay readers on the Sundays when no minister might be available and were duly licensed by Bishop Carruthers. Services are continuing without a break. On the first Sunday in each month the Rev. Waties R. Haynsworth of Charleston holds a communion service. The Rev. Michael P. Ollic, Jr., of St. Stephen's officiates on the third Sunday and visits among the congregation on the following

Tuesday. Philip Porcher with Paul Foster, and Francis Porcher with Francis Wayne read morning prayer with sermon, alternately, on the other Sundays.[9]

Besides the steadfast congregation, there are many other friends of the old church who venerate it as a sacred shrine, and gifts sometimes come from far-off places. Slowly the membership of the congregation is changing, as some new members come in and others are laid to rest in the churchyard. But the hope is still cherished that the day is not too distant when the venerable church may again achieve the status of a flourishing parish.

Isolated from the world until recent decades by waterways and slow ferries, Christ Church in the past has influenced only its own plantation parish. As the parish church, it was more concerned with the simple teachings of Jesus than with form or doctrine and has served all who came, regardless of denomination.

The records show that Christ Church also has been served many times without regard to denomination. Before the Revolution, a Lutheran minister held a service there, and the Congregationalists of Wappetaw were invited there to hear the evangelist George Whitefield preach. After the Revolution, a Congregational minister officiated in Christ Church for twelve years. In 1867 a good Baptist was elected to the Christ Church vestry, and in 1913 the first Sunday School at the church had a Presbyterian superintendent. For the parishioners of Christ Church in the old days, the ecumenical aspirations of the future were already the natural way of a Christian life.

May all the changes now at hand prove to be for the better.

APPENDIX

MEMORIALS

THE PINCKNEY CENOTAPH

The broken, ironbound, marble slab mounted on bricks near the church door is a discarded tombstone to the memory of Col. Charles Pinckney, 1732-1782, of Snee Farm. He died in St. Andrew's Parish while the British army held Charleston and was buried in St. Andrew's churchyard. As his will directed that he be buried at St. Philip's, Charleston, his remains were later removed there. The slab at Christ Church gives his age as 52 years instead of 50, and probably because of this error the stone for more than a century remained in the grove at Snee Farm. On April 11, 1892, the vestry granted Thomas Pinckney permission to place the slab in Christ Church. As the inscription was not religious, Mr. Philip Edward Porcher suggested that the churchyard was a more suitable place, and the stone now rests there.

STAINED GLASS WINDOW
(See page 132)

BRASS ALTAR CROSS

A memorial to Anne Palmer Porcher, 1855-1918, wife of Ferdinand Gregorie.

BRASS PRAYER DESK

In memory of Miss Emma C. Boylston, March 21, 1916, of St. Luke's Church, Charleston. When St. Luke's was united with St. Paul's and the building was sold to a Negro Baptist congregation, a relative of Miss Boylston transferred the memorial to Christ Church.

WICK ELECTRIC ORGAN
(See pages 137-138)

SILVER ALMS BASINS

One is a memorial to Philip Gendron Porcher, 1852-1909, and to his son, Francis Cordes Porcher, 1898-1938. The other is in memory of two other sons, Philip Gendron Porcher, 1877-1930, and Samuel Cordes Porcher, 1902-1954.

SILVER CRUETS AND WAFER BOX

These are memorials to Arthur Trezevant Wayne, 1863-1930, and his wife, Maria Louisa Porcher, 1870-1950.

[147]

ALPHABETICAL LIST OF MARKED GRAVES

The oldest graves have no markers. Existing burial records, 1723-1826, were published in *The South Carolina Historical Magazine*, XVIII, XX, XXI, XXII.

[The entries in this list depart from strict alphabetical order when the actual wording of the markers provides information on family relationships. The list has been brought up through 1960 by Miss Surles. —G. W. W.]

Ann Allan
    daughter of Richard A. & Elizabeth
    A. Allan
    died 19 April 1821
    age 8 mos 3 dys
Richard A. Allan
    died 29 April 1835
    age 50 yrs
Agnes H. Ashley Auld
    wife of I. D. Auld
    13 Jan. 1893—2 July 1948
Helen A. Auld
    daughter of Isaac & E. L. Auld
    15 Oct. 1887—2 Nov. 1909
Isaac Auld
    1858—1923
Martha B. S. Auld
    1871—1960
Sarah Ann Amelia Beand
    daughter of Ann & [*broken*]
Leonora Broughton Stack Bennett
    wife of John H. Bennett
    daughter of Leila Lawrence &
    Napoleon C. Stack
    19 April 1912—16 Oct. 1957
Samuel M. Bennett
    1892—1960
Margaret Ray Bissell
    died 28 March 1959
    age 41 yrs 4 mos 29 dys
James Alexander Blackard
    1867—1942
Ann Maybank Bonneau
    daughter of Winhorn Lawton, Jr., &
    Ann L. Maybank
    died 4 Oct. 1857
    age 8 mos 16 dys
[Two Boone family vaults in ruin,
    no names or dates]
Frank T. Boyd
    24 Oct. 1878—27 Feb. 1957
Ward D. Carpenter
    1882—1952

Joseph W. Casrin
    died 16 Dec. 1843
    age 33 yrs
    erected by his wife J. M. Casrin
Robert Clark
    born Lugar, Scotland
    10 Oct. 1886—30 April 1946
Ina Bonneau Clement
    3 June 1859—26 May 1939
Pinckney Clement
    10 Dec. 1881—21 Aug. 1903
Samuel M. Clement
    15 Aug. 1848—27 Sept. 1915
Robert F. Clute
    3 Jan. 1890—31 May 1932
Robert Netherton Clute
    7 Feb. 1860—19 Nov. 1937
Charles Lee Cluverius
    20 June 1869—18 Feb. 1936
    Addie Jane Haselden his wife
    15 Oct. 1871—6 March 1942
Millard F. Crary
    CWO (Retd) U. S. Army
    Pipe Major & Founder
    Citadel Bagpipe Band
    4 July 1913—23 Sept. 1960
George Ball Daniels
    18 March 1896—23 Aug. 1937
William Gadsden Daniels
    1st Lt. U. S. A. Air Force
    27 Aug. 1920—6 Oct. 1944
Gordon McGrath Darby
    3 Sept. 1875—13 Jan. 1936
Hattie Vernon Whitaker Darby
    25 April 1893—12 June 1956
Margaret Pinckney Darby
    12 June 1876—13 Jan. 1932
William Kirkland Darby
    2 Oct. 1906—28 March 1941
John Deliesseline
    son of John Tompson Deliesseline
    & Elizabeth Deliesseline

born at St. James' Santee 31 Oct.
1786
died at his residence Dewees Island
14 Jan. 1840
Elizabeth C. Doar
daughter of P. G. Porcher
wife of T. Screven Doar
28 Sept. 1878—22 Aug. 1904
Ann Marshall Sanders Donaldson
16 March 1872—6 Aug. 1954
Catherine L. Coleman Donaldson
wife of Robert J. Donaldson
9 Feb. 1911—22 Oct. 1936
Sidney Townley Donaldson
27 May 1866—14 Aug. 1939
James Thomas Edmondston
son of Juanita McLeod & Robert D.
Edmondston
11 Aug. 1943—1 March 1944
Robert Dorrill Edmondston
7 July 1889—28 Feb. 1959
Edith Porcher Elmore
wife of William H. Elmore
daughter of Philip G. & Lucia L.
Porcher
21 Dec. 1889 [1888]—23 Jan. 1919
Arthur A. Everett
Mus. Co. 1, 14 Pa. Inf. Sp. Am. War
George Fraser *
died 4 July 1814 in 26th yr
James Oswald Freeman
1 Feb. 1886—25 April 1956
James Oswald Freeman
son of J. O. & Mary F. Freeman
23 April 1909—29 Oct. 1926
John Thomas Freeman
13 Sept 1886—5 June 1956
Lockwood McC. Freeman
1893—1945
Mary Pope Frampton Freeman
wife of James Oswald Freeman
6 Dec. 1884—11 Aug. 1948
Christopher Edwards Gadsden
eldest son of Mary T. & Rev. T. S.
Gadsden
20 July 1867—4 Oct. 1876
Charlotte T. Gibbs
29 Jan. 1892—23 Feb. 1947
Annie M. Gordon
wife of J. L. W. Gordon
7 March 1871—4 May 1899
J. Lyde W. Gordon
5 Sept 1859—5 Oct 1902

Louise W. Gordon
daughter of J. L. W. & A. M.
Gordon
11 Feb. 1896—11 July 1896
Sallie W. Gordon, Sister
1849—1903
Lawrence C. Gordon, Brother
1853—1936
Ann Eliza Gregorie
daughter of Edmund & Emilie
Venning Gregorie
1871—1932
Anne King Gregorie
1887—1960
Anne Palmer Gregorie
daughter of Philip E. & Elizabeth C.
Porcher
wife of Ferdinand Gregorie
16 March 1855—18 Sept 1918
Edmund Gregorie
20 Jan. 1848—13 Feb. 1924
Emilie Gregorie
5 Sept. 1848—8 March 1921
Ferdinand Gregorie
son of Ferdinand & Anne V.
Gregorie
22 Jan. 1856—5 Oct. 1928
Gertrude Edmondston Gregorie
31 Oct. 1884—11 Sept. 1935
Margaret Gregorie
1917—1960
Margaret Narcissa Gregorie
28 March 1922—17 Aug. 1924
Philip Porcher Gregorie
son of Anne Palmer Porcher &
Ferdinand Gregorie
1 Dec. 1889—7 Feb. 1953
Richard Hutson Gregorie
22 Nov. 1880—3 Jan. 1931
Samuel Riley Gregorie
son of Edmund & Emilie Gregorie
died 2 Sept. 1880
age 3 yrs 24 dys
John Everette Guerry, Sr.
24 Aug. 1900—17 July 1958
Elizabeth C. Haselden Hale
23 March 1868—18 April 1939
Harry R. Hale
26 Aug. 1864—1 Nov. 1943
Harry V. Hale
20 March 1893—21 Nov. 1948
Porcher S. Hale
11 March 1891—13 Jan. 1917

* He is said to have been killed at Boone Hall when he frightened his horse by
lifting his plumed hat in a sweeping bow to his fiancée.

Wilhelmina J. Hale
14 June 1862—17 Dec. 1945
William Mauldin Hale
18 June 1862—26 Feb. 1930
Edward Octavus Hall
6 July 1837—23 Dec. 1913
Ellen Simons Hall
11 April 1830—11 Jan. 1913
John Simons Hall
born 19 Sept. 1860
died in infancy
Maria Theresa Hall
11 Oct. 1869—5 Oct. 1948
Theodore Sumner Hall
1871—1949
Mary Eliza Royall Hamlin
14 March 1852—1 Nov. 1939
Osgood Darby Hamlin
24 Aug. 1890—22 April 1931
Thomas John Hamlin
8 May 1852—15 Jan. 1924
Thomas Royall Hamlin
21 Dec. 1881—5 April 1960
James Manley Hare
1908—1960
Martha Ann Venning Haselden
wife of Edward A. Haselden
14 Nov. 1839—9 Jan. 1925
John Frederick Hutchting
9 Sept. 1887—30 April 1953
J. F. Hutchting, Jr.
1913—1959
Julius B. Hyer, grandfather
6 Feb. 1867—8 Oct. 1949
Dale LaVance Johnson
Cpl 161 FA/35 Inf. Div. World
War II P. H.
10 Feb. 1923—18 June 1958
Diane L. Johnson
1945—1948
Alice Jane Jordan
eldest daughter of James & Jane
Jordan
died 28 Oct. 1846
age 2 yrs 11 mos
Emily Agusta [sic] Jordan
daughter of James & Jane Jordan
died 27 Sept 1850
age 2 yrs 26 dys
Mrs. Jane Jordan
died 14 May 1855
age 32 yrs 6 mos 5 dys
William James Knox
1861—1947
Margaret Buffington Knox
wife of William J. Knox
1866—1947

Catherine Porcher Langley
wife of Philip Gendron Langley
1854—1947
Cordes Prioleau Langley
1876—1958
Philip Gendron Langley [Jr.]
1874—1944
Roy P. Langley
1887—1959
Capt. Fred R. Leepin
31 Oct. 1888—17 Feb. 1959
Louis A. Legay
died 24 May 1808
age 44 yrs
Mrs. Rebecca S. Legay
died 10 May 1827
age 70 yrs
Alonzo Linton Lemon
21 March 1892—27 April 1957
John G. Leopold
born in Hanover
20 Aug. 1808—13 Oct. 1856
Addie F. Lewis
1879—1958
Aubrey M. Lewis
Chf. Q. M., U. S. Navy
Span. Am. War, Puerto Rico,
Philippine Is.
71 yrs 2 mos 7 dys
Mrs. Rosalie Lewis
wife of P. Charles Lewis
died 10 Jan. 1857
age 21 yrs 11 mos 19 days
Julia M. Lindsay
1827—1864
Sarah Lindsay
1793—1877
William Lindsay
1812—1870
Samuel H. Lofton, Father
Susan Ann Lofton, Mother
Robert & George E., Brothers
All died the same week 1858
Clement Stevens McCants
20 Dec. 1878—21 April 1924
Lockwood Allison McCants
30 June 1834—10 Nov. 1888
Lockwood Alison [sic] McCants, Jr.
20 Nov. 1869—6 Sept. 1879
accidentally shot
Lockwood Allison McCants
10 Oct. 1900—23 June 1960
Mary Caroline McCants
6 Nov. 1873—11 July 1937
Mary Jane McCants
wife of Lockwood Allison McCants
10 May 1831—9 Sept. 1916

Thomas Gadsden McCants
19 Oct. 1867—28 March 1934
William McCants
born in St. Bartholomew's Parish
16 Sept. 1799—30 Nov. 1858
William Alison [sic] McCants
only son of Lockwood A. & Mary J.
McCants
died 1 Nov. 1858
age 3 yrs 9 mos 8 dys
Ann Eliza McElheran
wife of Rev. David McElheran
died 24 Aug. 1857
age 63 yrs 9 mos 23 dys
Rev. David McElheran
born in 1801, Liverpool, Eng.
ordained 1835
died 17 July 1875
Claude E. McElveen
12 April 1905—2 June 1955
William Whilden McIver
5 Nov. 1881—15 Nov. 1947
Carl Saint Clair McKinley
7 April 1875—21 Dec. 1941
Catherine Hall McKinley
6 Dec. 1874—8 Sept. 1949
Robert Charles MacNeal
7 Dec. 1879—7 Feb. 1959
Lewis E. Magwood
1903—1959
Col. Joseph Maybank
died 17 April 1844
age 44 yrs
William G. Mazyck, Jr.
1885—1960
Julian Theodore Melchers
26 Dec. 1889—3 Dec. 1958
Mary Porcher Mellichamp
wife of Henry L. Mellichamp
4 March 1884—14 April 1948
Florinda Knox Moore
wife of Judge Alfred S. Moore
1861—1940
W. Moultrie Moore
30 June 1880—16 Sept. 1956
Merle Hayes Muirhead
wife of J. Murray Muirhead, Jr.
14 July 1895—19 Dec. 1959
R. M. Muirhead *
born in Glasgow

Caroline Hauck Muirhead *
his first wife (1836)
R. M. Muirhead, Jr.*
Hampton's Cavalry, C. S. A.
May Pratt Edmonston Muirhead *
wife of R. M. Muirhead, Jr.
Sarah M. Muirhead *
daughter of R. M. Muirhead, Jr.
Florence A. Wayne Muirhead *
second wife of R. M. Muirhead
Florence A. Muirhead *
daughter of R. M. Muirhead
Two infant sons * of J. M. Muirhead,
Jr.
David J. Murphy
son of John D. & Lavina T. Murphy
died 8 Sept 1851
age 2 yrs 10 mos 8 dys
Gustaf L. Nielson
1885—1960
John Rowland Nowell
1879—1958
Anna E. Pearce
1849—1914
Harriet A. Pearce
1848—1924
William T. Pearce
buried in Lucas Cemetery
1819—1881
His wife Mary Pearce
1827—1892
William T. Pearce
1846—1904
Cornelia Jerman Pinckney
14 June 1874—24 Sept. 1946
Francis Douglas Pinckney
7 Oct. 1869—10 Feb. 1946
Annie Porcher
daughter of P. G. & L. B. W.
Porcher
died 5 Dec. 1882
age 1 yr
Camilla Lavinia Porcher
daughter of Mary Cordes & Philip
G. Porcher
2 April 1904—12 April 1950
Francis Cordes Porcher
son of Philip Gendron Porcher &
Mary Frances Cordes
21 Aug. 1898—28 July 1938

[* According to information from J. M. Muirhead, Jr., remains of members
of the Muirhead family were removed from the family cemetery at Hobcaw
Plantation on Wando River and re-interred at Christ Church. In 1960, a marker,
commemorating these persons (and other members of the family) was erected in
Christ Church cemetery.—F.B.S.]

James Palmer Porcher
son of Philip E. & Elizabeth P.
Porcher
1863—1936
Lucia Bellinger Waring Lockwood
Porcher
wife of Philip Gendron Porcher
28 March 1854—15 Dec. 1893
Lucian Lockwood Porcher
1890—1930
Marian Muirhead Porcher his wife
1889—1928
Infant sons James Murray & Lucian
Lockwood [Porcher]
Marie Screven Porcher
2 March 1888—24 Jan. 1926
Philip Edward Porcher
born in St. John's, Berkeley
2 March 1827—27 Oct. 1917
Elizabeth Catherine his wife
daughter of Dr. John S. Palmer
born in St. James, Santee
19 April 1833—24 July 1917
Philip Gendron Porcher
7 Oct. 1852—19 Sept. 1909
Philip Gendron Porcher
11 Sept. 1877—7 March 1930
Samuel Cordes Porcher
son of Philip Gendron Porcher &
Mary Frances Cordes
7 March 1902—4 Feb. 1954
Arthur Lee Rivers
10 Sept. 1870—13 May 1945
Constant Rivers
son of Constant H. & Mary Minott
Rivers
15 April 1865—27 July 1927
John Minott Rivers
13 April 1855—9 May 1929
Jennie Fell Rivers his wife
died 11 Dec. 1944
John Minott Rivers
son of J. M. & Jennie F. Rivers
23 Jan. 1883—27 July 1884
Sarah Ursula Edmondston Rivers
wife of Arthur Lee Rivers
3 Nov. 1876—2 Dec. 1932
John Thomas Ross
eldest child of John & Sarah Ann
Ross
31 March 1832—30 Jan. 1839
Rebecca Ann Ross
wife of James Ross
15 March 1822—28 June 1853
Frances A. Rotureau
1846—4 Sept. 1912

Andrew DuPre Royall
18 April 1880—24 June 1905
Anne Baily Royall
27 Oct. 1827—20 July 1920
Annie Claudia Royall
13 Sept. 1870—3 March 1952
Basil Manly Royall
1858—1920
Claudia Sanders Royall
1895—1948
Edward Manly Royall, M.D.
2 Dec. 1827—23 Nov. 1915
Emilie Marion Royall
27 Aug. 1867—5 March 1955
Esther Porcher Royall
1860—1929
Harriet H. M. Royall
1879—1959
Harriet Maybank Royall
daughter of Edward M., Jr. &
Norene H. Royall
3 Dec. 1932—13 Feb. 1942
John DuPre Royall
8 Feb. 1888—17 Jan. 1920
Lee Royall
son of Anne Venning & Edward M.
Royall
16 June 1866—22 July 1942
Robert Venning Royall
16 Feb. 1854—21 March 1935
Sallie Williams DuPre his wife
8 Feb. 1857—16 Aug. 1941
Robert V. Royall, Jr.
18 Oct. 1885—6 Nov. 1918
Anna Louisa Sams
eldest daughter of Mary J. &
Benjamin Freeman
wife of C. A. Sams
20 Dec. 1827—4 May 1875
Benjamin Freeman Sams
2d son of C. A. & A. L. Sams
11 March 1853—7 July 1862
George Evans Sams
3rd son of C. A. & A. L. Sams
12 Oct. 1856—13 Aug. 1858
Rev. William Bee Sams
29 Sept. 1875—15 May 1952
Edna Rivers Sassard
daughter of Edmund & Emilie
Gregorie
wife of Nelson DuPre Sassard
10 July 1885—23 March 1960
Charles William Schroder
31 Dec. 1891—3 July 1951
John L. Seabrook, Sr.
1911—1960

Benjamin Alston Simons
youngest son of John J. & Maria T.
Simons
died 27 Oct. 1857
age 14 yrs 10 mos 20 dys
John Alston Simons
son of John & Sarah Simons
died 18 Sept. 1855
age 56 yrs 3 mos 13 dys
John Peter S[imons]
eldest son of [John Alston Simons]
died 1856
Selina Sobieski
died 6 Jan. 1841 age 60 yrs
Alison Gay Squier
died 12 Aug. 1959 age 1 dy
Victoria Lynn Squier
Sharon Lee Squier
3 Dec. 1955—16 Feb. 1958
daughters of Lucius Robinson, Jr., &
Joyce Higgins Squier *
Harold Tatum
14 July 1887—30 April 1958
Louise F. Taylor
2 Feb. 1884—14 Aug. 1938
Henry Slade Tew
1805—1884
Sarah Jane Lindsay his wife
1818—1902
Ruth Hyer Tiencken, Mother
14 Jan. 1893—4 May 1951
Wiley Edward Tiencken, Father
24 Oct. 1892—27 April 1953
Sarah Townsend
died 24 Aug. 1804 age 51 yrs
Addie Venning
8 June 1853—24 July 1908
Charles S. Venning
18 June 1870—20 Sept. 1899
Elias Venning
5 March 1864—22 Nov. 1905
Gulielma Oswald Venning
daughter of Elias & Mary C.
Venning
died 27 June 1860
age 6 mos 22 dys
Hennie E. Venning
1 Nov. 1860—20 Nov. 1903
Jane Eliza Venning
wife of Mortimer W. Venning
died 5 July 1877
age 54 yrs
Margaret Venning
1872—1957

Martha Elizabeth Venning
wife of Mortimer W. Venning
died 11 Nov. 1843 in her 27th yr
Nicholas & Eugenia M., infants
Mortimer W. Venning
12 Sept. 1816—11 April 1905
Nicholas Venning
2d son of Samuel Venning, War of
1776
4 May 1788—11 Nov. 1855
Martha Allan his wife
daughter of Thomas Allan, an
Englishman
19 Dec. 1800—20 Jan. 1878
Samuel R. Venning
[no dates]
Sarah Ann Venning
daughter of Nicholas & Martha
Venning
died 13 May 1820
age 1 yr 15 dys
Nannie McCants Wagner
wife of Wm. H. Wagner
26 Aug. 1857—5 Aug. 1940
Theodore D. Wagner
son of Nannie M. & Wm. H.
Wagner
9 Nov. 1896—16 Oct. 1906
William H. Wagner
son of Esther C. & Theodore D.
Wagner
22 May 1849—23 April 1898
Arthur Trezevant Wayne
Ornithologist & Author
1 Jan. 1863—5 May 1930
Maria Louisa his wife
daughter of Philip E. & Elizabeth
C. Porcher
24 April 1870—26 Dec. 1950
Francis A. Wayne
6 March 1893—17 April 1953
Elizabeth Cooper Welch
1854—1935
Julian Bulkeley Weston
10 Oct. 1899—31 Oct. 1958
Elizabeth Whitesides
daughter of Moses & Eliza
Whitesides
died Oct. 1823
age 2 yrs 8 mos
Mrs. Mary Whitesides
died 16 Oct. 1848 in her 41st yr

[* These twins were burned to death when their house on Sullivans Island was
destroyed by fire.—F.B.S.]

Mrs. Mary E. Whitesides
    died 12 Dec. 1836
    age 42 yrs 9 mos 18 dys
Moses Whitesides
    died 1 Dec. 1852
    age 60 yrs
Susan E. M. Whitesides
    [no dates]

Agnes Mahoney Williams
    1907—1954
Patricia Ann Williams
    1936—1958
John Byrd Wilson
    1889—1960
Henrietta Parker Lining Workman
    wife of John J. Workman
    11 Oct. 1870—17 March 1950

NOTES

ONE: A Small Timber Church

[1] D. D. Wallace, *South Carolina: A Short History* (Chapel Hill, 1951), 58.

[2] *Statutes at Large of South Carolina* (cited as *S. C. Stat.*), II, 237, 240.

[3] Frederick Dalcho, *An Historical Account of the Protestant Episcopal Church in South Carolina* (Charleston, 1820, cited as Dalcho), 67, 69.

[4] A. S. Salley (ed.), *Journal of the Commons House of Assembly of South Carolina, March 6—April 9, 1706* (Columbia, 1937, cited as *JCHA*), 10.

[5] *Ibid.*, 21.

[6] *S. C. Stat.*, II, 282 ff., 247, 295.

[7] *Ibid.*, 594, 596. The Christ Church vestry, June 15, 1721, signed indentures binding Thomas Hickman as apprentice to Church Warden William Bollough and gave Bollough £20 to buy Hickman's clothes and other necessities. His trade is not given.

[8] The Proprietors repealed such election laws of 1716 and 1717. In 1721 these provisions were included in a permanent act. *S. C. Stat.*, III, 135 ff.

[9] F. J. Klingberg (ed), *Carolina Chronicle, The Papers of Gideon Johnston 1707-1716* (Los Angeles, 1946, cited as *Johnston*), 59, 60.

[10] Dalcho, 275; *S. C. Stat.*, II, 283, 284. At this time £150 in South Carolina money, currency, was worth about £100 in English money, sterling.

[11] Dalcho, 275; Gilbert Jones, report to Gov. Nicholson, June 8, 1721, microfilm positive (S. P. G. MSS, London) from Library of Congress British reproductions.

[12] *Johnston*, 19, n.3; F. J. Klingberg, *The Carolina Chronicle of Dr. Francis LeJau 1706-1717* (Los Angeles, 1956, cited as *LeJau*), 43; *The South Carolina Historical Magazine*, cited as *SCHM*), XIV (1915), 136; MS Minutes of Christ Church Vestry, 87. References for information from vestry minutes hereafter will not be given.

[13] Minutes of the vestry show oaths and signatures of members 1708, 1709, 1711, 1712. Later minutes merely state that members "were severally sworn according to law" or "qualified according to law."

[14] *SCHM*, V, 101; XL, 115.

[15] *S. C. Stat.*, II, 288; *JCHA*, Nov. 1706-Feb. 1707 (Columbia, 1939) and *Journal of the Commissioners of the Indian Trade* (Columbia, 1926), *passim*.

[16] *SCHM*, II, 273 n., 274; A. S. Salley (ed.), *Warrants for Lands in South Carolina 1692-1711* (Columbia, 1915, cited as *Warrants*), 39, 67, 176, 182.

[17] *Ibid.*, 180, 185.

[18] F. H. James, "Richard Marsden, Wayward Clergyman," *William and Mary Quarterly*, Ser. 3, XI (October 1954), 578-580; *Johnston*, 46.

[19] *Johnston*, 46, 47, 48.

[20] *S. C. Stat.*, II, 328, 329. Acreage is from Gilbert Jones' report of 1721.

[21] *SCHM*, XIII, 2-5.

[22] *Warrants*, 143, 189, 196.

[23] *SCHM*, XIII, 112, 113. Salt Hope and Salt Ponds are shown on the accompanying map.

[24] *Warrants*, 56, 205.

[25] *Ibid.*, 176-177.

[26] *Johnston*, 49.

[27] *LeJau*, 94.

[28] "The State of Mr. Jones' Case," to the Society, 1711, microfilm positive from Library of Congress.

²⁹ B. R. Carroll (ed.), *Historical Collections of South Carolina* (New York, 1836), I, 121; G. N. Edwards, *A History of the Independent or Congregational Church of Charleston, South Carolina* (Boston, 1947), 9.

³⁰ A. K. Gregorie (ed.), *Records of the Court of Chancery of South Carolina* (Washington, 1950), 70, n. 22.

³¹ Gilbert Jones to the Society, Nov. 6, 1716, microfilm positive from Library of Congress, and his report of 1721.

³² *Ibid.*

³³ *Johnston*, 155 and n.

³⁴ *Ibid.*

³⁵ Jones' report of 1721.

³⁶ In 1707 the Assembly ordered these paths broadened to 16 feet. *S. C. Stat.*, IX, 9. Today they are (1) Long Point road from Belvue-Bermuda plantation along by Boone Hall to Christ Church, where it enters U. S. Highway 17, which at Wando Neck is entered by (3) the Sewee road.

³⁷ Jones to the Society, Nov. 6, 1716.

³⁸ *Ibid.* At this time South Carolina currency was worth half of the English sterling.

³⁹ *Ibid.*

⁴⁰ Jones' report of 1721.

⁴¹ Jones to the Society, March 28, 1717, microfilm positive from Library of Congress.

⁴² *Ibid.*

⁴³ David D. Van Antwerp, *Church History in Three Volumes* (4th ed.; Claremont, N. H., 1880), III, 108-109.

⁴⁴ Microfilm positive from Library of Congress.

⁴⁵ Microfilm positive from Library of Congress.

⁴⁶ See note 10 *supra*.

⁴⁷ At a vestry meeting, Dec. 3, 1731, "Thomas Barton Senior produced his Affidavit concerning the parsonage land and that it was to be presented to the Church Commissioners by Mr. George Haddrell one of the Vestry."

⁴⁸ Dalcho, 279.

TWO: The Brick Church

¹ *JCHA*, Feb.-June 1725, 60. At this time £400 currency was worth about £100 sterling.

² MS Will Book 1671-1721, 262, Probate Court, Charleston County courthouse

³ Dec. 4, 1730, photostat from Library of Congress, S.P.G. transcripts.

⁴ The House Committee on Grievances in January 1727 said "the Law wch obliged people to go arm'd to Church &c wants strengthening." *JCHA*, Nov. 1726-March 1727, 69; *Stat.*, VII, 417.

⁵ In 1730 Mr. Fulton reported the church had no chancel. In 1732, the vestry voted for an addition to the church. In 1744 Mrs. Charlotta Durand was buried "in the Chancel under the Altar."

⁶ Dalcho, 281.

⁷ *JCHA*, 1736-1739, 632; *S. C. Stat.*, III, 539.

⁸ *SCHM*, XXV, 1-4, 12.

⁹ *SCHM*, II, 130-131, 133.

¹⁰ *SCHM*, XXXIX, 17, 21.

¹¹ Dalcho, 281.

¹² John Atkin and his brother Edmund, Charleston merchants, born in England, had been in Carolina since boyhood. They owned 208 acres in the parish between Hobcaw and Shem creeks.

¹³ April 19, 1744, photostat, Library of Congress S. P. G. transcripts.

¹⁴ Photostat, Library of Congress S. P. G. transcripts.

[15] Photostat, Library of Congress S. P. G. transcripts. Further family sorrows may account for his gloom, for a conveyance of 1748 states his then wife was Susannah, widow of Amias Hext. Register of Mesne Conveyance, Book NN, 13, Charleston County courthouse.

[16] *South Carolina Gazette* (cited as *SCG*), Jan. 19, 1749, Jan. 1, 1750.

[17] *SCG*, Apr. 9, 1750.

[18] *SCHM*, XXXI, 11-14.

[19] Edmund Atkin (1707-1761), member of his Majesty's Council in 1738, closed his business in 1750, went to England, and six years later returned as first superintendent of Indian affairs in the Southern Department. In 1760 he married Lady Anne Mackenzie, and died the next year at his Mars Bluff plantation on Pedee River.

[20] John Drayton, *A View of South Carolina* (Charleston, 1802), 99.

[21] He then advertised (*SCG*, June 9, 1757), to teach reading, writing, and arithmetic.

[22] Dalcho, 282.

[23] Wallace, *S. C. Short History*, 174.

[24] Dalcho, 180, 192, 349.

[25] John Bartram, *Diary of a Journey through the Carolinas, Georgia, and Florida, 1765-66*. Annotated by Francis Harper (Philadelphia, 1942), 14.

[26] *SCG and Country Journal*, March 4, 1766.

[27] Dalcho, 198, 199, 341.

[28] This and documents quoted below are from papers in the files of Christ Church. Any cited hereafter will be as Christ Church papers.

[29] This suggestion is from Mrs. W. W. McIver, a descendant of Andrew Hibben, who owns his home in Mount Pleasant. She also loaned the writer her Hibben notes and a clipping, "The Village of Mount Pleasant," by John A. Leland (*The News and Courier*, Sept. 5, 1880).

[30] *SCG*, March 8, 1770.

[31] Christ Church papers.

[32] A draft for £600 currency was drawn April 7, 1770, for materials for parsonage buildings. Specifications for outbuildings—a storeroom, a dairy, a cornhouse, and a Negro house—were advertised in June 1772, and were built by Levi Durand, son of the former rector, for £71. Subscriptions were being taken for the parsonage as late as March 1772, when more than £1,000 was pledged. The writer has been in the house many times, and once drew measured drawings of the plan, now lost. Woodwork of the living room was removed to the Charleston Museum shortly before the house fell. The stairway is in the home of Laura M. Bragg, 38 Chalmers Street, Charleston.

[33] Thomas Shubrick, A. Vanderhorst, Andrew Rutledge, Hugh Rutledge, J. Rutledge, William Hort, Clem't Lemprière, William Gibbes, David Linn, Alex'r Rose, John Ash, Levi Durand, John Boone, Peter Croft, Pet'r Sanders, Andrew Hibben, Robt Dorrill, Wm Cook, Jacob Bond, Jos Maybank, Peter Manigault, Thomas Lynch, Jr., John Huger, Wm Hopton, Joseph Wigfall, John Dart, Thomas Barton.

[34] G. W. Williams, *St. Michael's, Charleston, 1751-1951* (Columbia, 1951), 313.

[35] A. H. Hirsch, *The Huguenots of Colonial South Carolina* (Durham, N. C., 1928), 87.

[36] Joseph Johnson, *Traditions and Reminiscences Chiefly of the American Revolution in the South* (Charleston, 1851), 580.

[37] Mesne Conveyance records (Book D, 112) in Charleston County courthouse attribute Lynch's Grove to John Lynch, which perhaps should be Jonah Lynch; for burial ground, see Book PP, 635.

[38] Constitution of 1778, art. XXXVIII; *S. C. Stat.* I, 144.

[39] Johnson, *Traditions*, 580; George Howe, *History of the Presbyterian Church in South Carolina* (Columbia, 1870, 1883, 2 vols.), I, 461.

[40] The officer of Christ Church was probably John Sandford Dart, son-in-law of Jacob Motte.

THREE: A Second Resurgence

[1] Dalcho, 463, 465, 466, 475.

[2] *S. C. Stat.*, VIII, 140, dated March 27, 1787.

[3] *The State Gazette,* April 24, 1787.

[4] Paul Pritchard's itemized account shows shingles, timbers, nails, and boards were bought, but no bricks, so it is evident that the walls were intact.

[5] A. M. Shipp, *The History of Methodism in South Carolina* (Nashville, 1884), 160.

[6] *S. C. Stat.*, VIII, March 22, 1787.

[7] Howe, *Presbyterian Church*, I, 462.

[8] *Ibid.*, 462-463.

[9] S. Dubose, "Remininiscences of St. Stephen's Parish," in T. G. Thomas, *A Contribution to the History of the Huguenots of South Carolina* (New York, 1887), 84.

[10] Dalcho, 428, 436.

[11] *S. C. Stat.*, IX, 346, 389, 396.

[12] *S. C. Stat.*, VIII, 254, 259.

[13] *SCHM*, XXV, 140; Howe, *Presbyterian Church*, I, 462.

[14] "William Hort's Journal," *SCHM*, XXIV, 40; "Antiquities of Mount Pleasant," *News and Courier*, Aug. 8, 1878.

[15] Dalcho, 509-510.

[16] Albert Sidney Thomas, *A Historical Account of the Protestant Episcopal Church in South Carolina 1820-1957* (Columbia, 1957, cited as Thomas), 14, 658.

[17] Unsigned copy of letter from James W. Brandt, Dec. 21, 1810, in Christ Church files. There is also a similar letter to C. L. Prince.

[18] Book I-8, 38, Register of Mesne Conveyance, Charleston County.

[19] *S. C. Stat.*, VIII, 310.

FOUR: The First Rector of the American Church

[1] Mr. Muller's letters, 1819-1823, are in Christ Church files. At the Diocesan Convention in February 1819, he reported for Christ Church as "visitor" and for the Sullivans Island church as "Rector."

[2] Book F-9, 145, Register of Mesne Conveyance, Charleston County Courthouse.

[3] A bill from Frederick Richards, Feb. 26, 1820, shows he had removed old plaster and replastered the parsonage, built a kitchen chimney and oven, brick pillars for house and piazza, and three flights of steps, and had dug a well 14 feet deep.

[4] At the Convention that month, Mr. Muller at his own request was tried on charges brought by Grace Church vestry:

> First.—That on Sullivan's Island, when an Officiating Minister of this Church, in the summer of 1818, or at some other time within the last three years, he, Mr. Muller, had violated the Seventh Commandment.

> Second.—That at sundry times, he, Mr. Muller, had been guilty of uttering that which he knew at the time to be false.

The Convention unanimously found him not guilty on both charges.

[5] The Rev. William H. Mitchell, deacon, officiated that summer at Grace Church. In 1822 the Rev. Joseph M. Gilbert resigned Edisto Island church and became rector of Grace, where he remained until his death in October 1824.

[6] His beautifully written letter book and three financial books attest Mr. Barksdale's zeal. In 1811 he had declined election to the vestry because he already had "as much business of that kind" as he could do.

[7] The vestry also authorized Mr. Hort to pay the rector $215 and to reimburse himself from any church funds collected.

[8] Records of this Auxiliary from that year until 1842 are in Christ Church files.

[9] In 1851 Mr. Rutledge was consecrated Bishop of Florida, and died three weeks later.

FIVE: A Great Missionary

[1] In Convention reports 1829, 1835, he says that he came into the Parish to reside on Nov. 10, 1827. On April 15, 1823, he had married in St. Augustine his second wife, Henrietta H. Payne, of Nassau, N. P. Their son, Andrew Dehon Fowler was born in Mount Pleasant in 1830. Mr. Fowler served at Christ Church before he became rector, and occasionally as late as 1844.

[2] Thomas, 661; Dalcho, 373.

[3] Will of Andrew Fowler, July 13, 1832, Book K, 464, Probate Court, Charleston County Courthouse.

[4] Dalcho, 267-268.

[5] S. C. Stat. III, 25, 438; IV, 256.

[6] Ibid., III, 651, 252, 699.

[7] Journal, Convention of 1843, 20-21.

SIX: Two Chancery Suits

[1] The charter stated that several pious persons "have given divers sums of money for rebuilding and fitting up the said church, and for providing for the maintenance of a minister and the payment of the proper officers of the same," and for carrying out these purposes, the vestry sought incorporaton. S. C. Stat., VIII, 140.

[2] It "is my intention (if not all) a large proportion of my commission will be returned to the Parish Church." Undated copy of Mr. Barksdale's letter to the commissioner in equity when delivering church bonds and records into custody of the court.

[3] Mr. Fell was ordained deacon in 1844 and was appointed missionary to Christ Church. He married a daughter of John Hamlin.

[4] The Ferdinand Gregorie family owned and resided on Myrtle Grove plantation, adjoining John Hamlin's Seaside, and the two families were intimate. The father of the writer told her these details in her youth, and she immediately recorded them in a notebook.

[5] Copies of the bill and the decree are in the Christ Church files.

SEVEN: Catastrophes and Abandonment

[1] The embankment along the northeast side of the churchyard, extending all the way from a creek of the Wando River at Boone Hall to the seacoast at Palmetto Fort subdivision, was thrown up in 1865 when federal troops were expected to land at Bulls Bay to attack Charleston. Philip Edward Porcher, lieutenant of engineers in charge of the construction, told the writer that it was built with Negro labor, and that all pines along the earthwork were felled with their tops pointing northeast to deter the expected enemy. The work was manned with Confederate troops only one day, when news came that the enemy was approaching Charleston from the south.

[2] The family of Philip Edward Porcher at Oakland, and the family of Ferdinand Gregorie at Myrtle Grove. Information in the two paragraphs above is from them to the author.

[3] His $900 included $620, a legacy from his father; $130, a loan from his mother; and $150, a gift from James Welsman & Son, Charleston.

4 The parsonage was sold under execution in July 1872 for non-payment of three years' taxes, $140.70.

5 The present benches to be furnished with regular pew ends and doors, to be closed up under the seats, to have the backs lowered and made all alike—the back rail to be made smaller—pews to have the regular pew hinges and buttons $112.00

Cupola to have 1 coat of paint; pews and doors to have stain and 1 coat of varnish 45.00

Repairing space on the walls where the old tablets stood 5.00

A bank and ditch to be placed around the graveyard, 887 feet 11.00

2 posts and a plan gate and fastenings 12.00

Cleaning up the graveyard 2.00

_____

$187.00

6 The resolutions adopted by the vestry noted that "With a mind of no ordinary stamp, enriched by judicious reading and illustrated by travel, he was ever a welcome guest at our hearths."

7 There he served until his death, Dec. 1, 1891. Thomas, 498.

8 In July 1885, when Mount Pleasant was the county seat of Berkeley County, the vestry purchased part of the courthouse grounds and erected a building for lawyers' offices called "law range." The total cost of $628 was financed by the remnant of the Christ Church endowment and a loan secured by a mortgage on the property. Mount Pleasant ceased to be county seat in 1895, and law range became useless. In 1900 it was sold for $350 and the last of the Christ Church endowment vanished.

9 The melodeon, first musical instrument used in Christ Church, had been bought for Mary Eliza, daughter of Dr. E. M. Royall. Later it was acquired by Philip G. Langley, and is now in possession of his daughters at Porcher's Bluff.

10 He wrote a treatise on the eucharist, and forty Lenten sermons published as _Sin and Our Saviour_ (Milwaukee, 1895). He edited Sunday School _Lesson Leaflets_ and _Teachers' Helps_. Later he taught history at Christ School, Arden, N. C.

11 Thomas, 280.

EIGHT: A Woman's Congregation

1 Born Jan. 22, 1856, died Oct. 29, 1928.

2 This writer induced her to write a brief account for the family record.

3 Thereafter for several years, one meeting a year was held at Christ Church. In 1923 the vestry agreed to hold every third meeting at Christ Church, but this continued for only two meetings.

4 In June 1921, the vestry gave to F. Gregorie, Jr., and P. G. Porcher, representing the church, a check for $502 from the war damage fund, to fence the churchyard. Because the highway had encroached on the churchyard and efforts were being made to have it removed, erection of the fence was delayed.

5 A descendant of David Maybank, church warden on the first Christ Church vestry.

6 The cemetery was 402 feet long and 220 feet wide.

7 The work was begun April 20, 1924, and completed in time for a service on Sept. 28, 1924.

8 Formerly Wilhelmina Weldon.

9 Born Jan. 26, 1908.

NINE: Rebirth in Old Age

[1] Born July 29, 1924.

[2] Philip G. Porcher, Ferdinand Gregorie, Jr., I. Dennis Auld, Jr., and Mrs. Wilhelmina Porcher, for the church; D. M. White, Jr., and Louis Sams for the chapel.

[3] Mr. Bywater was ordained deacon, Feb. 25, 1956, in St. Andrew's Parish Church, and to the priesthood, June 1, 1957, at Holy Cross, Sullivans Island.

[4] Osgood D. Hamlin and Ferdinand Gregorie, Jr., cleared the ground with their own machinery at no cost to the church.

[5] Letter of F. E. Bliven to Kate P. Langley, Jan. 16, 1955.

[6] The plan was drawn by Francis Peyre Porcher. Mr. and Mrs. P. G. Porcher donated the refrigerator. Mr. Paul A. Foster gave the kitchen ware.

[7] Born March 12, 1932.

[[8] The addition was begun December 6, 1960, and completed in January 1961.]

[[9] Because he was needed for other duties, the Rev. Mr. Haynesworth was recalled in 1960 by Bishop Carruthers, who assigned the Rev. Mr. Ollic as part-time rector. In February 1961, the Vestry, with the permission of the Rt. Rev. Gray Temple, eleventh Bishop of South Carolina, invited Mr. Ollic to be full-time rector of Christ Church and St. James', McClellanville; he accepted the call and took up his duties March 15, 1961. The engaging of a full-time rector was an important step in the process of regaining full parish status. (Cf. *News and Courier*, March 12, 1961.)—F.B.S. and G.W.W.]

INDEX OF NAMES

Names in the Alphabetical List of Marked Graves (pp. 148-154) are not included in this Index.